THE LADY DOC

THE FIRST CARTRIDGE HAD JAMMED AND
EVERY OTHER CHAMBER WAS FILLED.

THE LADY DOC

BY

CAROLINE LOCKHART

AUTHOR OF "ME-SMITH"

WITH ILLUSTRATIONS BY
GAYLE HOSKINS

PHILADELPHIA & LONDON
J. B. LIPPINCOTT COMPANY
1912

1285 Sheridan Avenue, No. 275
Cody, Wyoming 82414

First edition published 1912, J.P. Lippincott Company

Printed in the United States of America.

ISBN 0-9652942-8-5

Lockhart, Boomtown, and the Lady Doc

by Paul Fees, Ph.D.

"[A] town hall, post office, railroad station, livery stable, blacksmith shop, two water wagons, two churches, three newspapers, four hotels, six saloons, a dozen stores and shops, 44 bronchos, half a hundred dwellings, 450 residents, one brothel, three chained bears, one corralled elk, and a caged eagle."

— Charles Wayland Towne

When he saw it in 1902, journalist Charles Wayland Towne dubbed Cody "Boomtown," a place "where everybody and everything hustled — including the wind." It was the same town, not much to look at, when Caroline Lockhart decided in 1904 to make it her home. Cody was "considubble of a skeleton yet," as one old timer, Dad Pearce, put it, "but," he predicted, "I 'spect it'll rib up soon."

Lockhart was seeking the raw West, and she found Cody just in time. The "ribbing up" was just about to begin. Buffalo Bill Cody and his partners George Beck, Nate Salsbury, Bronson Rumsey, George Bleistein, Henry Gerrans, and Horace Alger (all to be immortalized in the names of Cody streets running, with the flow of capital, from east to west), had happily surrendered most of their Bighorn Basin irrigation scheme to the federal government's newly formed Reclamation Service. Construction of the huge Shoshone (later Buffalo Bill) Dam would begin in 1905. Within three years the population would almost triple, automobiles would update the smells of horses and the clanking of wagons and coaches, and businessmen would be dressing up in Hart, Shaffner, and Marx suits purchased at Jakie Schwoob's Big Store or Dave Jones' men's store.

By 1912, the town would settle into the pattern of hardscrabble and occasional prosperity, hard-partying and boredom, haves and have-nots, and slow but steady population growth that characterized most of its 20th century. As Cody gentrified on the one hand, and stratified on the other, Lockhart would publish a bombshell of a novel to polarize, scandalize, and, perhaps better than any non-fiction could, characterize the town of Cody. After almost two decades of adventuring, she had found home.

Lockhart was born in Illinois in 1870 and reared on her family's ranch in Kansas. She attended college briefly before striking out at age 18 to be a writer, and in 1888 she landed a job as reporter with the Boston *Post.* Very likely her example was the famous and fearless Nellie Bly who had begun turning heads as a staff writer for the New York *World* only a year before. With the Chicago *Sun's* Amy Leslie, Lockhart and Bly formed a triumvirate that made the crusading woman reporter almost a cliché of American newspaper culture by the early 20th century. And Caroline was a crusader.

In Boston she admitted herself to a female "asylum" to do an expose and barely escaped to write her story. She was photographed in a diving suit after descending to the depths of Boston Harbor. She leapt from a four-story building in a demonstration of the fire department's life-saving net. After a while it became evident that, to Caroline, the risk was becoming its own reward. As her notoriety grew, she moved on to the Philadelphia *Bulletin* where she was given her own celebrity byline and a *nom de plume*, "Suzette."

One of her delights was to scoop her male counterparts with interviews of the famous and infamous. In Boston she arranged to interview the most widely known American of the day, Colonel William F. Cody, "Buffalo Bill," touring with his Wild West show. She found him in his private railroad car, she said, in dressing gown and slippers, gracious in his hospitality, indifferent to her stumbling questions, and generous with his time.

Cody may have been for her as close to the ideal man as she would hope to find. His early life had been one of risk and adventure. He was tall and gentlemanly, still handsome in his mid fifties. His credentials as a rugged and self-reliant individual were impeccable. He was the companion of Indian chiefs, royalty, the rich and powerful, yet he also was a perfect democrat, unaffected in his dealings with persons of any station, including girl reporters. Though Caroline painted him as the archetypal laconic westerner, Buffalo Bill was full of his plans for the Bighorn Basin and the new town of Cody. He described the glories of the Yellowstone country and the prospects for development. It was his persuasive powers that would lead Charles Wayland Towne to see what all the fuss was about, and it may have been, as she later claimed, a similar invitation that led Lockhart to Cody.

But the call to adventure was a constant in Lockhart's life. In 1898 she traveled with her former *Post* editor Andrew MacKenzie to New Mexico where they spent several months, both of them intending to find material and inspiration to move from journalism to literary fiction. She began publishing short stories featuring unusual characters and exotic locations. During the next five years Caroline would sail to Europe and the Canadian Arctic and explore the Maine coast. But, Buffalo Bill or not, it was the West that beckoned. In 1904 the *Bulletin* sent her to Montana for a feature on the Blackfeet Indians. Her reporting chore done, she took the train to Cody at least in part because Andrew MacKenzie had settled nearby. Not long afterward MacKenzie left, never to return. Caroline stayed.

The rawness of Cody as a town on the make appealed to her. The inhabitants seemed less like a community of townspeople than a congregation of colorful character types. Yet it was a skeleton community of mostly married couples and single men — seemingly evenly divided among old timers and speculators — who shared a common optimism in the future of their place. The oracle of their faith was the Cody *Enterprise* which was hardly a newspaper like those she had known but more like a cheerleader for the boom that seemed the inevitable outcome of the energy in the air. Cowboys, sheepherders, and capitalists mingled at the Irma or any of the bars that outnumbered the other businesses on Main Street. The wives all knew each other as self-conscious pioneers of the civilization to

George Beck's Shoshone Land and Irrigation Company offices on the northeast corner of Sheridan Avenue and 13th Street. Beck/Gerber Collection. Park County Historical Archives.

come. Lockhart was welcomed as a celebrity journalist, and she reveled in the opportunities she sensed for an attractive single woman. And in her eagerness to find a slice of the frontier, Caroline at first read the town wrong.

It has been said that the defining element in American culture has been the tension between individualism and authority, between freedom and responsibility. The West of Caroline's imagination was a perpetual frontier where the institutions of order were forever thwarted by eccentric and powerful characters. Buffalo Bill to her was at first the romantic and morally-free individual who forever represented the unfettered breeziness of the plains, and his town was the antidote to the class-bound societies of the East and Europe. To Caroline the meaning of America, at least as she sought it in the West, was clear. It was a democracy of character over money or name, the home of initiative and personal responsibility over law and lawyers, the place where the duel — in her case, the duel of words — was the test of backbone and honor. A person of substance might be measured by his (or her) enemies, but in the West even enemies found common cause in the preservation of the rough democracy and sociability that encouraged individualistic and chivalric solutions to public problems.

Cody seemed to be frozen in time, an ideal laboratory for Lockhart's study of character and characters. Perhaps even more, Cody seemed at first to be isolated, perhaps even immune, from the social posturing that made the East seem so stifling. As the town began to change, Caroline refused to change with it and resented the coming of the civilizers she called "scissorbills." And as the characters, the locals, she had initially admired for their grit and independence began to seem to her to be no better, perhaps even worse, than the Bostonians and Philadelphians she had left behind, she acted as if she had been betrayed and grew bitingly satirical in her literary treatment of them.

During her first few years in Cody, Lockhart seemed to relish the activity that came with growth. Everyone seemed to have a scheme to make money. Irrigation projects limped along with little capital but great fanfare. The Shoshone Project, initially underwritten by Buffalo Bill and his partners and managed by George Beck, was matched in promotional spirit by the planned flooding of the Oregon Basin a few miles south, the brainchild of entrepreneur Solon Wiley who brought train cars of potential investors and settlers to town. Few of them stayed. Though the project mostly failed (seemingly inevitably), Wiley had had the good sense (a quality generally lacking in Boomtown, Lockhart thought) to acquire mineral rights in Oregon Basin to what became one of Wyoming's first producing oilfields. The Cody Club, a loosely organized and undercapitalized predecessor to the current chamber of commerce, cajoled and wheedled to attract money and attention for civic needs, such as building and maintaining the tourist road to Yellowstone National Park. The economic stakes were so trifling by urban standards — $25 was allocated one spring for road repairs, for instance — that Lockhart recognized and lampooned the eternal money squabbles and the petty larcenies that grew out of scarcity.

Caroline's crusade turned to the celebration — with an edge — and the preservation of the freewheeling Old West she was sure she had discovered. Her output was prodigious. She found abundant material among the local sheepmen and barkeeps for the numerous satirical commentaries and short stories she published in the eastern and regional press. Her social life as a liberated and single professional woman flourished as well. Though Andrew MacKenzie left Cody for parts unknown, two old friends and, quite likely, former lovers came to town. One of them, Harry Thurston, put himself out of reach when he married a niece of Buffalo Bill's, became supervisor of the Shoshone National Forest, and eventually settled into the staid life of a businessman. But Lockhart would not long be dismayed. A second, the dashing and wealthy Philadelphian John Painter, showed up as a speculator, prospecting for land and mineral riches. That he was married with children did not dampen his and Caroline's ardent interest in one another. His adventures became hers, and she later celebrated him in a 1915 novel, *The Man from the Bitter Roots.*

A young John Painter, before he arrived in Sunlight Basin. Jack Richard Collection. Park County Historical Archive.

Her first six years in Cody had given Caroline a great deal more than lovers and local color and a mission to preserve her West. It also had provided her with the material for her first and possibly most successful novel. Published in 1911, *Me-Smith* was a western, yet it wasn't a western. Some critics compared it favorably to Owen Wister's *The Virginian* (1902), but the book, like Lockhart herself, challenged traditions and stereotypes. The protagonist was an anti-hero, a bad guy/good guy infected with too much of the freedom and too little of the responsibility that represented the complexity of the changes that Caroline was witnessing and beginning to understand. Most important, it was a big seller, going into several printings in its first year and giving Caroline a new status among her Cody neighbors. In the spring of the pivotal year 1912, the Cody *Enterprise* took space from its sensational coverage of the *Titanic* disaster to boast that "Miss Caroline Lockhart's now famous novel" was "running in the Big Dailies," notably, for the region's pride, in the Denver *Times.* Cody was on the map even when Buffalo Bill was off roaming the world.

In fact, Cody was in the process of congratulating itself on the splendid Shoshone Dam, completed in 1910, and the filling of the reservoir. The town was "ribbing up," as Dad Pearce had predicted, with over a thousand permanent residents, a volunteer fire department, banks, hotels, electricity, telephones, churches, a world-renowned patron saint in the person of Buffalo Bill, and a resident literary lioness, Caroline Lockhart. There even was a public library in its own stone building, a project of the women's club led by Dr. Frances Lane.

Lockhart's neighbors had many reasons to be proud, and they had every reason to expect her next book to reflect new glamour on Cody. But Caroline's crusade was taking a dark turn, and her satirical wit was aimed at the small-town smugness she detected and detested. She must have been amused by the irony and piqued by the pretension of a weekly column in the *Enterprise* entitled "Pioneer Days in Cody" which celebrated events of just a decade before. Even as she had been writing *Me-Smith,* Lockhart had been collecting material for what she may have intended originally as a journalistic expose but which became her novel, *The Lady Doc.*

During the construction of the dam between 1905 and 1910, Lockhart had watched Cody veer away from the western ideal she had envisioned for it, and to her eyes the community of colorful characters struggling openly and equally to thrive in the democratic air of Wyoming had been betrayed by the grasping of some of them for money and social status. The most visible and most galling symbol of naked greed, in her view, was the hospital established by Dr. Lane and her partner, Dr. James T. Bradbury, not so much to serve the workers on the government project as to profit unscrupulously from them.

Lane and Bradbury had contracted with the Reclamation Service to provide medical care, and all of the laborers were assessed a monthly fee as a sort of health insurance. The fee was just one dollar, but few of the workers were paid more than three dollars per day. Lockhart conducted her own investigation into what she perceived as fraud and malpractice. She heard allegations of theft, poor sanitation, shoddy care, and downright negligent homicide. While officially only seven workers were documented to have died during the construction project, dozens of patients were said to have perished at the hands of the two doctors only to be buried quietly in paupers' graves. Most grievously, in Caroline's eyes, the scandal was compounded by a conspiracy of silence among the town's first citizens and the taint not only of shameful mistreatment but of the emergence of a complicit power structure in Cody.

In *The Lady Doc*, the town of "Crowheart" is, of course, Cody. Many of the characters are suggested by or based on Cody residents. Some are thinly disguised, indeed. Lockhart meant for some of the townspeople to recognize themselves. Her two primary targets in the novel were the title character, Dr. Frances Lane, and the town's leading citizen, George Beck. As Dr. Emma Harpe and Andrew Symes, they are portrayed unsparingly but not entirely unsympathetically. As a medical practitioner, Dr. Harpe's partner, modeled after Dr. Bradbury, is even more of a butcher than Dr. Harpe but is not much more than a cipher in the novel, possibly in part because he had left Cody in 1911. Lockhart's motivation in attacking Lane and Beck so unambiguously may have had a great deal to do with her earlier friendship with the two. Caroline had written admiringly of Lane's caring courage in 1904 in reporting a Cody bank robbery during which the cashier was fatally shot. Beck had been the town's perfect

Daisy and George Beck, central figures in The Lady Doc *and leading lights of Cody's early history.* Park County Historical Society.

host, the quiet and generous power behind the scenes and fount of western hospitality. Their apparent betrayal of the principles which in Caroline's view separated the honest and friendly locals from the "scissorbills" earned them her particular scorn. Other characters are composites of identifiable sometime Cody characters. Ogden Van Lennop suggests investor Bronson Rumsey, for instance, a genuine and natural aristocrat whose qualities stand in stark contrast to

Hattie McFall, (left) and Dr. Frances Lane, both dressed fit to kill. Park County Historical Society.

those of the would-be gentleman, Symes. Mrs. Hank Terriberry is obviously modeled after the gaudily made-up and eccentric but lovable matron of the Hart Mountain Hotel, Hattie McFall, whose frank pioneer qualities are likewise intended to show up the pettiness of aspiring ladies such as the wife of the bank president, Mrs. Percy Parrott, patterned after the real-life Mrs. Sammie Parks.

Cody's reaction to *The Lady Doc* was (and is) complex. The book is remembered chiefly as an attack on several leading citizens and an indictment of the Lane-Bradbury Clinic. But the town was likely scandalized more by the almost explicit homosexuality of Dr. Emma Harpe who carries on a lesbian affair with Augusta Kunkel Symes, a very thinly disguised Daisy Beck. Lockhart may have recognized and indulged bisexual tendencies in herself though her preferences were made clear in her several passionate affairs with men such as J. R. Painter. Dr. Lane was unquestionably lesbian, and most of Cody understood. But she was at the same time admired for her loyalty to the town, her leadership in community causes, her medical skills, and the compassion that Lockhart failed to see, and she continued to live and practice in Cody, her reputation mostly undamaged by *The Lady Doc* (and there is even a short street, Lane Drive, named for her)

The town was bitterly but tacitly divided by Lockhart's work. The book itself was discussed but possibly little read except by those who might have recognized themselves in its pages. Considering its sensation, few copies apparently survive in Cody collections. Caroline herself continued to live and work in and around Cody until her death in 1962, also honored locally for her sturdy integrity and quiet charities. She took up residence in Denver for a short time, but it was in 1918 and not because the novel's backlash chased her away.

Unfortunately for Lockhart, the novel was little read elsewhere as well. The literary world in 1912 was coincidentally celebrating the dean of America's genteel realism, William Dean Howells. The best-selling novelist of the day, Winston Churchill (who was so well-known that until the eve of the Second World War, references in the U.S. to the British statesman usually identified him as the "English Winston Churchill"), was one of those who toasted Howells for his unswerving adherence to eternal moral values and the happy certainty of Progress, neither of which is left unscathed in *The Lady Doc.* Churchill is little remembered today for some of the same reasons Lockhart has been so neglected — his inability to avoid larding his novels with the contrived romances that characterized all of Caroline's work.

Daisy Beck (left) and Dr. Frances Lane were lifelong friends. A Beck granddaughter was named Frances Lane Beck in the doctor's honor. Park County Historical Society.

In her own day, Lockhart intended her works to be taken seriously for their social content rather than as formula westerns. Her parallel romantic plots subverted her purpose, however, and in the case of *The Lady Doc,* readers attracted to happy endings found the romance overwhelmed by the shocking revelation of a vile lesbian doctor. Modern readers will likely decide that that *The Lady Doc* has been unfairly neglected or suppressed. Lockhart's skill as a satirist and her story-telling powers make for a vivid and often funny portrait of a western town in the agonizing grip of change. It may be disquieting, but it is always fun to read.

For readers familiar with Cody, and with similar towns and cities, there may even be uncomfortable moments of recognition of the affectations of wealth and position and the artificial social distinctions that define the public face of the town and its institutions. Discerning critics have noted that Cody sometimes seems to have a split personality — an up-scale, progressive, and cosmopolitan city in apparent denial of the pervasive problems plaguing the rest of American urban society, problems such as drug use, crime, and high rates of teen-pregnancy and suicide. It is a city that Caroline, with a cool but witty eye, would have loathed, loved, and lampooned. Yet it is also, as she acknowledged by making it her lifetime home, a place where western chivalry still exists and where institutions do not yet overwhelm the individual. She would urge us to admit to our hypocrisies, to treat problems face to face, and to exalt our sense of humor above our sense of propriety. She also would urge us, of course, to read *The Lady Doc* and find our selves and our times reflected in the Crowheart of 1912.

Caroline Lockhart at work.
Park County Historical Society.

For further reading

Jeannie Cook *et al*, Buffalo Bill's Town in the Rockies (Virginia Beach: The Donning Company, 1996)

Necah Stewart Furman, Caroline Lockhart: Her Life and Legacy (Cody: Buffalo Bill Historical Center in association with the University of Washington Press, 1994)

Lucille Nichols Patrick Hicks, Caroline Lockhart: Liberated Lady, 1870-1962 (Cheyenne: Pioneer Printing, 1984)

Charles Wayland Towne, "Preacher's Son on the Loose with Buffalo Bill Cody," Montana, the Magazine of Western History, XVII, 4 (Autumn, 1968)

Norris Yates, Caroline Lockhart (Boise: Boise State University Western Writers Series, 1994)

Other novels by Caroline Lockhart

Me-Smith (Philadelphia: Lippincott, 1911)

The Full of the Moon (Philadelphia: Lippincott, 1914)

The Man from the Bitter Roots (New York: A. L. Burt, 1915)

The Fighting Shepherdess (Boston: Small, 1919)

The Dude Wrangler (Garden City: Doubleday, 1933)

Old West and New (Garden City: Doubleday, 1933)

Some of the few exisiting copies of *The Lady Doc* still to be found on Cody family library shelves include a handwritten "key," identifying the novel's characters.

Character	*Cody resident*
Andy P. Symes	George T. Beck
Augusta Symes	Daisy Beck
Dr. Emma Harpe	Dr. Frances Lane
Essie Tisdale	Nellie DeMaris
Ogden Van Lennop	Bronson Rumsey
Tin Horn Frank	Frank Houx
Mrs. Alva Jackson	Mrs. Tex Holm
Edouard DuBois	Charles DeMaris
Dr. Lamb	Dr. James Bradbury
Hank Terriberry	Dave McFall
Mrs. Hank Terriberry	Hattie McFall
Percy Parrott	Samuel Parks
Mrs. Percy Parrott	Mrs. Samuel Parks
Prescott	Jakie Schwoob

CONTENTS

CHAPTER PAGE

I. The "Canuck" That Saved Flour Gold...... 9
II. The Humor of the Fate Lachesis.............. 17
III. A Mésalliance............................ 31
IV. "The Ground Floor"........................ 43
V. Another Case in Surgery.................... 56
VI. "The Church Racket"....................... 70
VII. The Sheep from the Goats................. 77
VIII. "The Chance of a Lifetime"............... 90
IX. The Ways of Polite Society................. 99
X. Essie Tisdale's Enforced Abnegation........ 110
XI. The Opening Wedge......................... 120
XII. Their First Clash........................ 127
XIII. Essie Tisdale's Colors.................. 139
XIV. "The Ethics of the Profession"........... 147
XV. Symes's Authority.......................... 165
XVI. The Top Wave.............................. 172
XVII. The Possible Investor.................... 179
XVIII. "Her Supreme Moment"..................... 188
XIX. "Down and Out"............................ 213
XX. An Unfortunate Affair...................... 234
XXI. Turning a Corner.......................... 248
XXII. Crowheart's First Murder Mystery......... 259
XXIII. Symes Meets the Homeseekers 271
XXIV. The Dago Duke and Dan Treu Exchange Confidences............................ 280
XXV. Crowheart Demands Justice.................. 288
XXVI. Latin Methods 294
XXVII. Essie Tisdale's Moment................... 303
XXVIII. The Sweetest Thing in the World........ 312
XXIX. "The Bitter End"......................... 325
XXX. "Thicker Than Water"....................... 332

ILLUSTRATIONS

PAGE

The First Cartridge Had Jammed and Every Other Chamber Was Filled . . . *Frontispiece*

"Old Hoss, You Oughtn't to Lie to Me Like That" . . . 62

"No, Essie Tisdale, I Can't Just See You in any Such Setting as That" . . . 113

He Laid His Huge Hand Upon Her Shoulder and Thrust Her Into a Chair . . . 322

THE LADY DOC

I

The "Canuck" That Saved Flour Gold

"A fellow must have something against himself—he certainly must—to live down here year in and year out and never do a lick of work on a trail like this that he's usin' constant. Gettin' off half a dozen times to lift the front end of your horse around a point, and then the back end—there's nothin' *to* it!"

Grumbling to himself and talking whimsically to the three horses stringing behind him, Dick Kincaid picked his way down the zigzag, sidling trail which led from the saddleback between two peaks of the Bitter Root Mountains into the valley which still lay far below him.

"Quit your crowdin', can't you, Baldy!" He laid a restraining hand upon the white nose of the horse following close at his heels. "Want to jam me off this ledge and send me rollin' two thousand feet down onto their roof? Good as I've been to you, too!"

He stopped and peered over the edge of the precipice along which the faint trail ran.

"Looks like smoke." He nodded in satisfaction. "Yes, *'tis* smoke. Long past dinner time, but then these squaws go to cookin' whenever they happen to think about it. Lord, but I'm hungry! Wish some good-lookin' squaw would get took with me and follow me off, for I sure hates cookin' and housework."

Still talking to himself he resumed the descent, slipping and sliding and digging his heels hard to hold himself back.

"They say she sticks like beeswax, Dubois's squaw, never tries to run off but stays right to home raisin' up a batch of young 'uns. You take these Nez Perces and they're good Injuns as Injuns go. Smarter'n most, fair lookers, and tolerable clean. Will you look at that infernal pack slippin' again, and right here where there's no chance to fix it!

"Say, but I'd like to get my thumb in the eye of the fellow that made these pack-saddles. Too narrow by four inches for any horse not just off grass and rollin' fat. Won't fit any horse that packs in *these* hills. Doggone it, his back'll be as raw as a piece of beefsteak and if there's anything in this world that I hate it's to pack a sore-backed horse.

"You can bet I wouldn't a made this trip for money if I wasn't so plumb anxious to see how Dubois saves that flour gold. You take one of these here 'canucks' and he 's blamed near as good if not a better placer miner than a Chink; more ingenious and just as savin'. Say, Baldy, will you keep off my heels? If I have to tell you again about walkin' up my pant leg I aim to break your head in. It's bad enough to come down a trail so steep it wears your back hair off t'hout havin' your clothes tore off you into the bargain."

And so, entertaining himself with his own conversation and scolding amiably at his saddle and pack horses, the youthful prospector slid for another hour down the mountain trail, though, as a rock would fall, the log house of the French Canadian was not more than a thousand yards below.

It was the middle of May and the deep snows of winter still lay in the passes and upon the summit, but in the valley the violets made purple blotches along the stream now foaming with the force of the water trickling from the melting drifts above. The thorn bushes were white with blossoms and the service-berry bushes were like fragrant banks of snow. Accustomed as he was to the beauty of valleys and the grandeur of peaks, something in the peaceful scene below him stirred the soul of young Dick Kincaid, and he stopped to look before he made the last drop into the valley.

"Ain't that a young paradise?" He breathed deep of the odorous air. "Ain't it, now?"

The faint blue smoke rising straight among the white blossoms reminded him again of his hunger, so, wiping the perspiration from his snow-burned face, he started on again, but when he came to the ditch which carried water from the stream through a hundred and fifty feet of sluice-boxes he stopped and examined with eager interest the methods used for saving fine gold, for, keen as was his hunger, the miner's instinct within him was keener.

"Will you look at the lumber he's whip-sawed!" Astonishment was in his voice! "Whip-sawin' lumber is the hardest work a man ever did. I'll bet the squaw was on the other end of that saw; I never heard of Dubois hiring help. Uh-huh, he uses the Carriboo riffles. Look at the work he's been to—punchin' all those holes in that sheet-iron. And here's two boxes of pole riffles, and a set of Hungarian riffles, not to mention three distributin' boxes and a table. Say, he isn't takin' any chances on losin' anything, is he? But it's all right you gotta be careful with this light gold and heavy sand. I'm liable to learn something down here. Lord I'm hungry! Come on, Baldy!"

As he pulled his saddle horse in the direction of the smoke he noticed that there were no footprints in the trail and a stillness which impressed him as peculiar pervaded the place. There was something which he missed—what was it? To be sure—dogs! There were no barking dogs to greet him. It was curious, he thought, for these isolated families always had plenty of dogs and no "breed" or "Injun" outfit ever kept fewer than six. There were no shrill voices of children at play, no sound of an axe or a saw or a hammer.

"Blamed funny," he muttered, yet he knew where there was smoke there must be human beings.

He stopped short at some sound and listened attentively. A whimpering minor wail reached him faintly. It was unlike any sound he ever had heard, yet he knew it was a woman's voice. There was something in the cadence which sent a chill over him. He dropped the bridle reins and walked softly down the trail. Suddenly he halted and his lips parted in a whispered ejaculation of astonishment and horror. He was young then, Dick Kincaid, but the sight which met his eyes stayed with him distinct in every detail, through all his adventurous life.

Two children, boys of eleven and thirteen or thereabouts, were roasting a ground squirrel in the smouldering embers of what had been a cabin. A dead baby lay on a ragged soogan near a partially dug grave. Cross-legged on the ground beside it was a woman wailing unceasingly as she rocked her gaunt and nearly naked body to and fro. The eagerness of famished animals gleamed in the boys' eyes as they tore the half-cooked squirrel in two, yet each offered his share to his mother, who seemed not to see the proffered food.

"Just a little piece, mother," coaxed the elder, and he extended an emaciated arm from which hung the rags of a tattered shirt sleeve.

Both children were dressed in the remnants of copper-riveted overalls and their feet were bound in strips of canvas torn from a "tarp." Their straight black hair hung over faces sunken and sallow and from the waist up they were naked.

The boy held the food before her as long as he could endure it, then he tore it with his teeth in the ferocity of starvation.

"Can you *beat* it! Can you beat *that!*" The boys did not hear Kincaid's shocked exclamation.

It was not until he cleared his throat and called in a friendly, reassuring voice that they learned they were not alone. Then they jumped in fright and scurried into a nearby thicket like two scared rabbits, each holding tight his food. But Dick Kincaid's face was one to inspire confidence, and as he approached they came forth timidly. Their first fright gave place to delirious joy. The smaller threw his arms about Kincaid's long legs and hugged them in an ecstasy of delight while the elder clung to his hand as though afraid he might vanish. The woman merely glanced at him with vacant eyes and went on wailing.

While he took cold biscuits and bacon from his pack they told him what had happened—briefly, simply, without the smallest attempt to color the story for his sympathy.

"We couldn't have held out much longer, m'sieu, we're so weak." The elder boy was the spokesman.

"And the strawberries and sarvis-berries won't be ripe for a long time yet. It wasn't so bad till the cabin burned. We could keep warm. But we went off in the woods to see if we could kill something, and when we came back the cabin was burned and the baby dead. Mother went crazy more than a month ago, I guess it was. She wouldn't let us bury the baby till yesterday, and when we started to dig we found we could only dig a little at a time. We got tired so quick, and besides, we had to try and keep a fire, for we have no more matches."

"I could dig longer nor you," chimed in the younger boy boastfully. The other smiled wanly.

"I know it, Petie, but you had more to eat. You had two trout and a bird more nor me."

"You have a gun, then? and fish-hooks?"

"Not now. We lost our hooks and shot our shells away long ago. We kill things with rocks but it takes muscle, m'sieu, to throw hard enough. The dog was starvin' and we killed and ate him. We couldn't try to get out because mother wouldn't leave and she'd a been dead before we got back. We couldn't have wallered through the snow anyhow. We'd never have made it if we'd gone. There wasn't anything to do but to try and hang on till spring; then we hoped somebody would come down like you have."

The boy did not cry as he told the story nor did his lip so much as quiver at the recollection of their sufferings. He made no effort to describe them, but the hollows in his cheeks and the dreadful thinness of his arms and little body told it all more eloquently than words.

Kincaid noticed that he had not mentioned his father's name, so he asked finally:

"Where's Dubois? Where's your father? I came to see him."

The childish face hardened instantly.

"I don't know. He cleaned up the sluice-boxes late last fall after the first freeze. Mother helped him clean up. He got a lot of gold—the most yet—and he took it with him and all the horses. He said he was going out for grub but he never came back. Then the big snows came in the mountains and we knew he couldn't get in. We ate our bacon up first, then the flour give out, and the beans. The baby cried all the time 'cause 'twas hungry and Petie and me wore our shoes out huntin' through the hills. It was awful, m'sieu."

Kincaid swallowed a lump in his throat.

"Do you think he'll come back?" the younger boy asked eagerly.

"He might have stayed outside longer than he intended and found he couldn't get in for the snow, or he might have tried and froze in the pass. It's deep there yet," was Kincaid's evasive reply.

"He'll never come back," said the older boy slowly, "and—he wasn't froze in the pass."

It was still May when Dick Kincaid climbed out of the valley with the whimpering squaw clinging to the horn of his saddle while the swarthy little "breeds" trudged manfully in the trail close to his heels. The violets still made purple blotches along the bank of the noisy stream, the thorn trees and the service-berry bushes were still like fragrant banks of snow, the grass in the valley was as green and the picture as serenely beautiful as when first he had stopped to gaze upon it, but it no longer looked like paradise to Dick Kincaid.

They stopped to rest and let the horses get their breath when they reached the edge of the snows, and for a time they stood in silence looking their last upon the valley below them. The older boy drew his thin hand from Kincaid's big palm and touched the gun swinging in its holster on his hip.

"Do they cost much, a gun like this?"

"Not much, boy. Why?"

The younger answered for him, smiling at the shrewdness of his guess.

"I know. He's goin' to hunt for father when he's big."

There was no answering smile upon his brother's face, the gravity of manhood sat strangely upon it as he answered without boastfulness or bitterness but rather in the tone of one who speaks of a duty:

"I'm goin' to find him, m'sieu, and when I do I'll get him *sure!*"

Dick Kincaid regarded him for a moment from the shadow of his wide-brimmed hat.

"If you do, boy, and I find it out, I don't know as I'll give you away."

II

THE HUMOR OF THE FATE LACHESIS

WHAT possible connection, however remote, this tragedy of the Bitter Root Mountains could have with the future of Doctor Emma Harpe, who, nearly twenty years later, sat at a pine table in a forlorn Nebraska town filling out a death certificate, or what part it could play in the life of Essie Tisdale, the belle of the still smaller frontier town of Crowheart, in a distant State, who at the moment was cleaning her white slippers with gasoline, only the Fate Lachesis spinning the thread of human life from Clotho's distaff could foresee.

When Dr. Harpe, whose fingers were cold with nervousness, made tremulous strokes which caused the words to look like a forgery, the ugly Fate Lachesis grinned, and grinned again when Essie Tisdale, many hundred miles away, held the slipper up before her and dimpled at its arched smallness; then Lachesis rearranged her threads.

Dr. Harpe arose when the certificate was blotted and, thrusting her hands deep in the pockets of her loose, square-cut coat, made a turn or two the length of the office, walking with the long strides of a man. Unexpectedly her pallid, clear-cut features crumpled, the strained muscles relaxed, and she dropped into a chair, her elbows on her knees, her feet wide apart, her face buried in her hands. She was unfeminine even in her tears.

Alice Freoff was dead! Alice Freoff was dead! Dr. Harpe was still numb with the chilling shock of it. She had not expected it. Such a result had not entered into her calculations—not until she had seen her best friend slipping into the other world had she considered it; then she had fought frantically to hold her back. Her efforts had been useless and with a frightful clutching at her heart she had watched the woman sink. Alexander Freoff was away from home. What would he say when he learned that his wife had died of an operation which he had forbidden Dr. Harpe to attempt? Fear checked the tears of grief with which her cheeks were wet. He was a man of violent temper and he had not liked the intimacy between herself and his wife. He did not like *her*—Dr. Emma Harpe—and now that Alice was dead and the fact that she, as a physician, had blundered, was too obvious to be denied, the situation held alarming possibilities. Consternation replaced her grief and the tears dried on her cheeks while again she paced the floor.

She was tired almost to exhaustion when she stopped suddenly and flung her shoulder in defiance and self-disgust. "Bah! I'm going to pieces like a schoolgirl. I must pull myself together. Twenty-four hours will tell the tale and I must keep my nerve. The doctors will—they *must* stand by me!"

Dr. Harpe was correct in her surmise that her suspense would be short. The interview between herself and the husband of her dead friend was one she was not likely to forget. Then the coroner, himself a physician, sent for her and she found him waiting at his desk. All the former friendliness was gone from his eyes when he swung in his office chair and looked at her.

"It will not be necessary, I believe, to explain why

I have sent for you, Dr. Harpe.'' His cool, impersonal voice was more ominous, more final than anger, and she found it hard to preserve her elaborate assumption of ease.

A dull red mounted slowly to her cheeks and faded, leaving them ashen.

''Two doors are open to you.'' He weighed his words carefully. ''If you remain here, suit will be brought against you by Alexander Freoff; and since, in this case, you have acted in violation of all recognized methods of medical science, I will not uphold you. As a matter of fact, immediate action will be taken by the State Medical Board, of which I am a member, to disqualify you. If you leave town within twenty-four hours you will be permitted to go unmolested. This concession I am willing to make; not for your sake but for the sake of the profession which you have disgraced. You have my ultimatum; you may take your choice.''

She gripped the arms of her chair hard, silent from an inability to speak. At last she arose uncertainly and said in a voice which was barely audible:

''I will go.''

And so it happened that while Dr. Emma Harpe was saying good-by to a few wondering acquaintances who accompanied her to the station, Essie Tisdale was making preparations for a dance which was an event in the embryotic metropolis of Crowheart, several hundred miles away.

Crowheart was booming and the news of its prosperity had spread. Settlers were hurrying toward it from the Middle West to take up homesteads and desert claims in the surrounding country. There was no specific reason why the town should boom, but it did boom in that mysterious fashion which far western towns have, up to a certain stage, after which the reaction sets in.

But there was no thought of reaction now. All was life, eagerness, good-nature, boundless belief in a great and coming prosperity. The Far West and the Middle West greeted each other with cordial, outstretched hands and this dance, though given by a single individual, was in the nature of a reception from the old settlers to the new as well as to celebrate the inception of an undertaking which was to insure Crowheart's prosperity for all time.

Crowheart was platted on a sagebrush "bench" on a spur of a branch railroad. The snow-covered peaks of a lofty range rose skyward in the west. To the north was the solitary butte from which the town received its name. To the south was a line of dimpled foothills, while eastward stretched a barren vista of cactus, sand, and sagebrush. A shallow stream flowed between alkali-coated banks on two sides of the town. In the spring when melting mountain snows filled it to overflowing, it ran swift and yellow; but in the late fall and winter it dropped to an inconsequential creek of clear water, hard with alkali. The inevitable "Main Street" was wide and its two business blocks consisted of one-story buildings of log and unpainted pine lumber. There was the inevitable General Merchandise Store with its huge sign on the high front, and the inevitable newspaper which always exists, like the faithful at prayer, where two or three are gathered together. There were saloons in plenty with irrelevant and picturesque names, a dance hall and a blacksmith shop. The most conspicuous and pretentious building in Crowheart was the Terriberry

House, bilious in color and Spartan in its architecture, located in the centre of Main Street on a corner. The houses as yet were chiefly tar-paper shacks or floored and partially boarded tents, but the sound of the saw and the hammer was heard week-days and Sundays so no one could doubt but that it was only a question of time when Crowheart would be comfortably housed. There was nothing distinctive about Crowheart; it had its prototype in a thousand towns between Peace River and the Rio Grande; it was typical of the settlements which are springing up every year along the lines of those railroads that are stretching their tentacles over the Far West. Yet the hopes of Crowheart expressed themselves in boulevards outlined with new stakes and in a park which should, some day, be a breathing spot for a great city. It was Crowheart's last thought that it should remain stationary and obscure.

To Dr. Harpe swinging down from the high step of the single passenger coach in the mixed train of coal and cattle cars, it looked like a highly colored picture on a drop-curtain. The effect was impressionistic and bizarre as it lay in the gorgeous light of the setting sun, yet it pleased and rested the eye of the woman whose thoughts had not been conducive to an appreciation of scenery during the journey past.

As she drew a deep breath of the thin, stimulating air, the tension lessened on her strained nerves. She looked back at the interminable miles over which she had come, the miles which lay between her and the nightmare of disgrace and failure she had left, and then at the new, untried field before her. The light of new hope shone in her handsome hazel eyes, and there was fresh life in her step as she picked up her suitcase and started across the railroad track toward the town.

"Emma Harpe. . . . St. Louis," she wrote boldly upon the bethumbed register of the Terriberry House.

The loungers in the office studied her signature earnestly but it told them nothing of that which they most wished to know—her business. She might be selling books upon the instalment plan: she might be peddling skin-food warranted to restore their weather-beaten complexions to the texture of a baby's: she *might* be a new inmate for the dance hall. Anything was possible in Crowheart.

She was the object of interested glances as she ate her supper in the long dining-room for, although she was nearly thirty, there was still something of girlhood in her tired face. But she seemed engrossed in her own thoughts and returned to her room as soon as she had eaten. There she lay down upon the patchwork quilt which covered her bed, with her hands clasped above her head, staring at the ceiling and trying to forget the past in conjecturing the future.

The clatter of dishes ceased after a time and with the darkness came the sound of many voices in the hall below. There was laughter and much scurrying to and fro. Then she heard the explanatory tuning of a violin and finally a loud and masterful voice urging the selection of partners for a quadrille. Whoops of exuberance, shrill feminine laughter, and jocose personalities shouted across the room followed. Then, simultaneous with a burst of music, the scuffling of sliding soles and stamping heels told her that the dance was on.

The jubilant shriek of the violin, the lively twang of a guitar, the "boom! boom" of a drum marking time, the stentorian voice of the master of ceremonies, reached her plainly as she lay staring at the stars through the single window of her room. She liked the sounds; they were cheerful; they helped to shut out the dying face of Alice Freoff and to dull the pitiless voice of the coroner. She found herself keeping time with her foot to the music below.

An hour passed with no diminution of the hilarity downstairs and having no desire to sleep she still lay with her lamp unlighted. While she listened her ear caught a sound which had no part in the gayety below. It came faintly at first, then louder as a smothered sob became a sharp intake of breath.

Dr. Harpe sat up and listened intently. The sound was close, apparently at the head of the stairs. She was not mistaken, a woman was crying—so she opened the door.

A crouching figure on the top step shrank farther into the shadow.

"Is that you crying?"

Another sob was the answer.

"What ails you? Come in here."

While she struck a match to light the lamp the girl obeyed mechanically.

Dr. Harpe shoved a chair toward her with her foot.

"Now what's the trouble?" she demanded half humorously. "Are you a wall-flower or is your beau dancing with another girl?"

There was a rush of tears which the girl covered her face with her hands to hide.

"Huh—I hit it, did I?"

While she wept softly, Dr. Harpe inspected her with deliberation. She was tall and awkward, with long, flat feet, and a wide face with high cheek bones that was Scandinavian in its type. Her straight hair was the drab shade which flaxen hair becomes before it darkens, and her large mouth had a solemn, unsmiling droop. Her best feature was her brown, melancholy, imaginative eyes. She looked like the American-born daughter of Swedish or Norwegian emigrants and her large-knuckled hands, too, bespoke the peasant strain.

"Quit it, Niobe, and tell me your name."

The girl raised her tearful eyes.

"Kunkel—Augusta Kunkel."

"Oh, German?"

The girl nodded.

"Well, Miss Kunkel"—she suppressed a smile—"tell me your troubles and perhaps you'll feel better."

More tears was the girl's reply.

"Look here"—there was impatience in her voice—"there's no man worth bawling over."

"But—but——" wept the girl, "he said he'd marry me!"

"Isn't he going to?"

"I don't know—he's going away in a few days and he won't talk any more about it. He's waltzed every waltz to-night with Essie Tisdale and has not danced once with me."

"So? And who's Essie Tisdale?"

"She's the waitress here."

"Downstairs? In this hotel?"

Augusta Kunkel nodded.

"I don't blame him," Dr. Harpe replied bluntly, "I saw her at supper. She's a peach!"

"She's the belle of Crowheart," admitted the girl reluctantly.

"And who is *he?* What's *his name?*"

The girl hesitated but as though yielding to a stronger will than her own, she whimpered:

"Symes—Andy P. Symes."

"Why don't you let Andy P. Symes go if he wants to? He isn't the only man in Crowheart, is he?"

"But he promised!" The girl wrung her hands convulsively. "He promised *sure!*"

A look of quick suspicion flashed across Dr. Harpe's face.

" He *promised*—oh, I *see!*"

She arose and closed the door.

The interview was interrupted by a bounding step upon the stairs and a little tap upon the door, and when it was opened the belle of Crowheart stood flushed and radiant on the threshold.

"We want you to come down," she said in her vivacious, friendly voice. "It must be lonely for you up here, and Mr. Symes—he's giving the dance, you know—he sent me up to ask you." She caught sight of the girl's tear-stained face and stepped quickly into the room. "Why, Gussie." She laid her arm about her shoulder. "What's the matter?"

Augusta Kunkel drew away with frank hostility in her brown eyes and answered:

"Nothing's the matter—I'm tired, that's all."

Though she flushed at the rebuff, she murmured gently: "I'm sorry, Gussie." Turning to Dr. Harpe, she urged persuasively:

"Please come down. We're having the best time *ever!*"

Dr. Harpe hesitated, for she thought of Alice

Freoff, but the violin was shrieking enticingly and the voice of the master of ceremonies in alluring command floated up the stairway:

"Choose your partners for a waltz, gents!"

She jerked her head at Augusta Kunkel.

"Come along—don't sit up here and mope."

Andy P. Symes, waiting in the hall below, was a little puzzled by the intentness of the newcomer's gaze as she descended the stairs, but at the bottom he extended a huge hand:

"I'm glad you decided to join us, Miss——"

"Harpe—Doctor Emma Harpe."

"Oh," surprised amusement was in his tone, "you've come to settle among us, perhaps? Permit me to welcome you, Dr. Harpe. We are to be congratulated. Our nearest physician is sixty miles away, so you will have the field to yourself. You should prosper. Do you come from the East?"

She looked him in the eyes.

"St. Louis."

"Take your pardners for the waltz, gents!"

Andy P. Symes held out his arms in smiling invitation while the news flashed round the room that the newcomer with the cold, immobile face, the peculiar pallor of which contrasted strongly with their own sun-blistered skins, was a "lady-doctor" who had come to live in Crowheart.

The abandon, the freedom of it all, appealed strongly to Dr. Harpe. The atmosphere was congenial, and when the waltz was done she asked that she might be allowed to sit quietly for a time since she found herself more fatigued by her long journey than she had realized; but, in truth, she desired to familiarize herself with the character of the people among whom her future work lay.

A noisy, heterogeneous gathering it was, boisterous without vulgarity, free without familiarity. There were no covert glances of dislike or envy, no shrugs of disdain, no whispered innuendoes. The social lines which breed these things did not exist. Every man considered his neighbor and his neighbor's wife as good as himself and his genuine liking was in his frank glance, his hearty tones, his beaming, friendly smile. Men and women looked at each other clear-eyed and straight.

The piercing "yips" of cowboys meant nothing but an excess of spirits. The stamping of feet, the shouts and laughter were indicative only of effervescent youth seeking an outlet. Most were young, all were full of life and hope, and the world was far away, that world where clothes and money matter.

The scene was typical of a new town in the frontier West. The old settlers and the new mingled gaily. The old timers with their indifferent dress, their vernacular and free manners of the mountains and ranges brushed elbows with the more modern folk of the poor and the middle class of the Middle West. They were uninteresting and mediocre, these newcomers, yet the sort who thrive astonishingly upon new soil, who become prosperous and self-important in an atmosphere of equality. There were, too, educated failures from the East and—people who had blundered. But all alike to-night, irrespective of pasts or presents or futures, were bent upon enjoying themselves to their capacities.

Callous-handed ranchers and their faded wives promenaded arm in arm. Sheep-herders and cowpunchers passed in the figures of the dance eyeing each other in mutual antipathy. The neat "hand-me-downs" of grocery clerks contrasted with the copper-riveted overalls of shy and silent prospectors from the hills who stood against the walls envying their dapper ease. A remittance man from Devonshire whose ancestral halls had sheltered an hundred knights danced with Faro Nell, who gambled for a living, while the station agent's attenuated daughter palpitated in the arms of a husky stage-driver. Mr. Percy Parrott, the sprightly cashier of the new bank, swung the new milliner from South Dakota. Sylvanus Starr, the gifted editor of the Crowheart *Courier,* schottisched with Mrs. "Hank" Terriberry, while his no less gifted wife swayed in the arms of the local barber, and his two lovely daughters, "Pearline" and "Planchette," tripped it respectively with the "barkeep" of the White Elephant Saloon and a Minneapolis shoe-drummer. In the centre of the floor the new plasterer and his wife moved through the figures of the French minuet with the stiff-kneed grace of two self-conscious giraffes, while Mrs. Percy Parrott, a long-limbed lady with a big, white, Hereford-like face, capered with "Tinhorn Frank," the oily, dark, craftily observant proprietor of the "Walla Walla Restaurant and Saloon." Mr. Abe Tutts, of the Flour and Feed Store, skimmed the floor with the darting ease of a water-spider dragging beside him his far less active wife, a belligerent-appearing and somewhat hard-featured lady several years his senior.

But the long, crowded dining-room held two central figures, one of which was Andy P. Symes, and the other was Essie Tisdale, the little waitress of the Terriberry House and the belle of Crowheart.

Symes moved among his guests with the air of a man who found amusement in mingling with those he deemed his inferiors even while patently bidding for their admiration and regard. His height and breadth of shoulder made him conspicuous even in this gathering of tall men. His finely shaped head was well set but in contrast his utterly inconsequential nose came as something of a shock. His face was florid and genial and he had a word for the most obscure.

Yet the trained and sensitive observer would have felt capabilities for boorishness beneath his amiability, a lack of sincerity in his impartial and too fulsome compliments. His manner denoted a degree of social training and a knowledge of social forms acquired in another than his present environment, but he was too fond of the limelight—it cheapened him; too broad in his attentions to women—it coarsened him; his waistcoat was the dingy waistcoat of a man of careless habits; his linen was not too immaculate and the nails of his blunt fingers showed lack of attention. He was the sort of man who is nearly, but not quite, a gentleman.

The slim little belle of Crowheart seemed to be everywhere, her youthful spirits were unflagging, and her contagious, merry laugh rang out constantly from the centre of lively groups. Her features were delicate and there was pride, sensitiveness and good-breeding in her mouth with its short, red upper lip. Her face held more than prettiness, for there was thoughtfulness, as well, in her blue eyes and innate kindness in its entire expression. Her light brown hair was soft and plentiful and added to her stature by its high dressing. She was natural of manner and graceful with the ease of happy youth and her flushed cheeks were pinker than her simple gown. She looked farther removed from her occupation than any woman in the room and to Dr. Harpe, following her with her eyes, the connection seemed incongruous.

"Moses!" she whispered to herself, "but that little biscuit-shooter would be a winner if she had clothes."

Other eyes than Dr. Harpe's were following Essie Tisdale and with an intentness which finally attracted her attention. She stopped as she was passing a swarthy, silent man in the corner, who had not moved from his chair since the beginning of the dance, and, arching her eyebrows, she asked mischievously:

"Don't you mean to ask me for a single dance, Mr. Dubois—not one?"

To her surprise, and the amusement of all who heard, he arose at once, bending his squat figure in an awkward bow, and replied:

"Certainly, m'amselle, if you will give me that pleasure."

And all the roomful stared in mingled astonishment and glee when old Edouard Dubois, the taciturn and little-liked sheepman from the "Limestone Rim," led Essie Tisdale out upon the floor to complete a set.

The evening was well along when Dr. Harpe laid her hand upon the unpainted railing which served as a bannister and turned to look once more at the roomful of hot, ecstatically happy dancers before she went upstairs.

"Harpe," she murmured, and her eyes narrowed, "Harpe, we're going to make good here. We're going to win out. We're going to make money hand over fist."

And even with her own boastful words there came a pang which had its source in a knowledge her dance with Symes had brought her. Something was dead within her! That something was the spirit of youth, and with it had gone the best of Emma Harpe.

III

A Mésalliance

Crowheart was surprised but not shocked when the engagement of Andy P. Symes to the blacksmith's sister was announced. It saw no mésalliance in the union. It was merely unaware that he had been attentive to Augusta Kunkel. Now they were to be married in the long dining-room of the Terriberry House and take the night train for Chicago on their honeymoon.

Dr. Harpe standing at the window of her new office on the second floor of the hotel smiled to herself as she saw the chairs going inside which served equally well for funerals or for social functions. The match, she felt, was really of her making.

"You've got to do it," she had told him. "You've simply got to do it."

He had come to see her at Augusta's insistence.

"But!" he had groaned; "a Kunkel! Perhaps you don't know—but I'm one of the Symes of Maine. Great-grandfather a personal friend of Alexander Hamilton's, and all that. My family don't expect *much* of me since I'm the black sheep, but," a dull red had surged over his face, "they expect something better of me than a Kunkel!"

She had shrugged her shoulders.

"Suit yourself, I'm only telling you how it looks to me. You'll queer yourself forever if you don't marry her, for this country is still western enough to respect women. You are just starting in to promote this irrigation project and if you succeed you can't tell what the future will hold for you politically; this is just the sort of thing to bob up and down you. You know I'm right."

"But she looks so obviously what she is," he had groaned miserably. "Some day I may want to go home—and think of introducing Augusta Kunkel!"

"You are wrong there," she had replied with conviction, "Augusta has possibilities. She has good eyes, her voice is low, her English is far better than you might expect, and, best of all, she's tall and slender. If she was short and fat I'd call her rather hopeless, but you hang good clothes on these slim ones and it works wonders. Besides, she's imitative as a parrot."

He had thrown his arms aloft in despair.

"But think of it!—the rest of my life—with a parrot."

"It's the lesser of two evils," she had urged, and in the end he had said dully:

"I guess you're right, Dr. Harpe. Your advice no doubt is good, though, like your medicine, a bitter dose just now. You've done me a favor, I suppose, and I'll not forget it."

When the door of her office had closed upon his broad back she had said to herself:

"I'll see that you don't forget it." And she repeated it again with renewed satisfaction. She liked the feeling that she already had become a factor in the affairs of Crowheart and she intended to remain one.

The practice of medicine with Dr. Harpe was frankly for personal gain. No ideals had influenced her in the choice of her profession and her practice of it had developed no ambition save the single one of building up a bank account. The ethical distinction between the trades and professions, which is based upon the fact that the professional man or woman is supposed to take up his or her life work primarily because he loves both his profession and the people whom it may benefit, was a distinction which she never had grasped. She practised medicine in the same commercial spirit that a cheap drummer builds up a trade. She had no sentiment regarding it, none of the ambitious dreams of high professional standing attained by meritorious work which inspire those who achieve. It was a business pure and simple; each patient was a customer.

Another consideration in her choice of this profession was the freedom it gave her. Because of it she was exempt from many of the restrictions and conventionalities which hampered her sex, and above all else she disliked restraint.

She was the single result of a "typhoid romance." Her mother, a trained nurse, had attended a St. Louis politician during a long illness. Upon his recovery he married his nurse and as promptly deserted her, providing a modest support for the child. She had grown to womanhood in a cheap boarding school, attaining thereby a superficial education but sufficient to enable her to pass the preliminary examinations necessary to begin her studies in the medical college which was an outcast among its kind and known among the profession as a "diploma mill." She selected it because the course was easy and the tuition light, though its equipment was a farce and its laboratory too meagre to deserve the name; one of the commercial medical colleges turning out each year by the hundreds, for a few dollars, illiterate graduates, totally unfitted by temperament and education for a profession that calls for the highest and best, sending them out in hordes like licensed murderers to prescribe and operate among the trusting and the ignorant.

Dr. Harpe had framed her sheep-skin and been duly photographed in her cap and gown; then, after a short hospital experience, she had gone to the little Nebraska town where perhaps the most forceful comment upon the success of her career there was that the small steamer trunk, which she was now opening, contained very comfortably both her summer and winter wardrobe.

Her pose was an air of camaraderie, of blunt good-nature. Her conspicuous walk was a swaggering stride, while in dress she affected the masculine severity of some professional women. Her hair was the dull red that is nearly brown and she wore it coiled in trying simplicity at the back of her head. Her handsome eyes were the hazel that is alternately brown and green and gray, sometimes an odd mixture of all three. Ordinarily there was a suspicion of hardness in her face but there was also upon occasions a kind of winsomeness, an unexpected peeping out of a personality which was like the wraith of the child which she once had been—a suggestion of girlish charm and spontaneity utterly unlike her usual self.

This attractive phase of her personality was uppermost as she sought in the trunk for something to wear, and a smile curved the corners of her straight lips and brought out a faint cleft in her square chin, as she inspected its contents.

She found what she wanted in a plain cloth skirt and a white tailored waist with stiffly starched cuffs, and a man's sleeve links. When she was dressed a man's linen waistcoat with a black silk watch-fob hanging from the pocket added further to the unfeminine *tout ensemble.* She liked the effect, and, as she thrust a scarf-pin in the long black "four-in-hand" before her mirror, she viewed the result with satisfaction.

Dr. Harpe regarded the wedding as exceedingly opportune for herself, bringing in as it did the settlers from the isolated ranches and outlying districts of the big county, and she meant it to serve as her real début in the community.

It was in fact a notable event for the reason that it was the first wedding in Crowheart, and, since the invitation was general, the guests were coming from far and near to show their approval and incidentally perhaps to partake of the champagne which it was rumored was to flow like water. Champagne was the standard by which Crowheart gauged the success of an entertainment and certainly Andy P. Symes was not the man to serve sarsaparilla at his own wedding.

When Dr. Harpe came downstairs she found the long dining-room cleared of its tables and already well filled with guests. "Curly" the camp cook was caressing his violin, and "Snake River Jim," tolerably drunk, was in his place beside him, while Ole Peterson, redolent of the livery-stable in which he worked, constantly felt his muscle to show that he was prepared to do his share with the big bass drum.

As Andy P. Symes moved through the rapidly growing crowd no one but Dr. Harpe guessed that he winced inwardly at the resounding slaps upon his back and the congratulations or that his heart all but failed him when he saw his bride-to-be in her bobinet veil, a flush upon her broad face and following his every movement with adoring eyes. To all but Dr. Harpe he looked the fortunate and beaming bridegroom and only she saw the tiny lines which sleeplessness had left about his eyes or detected the hollowness of his frequent laughter.

It was more or less of a relief to all when the ceremony was over and the nervous and perspiring Justice of the Peace, miserable in a collar, had wished them every known joy. It was a relief to Symes who kissed his bride perfunctorily and returned her to weeping "Grandmother" Kunkel's arms—a relief to those impatient to dance—a relief to the thirsty whose surreptitious glances wandered in spite of their best efforts toward the pile of champagne cases in the corner.

But the reward of patience came to all, and as the violin and guitar tuned up the popping of corks was assurance enough that the unsurpassed thirst created by alkali dust would shortly be assuaged. "Hank" Terriberry, in whose competent charge Symes had placed this portion of the wedding entertainment, realizing that, at best, pouring from a bottle and drinking from a glass is a slow and tedious process, to facilitate matters had provided two large, bright, new dish-pans which he filled with wine, also a plentiful supply of bright, new, tin dippers.

They drank Symes's health in long, deep draughts and it was with some forebodings that Symes noted the frequency with which the same guests appeared in line. Symes had no great desire that his wedding should go down in the annals of Crowheart as the most complete drunk in its history nor was his bank account inexhaustible. Also he observed with annoyance that his newly-created brother-in-law, Adolph Kunkel, had retired to a quiet corner where he might drink from the bottle unmolested. Adolph Kunkel, sober, was bad enough, but Adolph Kunkel, drunk, was worse.

That his fears were not unfounded was shortly made evident by the appearance of Sylvanus Starr with a bland, bucolic smile upon his wafer-like countenance and his scant foretop tied in a baby-blue ribbon which had embellished the dainty ham sandwiches provided by Mrs. Terriberry. By the time the dance was well under way eyes had brightened perceptibly and sunburned faces had taken on a deeper hue while Snake River Jim sat with a pickle behind his ear and his eyes rolled to the ceiling as though entranced by his own heavenly strains.

As the room grew warmer, the conversation waxed louder, the dance faster and the whoops of exuberance more frequent, until Bedlam reigned. Percy Parrot chancing to observe "Tinhorn Frank" sliding toward the door with two unopened bottles of champagne protruding from his coat pockets made a low tackle and clasped him about the ankles. As "Tinhorn" lay prone he was shamed in vivid English by the graceful barber while the new plasterer excused himself from his partner long enough to kick the prostrate ingrate in the ribs. Mrs. "Hank" Terriberry, whose hair looked like a pair of angora "chaps" in a high wind, returning from her third trip to the dish-pan, burst into tears at the man's depravity and inadvertently wiped her streaming eyes on the end of her long lace jabot instead of her handkerchief.

Sylvanus Starr, declaring that his chivalrous nature was unable to endure the sight of a woman's tears, sought to divert her by slipping his arm about her waist and whirling her dizzily the length of the room and back again where they were met by Mr. Terriberry who, while playfully endeavoring to snatch his wife from the editor's encircling arms, accidentally stepped on the train of her black satin skirt. There was a popping, ripping sound! In the brief but awful second while this handsome creation slid to the floor, Mrs. Terriberry stood panic-stricken in a short, red-flannel petticoat. She screamed piercingly and with the sound of her own voice recovered her presence of mind. Swooping, she picked up the garment and bounded out of the room, thereby revealing upon her plump calves the encircling stripes of a pair of white and black stockings.

The milliner, who was clairvoyant, covered her face with her gauze fan, while Pearline and Planchette Starr asked to be taken into the air, and left the room each leaning heavily upon an arm of the "Sheep King of Poison Crick."

The remittance man from Devonshire removed the crash towel from its roller in the wash-room off the hotel office, and spread it carefully on the floor in a corner to protect his clothing while he refreshed himself with a short nap.

A Roumanian prince who had that day returned from a big game hunt in the mountains and who had been cordially urged by Symes to honor his wedding, adjusted his monocle and stood on a chair under a kerosene wall-lamp that he might the better inspect the fig "filling" of Mrs. Terriberry's layer cake which he seemed to regard with some suspicion.

Mrs. Abe Tutts, who was reputed to have histrionic ability, of her own accord recited in a voice which made the welkin ring: "Shoot if you will this old gray head, But spare my country's flag." Whereupon "Baby" Briggs, six foot two in his cowboy boots, produced a six-shooter and humorously pretended to be about to take her at her word. Mrs. Tutts was revived from a fainting condition by a drink while "Baby" Briggs was relieved of his weapon.

"Take your pardners for a quadrille!" yelled Curly, the camp cook, rising from his chair.

The guests scrambled for places in the quickly formed sets.

"Swing your pardner!" he whooped.

Andy P. Symes slipped his arm about Essie Tisdale's waist and the dance moved fast and furious.

"Join your hands and circle to the left!"

Around they went in a giddy whirl and starched petticoats stood out like hoopskirts.

"First lady swing with the right hand round with the right hand gent!"

The train of Mrs. Abe Tutts's diaphanous "teagown" laid out on the breeze, thereby revealing the fact that she was wearing Congress gaiters, comfortable but not "dressy."

"Pardner with your left with your left hand round!"

Andy P. Symes held Essie Tisdale's hand in a lingering clasp and whispered in foolish flattery:

"Terpsichore herself outdone!"

"Swing in the centre and seven hands around. Birdie hop out and crow hop in! Take holt of paddies and run around agin!"

Abe Tutts executed a double shuffle on the corner.

"Allemande Joe! Right hand to pardner and around you go! Balance to corners, don't be slack! Turn right around and take a back track! When you git home, don't be afraid. Swing her agin and all promenade!"

It was a glorious dance and it moved unflaggingly to the end; but when it was done and the dancers laughing and exhausted sought their seats, it was discovered that Snake River Jim had fallen to weeping because he said it was his unhappy lot to work while others danced.

Therefore Sylvanus Starr suggested that out of a delicate regard for an artist's feelings, and no one could deny but Snake River Jim was that, the dance be temporarily suspended while the bridegroom and others expressed their sentiments and delight in the occasion by a few remarks, Sylvanus Starr himself setting the example by bursting into an eulogy which had the impassioned fervor of inspiration.

The vocabulary of laudatory adjectives gleaned in many years' experience in the obituary department of an eastern newspaper were ejected like volcanic matter, red hot and unrestrained, running over and around the name of Symes to harden into sentences of which "a magnificent specimen of manhood, a physical and intellectual giant, gallantly snatching from our midst the fairest flower that ever bloomed upon a desert waste," only moderately illustrates the editor's gift of language.

When Andy P. Symes stood on a chair and faced the expectant throng the few trite remarks which he had in mind all but fled when his eyes fell for the first time upon his bride buttoned into her "going away gown." As he mounted the chair his face wore the set smile of the man who means to die a nervy death on the gallows. His voice sounded strained and unnatural to himself as he began:

"Ladies and gentlemen."

"Wee-hee!" squealed a youth in a leather collar and a rattleskin necktie.

"This is the happiest moment of my life!"

"Wee-ough! It ought to be!" yelled the "Sheep King of Poison Crick" as he pressed the arms of the Misses Starr gently and impartially against his sides.

"Also the proudest moment." He looked at his bride, noting that she wore a broach which might have belonged on a set of harness.

"Yip! Yip! Yee-ough!"

"I am deeply conscious of my own unworthiness and not insensible to the fact that the gods have singled me out for special favor——"

Any reference to the gods was considered a mark of learning and eloquence, so Symes's humble admission was loudly applauded.

"Love, the Wise Ones say, 'is blind.' If this is true it is my earnest wish that I may remain so, for I desire to continue to regard my wife as the most beautiful, attractive, charming of her sex." He bowed elaborately toward the grotesque figure whose adoring eyes were fixed upon his face.

The guests howled in ecstasy at this flight of sentiment and only Dr. Harpe caught the sneering note beneath the commonplaces he uttered with such convincing fervor.

"What a cad," she thought, yet she looked in something like admiration at his towering figure. "If only he had brains in proportion to his body he might accomplish great things here," she murmured.

Shrugging her shoulder, she added: "I envy him his chance."

It did not occur to any person present that this wedding was an important, far-reaching event to any save the principals; but to Essie Tisdale and to Dr. Harpe it was a turning point in their careers. It meant waning triumphs to the merry little belle of Crowheart, while it spread a fallow field before Dr. Harpe the planting of which in deeds of good or evil was as surely in her hands as is the seed the farmer sows for his ultimate harvest. Which it was to be, can be surmised from the fact that already she was considering how soon, and in what way, she might utilize her knowledge after Symes's return from his wedding journey.

IV

"The Ground Floor"

While Andy P. Symes on his honeymoon was combining business with pleasure in that vague region known as "Back East," and his bride was learning not to fold the hotel napkin or call the waiter "sir," the population of Crowheart was increasing so rapidly that the town had growing pains. Where, last month, the cactus bloomed, tar-paper shacks surrounded by chicken-wire, kid-proof fences was home the next to families of tow-heads.

Crowheart, the citizens of the newly incorporated town told each other, was booming *right*.

They came in prairie schooners, travel-stained and weary, their horses thin and jaded from the long, heavy pull across the sandy trail of the sagebrush desert. With funds barely sufficient for horse feed and a few weeks' provisions, they came without definite knowledge of conditions or plans. A rumor had reached them back there in Minnesota or Iowa, Nebraska or Missouri, of the opportunities in this new country and, anyway, they wanted to move—*where* was not a matter of great moment. Others came by rail, all bearing the earmarks of straitened circumstances, and few of them with any but the most vague ideas as to what they had come for beyond the universal expectation of getting rich, somehow, somewhere, some time. They were poor alike, and the first efforts of the head of each household were spent in the construction of a place of shelter for himself and family. The makeshifts of poverty were seldom if ever the subject of ridicule or comment, for most had a sympathetic understanding of the emergencies which made them necessary. Kindness, helpfulness, good-fellowship were in the air.

When Ephriam Baskitt loomed up on the horizon with two freight wagons filled with the dust-covered canned goods of a defunct grocery store and twenty-four hours later was a fixture, nobody saw anything humorous in the headline in the *Courier* which heralded him as "The Merchant Prince of Crowheart." Two new saloons opened while "Curly" resigned as chef for the Lazy S Outfit to become the orchestra in a new dance hall which arrived about midnight in a prairie schooner.

As Dr. Harpe made friends with the newcomers and continued to ingratiate herself with the old, she sometimes felt that the death of Alice Freoff was not after all the tragedy it had at first seemed. She missed the woman—not the woman so much either, as the association—and there was no one in Crowheart to fill her place, so she was frequently lonely, often bored, with the intensely practical, unsophisticated women whom she attracted strongly. Sometimes she thought of Augusta Kunkel and a derisive smile always curved her lips as she attempted to picture her in a worldly setting and the smile grew when she tried to imagine Symes's sensations while presenting her to his friends. She indulged, too, in speculation as to the outcome of the marriage, but could not venture a prophecy since it was one of those affairs to which no ending would be improbable.

But while Dr. Harpe speculated, observation and the suggestions of Andy P. Symes were working wonders in the appearance of the gawky, long-limbed woman. A session with a hair-dresser had not been wasted, for she had learned to dress her hair in the prevailing mode. Symes had lost no time in rushing her to an establishment where the brown cashmere basque and many gored skirt had been exchanged for a gown of fashionable cut. A pair of French stays developed indications of a figure and the concho-like broach had been discarded, while Augusta herself had learned that black silk mitts had not been greatly in vogue for nearly a quarter of a century. The conspicuous marvel which had displayed the skill of the clairvoyant milliner from South Dakota had been replaced by a hat of good lines and simplicity, and, for the first time in her life, Augusta Kunkel rustled when she walked.

When the transformation was complete, Andy P. Symes sighed in a little more than relief, and mentally observed that in the course of human events he *might* be able to introduce her to his family.

Nor was Symes himself idle in a land where Capital hung like an over-ripe peach waiting to be plucked by the proper hand. Mr. Symes was convinced that his was the hand, so he lost no opportunity of widening his circle of desirable acquaintances.

In his wide-brimmed Stetson, with his broad shoulders towering above the average man, his genial smile and jovial manners, he was the typical free, big-hearted westerner of the eastern imagination. And he liked the rôle; also he played it well. Symes was essentially a poseur. He loved the limelight like a showman. To be foremost, to lead, was essential to his happiness. He demanded satellites and more satellites. His love of prominence amounted to a passion. Sycophancy was as acceptable as real regard, since each catered to his vanity.

It required money, much money, to live up to the popular conception of the type he chose to represent. To successfully carry out his rôle of the breezy, liberal, unconventional westerner required money enough to include the cabman on the pavement in his invitations to drink, money enough to donate bank notes to bell-boys, to wave change to waiters, to occupy boxes where he could lay his conspicuous Stetson upon the rail. Having indulged himself in these delightful extravagances, Symes was suddenly recalled one morning to a realization of the fact that earthly paradises end by a curt notification from his bank that he had overdrawn his account.

This was awkward. It was particularly awkward to Symes because he had no assets. With the singular improvidence which distinguished him he had not provided for this exigency before leaving Crowheart. True, he had made a vague calculation which would seem to indicate that he had sufficient funds to last the trip, but it was more extended than he had anticipated and he had forgotten to deduct the amount of the checks which he had given in payment for the champagne provided in such unstinted quantities by "Hank" Terriberry.

Not only was Symes without reserve funds but he had a large hotel bill owing. Yes, it was high time he was "doing something." "Doing something" to Mr. Symes, meant devising some means of securing an income without physical and no great mental effort, something which should be compatible with the notable House of Symes.

Had he borne any other than that sacred name he would have turned to insurance or a mail order business with the same unerring instinct with which the sunflower turns to the sun, but this avenue was closed to him by the necessity of preserving the dignity of his name. It was necessary for him as a Symes to promote some enterprise which would give him the power and prestige in the community which belonged to him.

Mr. Symes had been East before with this end in view. As he himself observed, "he never went East except to eat oysters and raise money." He had been much more successful as an oyster eater than a promoter. There was that vein of coking coal over beyond the "Limestone Rim"; he nearly landed that, but the investors discovered too soon that it was 150 miles from a railroad. There was an embryo coal mine back in the hills—a fine proposition but open to the same objection. Also an asbestos deposit, valueless for the same reason. He had tried copper prospects with startling assays and had found himself shunned nor had mountains of marble aroused the enthusiasm of Capital. They had listened with marked coldness to his story of a wonderful oil seepage and had turned a deaf ear on natural gas. He had baited a hook with a stratum of gypsum which would furnish the world with cement. Capital had barely sniffed at the bait. Nor had banks of shale adapted to the making of a perfect brick appealed to its jaded palate. But Symes was never at a loss for something to promote, for there was always a nebula of schemes vaguely present in his prolific brain. Irrigation was the opportunity of the moment and he meant to grab it with a strangle hold. He had been dilatory but now he intended to get down to business.

If only he could hang on until he accomplished his end! Symes stopped manicuring his nails with a pin, which he kept in the lapel of his coat for that commendable purpose, and counted his money. He was thankful that since he *had* overdrawn his account he had done it so liberally as, by strict economy, it would enable him to remain a short while and depart with his credit still unimpaired.

Augusta Symes regarded the pile of crisp bank-notes with pleased eyes. She could not recollect ever having seen so much money together before; the proceeds of horse-shoeing and wagon repairs came mostly in silver. Placing the bank-notes in his wallet with considerably more than his usual care, Mr. Symes paced the floor of their corner suite with the slow, measured strides of meditation, his noble head sunk upon his breast and his broad brow corrugated in thought. Mrs. Symes's eyes followed him in silent and respectful admiration.

When he stopped, finally, in the middle of the room, the fire of enthusiasm was newly kindled in his eyes and an unconscious squaring of his shoulders announced that he was now prepared to "do something."

Symes really had initial energy and the trait was most apparent when driven by necessity. The first step toward getting his enterprise under way was the bringing together of the people he hoped to interest. He reached for his hat and straightened his scarf before the mirror.

Augusta watched the preparations in some dismay; she dreaded being alone in the great hotel.

"Will you be gone long, Mr. Symes?"

"Good God! Don't call me Mister Symes," he burst out in unexpected exasperation.

Augusta's eyes filled with tears.

"But—but everybody calls you 'Andy' and—and just 'Symes' sounds so familiar. Why can't I call you 'Phidias?'"

"Phidias! Do, by all means, call me Phidias. I dote on Phidias! I love the combination—Phidias Symes. Father was drunk when he named me."

He slammed the door behind him, forgetting to explain that he was not returning for luncheon or dinner so, that evening, while Augusta wandered aimlessly through the rooms, both hungry and anxious yet afraid to venture into the big dining-room, Andy P. Symes was saying with impressive emphasis as he fumbled in a box of cabanas:

"Big opportunities, I am convinced, seldom come more than once to a man."

His guests listened to the trite axiom with the respect due one who has met and grappled successfully with his one great chance. His well-fed appearance, his genial, contented smile, gave an impression of prosperity even when his linen was frayed and his elbows glossy; now in the latest achievement of a good tailor it was difficult to conceive him as being anything less than a millionaire.

"And this," Symes looked squarely in each eager eye in turn, "this, gentlemen, is such an opportunity."

The timid voice of a man who had made a hundred thousand from a patent fly-trap broke the awed silence.

"It sounds good."

"*Sounds* good! It *is* good." Mr. Symes clenched his huge fist and emphasized the declaration with a blow upon the table which made the dishes rattle.

"Think of it," he went on, "two hundred thousand acres that can be made to bloom like the rose. An earthly paradise of our own making.'' The flowery figures were borrowed from a railroad folder but Mr. Symes had grasped them with the avidity of true genius and made them his own. ''And how?''

The waiter starting away with a tray load of dishes stopped to learn.

''By the mere introduction of water upon the most fertile soil in the world! Is there anything like it—a miracle worker!'' Mr. Symes shut one eye and peered into an empty bottle. ''And how can this be done?'' He answered himself. ''By the expenditure of a ridiculously small amount of money; the absurd sum of $250,000. And look at the returns!''

By the intentness of their gaze it was evident that all were willing enough to look. Symes lowered his voice to a dramatic whisper and swept the air with his outspread fingers.

''A clean million!''

The man who made only six thousand a year selling plumbers' supplies, gulped.

''But who's goin' to buy it?'' It was the timid voice of the Fly-trap King.

''*Buy it!*'' The questioner withered before Symes's scorn. ''Buy it? Why, the world is land-hungry—crying for land!—and water. But I've considered all that; I've arranged for it,'' Mr. Symes went on with a touch of impatience. ''We'll colonize it. We'll import Russian Jews to raise sugar-beets for the sugar-beet factory which we will establish. They will buy it for $50 an acre cash or $60 an acre with 10 per cent. interest upon the deferred payments. It's very simple.''

''But—but—I thought Russian Jews went in

mostly for collar buttons, shoe-strings and lace—mercantile enterprises—commercial natures, you know? Besides, where they going to get their money for the first payment?''

Symes curbed his irritation at the piffling objections of the Fly-trap King and responded tolerantly.

''We'll organize a bank and loan 'em the money. If they fail to come through at the specified time the land will return to the company and we'll have their improvements, making them a small allowance for same, at our discretion. We'll lay out a town and build an Opera House, get electric light and street railway franchises—a million? Why, there's millions in sight when you consider the possibilities.''

The painting of the roseate picture had flushed Mr. Symes's cheeks; already ''Symesville'' or ''Symeston'' rose clear before his mental vision, while his listeners endeavored to calculate their share of the millions when proportioned in accordance with the investment of all their available cash. Certainly the returns were temptingly large and the least optimistic among them believed he could convince his wife of the perfect safety of the investment, the success of which was practically assured by the fact that Andy P. Symes for an infinitesimal salary, as compared to his ability, was willing to assume the management.

A slender, blond gentleman, who derived a satisfactory income from the importation of Scotch woollens and Irish linens, confessed that for years he had cherished a secret desire to do something for mankind, providing he was assured of a reasonable return upon his investment, and, with the King of Brobdingnag, believed that the man who made, say, two sugar-beets grow where only one grew before, rendered an incalculable service to the human race.

The other guests expressed their admiration of the woollen importer's high sentiments, and while they admitted that no such noble impulse governed them they subscribed generously for stock in the company which was formed then and there to apply for the segregation of 200,000 acres of irrigable land.

Mr. Symes talked familiarly of State Land Boards, water rights, flood water, ditches, laterals, subsoil and seepage, the rotation of crops and general productiveness until even the cynical politician who controlled the negro vote in his ward began to realize that it was a liberal education merely to know Andy P. Symes, not to mention the distinction of being associated with him in business.

Inspired by the prospect of once again handling real money, Andy P. Symes talked with an earnestness and fluency which cast a hypnotic spell upon his listeners. Swiftly, graphically, he outlined the future of the country which would be opened up to settlement by this great irrigation project. His florid face turned a deeper red, his eyes sparkled as the winged imagination of the natural promoter began to play. It was of the dirigible kind, Symes's imagination, he could steer it in any direction. It could rise to any heights. It now shot upward and he saw himself at the head of a project which would make his name a household word throughout the State. He saw crowds of Russian Jews crying hosannas as he walked along the street of Symesville; he heard the clang of trolleys; he saw the smoke of factories; he heard the name of Symes upon the lips of little children; he saw, but the dazzling vision made him blink and he leaned back in his chair with the beneficent smile of a man who had just endowed a hospital for crippled children, while he permitted himself to accept a subscription for $15,000 from a guest who had cleared that modest sum in the manufacture of white lead and paint. A slow and laborious process compared to the sale of irrigated land to Russian Jews.

Symes's guests wrung his hand at parting, in silent gratitude at being permitted to get in on the ground floor of what was undoubtedly the greatest money making enterprise still open to investors. And they left him with the assurance of their hearty co-operation and willingness to endeavor to raise the balance among their friends.

While the subscribers for the stock of the Symes Irrigation Project were rousing their wives from their first sleep to gloat with them over the unprecedented good fortune which had thrown the big-hearted and shrewd but honest westerner in their paths, that person was returning from a night lunch cart with two hot frankfurter sandwiches for Augusta concealed in his pocket. The dinner, although so fruitful of results, had seriously reduced the roll of crisp bank notes.

Strict economy was imperative during the days which followed and it became no uncommon occurrence for Andy P. Symes to whisk Augusta into a caravansera where the gentlemen patrons ate large, filling plates of griddle cakes with their hats on. But such are the sordid straits to which the proudest spirits are sometimes reduced and depressing as it was to Andy P. Symes, who winced each time that he seated himself at the varnished pine table upon which the pewter castor was chained to the wall and selected a paper napkin from a glass tumbler, he consoled himself with the thought that it would not be for long. Also it was some little compensation to see traces of animation in Augusta's stolid face, for the atmosphere was vastly more congenial to his wife than that of the fashionable hotel restaurant where her appetite fled before the waiter's observant eye and the bewildering nightmare of a menu.

Invariably upon these humiliating occasions when Symes dined cheek by jowl with *hoi polloi* who left their spoons in their cups and departed using a toothpick like a peavy, his thoughts turned to his coming triumph in Crowheart. And although his gorge rose at the sight of a large, buck cockroach which scurried across the table and turned to wave a fraternal leg at him before it disappeared, the knowledge that he would soon take his rightful position as that city's leading citizen helped to restore his equanimity.

With an assured income, Company money to spend among the local merchants, work for many applicants, Symes felt that he could do little else than step into the niche which clearly belonged to him. The one smudge upon the picture was Augusta. Her eyes were ever upon him in adoring, dog-like fidelity and it irritated him. Her appearance had altered amazingly, she no longer called him "Mister Symes," and by repeated corrections he had succeeded in inducing her to refrain from folding her hands upon her abdomen, but the plebeian strain, the deficiency of gentle birth betrayed itself in a dozen little ways, by indelicacies none the less irritating because they were trifling.

Symes knew what a gentlewoman should be, for he had mingled with them in the past and he never had thought of his wife as being anything else than well born. Augusta's large knuckled hands, conspicuous in white kid gloves, her long, flat feet, the shiny, bald spots behind her ears, were sources of real mortification to him, and invariably he found himself growing red upon the occasions when it was necessary to present her to his friends.

In the presence of other women she sat bolt upright, a red spot burning on either cheek-bone, her eyes bright with nervous excitement while she answered the careless small talk with preternatural seriousness. At such times Symes himself talked rapidly to hide the gaucheries of her speech, and they were ordeals which he took care should be as few as possible.

If the yoke were chafing already, he asked himself frequently, what would its weight be in a year, five, ten years later?

V

'Another Case in Surgery

Dr. Emma Harpe walked briskly into her office and, taking ten silver dollars and some worn bank-notes from the pocket of her square-cut coat, piled them upon her office desk.

"Moses! I need that money, and," she sniggered at the recollection, "didn't old Dubois hate to dig."

She threw the Stetson hat she now affected upon a chair, her coat upon another, and rolling a cigarette with the skill of practice, sauntered up and down the room.

"He's sick all right—the old guinea. Looks like typhoid. If it is, it'll pull me out of this hole. Mileage counts up in this country at a dollar a mile. About five cases of typhoid would put me square again and see me through the summer; an epidemic would be a godsend. This is the infernalest healthy country I ever saw; die in their boots or dry up and blow off. Two cases of measles and the whooping cough in six weeks. Dubois comes like a shower of manna, for I can't stand off the Terriberrys forever. I'll go out and see him again in a couple of days and give him a dose of calomel. If he pulls through the credit is mine; if he dies, it's the will of God. Any way it goes, I'm squared. Harpe," she stopped and looked out of the window, "you belong to a noble profesh—you play a safe and genteel game where you can't lose."

She watched idly as a covered wagon accompanied by two men on horseback stopped on the vacant lot opposite the hotel which was much used as a camping-ground by freighters and campers. It was a common enough sight and she looked on indifferently while the team was unharnessed and the saddle horses led toward the livery stable by one of the riders and the driver of the wagon hastened across the street, looking, she thought, at the sign beneath her window.

She barely had time to throw away her cigarette and fan the smoke out of the air before the hurrying footsteps which had told her of his approach brought the man to her office door.

"Are you the doctor?" he asked in surprise at seeing a woman.

She nodded.

"Will you come over right away? My little girl fell over the wheel and one of the fellows that's along says her leg is broken. It only happened a little ways back but it's beginning to swell."

The man's face was pale beneath its tan and the dust of travel, and he plainly chafed at her deliberate movements as she took bandages from the drawer and adjusted her hat before a mirror. It was the first practical test of her theoretical knowledge of bone-setting and because of some misgivings her swagger was a little more pronounced than usual when she accompanied him across the street.

The child lay upon the bunk in the front of the wagon and her eyes were bright with the pain of the dull ache, and fear of more that the doctor might inflict.

"Is it hurtin' bad, Rosie?" Anxiety was in the man's voice.

"Not so very much, Daddy," she replied bravely.

"Your young'un?"

The man glanced at Dr. Harpe quickly in a mixture of surprise and resentment.

"My sister's—young'un," he answered curtly.

The child winced as Dr. Harpe picked up the foot roughly and ran her fingers along the bone.

"Yep; it's broken." She hesitated for an instant and added: "The job'll cost you fifty dollars."

"Fifty dollars!" Consternation was in the man's tone. "Ain't that pretty steep for settin' a leg?"

"That's my price." She added indifferently, "There's another sawbones sixty miles farther on."

"You know well enough that she can't wait to get there."

"Well," she shrugged her shoulder, "dig then."

"But I haven't got it," he pleaded.

"Sell a horse."

He looked to see if she was serious; undoubtedly she was.

"How am I to go on if I sell a horse?"

"That's your lookout."

He stared at her in real curiosity.

"What kind of a doctor are you, anyhow? What kind of a woman?"

"O Daddy—it's hurtin' worse!" moaned the child.

Dr. Harpe laughed disagreeably—

"I'm not in Crowheart for my health." Ignoring the displeasure which came into the man's eyes, she suggested: "Can't you borrow from those fellows that came with you?"

"They're strangers. We are all strangers to each other—we only fell in together on the road. The one lying under the wagon was on a tear in the last town; most likely he's broke."

The child in the bunk whimpered with the increasing pain.

"How much have you got yourself?" she haggled.

"Twenty-two dollars and fifty cents; it's *all* I've got and we're a hundred miles yet from the end of our road. I've got work there and I'll give you my note and send the balance as soon as I earn it."

Twenty-two dollars and fifty cents—it was more than she anticipated, but every extra dollar was "velvet" as she phrased it.

"See what you can do with that fellow outside."

The man's dark eyes flashed and his face went blood red, but he left the wagon abruptly, and she heard distinctly the angry explanation to his travelling companion lying on a saddle blanket in the shade of the wagon. The knowledge that she was forfeiting these strangers' respect did not disturb her. These indigent campers—gone on the morrow—could do her no harm in Crowheart where her reputation for blunt kindness and imperturbable good nature was already established. It was something of a luxury to indulge her hidden traits; in other words, she was enjoying her meanness.

A forceful ejaculation told her that the slumbering débauché had revived and grasped the situation. She listened intently to his response to the other's request for a loan.

"So the lady doc wants money? She wants to see the color of your dust before she can set the baby's broken leg, you say? Interesting—very. By all means give the kind lady money. How much money does the lady want?"

The color rose swiftly in her cheeks, not so much because of the mocking words as the intonation of the voice in which they were uttered—the most wonderfully musical speaking voice she ever had heard. The angry resentment of the child's foster-father had left her unmoved but this was different. The sneering, cutting insolence came from no ordinary person. It stung her. She thought she detected a slight foreign accent in the carefully articulated words, though the phraseology was distinctly western. The voice was high pitched without effeminacy, soft yet penetrating, polished yet conveying all the meaning of an insult. No Anglo-Saxon could express such mocking contempt by the voice alone—that accomplishment is almost exclusively a gift of the Latins.

She was hot and uncomfortable, conscious that the blood was still in her face, when she heard him scramble to his feet and walk to the back of the wagon. Ever after Dr. Harpe remembered him as she saw him first framed in the white canvas opening of the prairie schooner.

His unusually high-crowned Stetson was pushed to the back of his head, one slender, aristocratic hand rested carelessly upon his hip, a fallen lock of straight, black hair hung nearly to his eyebrows—eyebrows which all but met above a pair of narrow, brilliant eyes. The aquiline nose, the creamy, colorless complexion, the long face with its thin, slightly drooping lips was unmistakably foreign in its type while a loose, silk neck scarf containing the bright colors of the Roman stripe added an alien touch. There was at once high breeding and reckless *diablerie* in his handsome face.

In the antagonistic moment in which they eyed each other, Dr. Harpe endeavored to recall the something or somebody which his appearance suggested.

She groped for it in the dim gallery of youthful memories. What was it? It flashed upon her with the suddenness of a forgotten word. She remembered it plainly now—that treasured, highly colored lithograph of a brigand holding up a coach in a mountain pass! There was in this face the same mocking deviltry; his figure had the same lithe grace; he needed only the big hoop earrings to complete the resemblance.

He removed his hat with a long, sweeping gesture and bowed in exaggerated deference.

"At your service," he murmured.

"There was no need——" she began in a kind of apology.

"Fifty dollars is little enough to pay for the privilege of your skill, madam. Shall it be in advance? Of course; in advance."

She threw out her hand in a gesture of protest, which he ignored.

"Permit me at least to show you that we have it here. I feel sure that you can work with a freer mind if I count it out and lay it where you can see it." He took an odd, foreign purse from the belt of his "chaps" and she noted that it sagged with the weight of its contents.

"Gold," he explained; "nearly new from the Mint. You can have it tested at the bank before you begin—acids or something of the sort, I believe."

She crimsoned with anger, but he went on—

"Fifty dollars! What a very little sum to start the milk of human kindness flowing!"

"I told him he needn't mind—there was no rush—just when it was convenient. He misunderstood me." She found her tongue at last and lied glibly.

The child's foster-father stared at her as though he doubted his own ears. Her very audacity left him speechless.

"There you are, $50 in gold!" He flung the money into her lap. "Old hoss," he laid his hand upon the man's shoulder while his mocking laugh again made her cheeks tingle, "you oughtn't to lie to me like that."

When he had sauntered across the street with his careless, easy stride and disappeared inside the swinging doors of the bar-room of the Terriberry House, Dr. Harpe said brusquely:

"Here, you gotta help me yank this leg straight but, first, I want you to go over to the store and bust up a thin box—something for splints—strips off a fruit case would be best if you can get 'em."

"Haven't you splints?" the man asked in surprise.

"No; I've just come; I haven't got a stock yet and there's no drug store in this jay town. It's on the way but that doesn't help us now. We ought to have plaster of Paris but we haven't. Hurry up—get a move on before it swells any more."

The man did as he was bid, with a look of doubt and uncertainty upon his face.

He returned almost immediately with strips torn from a case of fruit.

"That's good." Dr. Harpe laid them on the bunk with the bandages. She added shortly: "She's going to howl."

"Can't you give her anything?"

"No; I can't give ether by myself. I'm not going to take a chance like that. If she'd die on my hands it'd queer me here on the jump. 'Twon't kill her.

"OLD HOSS, YOU OUGHTN'T TO LIE TO ME LIKE THAT."

She'll probably faint and then it'll be easy. When the muscles relax, hold on to her leg above her knee while I pull."

The man's face turned a ghastly hue as the child screamed and fainted away, nor did the color return as he watched the woman's clumsy fingers, the bungling movements which, unlettered as he was, told him of her inexperience—bungling movements which had not even compensating feminine gentleness.

When the child had revived and Dr. Harpe had finished, the man went outside and leaned against the wheel.

"Are you sure it'll be straight?"

She saw her own misgivings reflected in his face, and it exasperated her.

"What a fool question. Do you think I don't know my business?"

He did not answer, and she turned away.

"Daddy?"

"Yes, Rosie." He was at her side at once.

She lifted her clear eyes to his face.

"I don't like that woman."

"Like her!" he answered slowly. "Like her! Her heart is as black as my hat."

To herself Dr. Harpe was saying:

"Moses! I had to start in on somebody."

It was with relief that she looked through her office window after supper and saw that the wagon was gone from the vacant lot.

"Good riddance!" she muttered. "I wouldn't have that black-eyed devil hanging around this town for money. He 's onery enought to do me mischief. I wonder who he was? He might be anything or anybody; a dago duke or a hold-up—or both. Anyway, he's gone, and if I never see him again it'll be soon enough."

She sat down in her office chair and rested her heels on the window sill while her cigarette burned to ashes between her listless fingers. For a time she watched the white light of the June moon grow on the line of dimpled foothills, the myriad odors of spring were in the air and the balmy west wind lifted the hair at her temples as it came through the open window. She felt lonely—inexpressibly lonely. She thought of Alice Freoff and restlessness grew. Downstairs she heard Essie Tisdale's merry laughter and it changed the current of her thoughts.

She had learned her story now and the mystery of her identity had given the little belle of Crowheart an added attraction. Everybody in Crowheart knew her story for that matter; it was one of the stock tales of the country to be repeated to interest strangers.

In the old days when Crowheart was a blacksmith shop and the stamping ground of "Snow-shoe" Brown, whose log cabin hung on the edge of the bench overlooking the stream like a crow's nest in a cottonwood tree, "Snow-shoe" Brown had yelled in vain, one spring day, at a man and woman on the seat of a covered wagon who were preparing to ford the stream at the usual crossing. But the sullen roar of the water drowned his warning that it was swimming depth, and, even while he ran for his horse and uncoiled his saddle rope, the current was sweeping the wagon and the struggling horses down stream. He followed along the bank until the horse's feet came up and the wagon went down, while there floated from the open end, among other things, something that looked to his astonished eyes like a wooden cradle.

He threw his rope, and threw again, with the skill which long practice in roping mavericks had given him; and gently, gently, with a success which seemed miraculous even to "Snow-shoe" Brown, he had drawn the bobbing cradle gradually to shore. Inside, a baby smiled up at him with the bluest eyes he ever had seen. There was a picture primer tucked beneath the flannel coverlet and it contained the single clue to her identity. "Esther Tisdale" was written on the fly-leaf with a recent date.

"Snow-shoe" Brown said she was a maverick and unblushingly declared that he claimed all mavericks that he had had his rope on; therefore "Esther Tisdale" belonged to him. He left her in the care of the wife of a cattleman who hoped thereby to purchase immunity from "Snow-shoe's" activities, which he did, though that person rustled elsewhere with renewed energy, since he said he had a family to keep. So she learned to ride and shoot as straight as "Snow-shoe" himself and even as a child gave promise of a winsome, lovely girlhood. The unique relationship ended when her guardian died in his boots in the little cowtown over beyond the Limestone Rim. A hard winter and the inroads of sheep "broke" the cattleman who sold out and moved away, while Esther Tisdale shifted for herself that she might not be a burden. She was nearly twenty now, and, in the democratic community never had felt or been made to feel that her position was subservient or inferior. Therefore when her work was done and she bounded up the stairs to Dr. Harpe's door she felt sure of a welcome.

"It's only Essie Tisdale," she said in her merry voice as she rapped and peered into the room.

"Come in, Essie; I'm lonesome as the deuce!"

It was some time later that Mrs. Terriberry sailing through the corridor in her dressing-sacque and petticoat, with her feet scuffling in Mr. Terriberry's carpet-slippers, had the stone-china water-pitcher dashed from her hand as she turned a corner.

"Why, Essie!"

"Oh, I'm sorry, Mrs. Terriberry!"

"What's the matter?" She looked wonderingly at the girl's crimson face.

"Don't ask me! but don't expect me to be friends with that woman again!"

"Have you had words—have you quarrelled with Dr. Harpe?"

"Yes—yes; we quarrelled! But don't ask me any more! I won't—I can't tell you!" the girl replied fiercely as she rushed on and slammed the door of her room behind her.

In her office, Dr. Harpe was sitting by the window panic-stricken, sick with the fear of the one thing in the world of which she was most afraid, namely, Public Opinion.

She was deaf to the night sounds of the town; to the thick, argumentative voices beneath her window; to the scratched phonograph squeaking an ancient air in the office of the Terriberry House; to the banging of an erratic piano in the saloon two doors above; to the sleepy wails of the butcher's urchin in the tar-paper shack one door below, and to a heap of snarling dogs fighting in the deep, white dust of the street.

She glanced through the window and saw without seeing, the deputy-sheriff escorting an unsteady prisoner down the street followed by a boisterous crowd. In a way she was dimly conscious that there was something familiar in the prisoner's appearance, but the impression was not strong enough to rouse her from her preoccupation, and she turned to walk the floor without being cognizant of the fact that she was walking.

She suddenly threw both hands aloft.

"I've got it!" she cried exultingly. "The very thing to counteract her story. It'll work—it always does—and I know that I can do it!"

In her relief she laughed, a queer, cackling laugh which came strangely from the lips of a woman barely thirty. The laughter was still on her lips when a sound reached her ears which killed it as quickly as it came.

Addio mia bella Napoli, addio, addio!
La tua soave imagine chi mai, chi mai scordar potra!
Del ciel l'auzzurro fulgido, la placida marina,
Qual core non imebria, non bea non bea divolutta!
In tela terra el 'aura favellano d'amore;
Te sola al mio dolore conforto io sognero
Oh! addio mia bella Napoli, addio, addio!
Addio care memorie del tempo ah! che fuggi!

The voice rang out like a golden bell, vibrating, as sweetly penetrating. The strange words fell like the notes of the meadow lark in spring, easy, liquid, yet with the sureness of knowledge.

The incoherent argument beneath the window ceased, the piano and the phonograph were silenced, the wailing urchin dried its tears and all the raw little town of Crowheart seemed to hold its breath as the wonderful tenor voice rose and fell on the soft June night.

Adieu, my own dear Napoli! Adieu to thee, Adieu to thee!
Thy wondrous pictures in the sea, will ever fill my memory!
Thy skies of deepest, brightest blue, thy placid waves so soft and clear;
With heaving sigh and bitter tear, I bid a last, a sad adieu!
Adieu the fragrant orange grove, the scented air that breathes of love
Shall charm my heart with one bright ray, in dreams, wher'er I stray;
Oh, adieu, my own dear Napoli! Adieu to thee, Adieu to thee!
Adieu each soul-felt memory, of happy days long passed away!

The old street-song of Italy, the song of its people, never held a stranger audience in thraldom. If the song had been without words the result would have been the same, almost, for it was the voice which reached through liquor befuddled brains to find and stir remote and hidden recesses in natures long since hardened to sentiment. Rough speeches, ribald words and oaths died on the lips of those who crowded the doorway of saloons, and they stood spell-bound by the song which was sung as they felt dimly the angels must sing up there in that shadowy land back of the stars in which vaguely they believed.

Only those who have lived in isolated places can understand what music means to those who year after year are without it. Any sound that is not an actual discord becomes music then and the least gentle listen with pathetic eagerness. A worn phonograph screeching the popular songs of a past decade holds the rapt attention of such. It reminds them of that world they left long ago, a world which in the perspective of waning years looks all song and laughter, good company, good clothes, good food, and green things everywhere.

Therefore it is little wonder that this voice of

marvellous sweetness and power rising unexpectedly out of the moonlit night should lay an awed hush upon the music-starved town. To some it brought a flood of memories and lumps in aching throats while many a weather-beaten face was lifted from mediocrity by a momentary exultation that was of the soul.

That a human voice unaided by a visible personality could throw such a spell upon the listeners seems rather a tax upon credulity; but the singer himself appeared to have no misgivings. His face wore a look of smiling, mocking confidence as he stood with one hand on his hip, the other grasping a bar of the iron grating which covered the single window of Crowheart's calaboose, pouring forth the golden notes with an occasional imperious toss of his head and a flash of his black eyes which made him look like a royal prisoner.

When the last note had died away, Dr. Harpe breathed an ejaculation.

"The Dago Duke!"

"He sings like an angel," said "Slivers," a barkeep.

"And fights like a devil," replied Dan Treu, the deputy-sheriff. "He turned a knife in Tinhorn's shoulder."

VI

"THE CHURCH RACKET"

DR. HARPE went downstairs the next morning with her straight upper lip stretched in the set smile with which she met a crisis. "Hank" Terriberry passed through the hall as she descended the stairs and she watched him breathlessly.

"Mornin', Doc." He nodded in friendly nonchalance and her heart leaped in relief.

He knew nothing of the quarrel!

"Wait a minute, Mr. Terriberry," she called, and he stopped. "Say, what church do you belong to? What are you?"

Mr. Terriberry suffered from pyorrhea, and the row of upper teeth which he now displayed in a genial grin looked like a garden-rake, due to his shrinking gums.

"I'm a Presbyterian, Doc, but I don't work at it. Why?"

"Let's get together and build a church. I 'll go around with a subscription paper myself and raise the money. I feel lost without a church, I honestly do. It's downright heathenish."

"That's so," Mr. Terriberry agreed heartily, "there's something damned respectable about a church. It makes a good impression upon strangers to come into a town and hear a church bell ringin', even if nobody goes. Doc, you're all right," he patted her shoulder approvingly; "you're a rough diamond; you can put me down for $50."

When Mr. Terriberry had gone his pious way,

Dr. Harpe smiled and reiterated mentally: "There's nothing like the church racket; it always works."

She passed on into the dining-room where the Dago Duke who had sung himself out of the calaboose sprang to his feet and, laying his hand upon his heart, bowed low in a burlesqued bow of deference.

"A tribute to your skill and learning, madam."

She stared at him stonily and his white teeth flashed.

How she hated him! yet she felt helpless before his impudence and audacity. He had "presence," poise, and she knew instinctively that to whatever lengths she might go in retaliation he would go further. She would only bring upon herself discomfiture by such a course. She knew that she had forfeited his respect; more than that, she felt that she had incurred a deep and lasting enmity which seemed to her out of all proportion to the cause.

His horseback companion of the previous day was breakfasting beside him and she found the young man's cold, impersonal scrutiny as hard to bear as the Dago Duke's frank impudence as she swaggered to her seat at the end of the long dining-room and faced them. He was as different in his way from the men about him as the Dago Duke, yet he differed, too, from that conspicuous person. He seemed self-contained, reserved to the point of reticence, but with a quiet assurance of manner as pronounced as the other's effrontery. He was dressed in a blue flannel shirt and worn corduroys. His face was tanned but it was the sunburned face of an invalid. There were hollows in his cheeks and a tired look in his gray eyes. Having critically examined her, Dr. Harpe observed that he seemed to forget her.

Essie Tisdale passed her without a glance, but Mrs. Terriberry came behind with the breakfast of fried potatoes and the thin, fried beefsteak on the platter which served also as a plate, from which menu the Terriberry House never deviated by so much as a mutton chop.

"I'm sorry you and Essie fell out," said Mrs. Terriberry apologetically as she placed the dishes before her. "But she seems awful set on not waitin' on you."

Dr. Harpe dropped her eyes for an instant.

"It's up to her."

"She's as good-natured as anybody I ever saw but she's high-strung, too; she's got a temper."

Dr. Harpe lifted a shoulder.

"She'd better have my friendship than my enmity, even if she has a temper."

"Essie's mighty well liked here," Mrs. Terriberry returned quickly.

"Popularity is a mighty uncertain asset in a small town."

"Don't forget that yourself, Doc," returned Mrs. Terriberry, nettled by her tone.

Dr. Harpe laughed good-naturedly; she had no desire to antagonize Mrs. Terriberry.

She watched the Dago Duke hold up a warning finger as Essie placed the heavy hotel dishes before him.

"Be careful, Miss, be very careful not to nick this fragile ware. As a lover of ceramic art, it would pain me to see it injured."

The girl dimpled, and, in spite of herself, burst into a trill of laughter which was so merry and contagious that the grave stranger beside him looked up at her with an interested and amused smile as though seeing her for the first time.

"Breakfasting at the Terriberry House was a pleasure which seemed a long way off last night," observed the Dago Duke without embarrassment. "You heard the imprisoned bird singing for his liberty? Music to soothe the savage breast of your sheriff. When I am myself I can converse in five languages; when I am drunk it is my misfortune to be able only to sing or holler. Your jail is a disgrace to Crowheart; I've never been in a worse one. The mattress is lumpy and the pillow hard; I was voicing my protest."

"I don't care why you sing so long as you sing," said Essie, dimpling again. "It was beautiful, but isn't it bad for your health to get so—drunk?"

"Not at all," returned the Dago Duke airily. "Look at me—fresh as a rock-rose with the dew on it!"

Again the grave stranger smiled but rather at Essie Tisdale's laughter than his companion's brazen humor.

He interested Dr. Harpe, this other stranger, and as soon as her breakfast was finished she looked for his name upon the register.

"Ogden Van Lennop," she read, and his address was a little town in the county. She shook her head and said to herself: "He never came from this neck of the woods. Another black sheep, I wonder?"

Dr. Harpe lost no time in agitating the subject of a church and it tickled Crowheart's risibilities, since she was the last person to be suspected of spiritual yearnings—her personality seeming incongruous with religious fervor. But while they laughed it was with good-nature and approval for it merely confirmed them in their opinion that with all her idiosyncrasies she was at heart what she liked to be considered, "a rough diamond," sympathetic and kind of heart underneath her blunt candor. That she had never been known to refuse a drink to the knowledge of any inhabitant was one of the stock jokes of the town, yet it was never urged against her. Already she had come to be pointed out to strangers with a kind of affectionate pride as a local celebrity—a "character." She had a strong attraction for the women of Crowheart—an attraction that amounted to fascination. Her stronger personality overshadowed theirs as her stronger will dominated them. She quickly became a leader among them, and her leadership aroused no jealousy. They quoted her rude speeches as characteristic bits of wit and laughed at her uncouth manners. Her callousness passed for the confidence of knowledge.

"She's so different," they told each other. "She's a law unto herself." Yet the most timid among them had less fear of Public Opinion than Dr. Harpe to whom it was always a menacing juggernaut.

She returned at the end of the day tired but content in the knowledge that her efforts had produced exactly the effect she desired. She had raised enough money to insure the erection of a modest mission church, but the important thing was that in so doing she had built a stout bulwark about herself which would long withstand any explanation that Essie Tisdale might make as to the cause of the mysterious break between them.

While she congratulated herself upon the success of this inspired move on her part, circumstances due to other than her own efforts were conspiring to eliminate the girl as a dangerous factor in her life.

She retired early and, consequently, was in ignorance of the receipt of a telegram by Sylvanus Starr announcing the return of Andy P. Symes and the complete success of his eastern mission. So when she was awakened the next morning by a conflict of sounds which resembled the efforts of a Chinese orchestra and raised the shade to see the newly organized Cowboy band making superhuman endeavors to march and yet produce a sufficiently correct number of notes from the score of "A Hot Time in the Old Town" to make that American warcry recognizable, she knew that something unusual had developed in the interim of her long sleep.

It was like Andy P. Symes to announce his coming that he might extract all the glory possible from his arrival and he knew that he could depend upon Sylvanus Starr to make the most of the occasion.

The editor issued an "Extra" of dodger-like appearance, and it is doubtful if he would have used larger type to announce an anticipated visit of the President. He called upon every citizen with a spark of civic pride to turn out and give Andy P. Symes a fitting welcome; to do homage to the man who was to Crowheart what the patron saints are to the cities of the Old World.

The matutinal "Hot Time in the Old Town" and a majority of the population waiting on the cinders about the red water tank were the results of his impassioned plea.

Tears of gratified vanity stood in the eyes of Andy P. Symes as from the front platform of the passenger coach he saw his neighbors assembled to greet him.

It seemed an eminently fitting and proper tribute to the great-grandson of the man who had been a personal friend of Alexander Hamilton's. He viewed the welcoming throng through misty eyes as, with an entire appreciation of the imposing figure he presented, he bared his massive head in deference to Mrs. Terriberry, Mrs. Percy Parrott, Mrs. Starr and her two lovely daughters whose shrill shrieks were audible above the grinding of the car-wheels upon the rusty track.

Sylvanus Starr with many sweeping gestures of a hand which suggested a prehensile, well-inked claw, welcomed him in an outburst of oratory, iridescent with adjectives which gushed from him like a volume of water from a fire-plug, that made Crowheart's jaw drop. While Symes may have felt that the editor was going it rather strong when he compared him to the financial geniuses of the world beginning with Crœsus and ending with the Guggenheims, he made no protest.

Behind Mr. Symes, wide-eyed and solemn, and transformed nearly past recognition by a hobble skirt and "kimona" sleeves, stood Mrs. Symes with the growing feeling of complacent aloofness which comes from being the wife of a great man.

In contrast to Sylvanus Starr's fluency Symes's response seemed halting and slow, but it gained thereby in impressiveness. When he clenched his huge fist and struck at the air, declaring for the third time that "it was good to be home!" nobody doubted him. And they need not have doubted him, for, since his salary did not begin until his return to Crowheart, and the offerings of night-lunch carts are taxing upon the digestion, it was indeed "good to be home!"

VII

The Sheep from the Goats

Andy P. Symes decided to emphasize further his return to Crowheart by issuing invitations for a dinner to be given in the Terriberry House, reserving the announcement of his future plans for this occasion; and, although Crowheart did not realize it at the time, this dinner was an epoch-making function. It was not until the printed invitations worded with such elegance by Sylvanus Starr were issued, that Crowheart dimly suspected there were sheep and goats, and this was the initial step toward separating them.

The making up of a social list in any frontier town is not without its puzzling features and Mr. Symes in this instance found it particularly difficult once he began to discriminate.

First there came the awkward question of his relatives by marriage. At first glance it would have seemed rather necessary to head the list with Grandmother Kunkel, but the fact that she was also the hotel laundress at the time made it a subject for debate. Once, just once, he was willing to test the social possibilities of his brother-in-law, so Symes magnanimously gave him his chance and the name of Adolph Kunkel headed the list.

The Percy Parrotts, of course, went through the sieve, and the Starrs, and Dr. Emma Harpe, but there was the embarrassing question of Mrs. Alva Jackson who had but lately sold her dance hall, goodwill, and fixtures, to marry Alva Jackson, a prosperous cattleman—too prosperous, Mr. Symes finally decided, to ignore. Would the presence of the sprightly Faro Nell give a touch of piquancy to the occasion or lower its tone? Could rich old Edouard Dubois be induced to change his shirt if invited? The clairvoyant milliner was barred owing to the fact that she was "in trade," but "Tinhorn Frank," who no longer sat drunk and collarless in his dirt-floored saloon fumbling a deck of cards thick with grime, went down upon the list as "Mr. Rhodes," the citizens of Crowheart learning his name for the first time when it appeared on the sign above the door of his new real estate office.

When the difficult undertaking was complete Mrs. Symes looked over his shoulder and read the list.

"You haven't Essie Tisdale's name."

Mr. Symes laughed good-humoredly—

"Oh, she'll be there; she'll wait on the table."

"You don't mean to ask Essie Tisdale?" Mrs. Symes's eyes opened.

Symes shook his head.

"That seems awfully mean," insisted Mrs. Symes in feeble protest; "she's always been so nice to me at dances and things."

"My dear," Symes replied impatiently, "we can't invite all the people who have been nice to us. Won't you ever understand that society must draw the line somewhere?"

Mrs. Symes pondered this new thought a long time.

When the invitations were out and the news of the dinner spread it became the chief topic of conversation. The fact that the dinner was at seven instead of twelve o'clock, noon, occasioned much hilarity among the uninvited while the invited guests were more than delighted at the fashionable hour. A tinge of acerbity was noticeable in the comments of those who were unaccustomed to the sensation of being excluded, among them Mrs. Abe Tutts, whose quick recognition of slights led one to believe she had received a great many of them. Mrs. Tutts, who was personally distasteful to Mr. Symes, went so far as to inquire belligerently of Mrs. Symes why she had not been invited.

"I don't know," stammered Mrs. Symes who was still truthful rather than tactful, "but I'll ask Phidias."

"You find out and lemme know," said Mrs. Tutts menacingly. "They can't nobody in this town hand *me* nothin'!"

Since Mrs. Tutts's sensitiveness appeared always to show itself in a desire to do the offender bodily harm, Andy P. Symes took care not to commit himself.

Until the very last Essie Tisdale could not believe that she had been intentionally omitted. She was among the first thought of when any gathering was planned and in her naive way was as sure of her popularity as Symes himself, so she had pressed the wrinkles from her simple gown and cleaned once more the white slippers which were among her dearest treasures.

As a matter of course Mrs. Terriberry had engaged other help for the occasion and all the afternoon of the day set Essie Tisdale waited for the tardy invitation which she told herself was an oversight. She could not believe that Augusta Kunkel, who was indebted to her for more good times than she ever had had in her uneventful life, could find it in her heart to slight her.

But the afternoon waned and no belated invitation came, so when the hour had arrived for her to go below she hung her cheap little frock upon its nail and replaced the cherished slippers in their box, hurt and heavy hearted and still unaware that the day when she had tripped in them as the acknowledged belle of Crowheart was done and the old régime of charity and democratic, unpretentious hospitality was gone never to return.

Her shapely head was erect and her eyes bright with the pain of hurt pride when she knocked upon Mrs. Terriberry's door. That lady thrust a floured face through the crack.

"You needn't get anyone to take my place to-night," she said bravely, "I'm not invited."

"What!"

In the white expanse Mrs. Terriberry's mouth looked like a crack in a glacier.

Essie Tisdale shook her head.

"Come in." Mrs. Terriberry sank upon the bed which sagged like a hammock with her weight. "What do you 'spose is the reason?"

"I haven't the least idea in the world." Essie's chin quivered in spite of her.

"For half a cent I wouldn't budge!" Mrs. Terriberry shook a warlike coiffure. "Folks like that ought to be learned something."

"Oh, yes, you must go."

"If I do it'll be only to see what they wear and how they act; I don't expect to enjoy myself a bit after hearin' this. I've lost interest in it."

With a zest somewhat at variance with her words Mrs. Terriberry began to manipulate a pair of curling tongs which had been heating in the lamp.

A sizzling sound followed and a cloud of smoke rose in the air.

"There! I've burnt off my scoldin' locks." Mrs. Terriberry viewed the damage with dismay. "I'm just so upset I don't know what I'm doin'. Essie, if you don't want to wait on 'em you needn't."

"I won't mind much—after the first. It will be hard at first. Thank you, though."

"If I ever git me another pair of these 'pinch-ins'," panted Mrs. Terriberry, "you'll know it. Take holt and lay back on them strings, will you? They got to come closter than that or that skirt won't meet on me by an inch—and to think twenty-fours was loose on me onct! Wait a minute!" A startled look came in Mrs. Terriberry's bulging eyes. "I thought I felt somethin' give inside of me—don't take much to cave a rib in sometimes."

"More?"

"Yep; these things have gotta meet if I have to hitch the 'bus team onto 'em."

When she was finally encased in a steel-colored satin bodice her plump shoulders appeared to start directly beneath her ears, and her hands were not only purple, but slightly numb.

"How do I look, child?"

"How do you feel?" asked Essie evasively.

"As well as anybody could with their in'ards crowded up under their chin," replied Mrs. Terriberry grimly. "I hope the house don't ketch fire while we're eatin', for I sure aims to slide these slippers off onct we're set down, and there's one thing certain," Mrs. Terriberry continued savagely, "I'm sufferin' enough to git some good out of it."

As Essie turned away Mrs. Terriberry kissed her cheek kindly.

"Keep a stiff upper lip, Essie, don't let them see."

"I can do that," the girl replied proudly.

Innovations are nearly always attended by difficulties and embarrassments but even Andy P. Symes had not anticipated that his effort to establish a local aristocracy would entail so many awkward moments and painful situations.

If the printed invitations and the unusual hour had filled his guests with awe, the formalities of the dinner itself had the effect of temporarily paralyzing their faculties. In lieu of the merry scramble characteristic of Crowheart's festivities, there was a kind of a Death March into the dining-room from which Mrs. Terriberry had unceremoniously "fanned" the regular boarders.

The procession was headed by Andy P. Symes bearing Mrs. Starr, tittering hysterically, upon his arm. Mrs. Symes's newly acquired *savoir-faire* deserted her; her hands grew clammy and Sylvanus Starr's desperate conversational efforts evoked no other response than "Yes, sir—No, sir." Mrs. Terriberry, red and flustered, found herself engaged in a wrestling match with little Alva Jackson, which lasted all the way from the door of the dining-room to the long table at the end. Mr. Jackson in his panic was determined to take Mrs. Terriberry's arm, whereas she was equally determined that she would take his, having furtively observed her host gallantly offering support to Mrs. Starr.

A sure indication of the importance attached to the affair was the number of new boots and shoes purchased for the occasion. Now, thick-soled, lustrous, in the frozen silence of the procession, these boots and shoes clumping across the bare floor called attention to themselves in voices which seemed to shriek and with the fiendishness of inanimate objects screamed the louder at their owners' gingerly steps. A function of the Commune when Madame Guillotine presided must have been a frothy and frivolous affair compared to the beginning of this dinner.

Adolph Kunkel, who had attached himself to Dr. Harpe to the extent of walking within four feet of her side, darted from line and pulled out the nearest chair at the table. Observing too late that the other guests were still standing, he sprang to his feet and looked wildly about to see if he had been noticed. He had. Alva Jackson covered his mouth with his handkerchief and giggled.

There was a frozen smile upon the faces of the ladies who, sitting bolt upright, twisted their fingers under the kindly shelter of the table-cloth. Each trivial observation, humorous or otherwise, was greeted with a burst of laughter and the person brave enough to venture a remark seemed immediately appalled by the sound of his own voice. Adolph Kunkel, to show that he was perfectly at ease, stretched his arms behind his neighbor's chair and yawned.

In spite of the efforts which brought beads of perspiration out on the broad forehead of their host, Essie Tisdale appeared with the first course mid a ghastly silence.

"I hardly ever drink tea," observed Mr. Rhodes, for the purpose, merely, of making conversation.

"Oh, my Gawd, Tinhorn, that ain't tea, it's bullion!" Mrs. Terriberry's loud whisper was heard the length of the table as she tore the sugar bowl from his hand, but the warning came too late, for Mr. Rhodes already had sweetened his consommé.

The guests displayed their tact by assuming a wooden expression, and turning their heads away secretly relieved that they had not committed the *faux pas* themselves. Only Alva Jackson stared at Mr. Rhodes's embarrassment in unconcerned delight.

"Let Essie bring you another cup," suggested Mr. Symes.

"Oh, no! not at all; I take sweetenin' in everything," declared Mr. Rhodes.

There was a distinct relaxation of tension all around when Andy P. Symes took the initiative in the matter of spoons.

"This here soup makes me think of the time I had mountain fever and et it stiddy for three weeks." Adolph Kunkel whispered the reminiscence behind the back of his hand.

"My real favorite is bean soup," admitted Mr. Terriberry, and Mrs. Terriberry looked mortified at this confession of her husband's vulgar preferences.

"It's very nourishing," declared Mrs. Starr tremulously.

"And delicious, too, when properly served." Mrs. Percy Parrott curled her little finger elegantly and toyed with a spoon.

"It's a pretty good article in camp," said Mr. Symes desperately to keep the ball rolling.

The guests shrieked with mirthless laughter at the suggestion of rough camp life.

"Gosh! me and Gus was weaned and raised on bean soup—and liverwurst," interjected Adolph Kunkel in the lull which followed, and immediately squirmed under Mrs. Symes's blazing eyes. "Of course," he added lamely, "we et other things, too—mush and headcheese."

During these trying moments Dr. Harpe settled back in her chair with folded arms regarding the scene with the impersonal amusement with which she would have sat through a staged comedy. No sense of obligation toward her host and hostess impelled her to do her share toward lessening the strain, and Andy P. Symes felt a growing irritation at the faint smile of superiority upon her face. She was the one person present who might have helped him through the uncomfortable affair.

Formality was the keynote of the occasion. Ladies who had been at each other's back door a few hours previous borrowing starch or sugar now addressed each other in strained and distant tones while the men were frankly dumb. It was a relief to everybody when a heaping platter of fried chicken appeared upon the table followed by mounds of mashed potatoes and giblet gravy which made the guests' eyes gleam like bird-dogs gaunt from a run.

Fried chicken is only fried chicken to those who dwell in the country where chickens scratch in every backyard, but to those who dwell where they reckon time from the occasion when they last ate an egg, fried chicken bears the same relation to other food that nightingales' tongues bore to other dishes at epicurean Roman feasts. As a further evidence of Symes's prodigality there was champagne in hollow-stemmed glasses brought from the East.

It was a glorious feast with cold storage chicken expressed from the Main Line and potatoes freighted up from the Mormon settlement a hundred miles below.

"It's a durn shame," said Adolph Kunkel as he surreptitiously removed an olive, "that the plums is spiled, for this is the best supper I ever flopped my lip over."

Symes suppressed a groan.

Each guest devoted himself to his food with an abandon and singleness of purpose which left no doubt as to his enjoyment, and the effort of old Edouard Dubois to scrape the last vestige of potato from his plate brought out a suggestion from Adolph Kunkel to leave the gilt design on the bottom. And when tiny after-dinner coffee cups appeared, the guests felt that a new and valuable experience was being added to their lives.

"Holy smoke—but that's stout!" hinted Mr. Terriberry after looking the table over for the customary pitcher of tinned milk. But before Mr. Symes could act upon the hint his brother-in-law's eyes began to water and bulge. He groped for his napkin while he compressed his lips in an heroic effort to retain the hot and bitter coffee, but instead he grabbed the hanging edge of the table-cloth. His pitiful eyes were fixed upon the coldly disapproving face of Andy P. Symes, but there is a limit to human endurance and Adolph Kunkel quickly reached it. Simultaneous with a spurt of coffee Adolph rose and fled, upsetting his chair as he went, disgraced upon his only appearance in that exclusive set from which he was henceforth and forever barred.

He coughed significantly under the window to remind Mr. Symes that he might be induced to return, but the hint passed unheeded, for regret would not have been among Mr. Symes's emotions if his brother-in-law's removal had been complete and permanent.

Over the coffee and a superior brand of cigars to which Mr. Symes called particular attention, the conversation of his guests began to contain some degree of naturalness and their painful self-consciousness gradually vanished. When they seemed in a mellow and receptive mood he began to rehearse his achievements in the East and unfold his plans. As he talked, their imaginations stimulated by wine, they saw the future of Crowheart pass before them like a panorama.

The army of laborers who were to be employed upon this enormous ditch would spend their wages in Crowheart. The huge pay-roll would be a benefit to every citizen. The price of horses would jump to war-time values and every onery cayuse on the range would be hauling a scraper. Alfalfa and timothy would sell for $18 a ton in the stack and there would be work for every able-bodied man who applied. The grocery bills of the commissary would make the grocers rich and Crowheart would boom *right*. When the water was running swift and deep in the ditch the land-hungry housekeepers would fight for ground. And it was only a step from settlement to trolley cars, electric lights, sandstone business blocks and cement pavements, together with lawns growing real grass! Under the spell of his magnetic presence and convincing eloquence nothing seemed more plausible or possible than the fulfilment of these prophecies. And all this was to be brought about through the efforts of Andy P. Symes, who intimated that not one million but millions had been placed at his disposal by eager and trusting capitalists to be used by him if necessary in making the desert bloom like the rose.

Mr. Rhodes saw himself selling corner lots at twenty thousand each while space rates rose in the mind of Sylvanus Starr in leaps and bounds. The

Percy Parrots saw themselves lolling in a rubber-tired vehicle while the vulgar populace on the curb identified them by pointing with their grimy fingers. Each guest looked forward to the fulfilment of some cherished dream and Dr. Emma Harpe saw a picture, too, as she gazed at Symes with speculative, contemplative eyes.

He looked the embodiment of prosperity and success, did Symes, and if he subtly intimated that the road to prosperity lay through loyalty to him, that his friendship, support and approval were the steps by which they could best climb, they were willing to give it without quibbling. They were content to shine in his reflected glory, and they dispersed at a late hour feeling that they had been tacitly set apart—a chosen people.

The next issue of the Crowheart *Courier* referred to the dinner as a three-course banquet, and published the menu. If the description of the guests' costumes made Crowheart's eyes pop and none more than the wearers, the latter did not mention it.

Pleased but bewildered, Mrs. Terriberry read of herself as "queenly in gray satin and diamonds," being unable to place the diamonds until she recalled the rhinestone comb in her back hair which sparkled with the doubtful brilliancy of a row of alum cubes.

Mrs. Percy Parrott had some difficulty in recognizing herself as "ravishing in shot silk garnished with pearls," since the plaid taffeta which had come in a barrel from home with the collar tab pinned flat with a moonstone pin bore little resemblance to the elegance suggested in the paragraph.

And if the editor chose to refer to the pineapple pattern, No. 60 cotton, collarette which Mrs. Jackson had crocheted between beers in the good old Dance Hall days as an "exquisite effect in point lace," certainly Mrs. Jackson was not the lady to contradict him.

But this was merely the warming up exercise of the editor's vocabulary. When he really cut loose on Andy P. Symes the graves of dead and buried adjectives opened to do him honor. In the lurid lexicon of his eloquence there was no such word as obsolete and no known synonym failed to pay tribute to this "mental and physical colossus." In his shirt sleeves, minus his cuffs, with his brain in a lather, one might say, Sylvanus Starr painted a picture of the coming Utopia, experiencing in so doing such joys of creation as he had not known since his removal from the obituary department.

And reading, the citizens of Crowheart rejoiced or envied according to their individual natures.

VIII

"The Chance of a Lifetime"

Dr. Harpe was still young enough to be piqued by Ogden Van Lennop's utter indifference to herself. He was now established in the hotel, apparently for an indefinite stay, and they met frequently in the corridors and on the stairs. His attitude of impassive politeness nettled her far more than the alert hostility of the Dago Duke whom she saw occasionally.

The slight overtures she made met no response and she minded it the more that he made no attempt to disguise his liking for Essie Tisdale, whose laughing good-nature and quaint humor had penetrated the reserve which was in his manner toward every one else. He seemed even to have no desire to take advantage of the patronizing advances of Andy P. Symes, and was content enough to spend a portion of each day reading books with mystifying titles and to ride away into the hills to be gone for hours at a time. He still wore the regalia of the country, the Stetson hat, flannel shirt and corduroys that were too common to attract attention, but the hollows in his cheeks were filling out and the tired look was going from his eyes.

When he had been a month in Crowheart and had made not the smallest effort to "get a job" he began to be regarded with some suspicion. The fact that he seemed always to have money for which he did not work inspired distrust. Then, too, as Mr. Rhodes shrewdly pointed out, he had the long white hands of a high-toned crook. As a result of the various theories advanced, Ogden Van Lennop came gradually to be looked at askance—a fact of which he seemed totally oblivious. And when the clairvoyant milliner went into a trance and declared that a desperado was in their midst planning a raid on Crowheart the finger of suspicion pointed straight at the uncommunicative stranger, and the Iowa Notion Store installed a riot gun.

Dr. Harpe wondered with the rest but she did not share their ignorant mistrust, for she had sufficient worldly wisdom to recognize the nicety of his speech and the reticence of his manners as belonging to a gentleman—a gentleman under a cloud mayhap but still born a gentleman. She was intensely curious regarding his antecedents, and one day she had her curiosity gratified. A letter which came in the morning mail from a schoolmate in the East, read:

DEAR EMMY:

I have just learned through the papers here that Ogden Van Lennop is "roughing it" in your country and I thought I'd write and give you a hint in case you come across him. Grab him, my dear, if you have the ghost of a show, for he is the most eligible man in seven states. Money, family, social position—it makes me green to think of your chance, it's the chance of a lifetime—for I'd never meet him in my humble sphere in a thousand years. He's an awfully decent sort, too, they say. He overworked after he came out of college and he's there getting his health back. Good luck to you and I hope you appreciate my tip.

Lovingly,

ADELE

Dr. Harpe folded the letter and put it away.

"Don't I though?" she said grimly.

She frowned as Van Lennop's low, amused laugh,

mingling with Essie Tisdale's merry trill, reached her through the open window.

"The presumptuous little upstart! The biscuit-shooter!" Dr. Harpe's face was not pleasant to see.

She took care to keep to herself what she had learned for when they met, as she was now determined that they should, she wished the friendship she meant to proffer to seem above all else disinterested. While she realized that she had his prejudice to overcome, she believed that she could overcome it and she would wait now with eagerness for the opportunity to insert the opening wedge.

Heretofore the dubious compliment "a good fellow," from the men with whom she smoked and drank, had pleased and satisfied her. She had no desire to appeal to them in any other way; but this was different because Ogden Van Lennop was different, being the first really eligible man who had limited by her always straitened circumstances. She looked upon Van Lennop in the light of an exceptional business chance, and with a conceit oddly at variance with her eminently practical nature, she believed she had only to set about exerting herself in earnest to arouse his interest and attach him to herself.

Van Lennop found himself still smiling at Essie Tisdale's sallies as he came up the stairs. Her droll originality amused him as he had not been amused in a long time, and he found himself unbending to a degree which often surprised himself; besides, with her frankness, her naturalness and perfect unconsciousnesss of any social barrier, she seemed to him a perfect western type. He prized the novel friendship, for it had become that, and would have regretted keenly anything which might have interrupted it.

Her realistic descriptions of the episodes of a small town were irresistible and Van Lennop never found himself more genuinely entertained than when after a certain set form of greeting which they went through daily with the greatest gravity, he would inquire—

"Well, Miss Tisdale, what are the developments in the world to-day?" And with her quick, dimpling smile she would respond with some item of local news which took its humor chiefly from the telling.

When a sign on the tar-paper shack which bore the legend "Warshing" was replaced by "Plane Sewing Done," she reported the change and, again, the fact that he was aware of Mrs. Abe Tutts's existence was due to Essie Tisdale's graphic account of the outburst of temper in which that erratic lady, while rehearsing the rôle of a duchess in an amateur production, kicked, not figuratively but literally, the duke—a rôle essayed by the talented plasterer—down the stairs of Odd Fellow's Hall over the General Merchandise Store. The girl enjoyed life and its small incidents with the zest of exuberant youth and Van Lennop often declared himself as anxious that Mrs. Percy Parrott should accumulate enough from the sale of milk to buy screens before flytime as that lady herself since Essie sustained his interest by daily account of the addition to the screen fund. He was still thinking of the combative Mrs. Tutts when he opened a book and sat down by the open window.

A murmur of voices which began shortly underneath his window did not disturb him, though subconsciously he was aware that one of them belonged to Essie Tisdale. It was not until he heard his own name that he lifted his eyes from the interesting pages before him.

"You lak him I t'ink—dat loafer—dat fellow Van Lennop?"

Van Lennop recognized the thick, gutteral voice of old Edouard Dubois.

"Like him? Of course I like him, and"—there was asperity in Essie's tone now—"he isn't a loafer."

"Hold-up, then," substituted Dubois.

"Nor a hold-up."

"What you t'ink he is?"

"Something you would never recognize," she answered sharply; "a gentleman."

Van Lennop smiled, for in his mind's eye he could see the tense aggressiveness of her slim figure.

"Chentleman!" was the contemptuous snort. "Chentleman—and never buy de drinks for nobody all de time he is in Crowheart. Fine chentleman dat!"

"When do you buy any?" was the pointed inquiry.

"I haf to work for *my* money; his comes easy," he replied significantly.

"You said that before." The voice was growing shriller. "How do you know?"

"Robbin's easy."

"I must believe it if *you say* so."

"Why you get mad? Why you stick up for him so hard?" persisted the Frenchman stubbornly.

"Why wouldn't I stick up for him? He's a friend of mine."

"Fine fren—dat lazy cheap-skate!" There was real venom in the voice.

Van Lennop heard the stamp of Essie Tisdale's small foot upon the hard-trodden dooryard.

"You needn't think you'll advance your own interests by calling him such names as that! Let me tell you I wouldn't marry you if you asked me a million, million times!"

Van Lennop started. So he was asking Essie Tisdale to marry him—this old Edouard Dubois with the bullet-shaped head and the brutal face that Van Lennop had found so objectionable upon each occasion that he had been his vis-a-vis in the dining-room?

"Oh, you wouldn't marry me?"—the guttural voice was ugly now—"I offer you good home, good clothes, ze chance to travel when you lak and hear ze good music zat you love and you wouldn't marry me if I ask you million times? Maybe some time, Mees Teesdale, you be *glad* to marry me when I ask you once!"

"Maybe I will," the angry young voice flung back, "but that time hasn't come *yet*, Mr. Dubois!"

"And God forbid that it ever should," breathed Van Lennop to himself at the window above. His eyes had grown a little moist at this exhibition of her loyalty and somehow the genuineness of it made him glow, the more perhaps that he was never without a lurking suspicion of the disinterestedness of women's friendship for the reasons which Dr. Harpe, for instance, knew.

What Van Lennop had learned through his unintentional eavesdropping was something of a revelation. In his mild conjectures as to Crowheart's opinion of him it never had occurred to him that it considered him anything more interesting than an impecunious semi-invalid or possibly a houseseeker taking his own time to locate. But a hold-up! a loafer! a lazy cheap-skate! Van Lennop shook with silent laughter. A skinflint too mean to buy a drink! He had no notion of enlightening Crowheart in regard to himself because of the illuminating conversation he had overheard. The situation afforded him too much amusement and since Essie Tisdale liked him for himself and trusted him in the face of what was evidently Crowheart's opinion, nothing else mattered. The only result then was to give him a more minute interest in his surroundings. Heretofore he had viewed the life about him in the impersonal fashion in which persons of large interests and wide experience regard unimportant people doing unimportant things. In the light of what he had learned he placed a new interpretation upon the curious stares, averted faces, frankly disapproving looks or challenging insolence of glances such as he received from Mr. Rhodes's bold eyes. He smiled often in keen enjoyment of his shady reputation and kept adding to his unpopularity by steadfastly refusing to be drawn into poker games which bore evidence of having been arranged for his benefit.

The experience of being avoided by the respectably inclined and sought after by those who had no respectability to lose was a new experience to Van Lennop, who had been accustomed from infancy to the deference which is tacitly accorded those of unusual wealth; but even had he found the antagonistic atmosphere which he encountered frequently now annoying, he would have felt more than compensated by the knowledge that he had discovered in the little belle of

Crowheart a friend whose loyalty was strong enough to stand the difficult test of public opinion.

Essie Tisdale had no notion that Van Lennop had overheard her quarrel with the Frenchman, but her quick perceptions recognized an added friendliness in his manner—a kind of unbending gentleness which was new—and she needed it for she daily felt the growing lack of it in people whom she had called her friends.

In the days which followed, Van Lennop sometimes asked himself if anything had gone wrong with Essie Tisdale. Her shapely head had a proud uplift which was new and in unguarded moments her red, sensitive lips had a droop that he had not noticed before.

Essie Tisdale was not, in her feelings, unlike a frolicsome puppy that has received its first vicious kick. She was digesting the new knowledge that there were people who could hurt others deliberately, cruelly, and so far as she knew, without provocation; that there were people whom she had counted her friends that were capable of hurting her—who could wound her like enemies. And, like the puppy who runs from him who has inflicted his first pain and turns to look with bewilderment and reproach in his soft puppy eyes, Essie felt no resentment yet, only surprise and the pain of the blow together with a great and growing wonder as to what she had done.

The ordeal of the dinner had been greater even than she had anticipated. For the first time in her life she had been treated like an inferior—a situation which Essie Tisdale did not know how to meet. But it had remained for Andy P. Symes who but a few months previous had pressed her hand and called her the prettiest girl in Crowheart to inflict the blow that hurt most.

The guests were leaving when she had found a chance to whisper, "You look so well to-night, Gussie," and Andy P. Symes had interrupted coldly, "Mrs. Symes, if you please, Essie."

Her cheeks grew scarlet when she thought of it. She had meant to tell them in that way that the slight had not altered her friendship and Andy P. Symes had told her in his way that they did not want her friendship.

She did not understand yet, she only felt, and felt so keenly, that she could not bring herself to speak of it, even to Ogden Van Lennop, who still supposed that she had gone as an invited guest.

IX

The Ways of Polite Society

The change which a marcelled pompadour, kimona sleeves, a peach-basket hat, and a hobble skirt wrought in the appearance of Mrs. Andy P. Symes, nee Kunkel, was a source of amazement to Crowheart. Her apologetic diffidence was now replaced by an air of complacency arising from the fact that since her return she began to regard herself as a travelled lady who had seen much of life. The occasions upon which she had sat blushing and stammering in the presence of her husband's friends were fast fading from mind in the agreeable experience of finding herself treated with deference by those who formerly had seemed rather to tolerate than desire her society. Until her return to Crowheart she had not in the least realized what a difference her marriage was to make in her life.

In that other environment she had felt like a servant girl taken red-handed and heavy-footed from the kitchen and suddenly placed in the drawing-room upon terms of equality with her mistress and her mistresses's friends, but she had profited by her opportunities and now brought back with her something of the air and manner of speech and dress of those who had embarrassed her. While Crowheart laughed a little behind her back it was nevertheless impressed by the mild affectations.

It is no exaggeration to say that Crowheart's eyes protruded when Mrs. Symes returned the neighborly visits of the ladies who had "just run in to see how she was gettin' on,'' by a series of formal afternoon calls. No such fashionable sight ever had been witnessed in the town as Mrs. Symes presented when, in a pair of white kid gloves and a veil, she picked her way with ostentatious daintiness across several vacant lots still encumbered with cactus and sagebrush, to the log residence of Mr. and Mrs. Alva Jackson.

There was a pair of eyes staring unabashed at every front window in the neighborhood when Mrs. Symes stood on Mrs. Jackson's ''stoop'' and removed a piece of baling wire from the lace frill of her petticoat before she wrapped her handkerchief around her hand to protect her white kid knuckles and knocked with lady-like gentleness upon Mrs. Jackson's door.

Mrs. Jackson, who had been peering through the foliage of a potted geranium on the window-sill, was pinning frantically at her scolding locks, but retained sufficient presence of mind to let a proper length of time elapse before opening the door. When she did, it was with an elaborate bow from the waistline and a surprised—

''Why, how do you do, Mis' Symes!''

Mrs. Symes smiled in prim sweetness, and noting that Mrs. Jackson's hands looked reasonably clean, extended one of the first two white kid gloves in Crowheart which Mrs. Jackson shook with heartiness before bouncing back and inquiring—

''Won't you come in, Mis' Symes?''

''Thanks.'' Mrs. Symes took a pinch of the front breadth of her skirt between her thumb and finger and stepped daintily over the door-sill.

''Set down,'' urged Mrs. Jackson making a dash at a blue plush rocking-chair which she rolled into the centre of the room with great energy.

When the chair tipped and sent Mrs. Symes's feet into the air Mrs. Jackson's burst of laughter was heard distinctly by Mrs. Tutts across the street.

"Trash!" exclaimed that person in unfathomable contempt.

Mrs. Jackson had two missing front teeth which she had lost upon an occasion to which she no longer referred, also a voice strained and husky from the many midnight choruses in which she had joined before she sold her good-will and fixtures. She now rested her outspread fingers upon each knee and wildly ransacked her brain for something light and airy in the way of conversation.

Mrs. Symes, sitting bolt upright on the edge of the plush rocking-chair with her long, flat feet pressed tightly together, tweaked at the only veil in Crowheart and cleared her throat with subdued and lady-like restraint before she inquired—

"Isn't it a lovely day?"

"Oh, lovely!" Mrs. Jackson answered with husky vivacity. "Perfeckly lovely!"

Another silence followed and something of Mrs. Jackson's mental state could be read in her dilated pupils and excited, restless eyes. Finally she said in a desperate voice—

"It's a grand climate anyhow."

"If it wasn't for the wind; it's one drawback."

Another burst of laughter from Mrs. Jackson who covered her mouth with her hand after the manner of those who have been unfortunate in the matter of front teeth.

"Cats!" hissed Mrs. Tutts across the street. "I'll bet they are laffin' at me!"

"We had charming weather while we were gone," continued Mrs. Symes easily. The word was new to her vocabulary and its elegance did not escape Mrs. Jackson.

"That's good."

"The change was so beneficial to me. One so soon exhausts a small town, don't you think so, Mrs. Jackson?"

Mrs. Jackson could not truthfully say that she ever had felt that she had exhausted Crowheart, but she agreed weakly—

"Uh-huh."

"I had so many new and delightful experiences, too." Mrs. Symes smiled a sweetly reminiscent smile.

"You musta had."

"Going out in the train we had cantelope with cracked ice in it. You must try it sometimes, Mrs. Jackson—it's delicious."

"I can't say when I've et a cantelope but, Oh Lord, I has a hankerin' for eggs! I tell Jackson the next time he ships he's gotta take me along, for I want to git out where I can git my mitt on a pair of eggs."

"We became quite surfeited with eggs, Phidias and I," observed Mrs. Symes with an air of ennui.

Mrs. Jackson blinked.

"I can't go 'em onless their plumb fresh," she replied non-committally.

"I've had *such* a pleasant call." Mrs. Symes rose.

"Run in agin." Mrs. Jackson's eyes were glued upon the leather card-case from which Mrs. Symes was edeavoring to extract a card with fingers which she was unable to bend.

"Thanks. I've been so busy getting settled and all but now I mean to keep a servant and shall have more time."

Mrs. Jackson had read of ladies who kept servants but never had hoped to know one.

"Where you goin' to git—it? From Omyhaw or K. C.?"

"Grandmother has promised to come to me," said Mrs. Symes languidly.

Mrs. Jackson's jaw dropped.

"Gramma Kunkel ain't a servant, is she? she's 'help.'"

"'Help' are servants," explained Mrs. Symes with gentle patience as she laid her printed visiting card upon the centre table.

"Gosh! that strikes me funny." Mrs. Jackson was natural at last.

"Not at all," replied Mrs. Symes with hauteur. "She must work, so why not for me? She's strong and very, very capable."

"Oh, she's capable all right, but," persisted Mrs. Jackson unconvinced, "it strikes me funny. Say, is Essie Tisdale a servant, too?"

Mrs. Symes smiled ever so slightly as she fumbled with her visiting card and laid it in a more conspicuous place.

"Certainly."

"Was that why she wasn't ast to the banquet?"

Again Mrs. Symes smiled the slow, deprecating smile which she was assiduously cultivating.

"Society must draw the line somewhere, Mrs. Jackson."

Mrs. Jackson gulped with a clicking sound, and at the door shook hands with Mrs. Symes, wearing the dazed expression of one who has bumped his head on a shelf corner. Through the potted geranium she watched Mrs. Symes picking her way across another vacant lot to the dwelling of the Sylvanus Starr's.

Mrs. Abe Tutts with her blue flannel yachting cap set at an aggressive angle over one eye paddled across the street and was upon Mrs. Jackson before that person was aware of her presence.

"Has that guttersnipe gone?" A quite superfluous question, as Mrs. Jackson was well aware.

"Of who are you speakin'?" inquired Mrs. Jackson coldly.

"Who would I be speakin' of but Gus Kunkel?" demanded Mrs. Tutts belligerently.

"Look here, Mis' Tutts, I don't want to have no words with you, but——"

"What's that?" interrupted Mrs. Tutts eyeing the visiting card which Mrs. Jackson had been studying intently. "Is she leavin' tickets for somethin'?"

"Oh, no," replied Mrs. Jackson in a blasé tone, "this is merely her callin' card."

"Callin' card! You was to home, wasn't you?"

"It's the new style to leave your callin' card whether they're to home or not," explained Mrs. Jackson, hazarding a guess.

Mrs. Jackson's air of familiarity with social mysteries was most exasperating to Mrs. Tutts.

"What's the sense of that? Lemme see it."

Mrs. Tutts read laboriously and with unmitigated scorn:

MRS. ANDREW PHIDIAS SYMES

At Home

Thursday 2–4

She sank cautiously into the blue rocking-chair and removed a hatpin which skewered her yachting cap to a knob of hair.

"That beats *me!* 'Mrs. Andrew Phidias Symes!'" Mrs. Tutts saw no reason to slight the letter p and pronounced it distinctly. "At home Thursdays between two and four! What of it? Ain't we all generally home Thursdays between two and four?"

"Gussie has improved wonderful," replied Mrs. Jackson pacifically.

"*Improved!* If you call goin' around passin' of them up that she's knowed well 'improved' why then she has improved wonderful. Snip!"

"I don't think she really aimed to pass you up."

"I wasn't thinkin' of myself," replied Mrs. Tutts hotly, "I was thinking of Essie Tisdale. I hope Mis' Symes don't come around to call on me—I'm kind of perticular who I entertain."

Mrs. Jackson's hard blue eyes began to shine, but Mrs. Jackson had been something of a warrior herself in her day and knew a warrior when she saw one. She had no desire to engage in a hand to hand conflict with Mrs. Tutts, whose fierceness she was well aware was more than surface deep, and she read in that person's alert pose a disconcerting readiness for action. It was a critical moment, one which required tact, for a single injudicious word would precipitate a fray of which Mrs. Jackson could not be altogether sure of the result. Besides, poised as she was like a winged Mercury on the threshold of Society, she could not afford any low scene with Mrs. Tutts. Conquering her resentment, Mrs. Jackson said conciliatingly—

"Yes, of course, now we're married it's different—we *have* to be perticular who we entertain. As Mis'

Symes says—'Society must draw the line somewhere!' "

Mrs. Tutts searched her face in quick suspicion.

"Who'd she say it about?"

"Promise me that this won't go no further—hope to die?—but to tell the truth we was speakin' of Essie Tisdale."

Mrs. Tutts looked mystified.

"What's she done?"

In unconscious imitation of Mrs. Symes, Mrs. Jackson curled her little finger and smiled a slow, deprecating smile—

"You see she works *out*—she's really a servant."

Mrs. Tutts nodded in entire comprehension.

"I know; back East in Dakoty we always looked down on them more or less as was out'n out hired girls. But out here I've aimed to treat everybody the same."

"I'll say that for you, Mis' Tutts," declared Mrs. Jackson generously, "you've never showed no diffrunce to nobody."

"I'm glad you think so," said Mrs. Tutts modestly, "and I don't mean to pass Essie Tisdale up altogether."

"Ner me," declared Mrs. Jackson, "she's a perfeckly good girl so far as I know."

"Where do you suppose Mis' Symes got them cards printed?" inquired Mrs. Tutts. "I gotta git Tutts to git to work and git me some."

"Over to the *Courier* office I should think," Mrs. Jackson added. "It's lucky I got some in the house since they've started in usin' em."

There was a moment's silence in which Mrs. Tutts eyed Mrs. Jackson with unfriendly eyes. It seemed very plain to her that her neighbor was trying to "put it over her." The temptation against which she struggled was too strong and she inquired pointedly while she discreetly arose to go—

"Business cards, Mis' Jackson—some you had left over?"

Diplomacy was scattered to the four winds.

"No; not business cards, Mis' Tutts! Callin' cards. I'll show you one since I've no notion you ever saw one back there in that beer garden where you cracked your voice singin'!"

Mrs. Tutts put on her yachting cap and pulling it down on her head until her hair was well covered, advanced menacingly.

"You gotta eat them words, Mis' Jackson," she said with ominous calm.

Mrs. Jackson retreated until the marble-topped centre table formed a protecting barrier.

"Don't you start no rough-house here, Mis' Tutts."

Mrs. Tutts continued to advance and her lips had contracted as though an invisible gathering string had been jerked violently.

"You gotta eat them words, Mis' Jackson." Unwavering purpose was in her voice.

"I'll have the law on you if you begin a ruckus here." Mrs. Jackson moved to the opposite side of the table.

"The law's nothin' to me." Mrs. Tutts went around the table.

"I haven't forgot I'm a lady!" Mrs. Jackson quickened her gait.

"Everybody else has." Mrs. Tutts also accelerated her pace.

"Don't you dast lay hands on me!" Mrs. Jackson broke into a trot.

"Not if I can stomp on you," declared Mrs. Tutts as the back fulness of Mrs. Jackson's skirt slipped through her fingers.

"What's the use of this? I don't want to fight, Mis' Tutts." Mrs. Jackson was galloping and slightly dizzy.

"You will onct you git into it," encouraged Mrs. Tutts, grimly measuring the distance between them with her eye.

"You ought to have your brains beat out for this!" On the thirteenth lap around the table Mrs. Jackson was panting audibly.

"Couldn't reach yours th'out cuttin' your feet off!" responded Mrs. Tutts, in whose eyes gleamed what sporting writers describe as "the joy of battle."

The strength of the hunted hostess was waning visibly.

"I've got heart trouble, Mis' Tutts," she gasped in desperation, "and I'm liable to drop dead any jump!"

"No such luck." Mrs. Tutts made a pass at her across the table.

"This is perfeckly ridic'lous; do you atall realize what you're doin'?"

"I won't," Mrs. Tutts spoke with full knowledge of the deadly insult; "I won't until I git a few handfuls of your *red* hair!"

Mrs. Jackson stopped in her tracks and fear fell from her. Her roving eye searched the room for a weapon and her glance fell upon the potted geranium. Mrs. Tutts already had possessed herself of the scissors.

"My hair may be red, Mis' Tutts," her shrill voice whistled through the space left by her missing teeth, as she stood with the geranium poised aloft, "but it's *my own!"*

Mrs. Tutts staggered under the crash of pottery and the thud of packed dirt upon her head. She sank to the floor, but rose again, dazed and blinking, her warlike spirit temporarily crushed.

"There's the door, Mis' Tutts." Mrs. Jackson drew herself up with regal hauteur and pointed. "Now get the hell out of here!"

X

Essie Tisdale's Enforced Abnegation

There was one place at least where the popularity of the little belle of Crowheart showed no signs of diminution and this was in the menagerie of domestic animals which occupied quarters in the rear of the large backyard of the hotel. The phlegmatic black omnibus and dray horses neighed for sugar at her coming, the calf she had weaned from the wild range cow bawled at sight of her, while various useless dogs leaped about her in ecstasy, and a mere glimpse of her skirt through the kitchen doorway was sufficient to start such a duet from the two excessively vital and omniverous mammals whom Essie had ironically named Alphonse and Gaston that Van Lennop, who had the full benefit of this chorus, often wished the time had arrived for Alphonse and Gaston to fulfil their destiny. Yet he found diversion, too, in her efforts to instil into their minds the importance of politeness and unselfishness and frequently he laughed aloud at the fragments of conversation which reached him when he heard her laboring with them in the interest of their manners.

A loud and persistent squealing caused Van Lennop to raise his eyes from his book and look out upon the pole corral wherein the vociferous Alphonse and Gaston were confined. Essie Tisdale was perched upon the top pole, seemingly deaf to their shrill importunities; depression was in every line of her slim figure, despondency in the droop of her head. Her attitude held his attention and set him wondering, for he thought of her always as the embodiment of laughter, good-humor, and exuberant youth. Of all the women he ever had known, either well or casually, she had seemed the farthest from moods or nerves or anything even dimly suggestive of the neurasthenic.

Moved by an impulse Van Lennop laid down his book and went below.

"Air-castles, Miss Tisdale?" he asked as he sauntered toward her. He still insisted upon the whimsical formality of "Miss Tisdale," although to all Crowheart, naturally, she was "Essie."

The girl lifted her sombre eyes at the sound of his voice and the shadow in them gave them the look of deep blue velvet, Van Lennop thought.

"You only build air-castles when you are happy, don't you? and hopeful?"

"And are you not happy and hopeful, Miss Tisdale?" Amusement glimmered in his eyes. "I thought you were quite the happiest person I know, and to be happy is to be hopeful."

"What have I to make me happy?" she demanded with an intensity which startled him. "What have I to hope for?"

"Fishing, Miss Tisdale?" He still smiled at her.

"For what? To be told that I'm pretty?"

"And young," Van Lennop supplemented. "I know women who would give a king's ransom to be young and pretty. Isn't that enough to make one person happy?"

"And what good will being either ever do me?" she demanded bitterly; "me, a biscuit-shooter!" Her musical voice was almost harsh in its bitterness. She turned upon him fiercely. "I've been happy because I was ignorant, but I've been enlightened; I've been made to see; I've been shown my place!"

That was it then; some one had hurt her, some one had found it in his heart to hurt Essie Tisdale whose friendliness was as impartial and as boundless as the sunshine itself. He looked at her inquiringly and she went on—

"Don't you think I see what's ahead of me? It's as plain as though it had happened and there's nothing else possible for me."

"And what is it?" he asked gently.

"There'll come a day when I'm tired and discouraged and utterly, utterly hopeless that some cow-puncher will ask me to marry him and I'll say yes. Then he'll file on a homestead away off somewhere in the foothills where the range is good and there's no sheep and it's fifty miles to a neighbor and a two days' trip to town." She stared straight ahead as though visualizing the picture. "He'll build a log house with a slat bunk in one end and set up a camp-stove with cracked lids in the other. There'll be a home-made table with a red oilcloth table cover and a bench and a home-made rocking chair with a woven bottom of cowhide for me. He'll buy a little bunch of yearlings with his savings and what he can borrow and in the spring I'll herd them off the poison while he breaks ground to put in a little crop of alfalfa. I'll get wrinkles at the corners of my eyes from squinting in the sun and a weatherbeaten skin from riding in the wind and lines about my mouth from worrying over paying interest on our loan.

"In the winter we'll be snowed up for weeks at a time and spend the hours looking at the pictures in a mail order catalogue and threshing the affairs of our acquaintances threadbare. Twice a year we'll go to town in a second-hand Studebaker. I'll be dressed in

"NO, ESSIE TISDALE. I CAN'T JUST SEE YOU IN ANY SUCH SETTING AS THAT."

the clothes I wore before I was married and he'll wear overalls and boots with run-over heels. A dollar will look a shade smaller than a full moon and I'll cry for joy when I get a clothes-wringer or a washing machine for a Christmas present. That," she concluded laconically, "is my finish."

Van Lennop did not smile, instead he shook his head gravely.

"No, Essie Tisdale, I can't just see you in any such setting as that."

"Why not? I've seen it happen to others."

"But," he spoke decisively, "you're different."

"Yes," she cried with a vehemence which sent the color flying under her fair skin, "I *am* different! If I wasn't I wouldn't mind. But I care for things that the girls who have married like that do not care for, and I can't help it. They save their money to buy useful things and I spend all mine buying books. Perhaps it's wrong, for that may be the reason of my shrinking from a life such as I've described since books have taught me there's something else outside. Being different only makes it all the harder."

"And yet," said Van Lennop, " I'm somehow glad you are. But what has happened? Who has hurt you? Did something go wrong at this wonderful dinner of which you told me? Were you not after all quite the prettiest girl there?"

"I wasn't asked!"

Van Lennop's eyes widened.

"You were not? Why, I thought the belle of Crowheart was always asked."

"Not now; I'm a biscuit-shooter; I work—and—'Society must draw the line somewhere.' "

"Who said that?" Amazement was in Van Lennop's tone.

"Mr. Symes said it to Mrs. Symes, Mrs. Symes said it to Mrs. Jackson, Mrs. Jackson said it to Mrs. Tutts, Mrs. Tutts said it to me."

"Of whom?"

"Of me."

"But what society?" Van Lennop's face still wore a puzzled look.

"Crowheart society."

A light broke over his face; then he laughed aloud, such a shout of unadulterated glee that Alphonse and Gaston ceased to squeal and fixed their twinkling eyes upon him in momentary wonder.

"When I told you I was going I thought of course they would ask me. I thought the tardy invitation was just an oversight, but now I know"—her chin quivered suddenly like a hurt child's—"that they never meant to ask me."

Van Lennop's face had quickly sobered.

"You are sure he really said that—this Andy P. Symes?"

"I think there's no mistake. It was the easiest way to rid themselves of my friendship." She told him then of the reproof Symes had administered.

An unwonted shine came into Van Lennop's calm eyes as he listened. This put a different face upon the affair, this intentional injury to the feelings of his stanch little champion, it somehow made it a more personal matter. The "social line" amused him merely, though, in a way, it held a sociological interest for him, too. It was, he told himself, like being privileged to witness the awakening of social ambitions in a tribe of bushmen.

Van Lennop was silent, but the girl felt his unspoken sympathy, and it was balm to her sore little heart.

"This—society?" she asked after a time. "What is it? We've never had it before. Everybody knows everybody else out here and there are so few of us that we've always had our good times together and we have never left anybody out. The very last thing we wanted to do was to hurt anyone else's feelings in that way."

"You have left those halycon days behind, I'm afraid," Van Lennop replied. "The first instinct of a certain class of people is to hurt the feelings of others. It's the only way they know to proclaim their superiority, a superiority of which they are not at all sure, themselves. Just what 'society' is, is an old and threadbare subject and has been threshed out over and over again without greatly altering anybody's individual point of view. Good breeding, brains and money are generally conceded to be the essentials required by that complex institution and certainly one or all of them are necessary for any great social success."

Van Lennop watched her troubled face and waited.

"Then that's why old Edouard Dubois was asked, though he never speaks, and Alva Jackson, who is uncouth and ignorant? They represent money."

Van Lennop smiled.

"Undoubtedly."

"And the Starrs are brains."

He laughed outright now.

"The power of the press! Correct, Miss Tisdale."

"And Andy P. Symes——" Van Lennop supplied

dryly—"is family. He had a great-grandfather, I believe."

Van Lennop returned the persistent, pleading stare of Alphonse and Gaston while Essie pondered this bewildering subject.

"But out here it's mostly money that counts, or rather will count in the future."

"Yes, with a man of Symes's type it would be nearly the only qualification necessary. If you had been the 'rich Miss Tisdale' you undoubtedly would have been the guest of honor."

"Then," she said chokingly, "my good times are over, for I'm—nobody knows who—just Essie Tisdale—a biscuit-shooter whose friendship counts for nothing."

With feminine intuition she grasped Crowheart's new point of view, and Van Lennop, because he knew human nature, could not contradict her, but in the security of his own position he could not fully understand how much it all meant to her in her small world.

"You mustn't take this to heart," he said gently, conscious of a strong desire to comfort her. "If the cost of an invitation were a single tear it would be too high a price to pay. In explaining to you what the world recognizes in a general way as 'Society,' I had no thought of Crowheart in my mind. There can be no 'Society' in Crowheart with its present material. What it is obvious this man Symes means to attempt, is only an absurd imitation of something he can never hope to attain. The effort resembles the attempts of a group of amateurs to present a Boucicault comedy, while 'in front' the world laughs at them, not with them. It is a dangerous experiment to pretend to be anything other than what you are. It means loss of dignity, for you are merely absurd when you attempt to play a part which by birth and training and temperament you are nowise fitted to play. You become a target for the people whom you care most to impress.

"When one begins to imitate he loses his individuality and his individuality is the westerner's chief charm. Be yourself, Essie Tisdale, be simple, sincere, and you can never be absurd.

"I am sorry for what you have told me, since, if what seems threatening comes to pass, Crowheart will be only a middle class, commonplace town of which it has a thousand prototypes. Its strongest attraction now is its western flavor, the lingering atmosphere of the frontier. This must pass with time, of course, but it seems a shame that the change should be forced prematurely by the efforts of this man Symes. Really I feel a distinct sense of personal injury at his innovations." Van Lennop laughed slightly. "The old way was the best way for a long time to come, it seems to me. That was real democracy—a Utopian condition that had of necessity to go with the town's growth, but certainly not at this stage. In larger communities it is natural enough that those of similar tastes should seek each other, but, in a place like Crowheart where the interests and the mental calibre of its inhabitants are practically the same, the man who seeks to establish an 'aristocracy' proclaims himself a petty-minded, silly ass. Be a philosopher, Miss Tisdale."

But Essie Tisdale was not a philosopher; the experience was still too new and bewildering for philosophy to prove an instant remedy. She found Van Lennop's sympathy far more comforting than his logic, but through her heavy-heartedness there was creeping a growing appreciation of the superiority of this stranger in worn corduroys to his surroundings, a clearer conception of his calm mental poise.

Van Lennop himself was a living contradiction of the fallacious statement that all men are equal, and now, moved by her unhappiness, she caught a glimpse of that lying beneath the impregnable reserve of a polite and agreeable exterior which made the distinction. She realized more strongly than before that he lived upon a different plane from that of any man she ever had known.

"Do you know who I think must have been like you?" she asked him unexpectedly.

He shook his head smilingly.

"I can't imagine."

"Robert Louis Stevenson."

He flushed a little.

"You surely flatter me; there is no one whom I admire more." He looked at her in something of pleased surprise. "You read Stevenson—you like him?"

Her face lighted with enthusiasm.

"So very, very much. He seems so wise and so—human. I have all that he has written—his published letters, everything."

He continued to look at her oddly. Yes, Essie Tisdale was "different" and somehow he was glad. The personal conversation had shown him unexpected phases of her character. He saw beneath her youthful worldliness the latent ambitions, undeveloped, immature desires and something of the underlying strength concealed by her ordinarily light-hearted exuberance. While the readjustment of Crowheart's social affairs was hurting her on the raw he saw the sensitiveness of her nature, the quick pride and perceptions which he might otherwise have been long in discovering. Previously she had amused and interested him, now she awakened in him a real anxiety as to her future.

"Be brave," he said, "and keep on smiling, Essie Tisdale. You must work out your own salvation as must we all. This will pass and be forgotten; there will be triumphs with your failures, don't forget that, and the long years ahead of you which you so dread may hold better things than you dare dream. In some way that I don't see now I may be able to lend you a helping hand."

"Your friendship and your sympathy are enough," she said gratefully.

"You have them both," he answered, and on the strength of ten years' difference in their ages he patted her slim fingers with a quite paternal hand, in ignorance of the malevolent pair of eyes watching him from the window at the end of the upper corridor.

XI

The Opening Wedge

It was with mixed feelings that Dr. Harpe saw Van Lennop ride briskly from the livery stable leading a saddle horse behind his own. It was for Essie Tisdale, she surmised, and her conjecture was confirmed when she saw them gallop away.

While the sight galled her it pleased her, too, for it lent color to the impression she was discreetly but persistently endeavoring to spread in the community that the open rupture between herself and the girl was of her making and was necessitated by reasons which she could but did not care to make public. She made no definite charge, but with a deprecatory shrug of her shoulder and a casual observation that "it was a pity Essie Tisdale was making such a fool of herself and allowing a perfect stranger to make such a fool of her" she was gradually achieving the result she desired. The newcomers seized upon her insinuations with avidity, but the old settlers were loath to believe, though upon each, in the end, it had its effect, for Dr. Harpe was now firmly established in Crowheart's esteem. She had, she felt sure, safeguarded herself so far as Essie Tisdale was concerned, yet she was not satisfied, for she seemed no nearer overcoming Van Lennop's prejudice than the day she had aroused it. He distinctly avoided her, and she did not believe in forcing issues. Time, she often averred, would bring nearly every desired result, and she could wait; but she did not wait patiently, fretting more and more as the days drifted by without bringing to her the desired opportunity.

"I hate to be thwarted! I hate it! I hate it!" she often said angrily to herself, but she was helpless in the face of Van Lennop's cool avoidance.

In the meantime the bugbear of her existence was making history in his own way. The Dago Duke was no inconspicuous figure in Crowheart, for his daily life was punctuated with escapades which constantly furnished fresh topics of conversation to the populace. He fluctuated between periods of abject poverty and briefer periods of princely affluence, the latter seldom lasting longer than a night. He engaged in disputes over money where the sum involved rarely exceeded a dollar, with a night in the calaboose and a fine as a result, after which it was his wont to present his disfigured opponent with a munificent gift as a token of his esteem. Who or what he was and why he chose to honor Crowheart with his presence were questions which he showed no desire to answer. He was duly considered as a social possibility by Andy P. Symes, but rejected owing to the fact that he was seldom if ever sober, and, furthermore, in spite of his undeniably polished manners, showed a marked preference for the companionship of the element who were unmistakably goats in the social division.

At last there came a time when the Dago Duke was unable to raise a cup of coffee to his lips without scalding himself. He had no desire for food, his eyes were bloodshot, and his favorite bartender tied his scarf for him mornings. He moved from saloon to saloon haranguing the patrons upon the curse of wealth, encouraged in his socialistic views by the professional gamblers who presided over the poker games and roulette wheels. In view of their interest there seemed no likelihood that the curse would rest upon him long.

Then one night, or morning, to be exact, after the Dago Duke had been assisted to retire by his friend the bartender, and the washstand by actual count had chased the bureau sixty-two times around the room, the Dago Duke noticed a lizard on the wall. He was not entirely convinced that it was a lizard until he sat up in bed and noticed that there were two lizards.

He crept out and picked up his shoe for a weapon.

"Now if I can paste that first one," he told himself optimistically, "I know the other will leave."

He struck at it with the heel of his shoe, and it darted to the ceiling, whence it looked down upon him with a peculiarly tantalizing smile.

The Dago Duke stood on the bureau and endeavored to reach it, but it was surprisingly agile; besides other lizards were now appearing. They came from every crack and corner. They swarmed. Lizards though harmless are unpleasant and the perspiration stood out on the Dago Duke's brow as he watched their number grow. He struck a mighty blow at the lizard on the ceiling and the bureau toppled. He found himself uninjured, but the breaking of the glass made something of a crash. The floor was all but covered with lizards, so he decided to return to his bed before he was obliged to step on them. He was shaking as with a chill and his teeth clicked. They were on his bed! They were under his pillow! Then he laughed aloud when he discovered it was only a roll of banknotes he had placed there before his friend the bartender had blown out the light. But the rest were lizards, there was no doubt about that, and he would tell Terriberry in the morning what he thought of him and his hotel! They were darting over the walls and ceiling and wiggling over the floor.

"I can stand it to-night," he muttered, "but to-morrow——"

What was that in the corner? He had only to look twice to know. He had seen Gila monsters in Arizona! He had seen a cowpuncher ride into town with one biting his thumb in two. The puncher went crazy later. Yes, he knew a Gila monster when he saw one and this was plain enough; there were the orange and black markings, the wicked head, the beady, evil eyes—and this one was growing! It would soon be as big as a sea-turtle and it was blinking at him with malicious purpose in its fixed gaze.

The Dago Duke's hands and feet were like ice, while the cold sweat stood in beads on his forehead. Then he screamed. He had not intended to scream, but the monster had moved toward him, hypnotizing him with its stare. He could see clearly the poisonous vapor which it was said to exhale! He screamed again and a man's scream is a sound not to be forgotten. The Dago Duke "had them," as Crowheart phrased it, and "had them" right.

The bartender was the first to arrive and Van Lennop was not far behind, while others, hastily dressed, followed.

The Dago Duke gripped Van Lennop's hand in dreadful terror.

"Don't let it come across that seam in the carpet! Don't let it come!"

"I'll not; it shan't touch you; don't be afraid, old man." There was something wonderfully soothing in Van Lennop's quiet voice.

"I'll tell the lady doc to bounce out," said the

bartender. "He's got 'em bad. I had 'em twict myself and took the cure. It's fierce. He's gotta have some dope—a shot o' hop will fix him."

The bartender hurried away on his kindly mission, while the Dago Duke clung to Van Lennop like a horrified child to its mother.

Dr. Harpe came quickly, her hair loose about her shoulders, looking younger and more girlish in a soft negligee than Van Lennop had ever seen her. She saw the faint shade of prejudice cross his face as she entered, but satisfaction was in her own. Her chance had come at last in this unexpected way.

"Snakes," she said laconically.

"Yes," Van Lennop replied with equal brevity.

"I'll have to quiet him. Will you stay with him?" She addressed Van Lennop.

"Certainly."

"Look here," protested the bartender in an injured voice. "He's my best friend and havin' had snakes myself——"

"Aw—clear out—all of you. We'll take care of him."

"Folks that has snakes likes their bes' friends around 'em," declared the bartender stubbornly. "They has influence——"

"Get out," reiterated Dr. Harpe curtly, and he finally went with the rest.

"I'll give him a hypodermic," she said when the room was cleared, and hastened back to her office for the needle.

Together they watched the morphine do its work and sat in silence while the wrecked and jangling nerves relaxed and sleep came to the unregenerate Dago Duke.

Dr. Harpe's impassive face gave no indication of the activity of her mind. Now that the opportunity to "square herself," to use her own words, had arrived, she had no notion of letting it pass.

"He seems in a bad way," Van Lennop said at last in a formal tone.

"It had to come—the clip he was going," she replied, seating herself on the edge of the bed and wiping the moisture from his forehead with the corner of the sheet.

The action was womanly, she herself looked softer, more womanly, than she had appeared to Van Lennop, yet he felt no relenting and wondered at himself.

She ended another silence by turning to him suddenly and asking with something of a child's blunt candor—

"You don't like me, do you?"

The awkward and unexpected question surprised him and he did not immediately reply. His first impulse was to answer with a bluntness equal to her own, but he checked it and said instead—

"One's first impressions are often lasting and you must admit, Dr. Harpe, that my first knowledge of you——"

"Was extremely unfavorable," she finished for him. "I know it." She laughed in embarrassment. "You thought, and still think, that I'm one of these medicine sharks—a regular money grabber."

Van Lennop replied dryly—

"I do not recollect ever having known another physician quite so keen about his fee."

She flushed, but went on determinedly—

"I know how it must have looked to you—I've thought of it a thousand times—but there were extenuating circumstances. I came here 'broke' with only a little black case of pills and a few bandages. My hotel bill was overdue and my little drug stock exhausted. I was 'up against it'—desperate—and I believed if that fellow got away I'd never see or hear of him again. I've had that experience and I was just in a position where I couldn't afford to take a chance. There isn't much practiee here, it's a miserably healthful place, and necessity sometimes makes us seem sordid whether we are or not. I'd like your good opinion, Mr. Van Lennop. Won't you try and see my position from a more charitable point of view?"

He wanted to be fair to her, he intended to be just, and yet he found himself only able to say—

"I can't quite understand how you could find it in your heart even to hesitate in a case like that."

"I meant to do it in the end," she pleaded. "But I was wrong, I see that now, and I've been sorrier than you can know. Please be charitable."

She put out her hand impulsively and he took it—reluctantly. He wondered why she repelled him so strongly even while recognizing the odd charm of manner which was undoubtedly hers when she chose to display it.

"I hope we'll be good friends," she said earnestly.

"I trust so," he murmured, but in his heart he knew they never would be "good friends."

XII

Their First Clash

The Symes Irrigation Company was now well under way. The application for segregation of 200,000 acres of irrigable land had been granted. The surveyors had finished and the line of stakes stretching away across the hills was a mecca for Sunday sight-seers. The contracts for the moving of dirt from the intake to the first station had been let and when the first furrow was turned and the first scoop of dirt removed from the excavation, Crowheart all but carried Andy P. Symes on its shoulders.

"Nothing succeeds like success," he was wont to tell himself frequently but without bitterness or resentment for previous lack of appreciation. He could let bygones be bygones, for it was easy enough to be generous in the hour of his triumph.

"He had it in him," one-time sceptics admitted.

"Blood will tell," declared his supporters emphatically and there was now no dissenting voice to the oft-repeated aphorism.

Symes moved among his satellites with that benign unbending which is a recognized attribute of the truly great. The large and opulent air which formerly he had assumed when most in need of credit was now habitual, but his patronage was regarded as a favor; indeed the Crowheart Mercantile Company considered it the longest step in its career when the commissary of the Symes Irrigation Company owed it nearly $7000.

Conditions changed rapidly in Crowheart once work actually began. The call for laborers brought a new and strange class of people to its streets—swarthy, chattering persons with long backs and short legs, of frugal habits, yet, after all, leaving much silver in the town on the Saturday night which followed payday.

Symes's domestic life was moving as smoothly and as satisfactorily as his business affairs. A lifetime seemed to lie between that memorable journey on the "Main Line" with Augusta in her brown basque and dreadful hat, and the present. She was improving wonderfully. He had to admit that. "No, sir," he told himself occasionally, "Augusta isn't half bad." Her unconcealed adoration and devotion to himself had awakened affection in return, at least her gaucheries no longer exasperated him and they were daily growing less. Dr. Harpe had been right when she had told him that Augusta was as imitative as a parrot, and he often smiled to himself at her affectations, directly traceable to her diligent perusal of *The Ladies' Own* and the column devoted to the queries of troubled social aspirants. While it amused him he approved, for an imitation lady was better than the frankly impossible girl he had married. Something of this was in his mind while engaged one day in the absorbing occupation of buttoning Mrs. Symes's blouse up the back.

He raised his head at the sound of a step on the narrow porch.

"Who's that?"

"Dr. Harpe."

"What—again?"

There was a suspicion of irritation in his voice,

for now that he came to think of it, he and Augusta had not dined alone a single evening that week.

"What of it? Do you mind, Phidias?"

"Oh, no; only isn't she crowding the mourners a little? Isn't she rather regular?"

"I asked her," Mrs. Symes replied uneasily.

"It's all right; I'm not complaining—only why don't you ask some one else occasionally?"

"I don't want them," she answered bluntly.

"The best of reasons, my dear," and Symes turned away to complete his own toilet while Augusta hastened out of the room to greet the Doctor.

Symes wondered if the installation of a meal ticket system at the Terriberry House had anything to do with the frequency with which he found Dr. Harpe at his table, and was immediately ashamed of himself for the thought. It recalled, however, an incident which had amused him, though it had since slipped his mind. He had found a pie in his writing desk and had asked Grandma Kunkel, who still formed a part of his unique ménage, for an explanation.

"I'm hidin' it," she had answered shortly.

"From whom?"

"Dr. Harpe. I have to do it if I want anything for the next meal. She helps herself. She's got an awful appetite."

He had laughed at the time at her injured tone and angry eyes and he smiled now at the recollection. It was obvious that she did not like Dr. Harpe, and he was not sure, he could not exactly say, that he liked her himself, or rather, he did not entirely like this sudden and violent intimacy between her and Augusta, which brought her so constantly to the house.

Some time he meant to ask Grandmother Kunkel why she so resented Dr. Harpe's presence.

Dr. Harpe was seated in a porch chair, with one leg thrown over the arm, swinging her dangling foot, when Mrs. Symes appeared. She turned her head and eyed her critically, as she stood in the doorway.

"Gus, you're gettin' to be a looker."

Mrs. Symes smiled with pleasure at the compliment.

"You are for a fact; that's a nifty way you have of doin' your hair and you walk as if you had some gumption. Come here, Gus."

Dr. Harpe pushed her unpinned Stetson to the back of her head with a careless gesture; it was a man's gesture and her strong hand beneath the stiff cuff of her tailored shirtwaist strengthened the impression of masculinity.

She arose and motioned Mrs. Symes to take the chair she had vacated while she seated herself upon the arm.

"Where have you been all day?" There was reproach in Mrs. Symes's dark eyes as she raised them to the woman's face.

"Have you missed me?" A faint smile curved Dr. Harpe's lips.

"Missed you! I've been so nervous and restless all day that I couldn't sit still."

"Why didn't you come over to the hotel?" Dr. Harpe was watching her troubled face intently.

"I wanted to—I wanted to go so much that I determined not to give in to the feeling. Really it frightened me."

Dr. Harpe's eyes looked a muddy green, like the sea when it washes among the piling.

"Perhaps I was wishing for you—*willing* you to come."

"Were you? I felt as though something was *making* me go, making me almost against my will, and each time I started toward the door I simply had to force myself to go back. I can't explain exactly, but it was so strange."

"Very strange, Gus." Her eyes now held a curious gleam. "But the next time you want to come —*come*, do you hear? I shall be wishing for you."

"But why did you stay away all day?"

"I wanted to see if you would miss me—how much."

"I was miserably lonesome. Don't do it again—please!"

"You have your Phidias." There was a sneer in her voice.

"Oh, yes," Mrs. Symes responded simply, "but he has been gone all day."

"All day! Dreadful—how very sad!" She laughed disagreeably. "And are you still so desperately in love with Phidias?"

"Of course. Why not? He's very good to me. Did you imagine I was not?"

"Oh, no," the other returned carelessly.

"Then why did you ask?"

"No reason at all except that—I like you pretty well myself. Clothes have been the making of you, Gus. You're an attractive woman now."

Mrs. Symes flushed with pleasure at the unusual compliment from Doctor Harpe.

"Am I? Really?"

"You are. I like women anyhow; men bore me mostly. I had a desperate 'crush' at boarding-school, but she quit me cold when she married. I've taken a great shine to you, Gus; and there's one thing you mustn't forget."

"What's that?" Mrs. Symes asked, smiling.

"I'm jealous—of your Phidias."

"How absurd!" Mrs. Symes laughed aloud.

"I mean it." Dr. Harpe spoke lightly and there was a smile upon her straight lips, but earnestness, a kind of warning, was in her eyes.

A clatter of tinware at the kitchen window attracted Symes's attention as he came from the bedroom.

"What's the matter, grandmother?" he asked in the teasing tone he sometimes used in speaking to her. "Not the cooking sherry, I hope."

She did not smile at his badinage.

"There's enough drinkin' in this house without my help," she returned sharply.

"What do you mean?" Symes's eyes opened. "Are you serious?"

The question he saw was superfluous.

"It's nothin' I'd joke about."

"You amaze me. Do you mean Augusta—drinks?"

"Too much."

"By herself?"

"No; always with Dr. Harpe. Dr. Harpe drinks like a man—that size." She held up significant fingers.

Symes frowned.

"I know that Dr. Harpe's sentiments are not—er—strictly temperance, but Augusta—this is news to me, and I don't like it." He thrust his hands deep in his trousers pockets and leaned his shoulder against the door jamb.

"When did this commence?"

"With the comin' of that woman to this house."

"It's curious—I've never noticed it."

"They've taken care of that. She's a—nuisance."

"You don't like Dr. Harpe?" Watching her face, Symes saw the change which flashed over it with his question.

"Like her! Like Dr. Harpe?" She took a step toward him, and the intensity in her voice startled him. Her little gray eyes seemed to dart sparks as she answered—"I come nearer hatin' her than I ever have any human bein'!"

"But why?" he persisted. Perhaps in her answer he would find an answer to the question he had but recently asked himself.

There was confusion in the old woman's eyes as they fell before his.

"Because," she answered finally, with a tightening of her lips.

"There's no definite reason? Nothing except your prejudice and this matter you've mentioned?"

A red spot burned on either withered cheek. She hesitated.

"No; I guess not," she said, and turned away.

"If I thought for a moment that her influence over Augusta was not good I'd put an end to this intimacy at once; but I suppose it's natural that she should desire some woman friend and it seems only reasonable to believe that a professional woman would be a better companion than that illiterate Parrott creature or the tittering Starrs." Symes shifted his broad shoulders to the opposite side of the door and his tone was the essence of complacency as he went on—

"Yes, if I had the shadow of a reason for forbidding this silly schoolgirl friendship I'd stop it quick."

The old woman's lips twisted in a faintly cynical smile.

"And could you?"

Symes laughed. Nothing could have been more preposterous than the suggestion that his control over Augusta was not absolute.

"Why, certainly. I mean to speak to Augusta at once in regard to this matter of drinking. I've never approved of it for women. There are two things that cannot be denied—Augusta is obedient and she's truthful." His good-nature restored by the contemplation of these facts, he turned away determined to demonstrate his control of the situation for his own and the old woman's benefit at the earliest opportunity. In fact, the present was as good as any.

He walked to the door opening upon the porch, where Dr. Harpe still sat on the arm of the chair, her hand resting upon Augusta's shoulder.

"One moment, Augusta, if you please."

She arose at once with a slightly inquiring look and followed him inside.

"I have reason to believe, or rather to know, that you have fallen into the way of doing something of which I do not at all approve," he began. "I mean drinking, Augusta. It's nothing serious, I am aware of that, it's only that I do not like it, so oblige me by not doing that sort of thing again." His tone was kindly but final.

He expected to see contrition in Augusta's face,

her usual penitence for mistakes; instead of which there was a sullen resentment in the glance she flashed at him from her dark eyes.

"It's true, isn't it? You do not mean to deny it?"

"No."

"You intend to respect my wishes, of course?"

"Of course." She turned from him abruptly and went back to the porch.

The action was unlike her. He was still thinking of it when he put on his hat and went down town to attend to an errand before dinner.

As the gate swung behind him Dr. Harpe said unpleasantly—

"You were raked over the coals, eh, Gus?"

Mrs. Symes flushed in discomfiture.

"Oh, no—not exactly."

"Oh, yes, you were. Don't deny it; you're as transparent as a window-pane. What was it?"

"He has found out—some one has told him that we—that I have been drinking occasionally."

"That old woman." Dr. Harpe jerked her head contemptuously toward the kitchen.

"Probably it was grandma—she doesn't like it, I'm sure, for I never was allowed to do anything of the sort; in fact, I never thought of it or cared to."

"You are a free human being, aren't you? You can do what you like?"

"I've always preferred to do what Phidias liked since we've been married."

"Phidias! Phidias! You make me tired! You talk like a peon!"

Her hand rested heavily upon Mrs. Symes's shoulder. "Assert yourself—don't be a fool! Let's have a drink." Mrs. Symes winced under her tightening grip.

"Oh, no, no," she replied hastily. "Phidias would be furious. I—I wouldn't dare."

"Look here." She took Mrs. Symes's chin in her hand and raised her face, looking deep into her eyes. "Won't you do it for me? because I ask you?"

"I can't." There was an appeal in her eyes as she lifted them to the determined face above her.

"You can. You *will*. Do you want me to stay away again?"

"No, no, no!"

"Then do what I ask you—just this once, and I'll not ask it again." She saw the weakening in the other woman's face. "Come on," she urged.

Mrs. Symes rose mechanically with a doubting, dazed expression and Dr. Harpe followed her inside.

Throughout the constraint of the dinner Dr. Harpe sat with a lurking smile upon her face. The domestic storm she had raised had been prompted solely by one of those impulses of deviltry which she seemed sometimes unable to restrain. It was not the part of wisdom to antagonize Symes, but her desire to convince him, and Augusta, and herself, that hers was the stronger will when it came to a test, was greater than her discretion. This was an occasion when she could not resist the temptation to show her power, and Symes with his eyes shining ominously found her illy-concealed smirk of amusement and triumph far harder to bear than Augusta's tittering, half-hysterical defiance.

When she had gone and Symes had closed the door of their sleeping apartment behind him he turned to Augusta.

"Well, what explanation have you to make?"

The cold interrogation brought her to herself like a dash of water.

"Oh, Phidias!" she whimpered, and sank down upon the edge of the bed, rolling her handkerchief into a ball between her palms, like an abashed and frightened child.

Her uncertain dignity, her veneer of breeding dropped from her like a cloak and she was again the blacksmith's sister, self-conscious, awed and tongue-tied in the imposing presence of Andy P. Symes. Her prominent knees visible beneath her thin skirt, her flat feet sprawling at an awkward angle, unconsciously added to Symes's anger. She looked, he thought, like a terrified servant that has broken the cut-glass berry bowl. Yet subconsciously he was aware that he was wounded deeper than his vanity by her disregard of his wishes.

"I insist upon an answer."

"I—I haven't any answer except—that—that I'm sorry."

"Did you drink at Dr. Harpe's suggestion?" he demanded in growing wrath.

She wadded the handkerchief between her palms and swallowed hard before she shook her head.

"No."

"She should never come here again if I thought you were not telling me the truth."

Agitation leaped into her eyes beneath their lowered lids and she blurted in a kind of desperation—

"But I am—it was my fault—I suggested it—she had nothing to do with it!"

"Am I to understand that you have no intention of respecting my wishes in this matter?"

She arose suddenly and began weeping upon his shoulder. The action and her tears softened him a little.

"Am I, Augusta?"

"No; I'll never do it again—honest truly."

"That's enough, then—we'll say no more about it. This is a small matter comparatively, but it is our first clash and we must understand each other. Where questions arise which concern your welfare and mine you must abide by my judgment, and this is one of them. I am old-fashioned in my ideas concerning women, or, rather, concerning the woman that is my wife, and I do not like the notion of your drinking alone or with another woman; with anyone else, in fact, except when you are with me—and then moderately. Personally, I like a womanly woman; Dr. Harpe is—amusing—but I should not care to see you imitate her. One does not fancy eccentricity in one's wife. There, there," he kissed her magnanimously, "now we'll forget this ever happened."

XIII

Essie Tisdale's Colors

Essie Tisdale's ostracism was practically complete, her position was all that even Dr. Harpe could desire, yet it left that person unsatisfied. There was something in the girl she could not crush, but more disquieting than that was the fact that her isolation seemed only to cement the friendship between her and Van Lennop, while her own progressed no farther than a bowing acquaintance. His imperturbable politeness formed a barrier she was too wise to attempt to cross until another opportune time arrived. But she fretted none the less and her eagerness to know him better increased with the delay.

She had plenty of time, too, in which to fret, for her practice was far from what she desired, owing to the climate, the exasperating healthfulness of which she so frequently lamented, and the arrival of a pale personality named Lamb who somehow had managed to pass the State Board of Medical Examiners. The only gratifying feature of her present life was the belief that Essie Tisdale was feeling keenly her altered position in Crowheart. The girl gave no outward sign, yet Dr. Harpe knew that it must be so.

The change in people Essie Tisdale had known well was so gradual, so elusive, so difficult of description that in her brighter moments she told herself that it was imaginary and due to her own supersensitiveness. But it was not for long that she could so convince herself, for her intuitions were too sure to admit of her going far astray in her conclusions.

She detected the note of uneasiness in Mrs. Percy Parrott's hysterical mirth when they met in public, although she was entirely herself if no one was about. The Percy Parrotts, with nearly $400 in the bank to their credit, were climbing rapidly, and Mrs. Parrott lost no opportunity to explain how dreadfully shocked mamma was when she learned that her only daughter was doing her own work—Mrs. Parrott being still in ignorance of the fact that local sleuths had learned to a certainty that Mrs. Parrott formerly had lived on a street where the male residents left with their dinner pails when the whistle blew in the morning.

Essie Tisdale saw Mrs. Alva Jackson's furtive glances toward the Symes's home when they met for a moment on the street and she interpreted correctly the trend of events when Mrs. Abe Tutts ceased to invite her to "run in and set a spell."

Pearline and Planchette Starr no longer laid their arms about her shoulders and there was constraint in the voices of the younger sisters, Lucille and Camille when they sang out " Hullo" on their way to school.

The only persons in whom Essie could detect no change were "Hank" and Mrs. Terriberry, the latter herself clinging desperately to the fringe of Crowheart's social life, determined that no ordinary jar should shake her loose.

Van Lennop himself saw, since Essie had made the situation clear to him, the patronizing manner of her erstwhile friends, the small discourtesies, the petty slights, and he found springing up within him a feeling of partisanship so vigorous as frequently to surprise himself. Were they really so ignorant, so blind, he asked himself, as to be unable to see that the girl, regardless of her occupation or antecedents, had a distinction of mind and manner which they could never hope to achieve? Of her parentage he knew nothing, for she seldom talked of herself, but he felt there was breeding somewhere to account for her clean, bright mind, the shapeliness of her hands, the slender feet and ankles and that rare carriage of her head. Imigrant stock, he assured himself, did not produce small pink ears, short upper lips, and a grace as natural as an antelope's.

But it was a small thing in itself—it is nearly always small things which precipitate great ones—that at last stirred Van Lennop to his depth.

They were riding that afternoon and the saddle horses were at the long hitching post in front of the hotel when Symes came down the street as Essie stepped from the doorway. She bowed as he passed, while Van Lennop mechanically raised his hat. The half-burnt cigar stayed in the corner of Symes's mouth, his hands in his trousers pockets, and his grudging nod was an insult, the greater that a few steps on he lifted his hat with a sweeping bow to Mrs. Alva Jackson.

Van Lennop's face reddened under its tan.

"Does he—do that often?" His voice was quiet, but there was a quaver in it.

"Often," Essie Tisdale answered.

They galloped out of town in silence. The incident seemed to have robbed the day of its brightness for the girl and a frown rested upon Van Lennop's usually calm face. They often rode in silence, but it was the silence of comradeship and understanding; it was nothing like this which was lasting for a mile or more. She made an effort at speech after awhile, but it was plainly an effort, and he answered in monosyllables. She glanced at him sideways once or twice and she saw that his eyes were narrowed in thought and their grayness was steel.

When the town was lost to sight and their horses had dropped to a walk on the sandy road which stretched to the horizon, Essie turned in her saddle and looked behind her.

"I wish we were never going back!" she said impulsively. "I hate it all! I wish we were going on and on—anywhere—but back—don't you?"

His eyes were upon her as she spoke, and he had no notion how they softened, while her color rose at something in his voice as he answered—

"I can imagine worse things in life than riding 'on and on' with Essie Tisdale. But"—his tone took on a new and vigorous inflection—"I want to go back. I want to stay. As a matter of fact I'm just getting interested in Crowheart."

She looked at him questioningly and then explained—

"It couldn't be, of course; I was only wishing, but you don't understand quite—about things."

He spoke promptly—

"I think I do—far better than you believe—and I've about made up my mind to take a hand myself. I cannot well be less chivalrous, less loyal than you."

She looked puzzled, but he did not explain that he had overheard her valiant defence of himself to old Edouard Dubois.

"You're not vindictive, are you?"

She shook her head.

"I think not, but I am what is just as bad, perhaps—terribly unforgiving."

"Even your beloved Stevenson was not too meek," he reminded her. "Do you remember his essay 'Ordered South'?"

She nodded.

"If I am quoting correctly, he says in speaking of a man's duties: 'He, as a living man, has some to help, some to love, some to correct; it may be, some to punish.' And," he was speaking to himself now rather than to her, "the spirit of retaliation is strong within me."

She answered, "They've been very unjust to you, but I did not think you'd noticed."

He laughed aloud.

"To me? Do you think I'd trouble myself for anything they might say or do to me?"

Her eyes widened—

"You don't mean because of——"

"You? Exactly. Aren't we friends—the best of friends—Essie Tisdale?"

The quick tears filled her eyes.

"Sometimes," she answered chokingly, "I think you are my only friend." She continued, "And that's the reason I want you to be careful. Don't resent anything on my account——"

"That's the privilege of friendship," he answered with a reassuring smile. "But why be careful—of whom?" There was some curtness in his voice. "Symes?"

"Yes—of Symes."

"And why Symes?"

"You must remember that you are in a country where the people are poor and struggling. Money is power, and influence, and friends. He has all, and we have neither. I appreciate your reasons, and am more grateful than I can tell you, but you would only hurt yourself, and Andy P. Symes cannot be—reached; is that the word?"

Van Lennop's lips twitched ever so slightly and he turned his head away that she might not see the betraying twinkle which he felt was in his eyes. When his face was quite grave again, he replied—

"Yes, 'reached' is the word, but there are few of us who cannot be reached when it comes to that, for somewhere there is some one who has the 'long arm.' " Once more the shadow of a smile rested upon his lips. "I still believe that Andy P. Symes might be 'reached.' "

"But," she argued, "it is his privilege to withdraw his friendship, if he likes."

"But not his privilege to treat you with disrespect—to insult you both openly and covertly. I like fair play, and Symes fights with a woman's weapons. Listen, Essie Tisdale. I mean from now on to wear your colors in the arena where *men* fight—the arena where I have moderately indulged my combative proclivities with the weapons I know best how to use—the arena where there is no quarter given or received. The most satisfying retaliation is to make money out of your enemies. Concentrate your energy; don't waste it in words. Allow me to add to my income."

He concluded with a whimsical smile, but she had been studying his face wonderingly as he talked, for it wore an expression which was new to her. The keen, worldly look of a man of affairs when his mind reverts to business had come into his eyes and his voice was curt, assured, containing the unconscious authority of one who knows his power.

Essie Tisdale's knowledge of the world was too

limited for her to entirely grasp the significance of his words; she felt, rather, the chivalry which inspired them, that spirit of defence of the weaker which lies close to the surface in all good men.

She put out her hand with a gesture of protest.

"Don't antagonize him. Your friendship and your sympathy are enough. To know that you are too big, too strong, to be influenced by the reasons which have made cowards of those upon whom I counted, is all I want. You can't tell to what lengths these people here will go when their private interests are attacked, and that is what Andy P. Symes represents to them."

"You are not very complimentary," he laughed "You don't think highly of my ability, I'm afraid. What you tell me is not news. Self-interest is the controlling factor in the affairs of human life. I've learned this largely by having my cuticle removed in many quarters of the globe. The methods here are rather raw and shameless, also more novel and picturesque. We accomplish the same result with more finesse in the East."

"I wasn't thinking of your ability, but of your safety," she said quickly. "I know this world out here as you know yours, and——"

"Remember this, Essie Tisdale," he interrupted, and unexpectedly he leaned and laid his gloved hand upon her fingers as they rested on the saddle horn, "whatever I may do, I do of my own volition, freely, gladly—yes, eagerly."

He spoke more lightly as he withdrew his hand and continued—

"The situation appeals to my sporting blood which I believe has been greatly underrated in Crowheart."

He laughed as he remembered Dubois's complaints. "Whatever I may chose to do in the future, please consider that I regard it solely in the light of recreation. It's one's enemies that give a zest to life, you know, and if I choose to match my wits against the wits of Andy P. Symes—my wits and resources—don't grudge me the pleasure, for it is in much the same spirit in which I might play the races or work out a game of chess."

"But," she shook her head dubiously, "with less chance of success."

XIV

The Ethics of the Profession"

Andy P. Symes sat in his comfortable porch chair in the cool of the evening, at peace with all the world. His frame of mind was enviable; indeed, that person would be hard to please who could look down the vista of pleasant probabilities which stretched before his mental vision and not feel tolerably serene.

His enterprise had been singularly free from the obstacles, delays, and annoyances which so often attend the getting under way of a new undertaking Mudge, the Chicago promoter, had been particularly successful in disposing of the Company's bonds, at least a sufficient number to keep the work going and meet the local obligations. Save in a few instances, the contractors had made money on their contracts and were eager for more. The commissary was a source of revenue and there were certain commissions and rebates in the purchase of equipment which he did not mention but which added materially to his income. His salary, thus far, had been ample and sure. Symes told himself, and sometimes others, that he had nothing in life to trouble him, that he was, in fact, that rare anomaly—a perfectly happy man.

This evening in the agreeable picture which he could see quite plainly by merely closing his eyes, there was an imposing residence that bore the same relation to Crowheart which the manor house does to the retainers upon a great English estate. He could see a touring car which sent the coyotes loping to their dens and made the natives gape; not so close, but equally distinct, a friendly hand was pointing the way to political honors whose only limit was his own desires. And Augusta—his smile of complacency did not fade—she was equal to any emergency now, he believed. She had not only changed amazingly but she was still changing and Symes watched the various stages of her development with quiet interest and approval. It is true he missed her former demonstrativeness and open admiration of himself, but he considered her self-repression a mark of advancement, an evidence of the repose of manner which she was cultivating. There were times, he thought, when she carried it a bit too far, when she seemed indifferent, unresponsive to his moods, but at such moments he would assure himself that not for the world would he have had her as she was in the beginning.

She was happy, too; he could hear her occasional laughter and the murmur of her voice as she swung in the hammock at the corner of the house with Dr. Harpe. On his right, he heard the unceasing click of Grandmother Kunkel's needles as they flew in and out upon the top row of the woollen stocking that was never done. It was a pleasing domestic scene and he opened his eyes lazily to enjoy it. They sought the hammock and their listlessness was gradually replaced by an intentness of gaze which became a stare.

"Grandmother," he said after a time, and he noticed that her mouth was a tight pucker of displeasure, though she seemed to have eyes only for her work. "You remember our conversation some time ago—have you changed your opinion in regard to the person we discussed?"

In the look she flashed at him he read not only the

answer to his question but something of the fierce emotion which was finding vent in her flying needles.

"I haven't!" she snapped.

"You truly believe that her influence over Augusta is not good?"

She leaned toward him in quiet intensity—

"Believe it? I *know* it! I've been prayin' that you might see it yourself before it is too late."

"Too late? What do you mean?"

"Just what I say." Her old chin trembled. "Before Augusta has lost every spark of affection for you and me—before I am sent away."

He looked at her incredulously.

"You don't mean that?"

She nodded.

"I've been warned already. I'm in Dr. Harpe's way; she knows what I think of her, and she'd rather have some stranger here."

"You amaze me. Does she dominate Augusta to such an extent as that!"

His mind ran back over the events of the past few weeks and he could see that those occasions from which Dr. Harpe had been excluded had seemed flat, stale, footless to Augusta. She had been absent-minded, preoccupied, even openly bored. He recalled the fact now that it was only at this woman's coming that animation had returned and that she had hung absorbed, fascinated upon her words. She became alive in her presence as though she drew her very vitality from this stronger-willed woman.

"I've noticed a change—but I thought it was nerves—the altitude, perhaps—and I've intended taking her with me on my next trip East."

"She wouldn't go."

"I can't believe that."

"Ask her," was the grim reply.

"She obeyed me in that other matter," Symes argued.

"Because she was *allowed* to do so."

"I'm going to stop this intimacy; I'm tired of her interference—tired of seeing her around—tired of boarding her, as a matter of fact, and I *will* end it." He spoke in intense exasperation.

"Look out, Andy P., you'll make a mistake if you try in that way. You might have done it in the beginnin' or when I first warned you; but Augusta's like putty in her hands now. She don't seem to have any will of her own or gratitude—or affection. I'm tellin' you straight, Andy P."

Symes considered.

"There is a way, if I could bring myself to do it."

"What's that?"

"Make Augusta jealous. Touch her pride, wound her vanity by making love to Dr. Harpe. No," he put the thought from him vehemently, "I'm not that kind of a hypocrite. But she can't be invulnerable—tell me her weaknesses. You women know each other."

The old woman assented vigorously—

"I know her you kin be sure. For one thing she's a coward. She's brave only when she thinks she's safe. She's afraid of people—of what they'll say of her, and she's crazy for money."

They were getting up, the two in the hammock, and as Dr. Harpe sauntered to the porch, Andy P. Symes looked at her in a sudden and violent dislike which he took no pains to conceal. Her hands were shoved deep in her jacket pockets as she swaggered toward him, straight strands of hair hung in dishevelment about her colorless, immobile face, while her muddy hazel eyes became alternately shifting or bold as she noted the intentness of his gaze. No detail of her slovenly appearance, her strange personality, escaped him.

"I'll be goin', Gus; good-night," Dr. Harpe said shortly. She felt both uneasy and irritated by the expression on his face.

Symes watched her swaggering down the sidewalk to the gate, and when it had slammed behind her, he said, sharply—

"I'll be greatly obliged to you, Augusta, if you will ask Dr. Harpe not to abbreviate your name. It's vulgar and I detest it."

Mrs. Symes turned and regarded him coolly for a moment before answering.

"I do not in the least mind what Dr. Harpe calls me."

"That is obvious"—his voice was harsh—"but I do—most emphatically."

Her eyes flashed defiance.

"Then tell her yourself, for I have no notion of doing so," and she stalked inside the house.

The incident of the evening brought to a head certain plans which long had been formulating in Dr. Harpe's mind; and the result was a note which made his lip curl as he read and re-read it the next morning with various shadings of angry scorn.

My dear Mr. Symes:

Kindly call at your earliest convenience, and oblige,

Faithfully yours,

Emma Harie

Symes had spent a sleepless night and his mood was savage. Another defiant interview before leaving the house had not improved it and now this communication from Dr. Harpe came as a climax.

He swung in his office chair.

"'My earliest convenience!' If that isn't like her confounded impudence—her colossal nerve! When she's stalking past here every fifteen minutes all day long. 'My earliest convenience!' By gad!"—he struck the desk in sudden determination—"I'm just in the mood to humor her. Things have come to a pretty pass when Andy P. Symes can't say who and who not shall be admitted to his home. If she wants to know what's the matter with me, I'll tell her!"

He closed his desk with a slam and slung his broad-brimmed hat upon his head. Dr. Harpe, glancing through her window, read purpose in his stride as he came down the street. Her green eyes took on the gleam of battle and to doubly fortify herself she wrenched open her desk drawer and filled a whiskey glass to the brim. When she had drained it without removing it from her lips she drew her shirtwaist sleeve across her mouth to dry it, in a fashion peculiarly her own. Then she tilted her desk chair at a comfortable angle and her crossed legs displayed a stocking wrinkled in its usual mosquetaire effect. She was without her jacket but wore a man's starched piqué waistcoat over her white shirtwaist, and from one pocket there dangled a man's watch-fob of braided leather. She threw an arm over the chair-back and toyed with a pencil on her desk, waiting in this studied pose of nonchalance the arrival of Symes.

The occasion when he had last climbed the stairs of the Terriberry House for the purpose of visiting Dr.

Harp was unpleasantly vivid and the secret they had in common nettled him for the first time. But secret or no secret he was in no humor to temporize or conciliate and there were only harsh thoughts of the woman in his mind.

"How are you, Mr. Symes?" She greeted him carelessly as he opened the door, without altering her position.

"Good morning," he responded curtly. There was no trace of his usual urbanity and he chewed nervously upon the end of an unlighted cigar.

"Sit down." She waved him casually to a chair, and there was that in her impudent assurance which made him shut his teeth hard upon the mutilated cigar.

"Thanks," he said stiffly, and did as she bid him.

"Light up," she urged, and fumbled in a pocket of her waistcoat for a match which she handed him. "Guess I'll smoke myself. It helps me talk, and that's what we're here for."

He had not known that she smoked, and as he watched her roll a cigarette with the skill of much practice the action filled him with fresh repugnance. Through rings of smoke he regarded her with coldly quizzical eyes while he waited for her to open the conversation.

"I've got a proposition to put up to you," she began, "a scheme that I had in the back of my head ever since you started in to 'make the desert bloom like the rose.'"

Her covert sneer did not escape him, but he made no sign.

She went on—

"It's an easy graft; it's done everywhere, and I know it'll work here like a breeze."

Graft was a raw word and Symes's face hardened slightly, but he waited to hear her out.

"You're putting a big force of men on the ditch, I understand. How many?"

"About five hundred."

"Give me a medical contract."

So that was it? His eyes lit up with understanding. She wanted to make money—through him? Her tone and attitude was not exactly that of a person asking a favor. A faint smile of derision curved his lips. She saw it and added—

"I'll give you a rake-off."

He resented both the words and her tone, but she only laughed at the frown which appeared for a moment.

"You're 'out for the stuff,' aren't you?" she demanded. "Well, so am I."

He regarded her silently. Had she always been so coarse of speech, he wondered, or for some reason he could not divine was she merely throwing off restraint? Brushing the ashes from his cigar with deliberation, he inquired non-committally—

"Just what *is* your scheme?"

"It's simple enough, and customary. Take a dollar a month out of your employees' wages for medical services and I'll look after them and put up some kind of a jimcrow hospital in case they get too bad to lie in the bunk-house on the works. I can run in some kind of a cheap woman to cook and look after them and you bet the grub won't founder 'em. Why, there's nothin' to it, Mr. Symes—I can run the joint, give you two bits out of every dollar, and still make money."

Symes scarcely heard what she said for looking

at her face. It seemed transformed by cupidity, a kind of mean penuriousness which he had observed in the faces of persons of small interests, but never to such a degree. "She's money mad," Grandmother Kunkel had said; the old woman was right.

He was not squeamish, Andy P. Symes, and it was true that he was "out for the stuff," but the woman's bald statement shocked him. Upon a few occasions Symes had been surprised to find that he had standards of conduct, unsuspected ideals, and somehow, her attitude toward her profession outraged his sense of decency. If a minister of the gospel had hung over his Bible and shouted from the pulpit "I'm out for the stuff!" the effect upon Symes would have been much the same.

Until she thrust her sordid views upon him he had not realized that he entertained for the medical profession any deeper respect than for any other class of persons engaged in earning a livelihood, but now he remembered that the best physicians he had known had seemed to look upon their life-work as a consecration of themselves to humanity and the most flippant among them, as men, had always a dignity apart from themselves when they became the physician, and he knew, too, that as a class they were jealous of the good name of their profession and sensitive to a degree where anything affected its honor. The viewpoint now presented was new to him and sufficiently interesting to investigate further; besides it shed a new light upon the woman's character.

"But supposing the men object to such a deduction," he said tentatively. "There's little sickness in this climate and the camps are sanitary."

"Object? What of it!" she argued eagerly.

"They'll have to submit if you say so; certainly they're not goin' to throw up their jobs for a dollar. Work's too scarce for that. They can't kick and they won't kick if you give 'em to understand that they've got to dig up this dollar or quit."

"But," Symes evaded, "the most of this work is let to contractors and it's for them to determine; I don't feel like dictating to them."

"Why not?" Her voice quavered with impatience. "They want new contracts. They'd make the arrangement if they thought it would please you?"

"But," Symes answered coolly, "I don't know that it would please me."

He saw the quick, antagonistic glitter which leaped into her eyes, but he went on calmly—

"Where the work is dangerous and the force is large your scheme is customary and practicable, I know, but upon a project of this size where the conditions are healthy, there is nothing to justify me in demanding a compulsory contribution of $500 a month for your benefit."

She controlled her temper with visible effort.

"But there will be dangerous work," she urged. "I've been over the ground and I know. There'll be a tunnel, lots of rock-work, blasting, and, in consequence, accidents."

"That would be my chief objection to giving you the contract."

"What do you mean?"

His smile was ironical as he answered—

"You are not a surgeon."

"Hell! I can plaster 'em up somehow."

Symes stared. His expression quickly brought her to a realization of the mistake into which her angry vehemence had led her and she colored to the roots of her hair.

"Your confidence is reassuring," he said dryly at the end of an uncomfortable pause. "But tell me," —her callousness aroused his curiosity—"would you, admittedly without experience or practical surgical knowledge, be willing to shoulder the responsibilities which would come to you in such a position?"

"I told you," she answered obstinately, "I can fix 'em up somehow; I can do the trick and get away with it. You needn't be afraid of *me.*"

"What *I'm* afraid of isn't the question; but haven't you any feeling of moral responsibility when it comes to tinkering and experimenting with the lives and limbs of workingmen who have families dependent upon them?"

"What's the use of worryin' over what hasn't happened?" she asked evasively. "I'll do the best I can."

"But supposing 'the best you can' isn't enough? Supposing through inexperience or ignorance you blunder, unmistakably, palpably blunder, what then?"

"Well," she shrugged her shoulder, "I wouldn't be the first."

"But," he suggested ironically, "a victim has redress."

She snorted.

"Not a doctor's victim. Did you ever hear of a patient winnin' a case against a doctor? Did you ever hear of a successful malpractice suit?"

He considered.

"I can't say that I've known the sort of doctors who figure in malpractice suits, but since I think of it I don't believe I ever read or heard of one who ever did."

"And you won't," she said tersely.

"Why not? The rest of the world must pay for the mistakes of incompetency."

"'The ethics of the profession,'" she quoted mockingly. "We protect each other. The last thing a doctor wants to do, or will do, is to testify against a fellow practitioner. He may despise him in his heart but he'll protect him on the witness stand. Besides, we're allowed a certain percentage of mistakes; the best are not infallible."

"That's true; but supposing," he persisted, "that the mistake to a competent surgeon was so obviously the result of ignorance that it could not be gotten around, would he still protect you?"

"Nine times in ten he would," she replied; "at least he'd be silent."

"And allow you to go on experimenting?"

He saw that she hesitated. She was thinking that she need not tell him she had known such an one.

"Of course there are high-brows who set the standards for themselves and others pretty high, and if I acted, or failed to act, in violation of all recognized methods of procedure, and with fatal results, they *might* make me trouble. But you can bet," she finished with a grin, "the ethics of the profession have saved many a poor quack's hide."

"Quack?"

"Oh, they may have diplomas. A diploma doesn't mean so much in these days of cheap medical colleges where they grind 'em out by the hundreds; you need only know where to go and have the price."

"This is—illuminating." Symes wondered at her

candor. She seemed very sure of her position with him, he thought.

"What difference does it make where your diploma's from to jays like these?" She waved her arm at Crowheart. "A little horse sense, a bold front, a hypodermic needle, and a few pills will put you a long way on your road among this class of people. I'm talkin' pretty free to an outsider, but," she looked at him significantly, "I know we can trust each other."

The implication irritated him, but he ignored it for the present.

"Do you mean to tell me," he demanded, "that there are medical schools where you can *buy* a diploma? Where *anybody* can get through?"

She laughed at his amazement.

"A quiz-compend and a good memory will put a farm-hand or a sheep-herder through if he can read and write; he doesn't have to have a High School education." She inquired jocularly, appearing to find enjoyment in shocking him: "You've seen me hated rival, haven't you—Lamb, the new M.D. that pulled in here the other day? His wife looks like a horse with a straw bonnet on and he ought to be jailed on sight if there's anything in Lombroso" theories. Have you noticed him?"

Symes nodded.

"He laid brick until he was thirty-five," she added nonchalantly. "I've thought some of taking him in with me on this contract, for some men, working men especially, are devilish prejudiced against women doctors."

Symes's eyes narrowed.

"Why share the—spoils?"

"It's a good thing to have somebody like him to slough the blame on in case of trouble."

"By gad!"—the exclamation burst from him involuntarily—"but you're a cold-blooded proposition."

She construed this as a compliment.

"Merely business foresight, my dear Mr. Symes," she smirked complacently. "Some fool, you know, might think he could get a judgment if he didn't like the way we handled him."

"And you're sure he couldn't?"

"Lord!—no. Not out here." Her leg slipped over her knee and her foot slumped to the floor. She slid lower in the chair, until her head rested on the back, her sprawling legs outstretched, her fingers clasped across her starched waistcoat, upon her face an expression of humorous disdain. "Let me tell you a story to illustrate what you can do and get away with it—to ease your mind if you're afraid of gettin' into trouble on my account. A friend of mine who had a diploma from my school came out West to practise and she had a case of a fellow with a slashed wrist—the tendons were plumb severed. She didn't know how to draw 'em together, so she just sewed up the outside skin. They shrunk, and he lost the use of his hand. Then he goes back East for treatment and comes home full of talk about damage suits and that sort of thing. Well, sir, she just bluffed him down. Told him she had fixed 'em all right, but when he was drunk he had torn the tendons loose and was tryin' to lay the blame on her. She made her bluff stick, too. Funny, wasn't it?"

"Excruciating," said Symes.

She seemed strangely indifferent to his sarcasm—to his opinion.

"I can promise you," she urged, "that I'll be equal to any emergency."

"I've no doubt of it," he returned.

Symes smoked hard; he was thinking, not of the contract which he intended to peremptorily refuse, but how best, in what words to tell this woman that now more than ever he wished the intimacy between her and his wife to end.

At the close of an impatient silence she demanded bluntly—

"Do I get the contract?"

With equal bluntness he responded—

"You do not."

She straightened herself instantly in the chair and he knew from the look in her eyes that the clash had come.

"Do you want a bigger rake-off?" she sneered offensively.

"Do you think I'm a petty thief?"

She shrugged her shoulder cynically, but answered—

"It's legitimate."

"Perhaps; but I don't choose to do it. I refuse to force your confessedly inexperienced and incompetent services upon my men. What you ask is impossible."

He expected an outburst but none came; instead, she sat looking at him with a twisted smile.

"You'd better reconsider," she said at last, and there was in her voice and manner the taunting confidence of a "gun-man" who has his hand at his hip.

Symes spat out a particle of tobacco with angry vehemence and his ruddy face turned redder.

"My answer is final."

Her composure grew with his loss of it.

"I hoped it wouldn't be necessary to remind you of your first visit here, but it seems it is."

That was it then—the source of her assurance—she meant to trade upon, to make capital of a professional secret. It was like her to remind him of an obligation, to attain her ends.

"I've not forgotten," he answered with an effort, "but the favor you ask is one I cannot conscientiously grant."

She laughed disagreeably.

"Since when has your conscience become a factor in your affairs?"

He could have throttled her for her insolence, but she gave him no chance to reply.

"Supposing I insist?"

"Insist?" Was she threatening him?

She answered coldly—

"That's what I said."

"Do you mean"—his voice dropped to an incredulous whisper—"that you are threatening to betray Augusta to attain your end?"

"I don't like to be thwarted for a whim—a senseless piece of sentiment. This contract means too much to me."

"But do I understand aright?" She gloated as she saw his fading color. "Do you intend to say that the price of your silence is this contract?"

"Something of the sort," she replied in cold stubbornness.

The full knowledge of her power swept over him; the helplessness of his position filled him with sudden fury. He sprang to his feet and hurled his cigar through the open window. His thick fingers twitched to choke the insolent smile from her face.

"You traitor! You blackmailer!"

She arose leisurely.

"Unpleasant words—but there are others as unpleasant."

With his hands thrust deep in his trousers pockets Symes faced her, eyeing her with an expression which would have made most women wince but which she returned with absolute composure. She was in control of the situation and realized it to the full. Symes was speechless nearly in the face of such effrontery, such disloyalty, such ingratitude.

"You would sacrifice your best friend for money!"

"Business is business, and I'm out for the stuff, as I told you, but there's no sense in letting it come to that. I don't *want* to do it, so don't be a fool!"

Symes groaned; she had attacked him in his most vulnerable spot, namely, his horror of scandal, of anything which would besmirch the name of which he was so inordinately proud. This pride was at once his strength and his weakness.

"And if I permit myself to be blackmailed—there is no use in mincing words—if I give you this contract in exchange for my wife's good name are you willing to consider every obligation wiped out."

Her eyes flashed their triumph at this quick collapse of his stand.

"I am."

"And, furthermore, will you agree to discontinue your visits to my house?"

"Why?" There was hard bravado in the question.

"Your influence is not good, Dr. Harpe."

"What does Augusta say?"

"I've not consulted her."

"And the contract is mine?—that is settled?"

"So long as you keep your word."

She smiled enigmatically.

"I'll keep my word."

A fumbling at the door ended the interview, for it opened to admit a white-faced woman with a child moaning in her arms.

"Oh, Doctor, I'm so glad you're here!" she cried in relief. "He's been like this since early this morning and I brought him in town as quick as I could. Is it anything serious?"

"Come here, my little man."

Symes saw the reddening of the ranchwoman's eyelids at the sympathy in the Doctor's voice, at the gentleness with which she took the child from her arms. Symes paused in the doorway to look longer at the swift transition which made her the woman that her patients knew. There was a softly maternal look in her face as she hung brooding over the child, a look so genuine that it bewildered him in the light of what had just transpired. Was this another phase of the woman's character or was it assumed for his benefit?

The child's shawl slipped to the floor and, as the mother stooped for it, Dr. Harpe flashed him a mocking glance which left him in no doubt.

XV

SYMES'S AUTHORITY

SYMES descended the stairs of the Terriberry House in a frame of mind that was very different from the determined arrogance with which he had ascended them less than an hour before. He was filled with a humiliating sense of defeat, and of having acted weakly. He returned mechanically the salutations of those he passed upon the street and sunk into his office chair with his hat upon his head, a dazed sense of shock and humiliation still upon him.

He had been blind as a bat, he told himself, blinder even, for a bat has an instinct which warns it of danger. The interview which had revealed the woman's character came in the nature of a revelation in spite of that he already knew. The part he had been forced to play did not become more heroic by contemplation, and the only satisfaction he could wring from it was that he was rid of her—that she would never pollute his home again. It had cost him his pride and the sacrifice of his conscience, but he tried to make himself believe that it was worth the purchase price; yet the thought always came back that he, Andy P. Symes, had allowed himself to be blackmailed.

The knowledge of Dr. Harpe's unbelievable perfidy would be a shock to Augusta, but it would terminate the friendship, he told himself, and he would be relieved of the disagreeable necessity of asserting his authority too strongly.

Symes removed his hat and flung it upon a near-by chair, then turned to his desk. A telegram propped conspicuously upon the ink-well proved to be from Mudge, the promoter, and read:

> Have possible investor who wants detailed information. Better come on at once.
>
> S. L. Mudge

Symes's face lighted.

"This is lucky! It couldn't have been more opportune! We'll go to-morrow and I'll tell Augusta while we're gone."

Thus the problem of abruptly ending the friendship without causing comment was solved. He had no misgivings as to the outcome when he issued his mandate concerning Dr. Harpe, but there might be a scene, and he had a man's instinctive dread of a family row in case that Augusta was loath to believe. She was loyal by nature and there was that possibility.

When his wife was removed from the influence which had undermined him in his own home, the old Augusta would return, he thought confidently; that adoring Augusta so flatteringly attentive to his opinions, so responsive to his moods. He wanted the old Augusta back more than he would have believed possible.

As his thoughts slipped in retrospect over the weeks past he could see that the change in her had come almost from the commencement of her friendship with Dr. Harpe. He shut his teeth hard as he thought of the banal influence she had exercised over a good woman; he always had considered Augusta that.

Well, it was ended. They would start once more with a better understanding of each other, in a clearer atmosphere. Something in the prospect made him glow; he felt a boyish eagerness to tell her of the proposed trip, but decided to wait until evening, as she would then have plenty of time to prepare.

The nervous strain of the day previous and the interview of the morning left Symes with a feeling of fatigue when evening came. As he stretched himself upon a couch watching Augusta moving to and fro freshly dressed for the dinner which had now wholly replaced the plebeian supper in the Symes household, he was again impressed by the improvement in her appearance.

The artificial wave in her straight, ash-blond hair softened greatly her prominent cheek bones, and a frill of lace partially hid the peasant hand that had so frequently distressed him. Her high-heeled slippers shortened and gave an instep to her long, flat foot. He smiled a little at the prim dignity which she unconsciously took on with her clothes; but that at which he did not smile was the air of cool toleration with which she listened to his few remarks. She seemed restless and went frequently to the door; when they faced each other at the dinner table he exerted himself to interest her and his reward was a shadowy smile. He was not at all sure that she was listening and he asked himself if this could be the woman who not so long ago had glowed with happiness merely to be noticed? As the meal progressed he became alternately chagrined and angry. Was the change in her more marked than usual, or was it only that he was awake? He felt that he could not endure her vacant, absent-minded stare much longer without comment, so it was a distinct relief when they arose from the table. He concluded to keep the pleasant surprise he had for her a little longer.

He felt something like a pang when she walked past the porch chair where he was sitting and went to the hammock at the corner of the house. She had a book and passed him without a glance, appearing not to notice the hand which he partially extended to detain her.

She looked often toward the street and he noticed that she only seemed to read. Would Dr. Harpe keep her word? Symes believed that she would.

The twilight deepened and he could plainly see her restlessness grow. She no longer made a pretence of reading but sat with her eyes upon the street. Symes remembered that it had been a long time since she had watched for him like that. Finally she threw down her book and stood up that she might have a better view of the door of the Terriberry House. When she started down the sidewalk toward the gate Symes called her.

"Augusta!"

"Yes?" impatiently.

"Come here."

"What is it?" She made no movement to return.

"If you please—one moment."

"I'll be back in a little while."

"But I want to speak to you now." His tone was a command.

"Pshaw!" She frowned in annoyance, but reluctantly obeyed.

"Where are you going?"

"Over to the hotel," she answered shortly.

"To look for Dr. Harpe?"

Resentment was in her curt answer—

"Yes."

"Don't go, Augusta."

"Why?"

"Because I want to talk to you."

"You can talk when I come back."

"I want to talk now; please sit down."

She made no motion to do so."

"What's the matter with you, Augusta?"

"Nothing,"—her face was sullen—"only I don't like to be ordered about."

"I'm not ordering you, as you put it, but I've a surprise for you and I want to tell you of it."

For answer she looked at him inquiringly.

"We're going to Chicago to-morrow."

Instead of the pleasure which he anticipated would light her dark eyes, there was a look rather of apprehension, of disapproval, of anything, in fact, but delight.

"Aren't you *glad?*" he asked in amazement.

"I'm not ready; I've no clothes."

"We can soon remedy that."

She stood before him in sullen silence and he finally asked—

"Well?"

"I don't *want* to go, if you must know!" She blurted the answer rudely and turned away.

"Augusta! Wait!"

"I'm going to the hotel," she flung over her shoulder.

She kept on walking.

"Come back."

Unlatching the gate she flung it open in defiance.

"No!" She seemed like a person obsessed.

Symes arose and walked quickly after her. She stopped then and Symes wondered at his own self-control as he faced her.

"Augusta," he said quietly, "Dr. Harpe is not coming here again."

He saw her face pale.

"Why not?" Her vehemence startled him.

"Because I have told her not to; she understands."

"How dare you?" Her voice rose shrill and her eyes blazed into his. "She's my friend!"

"No, she's not your friend or my friend." He grasped her wrist as she started to go. "You've got to listen; you've got to hear me out! I found her out to-day and I meant to tell you when we had gone from here, but you are forcing me to do it now." Still grasping her wrist he told her briefly of the interview and the price he had paid for her silence. When he had done she wrenched herself free.

"I don't believe it! Anyway, why shouldn't you give her the contract? Why shouldn't you? I tell you I'm going to her and you shan't stop me!"

"Augusta!" There was horror in his voice. "Do you realize what this means? Do you understand what you are doing—that you are choosing between this woman and me? Are you crazy? Are you mad?"

"Yes, yes, yes! Anything you like, but I'm going! I tell you, you shan't dictate who and who not shall be my friends!"

"But she isn't your friend!" he cried with savage bitterness. "She's your worst enemy. Augusta,"—the harshness went suddenly from his voice—"I beg of you don't let this woman come between us!"

"You're a nice one to criticise others."

He winced at the taunt.

"I've tried to make amends," he pleaded.

"Well—you haven't! And," she flung the challenge at him recklessly, "if you want to get a divorce, get it, for I'll quit you quick before I'll give up Dr. Harpe."

She stared into his eyes defiant, unabashed, and in her face he read his defeat—the utter uselessness and futility of commands, or threats, or appeals. He loosened his hold of her wrist without a word, and, flinging him a last glance of angry resentment and defiance, she walked swiftly toward the hotel.

XVI

THE TOP WAVE

MEDICAL contracts between Drs. Harpe and Lamb, Andy P. Symes and the several contractors upon the project, were properly executed before Symes left for Chicago—alone. It entailed a delay, but Dr. Harpe insisted upon immediate action, and her covert threats had the desired result.

"I've kept my word," she said, "and it's up to you to keep yours. If Gus comes to see me that's your lookout, not mine." And since Symes could not help himself, he consented, although he knew that the delay might mean the loss of an investor.

Dr. Harpe quickly realized that she had assailed him in his most vulnerable spot and Symes realized as surely that she would use this knowledge to the limit to attain her ends.

"Am I a coward or a hero?" Symes sometimes asked himself in his hours of humiliation and ignominy.

The day Andy P. Symes left for Chicago Dr. Harpe celebrated the era of prosperity upon which she was about to enter, by the purchase of a "top-buggy," which is usually the first evidence of affluence in the West.

"Doc's all right—she's smart," chuckled the populace when they heard the news of the contract and watched her sitting up very straight in the new vehicle with its shining red wheels and neatly folded top.

"Moses!" Dr. Harpe told herself frequently and

complacently, "'getting there' is easy enough if you've only the brains and the nerve to pull the right wire," and she considered that she had taken a turn around Opportunity's foretop in a manner which would have been creditable to a far more experienced hand than hers; also she had no reason to doubt that the "wire" upon which she now held an unshakable grip held manifold possibilities. By her astuteness and daring, she assured herself, she was in absolute control of a situation which promised as great a success as any person handicapped by petticoats could hope for. Assuredly the top wave made pleasant riding.

Lamb accepted her partnership proposition with an avidity which rather indicated that he needed the money. He had no objections to being a salaried scapegoat providing the pay was sure, but naturally it did not occur to Lamb to regard himself in any such light. If Dr. Harpe dubbed him her "peon," she took care to treat him and his opinions with flattering deference.

They rented a long, unpainted, one-story building which had been a boarding house, for hospital purposes. It was divided lengthwise by a narrow hall which ended in a dingy kitchen in the rear. Dr. Lamb who had some vague theories upon sanitation protested feebly when the operating room was located next to the kitchen, but the location was not changed on that account. The office in the front was furnished with a few imposing bottles and their combined display of cutlery was calculated to impress. Their ideas as to keeping expenses for equipment at a minimum were in perfect harmony, for Lamb as well as Dr. Harpe regarded it as a purely commercial venture.

The latter, however, was disposed to regard the purchase of an X-ray machine as a profitable investment because of the impression it would make upon their private patients.

"Moses!" She chortled at the notion. "Wouldn't their eyes bung out if I showed 'em their own bones! I could soak 'em twice the fee and they'd never peep."

Lamb discouraged the idea for the present on the grounds of economy and advised a sterilizing apparatus instead, which Dr. Harpe opposed for the same reason.

If Dr. Harpe had been given the opportunity of selecting an associate from a multitude of practitioners, it is doubtful if she could have found another better suited to her purpose than the man Lamb. Although, by some means, he had succeeded in being graduated from an institution of good repute, he was a charlatan in every instinct—greedy, unscrupulous, covering the ignorance of an untrained mind with a cloak of solemn and pious pretence which served its purpose in the uncritical, unsuspicious western community where a profession is always regarded with more or less awe.

Lamb's colorless personality had made no great impression upon Crowheart and as yet he was known chiefly through his professional card which appeared among the advertisements in the Crowheart *Courier*. Dr. Harpe had not reckoned him a formidable rival, but she recognized in him an invaluable associate; and often as she contemplated his pasty face, his close, deep-set eyes and listened to his nasal voice she congratulated herself upon her choice, for he was what she needed most of all, a pliable partner.

"Be you goin' to put up a sign?" inquired Lamb.

"Sure; we want all the advertisin' we can get out of this, don't we?" And soon the day came when the two partners stood across the street and read proudly:

HARPE AND LAMB HOSPITAL

In her new buggy with its flashing wheels Dr. Harpe was soon driving through the different camps along the project, and the laborers rather enjoyed the novelty of visits from the "lady doc," as they called her, and consented good-naturedly enough to the deduction of monthly dues for hospital benefits from their wages.

While they regarded her professionally and personally in a humorous light and made her more or less the target of coarse jokes, as is any woman who leaves the beaten track, yet the general feeling toward her was one of friendliness.

They laughed at her swaggering stride, her masculine dress, the vernacular which was their own speech, but there was quickly established between them and her a good-humored familiarity which was greatly to her liking. They become "Bill" and "Pat" and "Tony" to her and she was "Doc" to them.

While her horses trotted briskly the length of the ditch and she was returning smiling nods and flinging retorts that were not too delicate over her shoulder, she began to feel herself a personage; she was filled with a growing sense of importance and power.

There was everything to indicate that the contract would prove all that she and Lamb had hoped for. The general health was exceptionally good and she urged sanitary precautions upon the men to prevent long and expensive fevers; as yet there was no dangerous rock-work entailing the use of explosives to imperil the lives and limbs of the men. The remedies required were of the simplest and the running expenses of the hospital were nil.

When they received their first checks from the Company and the contractors, Lamb's joy was almost tearful.

"It's easier than layin' bricks, Doc," he said as they wrung each other's hands in mutual congratulation.

Dr. Harpes ambitions grew with her bank account, and among them there was one which began to take the shape of a fixed purpose. With her successful manipulations of conditions to further her own ends she came to believe herself in her small world invincible. The effect of this belief upon a nature like hers was to increase its natural arrogance and her tendency to domineer, while the strange, extravagant personal conceit which seemed so at variance with her practical nature became a paramount trait.

There was really no doubt in ner mind that she could marry Ogden Van Lennop if she really set about doing so. It was only of late that she had given the thought words. In the beginning when she had discovered his identity, the most she had hoped for was to be friends, for a friend of Van Lennop's importance might be useful. She felt that there would be some way of turning his friendship to account. The fact that they were still only acquaintances did not discourage her, nor the fact that he seemed entirely satisfied with the companionship of the erstwhile belle of Crowheart.

Rich men and rich men's sons had a way of amusing themselves with the society of their inferiors where they were unknown, was her disdainful explanation to herself, but it piqued and irritated her even while it furnished the material for her sly innuendoes, for the insidious attacks which were fast completing what Andy P. Symes's social dictatorship had begun. With her mounting arrogance Dr. Harpe believed that if her ultimate success in her new ambition demanded the entire removal of Essie Tisdale from the field, this too she could accomplish. Her overweening confidence now was such that she was persuaded that she could shape events and mould the lives of others and her own as she willed.

She was resting one day in her new office in the hospital after a long drive along the ditch, and from her window she watched Van Lennop at the Kunkel blacksmith shop across the street. He gave his horse a friendly pat between the eyes before he swung into the saddle and she stood up to watch him gallop the length of the street with the lithe and confident grace which made him a noticeable figure in the saddle.

"Moses!" she observed aloud, "but he has improved in looks since he landed here—his looks, however, are a mere incident compared to the value of his name on the business end of a check. Harpe,"—she sniggered at a mental picture—"how will you look anyhow hanging to a man's arm? As a clingin' vine you'll never be a conspicuous success, but you could give a fair imitation if the game was worth the candle, and this happens to be an instance where it is. Let's have a look at you, my child."

She took a small hand-mirror from beneath the papers of a drawer and regarded her reflection with a critically humorous smile.

"You're not the dimpled darling you once were,

Harpe,'' she said aloud. ''You're tired now and not at your best, but all the same there's a kind of a hard-boiled look coming that's a warning, a hint from Father Time, that you've got to do something in the matrimonial line before it gets chronic.''

Still viewing herself in the mirror she continued her soliloquy—

''By rights, Harpe, you ought to cut out these piqué vests and manly shirt bosoms and take to ruches and frills and ruffles. It would be the quickest way to make a dent in his heart. He's that sort, I can see, but, Lord! how I hate such prissy clothes! Your chance will come, Harpe, you'll wear the orange blossoms now you've set your mind on it, and, if the chance doesn't come soon you'll have to make it.''

XVII

The Possible Investor

The slender, mild-mannered young man to whom Symes was introduced in the office of Mudge, the promoter, was not a person Symes himself would have singled out as one entrusted with the handling and investment of the funds of a great estate. He had a slight impediment of speech, he was modest to diffidence, and modesty and money was a combination not easy for Symes to conceive, but Mudge had said anxiously upon Symes's arrival:

"I hope you make a good impression, Symes, and can put the proposition up to him right, because if we can land him at all we may be able to land him for the whole cheese, and it will take a load off me if we can. It's gettin' harder all the time to place these bonds; money is tighter and people seem leary of irrigation projects.

"I had no idea so many people had been pecked in the head until I began to handle this proposition. They're damned suspicious I can tell you. It's nearly as easy to sell mining stock and, compared to that, peddling needles and pins from door to door is a snap. Talk it up big but don't overdo it, for J. Collins Prescott is no yap."

"Leave him to me," Symes had replied confidently; "don't worry. If he has got real money and is looking for a place to put it, I'll see that he finds it." And Mudge, noting the warmth of his grasp, the heartiness of his big voice, the steady frankness of the look which the westerner sent into Prescott's eyes. felt that Symes was the man to do the trick and congratulated himself upon his wisdom in sending for him.

"I—I've been looking through you're prospectus, Mr. Symes," said J. Collins Prescott after he had been duly presented with a cabana by that gentleman, "and it is v-very attractive, I might say a-alluring."

Symes beamed benignly.

"You think so? I tell Mudge there's one fault I have to find with it—it's too conservative."

"A good fault," commended Mr. Prescott.

"Yes, yes, of course, better that than overdrawn, and then it's always an agreeable surprise to investors when they come out and look the proposition over. If you are thinking seriously of this thing, Mr. Prescott, I wish you could arrange to return with me. I invariably advise it. Mr. Mudge tells me you have some idle money and I feel sure that you could not place it where you'd get bigger returns."

"W-western irrigated lands have a-always interested me c-considerably," admitted Mr. Prescott, "but heretofore the estate which I represent has confined itself chiefly to the acquirement of water-power sites and their development. They—they're good investments in your opinion?"

"Undoubtedly," was Mr. Symes's emphatic reply. "Very; but they're gettin' scarce, while the irrigating of arid lands is as yet in its infancy."

"E-exactly. I feel that we should begin reaching out along those lines, and although I am not greatly c-conversant with investments of this nature, I can readily see their possibilities."

"No limit!" declared Symes. "Nothin' *but!* Takes capital of course, but the returns are big and sure. That's what we are all looking for."

"I know little if anything of the actual construction of a ditch, but I should presume that the personnel of the m-management would count for much," ventured Mr. Prescott.

"Rather!" Symes replied abruptly, "and if I may say so—if you will pardon me—the name of Symes is a valuable asset to any enterprise—prestige, you know, and all that."

Prescott looked slightly mystified.

"The Symes of Maine—grandfather personal friend of Alexander Hamilton's—father one-time Speaker of the House; naturally the name of Symes stands for something."

Not a muscle of J. Collins Prescott's face moved, but Mudge, watching him keenly, felt uncomfortable and a sudden annoyance at Symes's childish boastings, for so they sounded in Prescott's presence. Symes seemed unable to realize the importance of the unassuming young man who listened so attentively but non-committally to all that he was saying, and in the light of their relative positions Mudge felt that Symes was making himself a trifle ridiculous.

"Ah, yes," Prescott replied courteously, "Symes is a notable name, but I was considering the management from a business rather than a social point of view. You have a w-wide experience in this line? You c-can, I presume, furnish credentials as to past successes, Mr. Symes?"

Symes's natural impulse was to reply, "Certainly, to be sure, years of experience, delighted to furnish anything you like," but something, the voice of caution or Mudge's warning look, induced him to say instead:

"I can't say a *wide* experience, Mr. Prescott, not

truthfully a *wide* one, but some, of course, in fact considerable. Experience isn't really necessary; horse-sense is the thing, horse-sense, executive ability and large-mindedness—these qualifications I think I may conscientiously say I possess."

"I—I see."

Mudge pulled nervously at his mustache.

"As a matter of fact," continued Mr. Symes, "I never permit myself to be identified with failures. When I see that things are shootin' the chutes I pull out." Mr. Symes laughed heartily. "I get from under."

"V-very wise." For an instant, the infinitessimal part of a second, there was a glint of amusement in Prescott's mild eyes and, as he added, Mudge once more felt that uncomfortable warmth under his collar, "Symes and success are synonymous terms, I infer."

Symes laughed modestly.

But to get down to business,"—there was a suggestion of weariness in Prescott's tone—"the water supply is ample?"

"Oceans! Worlds of it, I might say."

"The water rights perfect—stand the severest legal scrutiny?"

"Absolutely!"

"Only engineers of recognized ability consulted and employed upon a project of such magnitude, I infer?"

Mr. Symes's hesitation was so slight as to be scarcely perceptible.

"The best obtainable."

"And approximately 200,000 acres of segregated land can be reclaimed under your project?"

"Every foot of it."

"At an expense of $250,000, according to the figures in your prospectus?"

"That's our estimate and the amount of our bond issue."

"You believe you will have no difficulty in disposing of this land at $50 an acre?"

"Dispose of it? They'll fight for it! Why," declared Mr. Symes, striking at the air with a gesture of conviction, "the whole country is land hungry."

"It's a liberal return upon the investment," murmured Prescott.

"It's a big thing! And think of the Russian Jews."

"Pardon me?"

"Colonization, you know, hundreds of Russian Jews out there raising sugar-beets for the sugar-beet factory, happy as larks."

"To be sure—I had forgotten." Mr. Prescott reached for a prospectus upon the table at his elbow and looked at the picture of a factory with smoke pouring from myriad chimneys and covering nothing short of an acre.

"The soil is deep then—strong enough to stand sugar-beets?"

"Rotation of crops—scientific farming," explained Symes, "gives it a chance to recover."

Prescott nodded.

"I see. The length of the ditch is——"

"Thirty-five miles and a fraction."

"What is the normal width and what amount of water does it carry?"

"Sixty-five feet and it carries six feet of water."

"What is the slope?"

"Two and a half feet per mile."

"How much water to the acre is applied in your State?"

Symes was showing some surprise. For a man who was not familiar with irrigation projects Prescott was asking decidedly pertinent questions, but Symes answered glibly—

"A cubic foot per second to each seventy acres."

"And the yardage? What are your engineer's figures on the yardage?"

Symes cleared his throat—a habit which manifested itself when he was nervous—

"It can be moved for ten to fifteen cents a cubic yard."

"C-cheap enough." Prescott looked at him with interested intentness. "And the loose rock?"

"Twenty-five to thirty." Symes stirred uneasily in his chair.

"And the cuts? the solid rock?"

"Fifty to sixty cents," Symes replied after an instant's hesitation.

"Ah, soft rock. These are your engineer's figures, of course?"

"Of course," Symes answered curtly, and added: "I should say that you had a good deal of practical knowledge of such matters, Mr. Prescott."

Prescott answered easily—

"Superficial, v-very superficial, just a little I picked up in railroad construction."

There were more questions as to loss of water by seepage, air and sub-soil drainage, drops, earth canals, character and depth of soil, possibilities of alkali, all of which questions Symes answered readily enough, but which at the conclusion left Symes with the exhausted feeling of a long session on the witness stand.

"There are still something like $150,000 worth of bonds in the market, I believe?"

"Approximately." It was Mudge who spoke up hopefully.

"And there is no doubt in your mind, Mr. Symes, but that with this amount you can finish the work at the specified time and in a manner satisfactory to the State engineers?"

Symes jingled the loose change in his trousers pockets and replied with a large air of confidence—

"None whatever, sir."

Mr. Prescott arose and stood for a moment thoughtfully stroking the back of one gray suede glove with the tips of the other.

"I—I will take the matter up with my p-people and give you their decision shortly."

His eyes were lowered so he did not see the look which made Symes's face radiant for an instant, but he may have imagined it was there, for his lips curved in ever so faint a smile.

"It has been a p-pleasure to meet you, Mr. Symes." Prescott extended a gray suede hand. "I do not feel that the hour has been wasted, since I have learned so m-much."

"Ask any question that occurs to you: my time is at your disposal as long as I am here." Symes shook his hand heartily in a strong western grip. "Great pleasure to converse with a gentleman again, I assure you."

Symes and Mudge looked at each other when the door had closed upon his back.

"Tractable as a kitten!" exclaimed Symes, beaming.

"Think so?" Mudge did not seem greatly elated.

"Why, yes; don't you?" Symes looked surprised.

"'Tractable' isn't just the word I'd ever apply to Prescott," he answered dryly. "You don't understand his kind."

"You're wrong there," Symes answered with asperity. "But don't you think we're goin' to land him?"

Mudge shrugged his shoulders.

"I'll bet you a hat!" cried Symes confidently. "I know the difference between a nibble and a bite. I tell you Prescott's hooked."

"I hope you're right"—Mudge's tone was doubtful—"but get it out of your head that he's an easy mark. I know that outfit; they're conservative as a country bank. Prescott didn't ask questions enough."

"Didn't ask questions enough? Lord amighty, he was cocked and primed."

Mudge smiled grimly.

"Not for Prescott. Besides, it's not like them to go into a proposition like this without further investigation. If they'd send an engineer back with you I'd begin to hope."

"Bosh!" Symes exclaimed impatiently. "My name counts for something in a game like this."

Mudge was unresponsive.

"Gentlemen understand each other," Symes went on complacently, "intuition—hunch—kind of a silent sympathy. I tell you. Mudge, I'm goin' to win a hat off you."

After leaving the office of Mudge, the promoter, J. Collins Prescott, sauntered into a secluded waiting room in a near-by hotel and sank into the depths of a huge leather chair. He took a voluminous type-written report from the pocket of his fashionable top-coat and fell to studying it with interest and care. He was engrossed in its contents for nearly an hour, and when he had finished he replaced it in his pocket. Then he sauntered to the telegrapher's station in the corner of the hotel office and wrote upon a blank with swift decision a telegram which seemed a trifle at variance with the almost foppish elegance of his appearance. The telegram read:

Crooked as a dog's hind leg. Buy.

XVIII

"Her Supreme Moment"

Dr. Harpe had surprisingly good shoulders for so slender a woman—white, well rounded, and with a gentle feminine slope. That she never had been given the opportunity of showing them to Crowheart had been a matter of some regret. Her chance came when Andy P. Symes celebrated the sale of $150,000 worth of bonds by an invitation ball in the dining-room of the Terriberry House.

Elation over the placing of these bonds with the estate represented by J. Collins Prescott mitigated in some slight degree the humiliation and bitterness of his feelings when, upon his return from his successful business trip, he found that not only had Grandmother Kunkel gone as she had foreseen she would go, but Dr. Harpe had resumed her visits as before and vouchsafed to him no word of explanation or apology at the deliberate violation of her promise.

In any case, as Symes saw clearly now, the fulfilment of it would have been futile so far as ending the intimacy was concerned, for the only result would have been that Augusta would have done the visiting. That he let the matter of Dr. Harpe's broken word pass without protest evidenced the completeness of his capitulation, his entire realization of the hopelessness of resistance to the situation, as did also the silence in which he accepted Augusta's cold explanation of Grandmother Kunkel's departure.

It is not likely that more time and care is devoted to the making up of the list for a court ball than

Symes bestowed upon the selection of guests for the proposed function, which he intended should leave an indelible impression upon Crowheart. It was a difficult task, but when completed the result was gratifying.

No person whom Symes could even dimly foresee as being of future use to himself was omitted and with real astuteness he singled out those who had within themselves the qualities which made for future importance. Even Mrs. Abe Tutts, who, he had learned, was second cousin to a railroad president, was thrown into a state of emotional intoxication by receiving the first printed invitation of her life. Besides, Mrs. Tutts had turned her talents churchward and now ruled the church choir with an iron hand. While her husky rendition of the solo parts of certain anthems was strongly suggestive of the Bijou Theatre with its adjoining beer garden, her efforts were highly praised. This invitation demonstrated clearly that Mrs. Tutts was rising in the social scale.

It was due to a suggestion from Dr. Harpe, made through Augusta, that Van Lennop also received his first social recognition in Crowheart.

"I don't know who the fellow is," Symes demurred. In reality his reluctance was largely due to a secret resentment that Van Lennop had seemed to withstand so easily the influence of his genial personality. Their acquaintance never had passed the nodding stage and the fact had piqued Symes more than he cared to admit. "Besides, he has elected to identify himself with rather singular company."

"No doubt he has been lonely," defended Mrs. Symes mildly, "and of course Essie *is* pretty."

When Van Lennop found the invitation in the

mail a couple of days later he frowned in mingled annoyance and amusement.

"Discovered," he said dryly, quickly guessing its import.

Dr. Harpe's increased friendliness had not escaped him and it had occurred to him that their frequent meetings were not entirely accidental. Past experiences had taught him the significance of certain signs, and when Dr. Harpe appeared with her hair curled and wearing a lingerie waist, the fact which roused the risibilities of her friends stirred in him a feeling which resembled the instinct of self-preservation.

Van Lennop's brow contracted as he re-read the invitation in his room.

"Confound it! I'm not ready to be discovered yet." Then he grinned, in spite of himself, at the hint in the corner—"full dress." He flung it contemptuously upon the washstand. "What an ass!" and it is to be feared he referred to the sole representative of the notable House of Symes.

The initial step in Crowheart toward preparing for any function was a hair washing, and the day following the mailing of the invitations saw the fortunate recipients drying their hair on their respective back steps or hanging over dividing fences with flowing locks in animated discussion of the coming event.

That there was some uncertainty as to the exact meaning of the request to wear "full dress" may be gathered from Mrs. Abe Tutts's observation, while drying a few dank hairs at Mrs. Jackson's front gate, that it was lucky she had not ripped up her accordion-pleated skirt which was as full as anybody could wear and hope to get around in!

"'Taint that," Mrs. Jackson snorted in her face.

"The fuller a dress is the less they is of it. You're thinkin' of a masquerade, maybe. Personally myself," declared Mrs. Jackson modestly, "I don't aim to expose my shoulder blades for nobody—not for *nobody.*"

"I'd do it if I was you," replied Mrs. Tutts significantly.

"Why, if you was me?" inquired Mrs. Jackson, biting guilelessly.

"Because"—Mrs. Tutts backed out of reach—"they's a law agin' carryin' concealed weapons."

Mrs. Tutts did not tarry to complete the drying of her hair, for Mrs. Jackson had succeeded in wrenching a paling from the fence and was fumbling at the catch on the gate.

The dining-room of the Terriberry House was a dazzling sight to the arriving guests, who were impressed to momentary speechlessness by such evidences of wealth and elegance as real carnations and smilax and a real orchestra imported from the nearest large town on the main line. The sight which held their eyes longest, however, was a large glass bowl on a table in an anteroom, beside which, self-conscious but splendid in new evening clothes, stood Mr. Symes urging an unknown but palatable beverage hospitably upon each arrival.

"This is cert'nly a swell affair," they confided to each other in whispers behind the back of their hands after the first formal greetings. "Trust Andy P. for doin' things right."

They frankly stared at each other in unaccustomed garb and sometimes as frankly laughed.

"Gosh!" said Mr. Terriberry as he sniffed the pungent atmosphere due to the odor of camphor emanating from clothing which had lain in the bottom of trunks since the wearers had "wagoned it" in from Iowa or Nebraska, "looks like you might call this here function a moth ball."

Mr. Terriberry himself gave distinction to the gathering by appearing in a dinner jacket, borrowed from the tailor, and his pearl gray wedding trousers, preserved sentimentally by Mrs. Terriberry.

Mr. Abe Tutts, in a frock coat of minstrel-like cut and plum-colored trousers of shiny diagonal cloth, claimed his share of public attention. For the sake of that peace which he had come to prize highly, Mr. Tutts had consented to make a "dude" of himself.

Mr. Abe Tutts, in a frock-coat of minstrel-like cut dinner clothes which upon a previous occasion had given Crowheart its first sight of the habiliment of polite society. If their exceeding snugness had caused him discomfiture then his present sensations were nothing less than anguish. His collar was too high, his collar-band too tight, the arm-holes of his jacket checked his circulation, and his waistcoat interfered with the normal action of his diaphragm, while Mr. Parrott firmly refused to sit out dances for reasons of his own. It was apparent too that he selected partners only for such numbers on the programme as called for steps of a sliding or gliding nature, for Mr. Parrott had the timid caution of an imaginative mind. Following him with anxious eyes was Mrs. Parrott looking like an India famine sufferer décolleté.

From the bottom of that mysterious wardrobe trunk, which resembled the widow's cruse in that it seemed to have no limitations, Mrs. Abe Tutts had resurrected an aigrette which sprouted from a knob of hair tightly twisted on the top of her head. As the evening advanced and the exercise of the dance loosened Mrs. Tutts's simple coiffure, the aigrette slipped forward until that lady resembled nothing so much as a sportive unicorn.

Mrs. Terriberry was unique and also warm in a long pink boa of curled chicken feathers which she kept wound closely about her neck.

The red and feverish appearance of Mrs. Alva Jackson's eyelids was easily accounted for by the numberless French knots on her new peach-blow silk, but she felt more than repaid for so small a matter as strained eyes by the look of astonishment and envy which she surprised from Mrs. Abe Tutts, who had exhausted her ingenuity in trying to discover what she meant to wear.

Mrs. "Ed" Ricketts in black jet and sequins, décolleté, en train, leaning on the arm of her husband, who was attired in a pair of copper-riveted overalls, new and neat, was as noticeable a figure as any lady present.

Mrs. Ricketts's French creation was a souvenir of a brief but memorable period in the history of the Ricketts family.

A few years previous Mr. Ricketts had washed $15,000 from a placer claim in an adjoining State and started at once for Europe to spend it, meaning to wash $15,000 more upon his return. In his absence some one washed it for him. When he came back with a wide knowledge of Parisian cafés, a carved bedstead, two four-foot cendelabra and six trunks filled with Mrs. Ricketts's gowns, but no cash, it was a shock to learn that financially he was nil. After months of endeavor in other lines there seemed no alternative but to light his four-foot candelabra and die of starvation in his carved bedside, or herd sheep, so he wisely decided upon the latter. Mrs. Ricketts adapted herself to the situation and made petticoats of her court trains and drove the sheep-wagon décolleté, so Crowheart was more or less accustomed to Mrs. Ricketts in silk and satin.

Dr. Harpe did not come down until the evening was well along, but the delay produced the effect she intended. As she appeared, fresh and cool with her hair in perfect order, at the end of a number which left the dancers red and dishevelled, she caused a sensation that could not well have been otherwise than flattering. Crowheart stared in candid amazement and admiration.

Her sheer, white gown fell from sloping, well powdered shoulders and its filminess softened wonderfully the lines which were beginning to harden her face. She had dressed with the eagerness of a débutante, and her eyes were luminous, her cheeks delicately flushed with the excitement of it and with happiness at the visible impression she was making.

Dr. Harpe could, upon occasions, assume an air which gave her a certain distinction of carriage and manner which was the direct antithesis of the careless, swaggering, unfeminine creature that Crowheart knew, and as she now came slowly into the ballroom it is little wonder that a buzz went round after the first flattering silence of astonishment, for even a stranger would have singled her out at a glance from the perspiring female crudities upon the floor.

She looked younger by years and with that unexpected winsomeness which was her charm. The murmur of approval was a tribute to her femininity that was music in her ears. The night promised to be one of triumph which she intended to enjoy to the utmost, but to her it ensured more than that, for Ogden Van Lennop was there, as she had seen in one swift glance, and it meant, perhaps, her "chance."

For reasons of his own Van Lennop finally decided to accept the invitation which at first thought he fully intended to refuse. He figured that he had time to telegraph for his clothes, and this he did with the result that Crowheart stared as hard almost at him as at Dr. Harpe's amazing transformation. The reserved, unapproachable stranger in worn corduroys, who had come to be tacitly recognized as an object of suspicion, was not readily reconciled with this suave, self-possessed young man in clothes which they felt intuitively were correct in every detail. He moved among them with a *savoir-faire* which was new to Crowheart, talking easily and with flattering deference to this neglected lady and that, agreeable to a point which left them animated and coquettish. He danced with Mrs. Terriberry, he escorted Mrs. Tutts to the punch bowl, he threw Mrs. Jackson's scarf about her shoulders with a gallantry that turned Jackson green, a neat compliment sent Mrs. Percy Parrott off in a series of the hysterical shrieks which always followed when Mrs. Parrott found herself at a loss for words. Long before Dr. Harpe's appearance it had begun to dawn upon Crowheart that in holding aloof in unfriendly suspicion the loss had been theirs, for it was being borne in even upon their ignorance that Van Lennop's sphere was one in which they did not "belong."

Dr. Harpe quickly demonstrated that she was easily the best dancer in the room, and there was no dearth of partners after the first awe of her had worn off, but her satisfaction in her night of triumph was not complete until Van Lennop's name was upon her programme.

Essie Tisdale, busy elsewhere, had her first glimpse of the ballroom where Van Lennop claimed his dance. She grew white even to her lips, and her knees shook unaccountably beneath her as she watched Dr. Harpe glide the length of the room in Van Lennop's arms. The momentary pain she felt in her heart had the poignancy of an actual stab. It was so—so unexpected; he had so unequivocally ranged himself upon her side, he had seen so plainly Dr. Harpe's illy-concealed venom and resented it in his quiet way, as she had thought, that this seemed like disloyalty, and in the first shock of bewilderment and pain Essie Tisdale was conscious only that the one person in all the world upon whom she had felt she could count was being taken from her.

Van Lennop had told her of his invitation in amusement and later had remarked carelessly that he might accept, but apparently had given it no further thought. Even in her unhappiness the girl was fair to her merciless enemy. She looked well—far, far more attractive than Essie would have believed possible, softer, more feminine and—more dangerous. Van Lennop was human; and, after all, as she was forced to recognize more and more fully, she was only the pretty biscuit-shooter of the Terriberry House. Essie Tisdale pushed the swinging doors from her with a shaking hand and managed somehow to get back into the kitchen where, as she thought, with a strange, new bitterness, she belonged.

Van Lennop did not leave Dr. Harpe when the

waltz was done, but seated himself beside her, first parting the curtain that she might get the air and showing a solicitude for her comfort so different from the cold, impersonal courtesy of months that her heart beat high with triumph. Verily, this propitious beginning was all she needed and, she told herself again, was all she asked. While she believed in herself and her personal charm when she chose to exercise it, Van Lennop's tacit recognition of it brightened her eyes and softened her face into smiling curves of happiness.

Van Lennop toyed with her fan and talked idly of impersonal things, but there was a veiled look of curiosity in his eyes, a kind of puzzled wonder each time that they rested upon her face. As he covertly studied her altered expression and manner, strongly conscious of the different atmosphere which she created, there rose persistently in his mind Stevenson's story of the strange case of Dr. Jekell and Mr. Hyde. He could not conceive a more striking example of dual personality or double consciousness than Dr. Harpe now presented. There was a girlish shyness in her fluttering glance, honesty in the depths of her limpid hazel eyes, while her white, unmarred forehead suggested the serenity of a good woman, and Van Lennop was dimly conscious that for some undefined reason he never had thought of her as that. She had personal magnetism—that he had conceded from the first, for invariably he had found himself sensible of her presence even when disliking her the most. To-night he was more strongly aware of it than ever.

"You are enjoying the evening?"

"Isn't that apparent?" A twinkle shone for a

moment in his eyes. "And you?" adding quickly, "An unnecessary question—your face is the answer."

She laughed lightly.

"It doesn't belie me, for I like this—immensely. Flossying up occasionally helps me keep my self-respect. You didn't expect to find this sort of thing out here, did you?"

He looked at her oddly, not sure that she was serious. Was it possible that she did not see the raw absurdity of it all? Somehow he had thought that she "belonged" a little more than this; her unusual self-possession gave the impression perhaps. He glanced at the attenuated Mrs. Percy Parrott, at Mrs. Sylvanus Starr, exhilarated by numerous glasses of punch, capering through an impromptu cakewalk with Tinhorn Frank, at Mrs. Andy P. Symes, solemn and as stiffly erect as a ramrod, trying to manage her first train, and Van Lennop's lips curved upward ever so slightly, but his voice had the proper gravity when he replied:

"Scarcely."

She shot a quick look at him.

"You *don't* like it," she asserted.

Van Lennop smiled slightly at her keenness.

"To be candid, I don't. The West has always been a bit of a hobby of mine since I was a lad and adored Davy Crockett and strained my eyes over the adventures of Lewis and Clark. I like the picturesqueness, the naturalness, the big, kind spirit of the old days and I'm sorry to see them go—prematurely—for that which takes their place makes no appeal to the heart or the imagination. It is only a—well—a poor imitation of something else.

"With no notion of criticising my host, I must say,

that in my opinion those who introduce these innovations''— he included the ballroom with a slight movement of her folded fan—''are robbing the West of its greatest charm. But then,'' he concluded lightly, and with a slight inclination of his head, ''if I were a woman and the results of—er—'flossying up' were as gratifying as in your case, for instance, I might welcome such opportunities.''

Dr. Harpe raised her eyes to his for one fluttering second and achieved a blush while he smiled down upon her with the faint, impersonal smile which was oftenest on his face.

''Just this once, my dear, and I won't ask you to go in there again. I know how hard it must be for you.''

''Not at all''—Essie had looked at Mrs. Terriberry bravely—''I will do whatever is to be done.''

She picked up a tray of fresh glasses for the table in the well patronized anteroom as she spoke and passed through the swinging door in time to see Dr. Harpe's uplifted eyes and blush and Van Lennop's answering smile.

The glases jingled upon the tray in her unsteady hand, but her little mouth shut in a red, straight line as she nerved herself for the ordeal of passing them. She came toward them with her head erect and a set look upon her young, almost childish face, and Van Lennop catching sight of her intuitively guessed something of her thoughts and interpreted aright the strained look upon her white face.

''She thinks me disloyal,'' flashed into his mind, and he all but smiled at the idea.

Swift as was the passing of the softly interested

expression upon Van Lennop's face, Dr. Harpe caught it and involuntarily turned her head to follow his gaze.

Essie Tisdale! Her face hardened and all her slumbering jealousy and hatred of the girl leaped to life in a mad, unreasoning desire to do her harm, bodily harm; she tingled with a longing to inflict physical pain.

The whirling dancers made it necessary for Essie to pass close, close enough to brush the skirts of the women occupying the chairs along the wall, and as she came toward them with her head erect, looking straight before her, Dr. Harpe acted upon an unconquerable impulse and slid her slippered toe from beneath her skirt. There was a crash of glass as the girl tripped and fell headlong. Tinhorn Frank guffawed; a few of his ilk did likewise, but the laughter died upon their lips at the blazing glance Van Lennop flashed them.

"Essie, you are hurt! Your hand is bleeding!"

Dr. Harpe shut her teeth hard at the concern in Van Lennop's voice as he helped the girl to her feet, but there was solicitude in her tone when she said:

"Let me see if there's glass in it, Essie."

The girl hesitated for an instant, then with an enigmatical smile extended her hand, but there was nothing enigmatical in the sidelong look which Van Lennop gave Dr. Harpe, a look that, had she seen it, would for once have made her grateful for her sex. Subconsciously he had seen the slight movement of her foot and leg as Essie Tisdale passed, but had not grasped its significance until the girl fell.

"I don't think there's any glass in it, but wash it

out well and bring me a bandage. You got a hard fall; you must have slipped."

"Yes, I must have slipped." Her smile this time was ironic.

The night fulfilled the promise of the evening. It was a succession of triumphs for Dr. Harpe. The floor was air beneath her feet and the combination of insidious punch and sensuous music turned her cold, slow-running blood to fire. She was the undisputed belle of the evening, and they took the trailing smilax from the side lamps on the wall and made her a wreath in laughing acknowledgment of the fact. It was such an hour as she had dreamed of and the reality fulfilled every expectation.

She had attracted Van Lennop to herself at last; she had aroused and held his interest as she had known she could and she had sent Essie Tisdale sprawling ridiculously at his feet. She had shown Crowheart how she could look when she tried—what she could do and be with only half an effort. In other words, she had proved to Van Lennop and to Crowheart that she was a success as a woman as well as a doctor. What more could any one person ask? The road to the end looked smooth before her. She wanted to scream, to shriek aloud in exultation. Her cheeks burned, her eyes blazed triumph. She had the feeling that it was the climax of her career, that no more satisfying hour could come to her unless perhaps it was the day she married Ogden Van Lennop. And she owed nothing, she thought as she whirled dizzily in Mr. Teriberry's arms, to anyone but herself. Every victory, every step forward since she arrived penniless and unknown in Crowheart had been due to her brains and efforts. She raised her chin arrogantly. She had never been thwarted and the person was not born who could defeat her ultimately in any ambition! Her mental elation gave her a feeling akin to omnipotence.

A clicking sound in Mr. Teriberry's throat due to an ineffectual effort to moisten his lips brought the realization that her own throat and mouth were parched.

"Let's stop and hit one up," she whispered feverishly. "I'm dry as a fish."

Mr. Terriberry seemed to check himself in mid-air.

"I kin hardly swaller."

He led the way to the anteroom and she followed, swaying a little both from the dizzy dance and the effects of previous visits to the punch bowl. The hour was late and the remaining guests were rapidly casting aside the strained dignity which their clothes and the occasion had seemed to demand. Observing that Van Lennop had made his adieux, Dr. Harpe also felt a sudden freedom from restraint.

Mr. Terriberry filled a glass to the brim and executed a notable bow as he handed it to her.

"To the fairest of the fair," said Mr. Terriberry gallantly, protruding his upper lip over the edge of his glass something in the manner of a horse gathering in the last oat in his box.

Dr. Harpe raised her glass to arms' length and cried exultantly—

"To my Supreme Moment!"

Mr. Terriberry, who had closed his eyes while the cooling beverage flowed down his throat, opened them again.

"Huh?"

Again she swung her glass above her head and shrilled—

"My Supreme Moment—drink to it if you're a friend of mine!"

"Frien' of yours? Frien' of yours! Why, Doc, I'd die fer you. But that's all same Ogollalah Sioux 'bout your S'preme Moment! Many of 'em, Doc, many of 'em, and here's t'you!"

They drained their glasses together.

"Always liked you, Doc. H'nest t'God, from the first minute I laid eyes on you." Mr. Terriberry reached for her fan dangling from the end of its chain and began to fan her with tender solicitude.

"Come on, let's have another drink; I don't cut loose often." Her eyes and voice were reckless.

"Me and you don't want to go out of here with our ropes draggin'," protested Mr. Terriberry in feeble hesitation. "Let's go out on the porch fer a minute an' look at the meller moon."

"Meller moon *nothin'!* Come on, don't be a piker." She was ladling punch into each of their glasses.

"Ah-h-h! Ain't that great cough mixture!" Mr. Teriberry rolled his eyes in ecstasy as he once more saw the bottom of his glass. "Doc, 'bout one more and me and you couldn't hit the groun' with our hats." Mr. Terriberry speared a bit of pineapple with the long nail of his forefinger and added ambiguously: "M'bet you."

"Aw, g'long! Food for infants, this—wish I had a barrel of it."

"Doc, you got a nawful capac'ty." Mr. Terriberry looked at her in languishing admiration. "That's why I like you. Honest t'God I hate to see a lady go under the table firs' shot out o' the box. Now my wife,''—suddenly remembering the existence of that lady Mr. Terriberry tiptoed to the door and endeavored to locate her—''my wife,'' he continued in a confidential whisper, ''can't take two drinks t'hout showing it. Doc,''—Mr. Terriberry's chin quivered as the pathos of the fact syept over him—''Doc, Merta's no sport.'' Mr. Terriberry buried his face in his highly perfumed handkerchief as he confessed his wife's shortcomings.

''Aw, dry up! Take another and forget it,'' replied his unsympathetic confidante crossly.

Mr. Terriberry looked up in quick cheerfulness.

''Le's do, Doc. Do you know I hate water—just plain water. If it'll rot your boots what'll it do to your stummick!''

A man breathless from haste appeared in the doorway of the anteroom.

''Dr. Harpe——''

''What is it?'' She did not turn around.

''A case came in at the hospital—feller shot, down the street.''

''Where's Lamb?'' she demanded irritably.

''Out of town.''

''Thunder!'' She stamped her foot impatiently. ''Who is it?'' she scowled.

''Billy Duncan. He's bleedin' bad, Doc.'' There was a note of entreaty in his voice.

''All right,'' she answered shortly, ''I'll be down.''

''Frien' of yours?'' inquired Terriberry.

''Friend? No. One of those damned hoboes on the Ditch. Looks like he might have taken some other night than this.''

''Don't blame you 'tall, Doc. I gotta get to work

and fin' Merta. If you see Merta——" Mr. Terriberry suddenly realized that he was talking to himself.

As Dr. Harpe made her way to the cloak-room she was conscious that it was well she was leaving. The lights were blurring rapidly, the dancers in the ballroom were unrecognizable and indistinct, she was sensible, too, of the increasing thickness of her tongue. Yet more than ever she wanted to laugh hysterically, to scream, to boast before them all of the things she had done and of those she meant to do. Yes, decidedly, it was time she was leaving, her saner self told her.

She fumbled among the wraps in the cloak-room until she found her own, then, steadying herself by running her finger-tips along the wall, she slipped from the hotel without being observed.

"Made a good get-away that time," she muttered.

Her lips felt stiff and dry and she moistened them frequently as she stumbled across the hummocks of sagebrush growing on the vacant lots between the hospital and the hotel. She fell, and cursed aloud as she felt the sting of cacti spines in her palm. She sat where she fell and tried to extract them by the light of the moon. Then she arose and stumbled on.

"God! I'm drunk—jus' plain drunk," she said thickly, and was glad that there would be no one but Nell Beecroft about.

Nell was safe. She had long since attended to that. They shared too many secrets in common for Nell to squeal. Nell was not easily shocked. She laughed foolishly at the thought of Nell being shocked and wondered what could do it.

Her contract with Symes called for a graduate nurse—Dr. Harpe snorted—a graduate nurse for hoboes! Nell was cheaper, and even if her reputation was more than doubtful she was big and husky—and they understood each other. The right woman in the right place, and with Lamb helped form a trio that stood for harmony and self-protection.

"Graduate nurse for hoboes!" She muttered it scornfully again. "Not on your tintype!"

She fell against the kitchen door and it opened with her weight.

"Hullo, Nell!" She blinked foolishly in the glare of the light.

The woman looked at her in silence.

"Hullo, I say!" The cloak slipped from her bare shoulders and she lunged toward a chair.

The flush on her face had faded and her color was ghastly, a grayish white, the pallor of an anæmic; the many short hairs on her forehead and temples hung straight in her eyes, the filmy flounce of her gown was torn and trailing, while a scraggly bunch of Russian thistle clung to the chiffon ruffles of her silk drop-skirt.

The woman stood in the centre of the kitchen with her arms akimbo—a huge raw-boned creature of a rough, frontier type.

She spoke at last.

"Well, you're a sight!"

"Been celebratin', Nell," she chuckled gleefully, "been celebratin' my S'preme Moment."

"You'd better git in there and fix that feller's arm or we'll be celebratin' a funeral," the woman answered curtly. "He's bleedin' like a stuck pig."

"That's what he is—good joke, Nell. Where'd it happen?" She seated herself in a chair and slid until her head rested on the back, her sprawling legs outstretched.

"Gun fight at the dance hall. Look here," she took her roughly by the arm, "I tell you he's bad off. You gotta git in there and do somethin'."

"Shut up! Lemme be!" She pulled loose from the nurse's grasp, but arose, nevertheless, and staggered down the long hallway into the room where the new patient lay moaning softly upon the narrow iron cot.

"Hullo, Bill Duncan!"

His moaning ceased and he said faintly in relief—

"Oh, I'm glad! I thought you'd never come, Doc."

"Say," her voice was quarrelsome, "do you think I've nothin' to do but wait at the beck and call of you wops?"

The boy, for he was only that, looked surprise and resentment at the epithet, but he was too weak to waste his strength in useless words.

She raised his arm bound in its blood-soaked rags roughly and he groaned.

"Keep still, you calf!"

He shut his teeth hard and the sweat of agony stood out on his pallid face as she twisted and pulled and probed with clumsy, drunken fingers.

"Nell!" she called thickly.

The woman was watching from the doorway.

"Get the hypodermic and I'll give him a shot of hop, then I'm goin' to bed. Lamb can look after him when he comes. I'm not goin' to monkey with him now."

"But, Doc," the boy protested, "don't leave me like this. The bullet's in there yet, and a piece of my shirt. The boys pulled out some, but they couldn't reach the rest. Ain't you goin' to clean out the hole or something? I'm scart of blood-poisonin', Doc, for I've seen how it works,'' he pleaded.

His protest angered her.

''God! but you're wise with your talk of blood-poisonin'! You bums from the Ditch give me more trouble and do more kickin' than all my private patients put together. What do you want for a dollar a month''—she sneered—''a special nurse? A shot in the arm will shut your mouth till morning anyhow.''

She shoved up the sleeve of his night clothes on the good arm and gripped his wrist; then she jabbed the needle viciously.

His colorless lips were shut in a straight line and in his pain-stricken eyes there was not so much anger now as a great wonder. Was this the woman of whose acquaintance he had been proud, by whose bow of recognition he always had felt flattered; this woman whose free speech and careless good-nature he had defended against the occasional criticism of coarser minds? This woman with her reeking breath and an expression which seen through a mist of pain made her face look like that of Satan himself, was it possible that she had had his liking and respect? He was still wondering when the drowsiness of the drug seized him and he slipped away into sleep.

Dr. Harpe gathered his clothes from the foot of the bed as she passed out.

''Did he have anything on him, Nell?''

''No.''

''They must have cleaned him out down below.'' She jerked her head toward the dance hall as she turned a pocket inside out. "A dollar watch and a jack-knife." She threw them both contemptuously upon the kitchen table. "If he wakes up bellerin', shove the needle into him—you can do it as well as I can. I'm goin' to bed."

She lunged down the corridor once more and Nell Beecroft stood looking after with a curious expression of derision and contempt upon her hard face.

Dr. Harpe threw herself upon the bed in one of the private rooms and soon her loud breathing told Nell Beecroft that she was in the heavy sleep of drink. The nurse opened the door and stood by the bedside looking down upon her as she lay dressed as she had come from the dance, on the outside of the counterpane. One bare arm was thrown over her head, the other was hanging limply over the edge of the bed, her loose hair was a snarled mass upon the pillow and her open mouth gave her face an empty, sodden look that was bestial.

"I wonder what your swell friends would say to you now?" the woman muttered, staring at her through narrowed lids. "Those private patients that you're always bragging swear by you? What would they say if I should tell 'em that just bein' plain drunk like any common prostitute was the least of——" she checked herself and glanced into the hallway. "What would they think if they knew you as I know you—what would they say if I told them only half?" Her mouth dropped in a contemptuous smile. "They wouldn't believe me—they'd say I lied about their 'lady doc.'"

She went on in sneering self-condemnation—

"I'm nothin'—just nothin'; drug up among the worst; no learnin'—no raisin'—but *her*—HER!" Nell

Beecroft's lips curled in indescribable scorn. "She's *worse* than nothin', for she's had her chanst!"

There was no color in the East, only a growing light which made Dr. Harpe look ashen and haggard when she crawled from the bed and looked at herself in a square of glass on the wall.

"You sure don't look like a spring chicken in the cold, gray dawn, Harpe," she said aloud as she made a wry face and ran out her tongue. "Bilious! A dose of nux vomica for you. That mixed stuff does knock a fellow's stomach out and no mistake. Moses! I look fierce."

Her head ached dully, her mouth and throat felt parched, and yet withal she had a feeling of contentment the reason for which did not immediately penetrate her dull consciousness. She realized only that some agreeable happening had left her with a sensation of warmth about her heart.

As she fumbled on the floor for hair-pins, yawning sleepily until her jaws cracked, she wondered what it was. She stopped in the midst of twisting her loose hair and her face lighted in sudden recollection. Ogden Van Lennop! Ah, that was it. She remembered now. She had broken down his prejudice; she had partially won him over; she had been the "hit" of the evening; further conquests were in sight and within easy reach if she played her cards right. And Essie Tisdale—her long upper lip stretched in its mirthless smile—she would not have her feelings this morning for a goodly sum.

The thought of Van Lennop accelerated her movements. She must get back to the hotel before Crowheart was astir, for it might be her ill-luck to bump into Van Lennop starting on one of his early morning rides. She had no desire that he should see her in her present plight.

The closeness of the illy-ventilated hospital, with its odors of disinfectants and sickness, nauseated her slightly as she opened the door and stepped into the hallway. She frowned at the delirious mutterings of a typhoid patient at the end of the corridor, for it reminded her of a threatening epidemic in one of the camps. The sharper moans of Billy Duncan, whose inflamed and swollen arm was wringing from him ejaculations of pain, recalled vaguely to her mind something of the incident of the night before.

Hearing her step, he called aloud as she passed the door—

"Won't somebody give me a drink? Please, please give me a drink! I'm choked!"

"Nell will be up directly," she answered over her shoulder. There was no time to lose, for the day was coming fast.

She lifted her torn and trailing flounce and pulled her cloak about her bare shoulders as she opened the street door. The air felt good upon her hot forehead and she breathed deep of it. The East was pink now, but the town was still as silent as the grave save for the sound of escaping steam from the early morning train. Happening to glance toward the station, something in the appearance of a man carrying a suit-case across the cinders attracted her attention and caused her to slacken her pace. It looked like Ogden Van Lennop. It *was* Ogden Van Lennop. He was leaving! What did it mean? Her air-castles collapsed with a thud which left her limp.

She kept on toward the hotel, but her step lagged. What did she care who saw her now? Surely, she reassured herself, he was not leaving for good—like this. It was certainly strange.

Entering the hotel through the unlocked office door she found the night lamp still burning and Terriberry was nowhere about. That was curious, for he was always up when any of his guests were leaving on the early train.

Van Lennop's decision must have been sudden. What could be the explanation?

There was a letter propped against the lamp on a table behind the office desk and, as she surmised, it was addressed to Mr. Terriberry in Van Lennop's handwriting. Looking closer she saw the end of a second envelope behind the first. To whom could he have written? In some respects Dr. Harpe had the curiosity of a servant and it now prompted her to walk behind the desk and gratify it.

"Miss Essie Tisdale" was the address on the second envelope. Instantly her face changed and the swift, jealous rage of the evening before swept over her again.

She ground her teeth together as she regarded the letter with malice glittering in her heavy eyes. He was writing to her, then, the little upstart, that infernal little biscuit-shooter!

Shorty, the cook, was rattling the kitchen range. She listened a moment. There was no other sound. She thrust the letter quickly beneath the line of her low-cut bodice and tiptoed up the stairs with slinking, feline stealth.

XIX

"Down and Out"

Dr. Harpe ripped open the envelope addressed to Essie Tisdale and devoured its contents standing by the window, bare-shouldered in the dawn. Long before she had finished reading her hand shook with excitement, and her nose looked pinched and drawn about the nostrils. As a matter of fact the woman was being dealt a staggering blow. Until the moment she had not herself realized how strongly she had built upon the outcome of this self-constructed romance of hers.

In her wildest dreams she had not considered Van Lennop's attentions to Essie Tisdale serious or, indeed, his motives good. That Ogden Van Lennop had entertained the remotest notion of asking Essie Tisdale to be his wife was furthest from her thoughts. Yet there it was in black and white, staring at her in words which burned themselves upon her brain, searing the deeper because she learned from them that her own deed had precipitated the crisis.

"I wasn't sure of myself until last night," Van Lennop wrote, "but that creature's disgraceful act left me in no doubt. If I had been sure of *you*, Essie Tisdale, I would have put my arm about you then and there and told that braying crowd that any indignity offered you was offered to my future wife.

"But I was not sure, I am not sure now, and only business of the utmost urgency could take me away from you in this state of uncertainty. If you want me to come back won't you send me a telegram telling me so to the address I am giving below? Just a word, Essie Tisdale, to let me know that you care a little bit, that your sweet friendship holds something more for me than just friendship? I shall haunt the office until I hear from you, so lose no time."

Further on she read:

"I love you mightily, Essie Tisdale, and I have not closed my eyes for making plans for you and me. It is quite the most delirious happiness I have ever known. I long to take you away from Crowheart and place you in the environment in which you rightly belong, for, while we know nothing of your parentage, I would stake my life that in it you have no cause for shame. I am filled with all a lover's eagerness to give, to heap upon you the things which women like—to share with you my possessions and my pleasures.

"But in the midst of my castle building comes the chilling thought that I am taking everything for granted and the fear that I have been presumptuous in mistaking your dear, loyal comradeship for something more makes me fairly tremble. I am very humble, Essie Tisdale, when I think of you, but I am going to believe you will say '*yes*' until you have said '*no*'."

Dr. Harpe crumpled the letter and hurled it into the farthermost corner of the room, half sick with a feeling of helplessness, of passionate regret and despair. She realized to the fullest what she was losing, or, as she phrased it to herself, what was "slipping through her fingers." And this was to be the future of the girl whom it seemed to her she hated above all others and all else in the world! The thought was maddening. She strode to and fro, kicking her torn flounce and trailing skirt out of the way with savage resentment. Van Lennop's letter temporarily punctured her conceit, chagrin and mortification adding to her feeling the anguish of that bad half hour. "That creature" he was calling her while in her ridiculous self-complacency she was drinking to her Supreme Moment. Oh, it was unbearable! She covered her reddening face with both hands.

When she raised it at last there was a light in her eyes, new purpose in her face. Her moment of weakness and defeat had passed. She would make good her boast that that person was not yet born who could ultimately defeat her. She would not go so far as to say that in the end she would marry Van Lennop nor would she admit that it was impossible, but she swore that whatever else might happen, Essie Tisdale should never be his wife. In every clash between herself and this girl she had won, so why not again? There must be—there was—some way to prevent it!

She had no plan in mind as yet, but something would suggest itself, she knew, for her crafty resourcefulness had helped her since her childhood in many a tight place, from seemingly hopeless situations. She picked up the crumpled letter and seating herself by the window smoothed the sheets upon her knee.

She read it through again, calmly, critically this time, lingering over the paragraph which hinted at the things he had to offer the woman who became his wife.

"Diamonds and good clothes that means, a box at the Opera, fine horses and a limousine. The trollop! the——!" The epithet was the most offensive that she knew. "He knows she would like such things," she reasoned.

Her mind was working in a circuitous way toward a definite goal which she herself had not as yet perceived, but when she did see it, it came with the flash of inspiration. She all but bounded to her feet and began to pace the floor in the quick strides of mental excitement. A plan suddenly outlined itself before her with the clearness of a written text. Her crushing disappointment was almost forgotten in the keen joy of working out the details of her plot. If only she could influence certain minds—could manipulate conditions.

"I can! I *will!*" She emphasized her determination with clenched fist.

After a hasty toilette she surveyed herself in the glass with satisfaction. The jaded look was fast fading under the stimulus of the congenial work ahead of her and little trace of her intemperate indulgence of the night remained.

"You're standing up well under the jolt, Harpe," she commented. "That letter was sure a body blow."

She seated herself at the breakfast table and in her habitual attitude of slouching nonchalance sat with half-lowered lids watching Essie Tisdale as she moved about the dining-room. There was something in her crouching pose, the cruel eagerness of her eyes, which suggested a bird of prey, but it was not until they were alone that she asked carelessly—

"How's the hand, Ess?"

The girl gave no sign of having heard.

"That was rather a bad fall you got."

Essie turned upon her with blazing eyes.

"Not so bad as you intended."

Dr. Harpe laughed softly and asked with a mocking pretence of surprise—

"Why, what do you mean?"

"You know perfectly well that I know you tripped

me. You need not pretend with me. Don't you think I know by this time that you would go to any length to injure me—in any way—that you already have done so?"

"You flatter me; you overestimate my power."

"Not at all. How can I when I see the evidence of it every day? You have left me practically without a friend; if that flatters you, enjoy it to the utmost." The girl's eyes filled with tears.

"Not without *one,*" she sneered significantly; "surely you don't mean that?"

The peach-blow color rose in the girl's cheeks.

"No," she answered with a touch of defiance, "not without one, or two when it comes to that."

"And who is—the other?"

"I can count on Mrs. Terriberry. Even you have no influence with her, Dr. Harpe."

"You are very sure of your two friends." The woman slouching over the table looked more than ever like a bird of prey.

"Very sure," Essie Tisdale answered, again in proud defiance.

"Then of course you know that Van Lennop left Crowheart this morning?" She drawled the words in cruel enjoyment with her eyes fixed upon the girl's face.

Her eyes shone malevolently as she saw it blanch.

"Didn't he tell you he was going? I'm amazed."

The girl stood in stunned silence.

"Yes, a telegram sent him to Mexico to look after some important interests there. Quite unexpected. He left a letter for me saying good-by and regretting that he would not be back. So you see, my dear Essie, that when it comes to the actual count your friends have simmered down to one." It was not enough that she should crush her, she wanted somehow to wring from her a cry of pain.

"You made a fool of yourself over him, Ess! The whole town laughed at you. You should have known that a man like Van Lennop, of his position, doesn't take a biscuit-shooter seriously. Green as you are you should have known that. You've ruined yourself in Crowheart, doggin' his footsteps every time he turned and all that sort of thing; he simply couldn't shake you. You're done for here; you're down and out and you might as well quit the flat. It's the best thing you can do, or marry the first man that asks you and settle down."

Essie Tisdale looked at her, speechless with pain and shock. She had no reply; in the face of such a leave-taking there seemed nothing for her to say. Every taunt was like a stab in her aching heart because she felt they must be true. It *was* true, else he would not have left her without a word. What did it all mean? How could such sincerity be false! Was no one true in all the world? Oh, the sickening misery of it all—of life!

She turned away and left the dining-room, swaying a little as she walked.

Dr. Harpe returned to her room with a smirk of deep satisfaction upon her face.

"I soaked the knife home *that* time," she murmured, pinning on her stiff-brimmed Stetson before the mirror, but, mingled with her gratification was a slight feeling of uneasiness because she had gone farther than she had intended in mentioning Van Lennop's letter and boasting that it had been left for her.

The pair of horses which she and Lamb owned in common was at the stable already harnessed for their semi-weekly trip to the camps along the Ditch, but Dr. Harpe turned their heads in the opposite direction and by noon had reached the sheep-camp of old Edouard Dubois.

She hitched her horses to the shearing-pen and opened the unlocked door of the cabin. A pan of freshly-made biscuit and a table covered with unwashed breakfast dishes told her that the cabin was being occupied, so she reasoned that it was safer to wait until some one returned than to search the hills for Dubois.

A barking sheep-dog told her of some one's approach, and in relief she went out to meet him, for she was restless and impatient of any delay. But instead of the lumbering old French Canadian she saw the Dago Duke coming leisurely from a near-by coulee, picturesque in the unpicturesque garb of a sheep-herder.

If there was no welcoming smile upon her face the Dago Duke was the last person to be embarrassed by the omission.

"Ah, 'Angels unawares' and so forth." The Dago Duke swept his hat from his head in a low bow. "A rare pleasure, Doctor, to return and find a lady——"

She flushed at the mocking emphasis.

"Cut that out; any fool can be sarcastic."

"You surprise and pain me. If it is sarcasm to refer to you as a lady——"

"Where's Dubois?"

He waved his hand toward the coulee and she walked away.

The Dago Duke looked after her with an expression of amused speculation in his handsome eyes. What deviltry was she up to now?

"Addio, mia bella Napoli," he whistled. "Addio! addio!" What difference did it make so long as she confined her activities to Dubois?—since he had no more liking for one than the other.

The Dago Duke had applied to Dubois for work as a sheep-herder and got it.

After the memorable midnight session with pink lizards and the Gila monster, the Dago Duke applied for work as a sheep-herder and got it, chiefly because of his indifference to the question of wages.

"I want to get away from the gilded palaces of vice and my solicitous friends; I want to lead the simple, virtuous life of a sheep-herder until my system recovers from a certain shock," explained the applicant glibly, "and something within me tells me that you are not the man to refuse a job to a youth filled with such a worthy ambition."

Dubois grinned understandingly and gave him work at half a sheep-herder's usual pay.

Whatever the nature of Dr. Harpe's business with his employer, the interview appeared to have been eminently satisfactory to them both, for she was smiling broadly, while Dubois seemed not only excited but elated when they returned together.

He looked after her buggy as she drove away, and chuckled—

"Ha—she brings me good news—zat woman!"

While the Dago Duke was warming up the fried potatoes and bacon, which remained from breakfast, over the rusty camp-stove, Dubois was diving under his bunk for a box from which he produced a yellowed shirt and collar, together with a suit of black clothes, nearly new.

"Per Iddio! 'Tis the Day of Judgment and you've gotten inside information!" jeered the Dago Duke.

Dubois showed his yellowed teeth.

"Mais oui, 'eet is ze Resurrection."

"I swear, you look like Napoleon, Dubois!" gibed the Dago Duke, when he was fully arrayed.

"Why not?" The Frenchman's face wore a complacent smirk. "Ze Little Corporal, *he* married a queen."

The frying-pan of fried potatoes all but dropped from the Dago Duke's hand, while his employer enjoyed to the utmost the amazement upon his face.

"The lady doc?"

Dubois threw up both hands in vehement protest.

"Non, non! Mon Dieu, non, non!"

The Dago Duke shrugged his shoulders impertinently.

"You aim higher, perhaps?"

"Mais certes," he leered. "Old Dubois has thirty thousand sheep."

"To exchange for——"

"A queen, ze belle of Crowheart—Mees Essie Teesdale!"

The Dago Duke stared and continued to regard his employer fixedly. Essie Tisdale! Had the solitude affected the old man's mind at last? Was he crazy? How else account for the preposterous suggestion, his colossal egotism? Why, Essie Tisdale, even to the Dago Duke's critical eye, was like a delicately tinted prairie rose, while old Dubois with his iron-gray hair bristling on his bullet-shaped head, his thick, furrow-encircled neck, his swarthy, obstinate, brutal face, was seventy, a remarkable seventy, it is true, but seventy, and far from prepossessing. It was too absurd! It must be one of the lady doc's practical jokes—it was sufficiently indelicate, he told himself. At any rate he would soon see Dubois returning crestfallen from his courting expedition, and the sight, he felt, was one he should relish.

"I'll reserve my congratulations until you come," said the Dago Duke as he picked up his sheep-herder's staff and returned to his band of sheep.

"You will have ze opportunity, my frien'," grinned Dubois confidently.

Dr. Harpe had advised—

"Give her a night to cry her eyes out. Twenty-four hours will put a crimp in her courage. Let the fact that she's jilted soak in. Give her time to realize what she's up against in Crowheart."

And the woman had been right in her reasoning, for a night of tears and grief, of shame and humiliation left Essie Tisdale with weakened courage, mentally and physically spent.

Back of everything, above all else loomed in black and gigantic proportions the fact that Van Lennop had gone away forever without a word to her, that he even had thought less of her when it came to leaving than of the woman whom he had seemed to avoid.

In the long hours of the night her tired brain constantly recalled the things which he had said that had made her glow with happiness at the time, but which she knew now were only the pleasant, idle words of the people who came from the world east of the big hills. Dr. Harpe was right when she had told her that in her ignorance of the world and its men she had misunderstood the kindness Van Lennop would have shown to any person in her position.

"But he didn't show it to her—he didn't show it to anyone else but me!" she would whisper in a fierce joy, which was short-lived, for, instantly, the crushing remembrance of his leave-taking confronted her.

Her face burned in the darkness when she remembered that Dr. Harpe had taunted her with having displayed her love to all the town. She no longer made any attempt to conceal it from herself, the sure knowledge had come with Van Lennop's departure, and she whispered it aloud in the darkness in glorious defiance, but the mood as quickly passed and her face flamed scarlet at the thought that she had unwittingly showed her precious secret to the unfriendly and curious.

She crept from bed and sat on the floor, with her folded arms upon the window-sill, finding the night air good upon her hot face. She felt weak, the weakness of black respair, for it seemed to her that her faith in human nature had received its final shock. If only there was some one upon whose shoulder she could lay her head she imagined that it might not be half so hard. There was Mrs. Terriberry, but after what had happened could she be sure even of Mrs. Terriberry? Could any inconsequential person like herself be sure of anybody if it conflicted with their interests? It seemed not. She shrank from voicing the thought, but the truth was she dared not put Mrs. Terriberry's friendship to any test.

"The best way to have friends," she whispered bitterly with a lump in her aching throat, "is not to need them."

She dreaded the beginning of another day, but

it must be gotten through somehow, and not only that day but the day after that and all the innumerable, dreary days ahead of her. Finally she crept shivering to bed to await the ordeal of another to-morrow.

The long shadows of the afternoon's sun lay in the backyard of the Terriberry House when Essie sat down in the doorway to rest before her evening's work began. The girl's sad face rested in the palm of her hand and her shoulders drooped wearily as Mrs. Abe Tutts in her blue flannel yachting cap came down the road beside her friend Mrs. Jackson, who rustled richly in the watered silk raincoat which advertised the fact that she was either going to or returning from a social function. Mrs. Jackson's raincoat was a sure signal of social activity.

"Let's walk up clost along the fence and see how she's takin' it," suggested Mrs. Tutts amiably. "Gittin' the mitten is some of a pill to swaller. Don't you speak to her, Mis' Jackson?"

Mrs. Jackson glanced furtively over her shoulder and observed that Mrs. Symes was still standing on the veranda.

"If I come upon her face to face, but I don't go out of my way a-tall," she added in unconscious imitation of Mrs. Symes's newly-acquired languor of speech. "One rully can't afford to after her bein' *so* indiscreet and all."

"Rotten, I says" declared Mrs. Tutts tersely.

"She looks kinda pale around the gills s'well as I can see from here," opined Mrs. Jackson, staring critically as they passed along. They tittered audibly. "I tell you what, Mrs. Tutts, Essie ought to get to work and marry some man what'll put her right up in society where Alva put me."

A biting comment which it caused Mrs. Tutts real suffering to suppress was upon the tip of that lady's tongue, but it was gradually being borne in upon her that the first families were not given to actual hand-to-hand conflicts, so she checked it and inquired significantly instead—

"But could he, after ridin' over the country t'hout no chaperon and all?"

Mrs. Tutts had only recently found out about chaperons and their function, but, since she had she insisted upon them fiercely, and Mrs. Jackson was finally forced to admit that this violation of the conventions was indeed hard to overlook.

Essie Tisdale was too unhappy either to observe the passing of the women or their failure to recognize her. In the presence of this new, real grief their friendliness or lack of it seemed a small affair. The only thing which mattered was Ogden Van Lennop's going. The sun, for her, had gone down and with the inexperience of youth she did not believe it ever would rise again.

The girl sat motionless, her chin still resting in her palm, until a tremulous voice behind her spoke her name.

"Essie."

She turned to see Mrs. Terriberry, buttoned into her steel-colored bodice and obviously flustered.

"Yes?" There was a trace of wonder in her voice.

At the sight of the pale face the girl upturned to her, Mrs. Terriberry's courage nearly failed her in the task to which she had nerved herself.

"Essie," she faltered, twisting her rings nervously, finally blurting out, "I'm afraid you'll have to go, Essie."

The girl started violently.

"Go?" she gasped. "Go?"

Mrs. Terriberry nodded, relieved that it was out.

"But why? Why?" It seemed too incredible to believe. This was the very last thing she had expected, or thought of.

Mrs. Terriberry avoided her eyes; it was even harder than she had anticipated. Why hadn't she let "Hank" Terriberry tell her himself! Mrs. Terriberry was one of that numerous class whose naturally kind hearts are ever warring with their bump of caution.

She was sorry now that she had been so impulsive in telling him all that Dr. Harpe had whispered over the afternoon tea at Mrs. Symes's now fashionable Thursday "At Home." It was the first of the coveted cards which Mrs. Terriberry had received and Dr. Harpe took care to adroitly convey the information that the invitation was due to her, and Mrs. Terriberry was correspondingly grateful.

"You can't afford to keep her; you simply can't afford it, Mrs. Terriberry," Dr. Harpe had whispered earnestly in a confidential corner.

But," she had protested in feeble loyalty, "but I *like* Essie."

"Of course you do," Dr. Harpe had agreed magnanimously; "so do I; she's a really beautiful girl, but you know how it is in a small town and I am telling you for your own good that you can't afford to harbor her."

"I couldn't think of turning her out just when she needs a friend," Mrs. Terriberry had replied with some decision, and Dr. Harpe's face had hardened slightly at the answer.

"It's your own affair, naturally," she had returned indifferently; "but I'll have to find accomodations elsewhere. If living in the same house would injure me professionally, merely a boarder, you can guess what it will do to you in a business way, and," she had added significantly, "socially."

Mrs. Terriberry had looked startled. After hanging to the fringe until she was all but exhausted, it was small wonder that she had no desire to again go through the harrowing experience of overcoming Society's objections to a hotelkeeper's wife.

"Certainly I don't blame you for hanging on to her as long as you can," Dr. Harpe had added, "and of course you would be the last to hear all the gossip that there is about her. But, on the whole, isn't it rather a high price to pay for—well, for a biscuit-shooter's friendship? Such people really don't count, you know."

Mrs. Terriberry who had once shot biscuits in a "Harvey's Eating House" murmured meekly—

"Of course not." But instantly ashamed of her weak disloyalty she had declared with a show of spirit, "However, unless Hank says she must go she can stay, for Essie has come pretty close to bein' like my own girl to me."

Dr. Harpe had been satisfied to let it rest at that, for she felt sure enough of Terriberry's answer.

"He needs my money, but if more pressure is necessary,"—she sniggered at the recollection of Mr. Terriberry's sentimental leanings—"I can spend an hour with him in the light of the 'meller moon.' "

Again Dr. Harpe was right. Mr. Terriberry needed the money, also his fears took instant alarm at the thought of losing so popular and influential a guest, one, who, as he told Mrs. Terriberry emphatically, could do him a power of harm. The actual dismissal of the girl who had grown to womanhood under his eyes he wisely left to his wife.

The girl stood up now, a slender, swaying figure: white, desolate, with uplifted arms outstretched, she looked like a storm-whipped flower.

"Oh, what shall I do! Where shall I go!"

The low, broken-hearted cry of despair set Mrs. Terriberry's plain face in lines of distress.

"Essie, Essie, don't feel so bad!" she begged chokingly.

The girl's answer was a swift look of bitter reproach.

"You can stay here until you find some place that suits you."

The girl shook her head.

"To-morrow I'll go—somewhere."

"Don't feel hard toward me, Essie," and she would have taken the girl's hand, but she drew it quietly away and stood with folded arms in an attitude of aloofness which was new to her.

"It's not that; it's only that I don't want your—pity. I don't think that I want anything you have to give. You have hurt me; you have cut me to the quick and something is happening—has happened—*here!*" She laid both hands upon her heart. "I feel still and cold and sort of—impersonal inside."

"Oh, Essie!"

"I understand perfectly, Mrs. Terriberry. You like me—you like me very much, but you are one kind of a coward, and of what value is a coward's friendship or regard? I don't mean to be impertinent—I'm just trying to explain how I feel. In your heart you believe in me, but you are afraid—afraid of public opinion—afraid of being left out of the teas and card parties which mean more to you than I do. You've known me all my life and fail me at the first test."

"I hate to hear you talk like that; it doesn't sound like Essie Tisdale." But in her heart she knew the girl was right. She was a coward; she had not the requisite courage to set her face against the crowd, but must needs turn and run with them while every impulse and instinct within her pulled the other way.

"Doesn't it?" The girl smiled bitterly. "Why should it? Can't you see—don't you understand that you've helped kill *that* Essie Tisdale—that blundering, ignorant Essie Tisdale who liked everybody and believed in everybody as she thought they liked and believed in her?"

"Dear me! oh, dear me!" Mrs. Terriberry rubbed her forehead and groaned pathetically.

Any consecutive line of thought outside the usual channels pulled Mrs. Terriberry down like a spell of sickness. She looked jaded from the present conversation and her thoughts ran together bewilderingly.

"I know to-night how an outlaw feels when the posse's at his heels and he rides with murder in his heart," the girl went on with hardness in her young voice. "I know to-night why he makes them pay dear for his life when he takes his last stand behind a rock."

"Oh, Essie, don't!" Mrs. Terriberry wrung her garnet and moonstone-ringed fingers together in distress. "You mustn't get reckless!"

"What real difference does it make to you or anybody else how I get?" she demanded fiercely, and added: "You are showing me how much when you advertise to all the town by turning me out that you believe their evil tongues."

"I'm goin' to talk to Hank again——" but Essie stopped her with a vehement gesture.

"You needn't. I don't want pity, I tell you, I don't want favors. I am going to-morrow. There is some way out. There is a place in the world for me somewhere and I'll find it."

She turned away and walked toward the corral where the black omnibus horses nickered softly at her coming, while Alphonse and Gaston stood on their hind legs and squealed a vociferous welcome.

"My only friends——" and she smiled bitterly.

She winced when she saw a new face passing the kitchen door and realized that Mr. Terriberry already had filled her place. It was only one small thing more, but it brought again the feeling that the world was sinking beneath her feet.

She stood for a long time with her forehead resting on her folded arms which lay upon the top rail of the corral. The big 'bus horses shoved her gently with their soft muzzles, impatient to be noticed, but she did not lift her head until a step upon the hard-trodden yard roused her from her apathy of dull misery. She glanced around indifferently to see old Edouard Dubois lumbering toward her in the fast gathering dusk.

Dubois's self-conscious, ingratiating smile did not fade because she drew her arched eyebrows together in a slight frown. It took more than an unwelcoming face to divert the obstinate old Frenchman from any purpose firmly fixed in his mind.

"Ha—I am ver' glad to find you alone, Mees Teesdale, I lak have leetle talk with you." There was a purposeful look behind his set smile of agreeableness.

She shrank from him a little as he came close to her, but he appeared not to notice the movement, and went on—

"I hear you are in trouble—eh? I hear you get fire from ze hotel?"

Again the girl's face took on its new look of bitterness. That was the way in which they were expressing it, spreading the news throughout the town. They were losing no time—her friends.

" 'Fired' is the word when a biscuit-shooter is dismissed," she returned coldly.

"I hear you get lef' by that loafer, too. I tole you, mam'selle, that fellow Van Lennop no good. I know that kind, I see that kind before, Mees Teesdale. Lak every pretty girl an' have good time, then 'pouf!—zat is all!"

She turned upon him hotly, her face a mixture of humiliation and angry resentment.

"You can't criticise him to me, Mr. Dubois! I won't listen. If I have been fool enough to misunderstand his kindness that's my fault, not his."

Dubois's eyes became suddenly inscrutable. After a moment's silence he said quietly—

"You love heem, I think. Zat iss too bad for you. What you do now, Mees Teesdale? Where you go?"

He saw that her clasped hands tightened at the question, though she replied calmly—

"I don't know, not yet."

"Perhaps you marry me, mam'selle? I ask you once—I haf not change my mind."

She stared at him with a kind of terror in her eyes.

Was *this* her way out! Was this the place that somewhere in the world she had declared defiantly was meant for her? Was it the purpose of the Fates to crowd her down and out—until she was glad to fill it—a punishment for her ambitions—for daring to believe she was intended for some other life than this?

Upon that previous occasion when the old Frenchman had made her the offer of marriage which had seemed so grotesque and impossible at the time, he had asserted in his pique, "You might be glad to marry old Edouard Dubois some day," and she had turned her back upon him in light contempt—now she was, not glad, she could never be that, but grateful.

"But I—don't love you." Her voice sounded strained and hoarse.

"Zat question I did not ask you—I ask you will you marry me?" He did not wait for an answer, but went on persuasively, yet stating the bald and hopeless facts that seemed so crushing to her youth and inexperience. "You have no parent—no home, Mees Teesdale; you have no money and not so many friend in Crowheart. You marry me and all is change. You have good home and many friends, because," he chuckled shrewdly, "when I die you have thirty thousand sheep. Plenty sheep, plenty friends, my girl. How you like be the richest woman in this big county, mam'selle?"

The girl was listening, that was something; and she was thinking hard.

Money! how they all harped upon it!—when she had thought the most important thing in the world was love. Even Ogden Van Lennop she remembered had called it the great essential and now she saw that old Edouard Dubois who had lived for seventy years regarded it in a wholly reverent light.

"When you marry me you have no more worry, no more trouble, no more tears."

Her lips moved; she was repeating to herself—

"No more worry, no more trouble, no more tears."

She was bewildered with the problems which confronted her, frightened by the overwhelming odds against her, tired of thinking, sick to death of the humiliation of her position. She stopped the guttural, wheedling voice with a quick, vehement gesture.

"Give me time to think—give me until to-morrow morning."

"What time to-morrow morning?"

"At ten o'clock,"—there was desperation in her face—"at ten to-morrow I will tell you 'yes' or 'no.'"

She was clutching at a straw, clinging to a faint hope which had not entirely deserted her: she might yet get a letter from Van Lennop, just a line to let her know that he cared enough to send it; and if it came, a single sentence, she knew well enough what her answer to Dubois would be.

"Until to-morrow." The old Frenchman bowed low in clumsy and unaccustomed politeness, but gloating satisfaction shone from his deep-set eyes, small and hard as two gray marbles.

XX

An Unfortunate Affair

Billy Duncan was in a bad way, so it was reported to the men upon the works, and the men to show their sympathy and liking for the fair-haired, happy-go-lucky Billy Duncan made up a purse of $90 and sent it to him by Dan Treu, the big deputy-sheriff, who also was Billy Duncan's friend.

"It'll buy fruit for the kid, something to read, and a special nurse if he needs one," they told the deputy and they gave the money with the warmest of good wishes.

Dan Treu took their gift to the hospital, and Billy Duncan burst into tears when he saw him.

"Oh, come, come! Buck up, Billy, you're goin' to pull through all right."

"Dan! Dan! Take me out of here—take me away! Quick!"

The deputy looked his surprise.

"What's the matter, Billy? What's wrong?"

"Everything's wrong, Dan, everything!" His voice was shrill in his weakness. "I'm goin' to croak if you don't get me out of here!"

Dan Treu bent over him and patted his shoulder as he would have comforted a child.

"There, there, don't talk like that, Billy. You're not goin' to croak. You're a little down in the mouth, that's all." He glanced around the tiny room. "It looks clean and comfortable here; you're lucky to have a place like this to go to and Doc's a blamed good fellow. She'll pull you through."

"But she ain't, Dan—she ain't anything that we thought. Lay here sick if you want to find her out. She thinks we don't count, us fellows on the works, and Lamb's no better, only he's more sneakin'—he hasn't her gall." He searched the deputy's face for a moment then cried pitifully, "You don't believe me, Dan. You think I'm sore about something and stretchin' the truth. It's so, Dan—I tell you they left me here the night I was brought in until the next forenoon without touchin' my arm. They've never half cleaned the hole out. It's swelled to the shoulder and little pieces of my shirt keep sloughing out. Any cowpuncher with a jack-knife could do a better job than they have done. They don't know how, Dan, and what's worse they don't care!"

He reached for the deputy's hand and clung to it as he begged again—

"My God! Dan, won't you believe me and get me out of here? Honest, honest, I'm goin' to die if you don't!"

In his growing excitement the boy's voice rose to a penetrating pitch and it brought Lamb quickly from the office in the front. He looked disconcerted for an instant when he saw the deputy, for he had not known of his presence in the hospital. Glancing from one to the other he read something of the situation in Billy Duncan's excited face and Dan Treu's puzzled look. Stepping back from the doorway he beckoned the deputy into the hall.

"I guess he was talkin' wild, wasn't he?" He walked out of the sick boy's hearing. "Kickin', wasn't he?"

Dan Treu hesitated.

"I thought as much," nodded Lamb. "But you

mustn't pay any attention to him. His fever's way up and he's out of his head most of the time."

"He seems to think his arm ain't had the care it should,"—Treu's voice was troubled—"that the wound ain't clean and it's swellin' bad."

Lamb laughed.

"His hallucination; he's way off at times. Everything's been done for him. We like the boy and he's havin the best of care. Why, we couldn't afford to have it get around that we neglect our patients, so you see what he says ain't sense."

The deputy-sheriff's face cleared gradually at Lamb's explanation and solicitude.

"Yes, I guess he is a little 'off,' though I must say he don't exactly look it. But do all you can for him, Lamb, for Billy's a fine chap at heart and he's a friend of mine. The boys have raised some money for any extras that he wants—I put it under his pillow."

Lamb brightened perceptibly.

"That's a good thing, because seein' as how he wasn't hurt on the works he'll have to pay like any private patient and of course we'd like to see where our money is comin' from. I've asked him for the money—his week is up to-day—but he don't seem to think he owes it."

"Kind of strikes me the same way," replied the deputy obviously surprised.

"That's accordin' to contract—that's the written agreement." Lamb's nasal voice immediately became argumentative.

"It may be that,"—the deputy looked at him soberly—"but it don't sound like common humanity to me—or fairness. He's been paying a dollar a month to you and your hospital ever since it started and hundreds of men who have no need of its services have been doin' the same, and I must say, Lamb, it sounds like pretty small potatoes for you to charge him for an outside accident like this because your contract will let you do it and get away with it."

"We ain't here for our health, be we?" demanded Lamb, offensively on the defensive.

"It don't look like it," Treu replied shortly.

"But he'll want for nothin' while he's under our care." Lamb's tone grew suddenly conciliatory. "You'd better go now, your presence excites him and he must have quiet. Step to the door and say good-by, if you like, but no conversation, please."

"Adios, Billy!" The deputy thrust his head and broad shoulders in the doorway. "I'll come again soon."

"Good-by, Dan, good-by for keeps, old man. I don't believe I'll be here when you come again." All the excitement was gone and the boy spoke in the quiet voice of conviction. "You're quittin' me, Dan. You don't believe me and the jig's up. You'd risk your life to save me if I was drowning or up against it in a fight, but you're walkin' away and leavin' me here to die. You don't believe me now, but I know you're goin' to find out some time for yourself that I'm tellin' the truth when I say that I've been murdered. There's more ways to kill a man than with a gun. Ignorance and neglect does the trick as well. Tell the boys 'much obliged,' Dan." He turned his white face to the wall and the tears slipped hot from beneath his lashes.

Dan Treu's troubled eyes sought Lamb's, who waited in the hallway.

"He'll be himself when you come again," said

Lamb reassuringly. "We're doin' everything to git his fever down. Don't let his talk worry you."

But in spite of Lamb's confident assurance Dan Treu walked away from the hospital filled with a sense of oppression which lasted throughout the day. The next morning he heard upon the street that they had amputated Billy Duncan's arm.

"Amputated Billy Duncan's arm!" The deputy-sheriff kept saying it over and over to himself as he hurried to the hospital. He was shocked; he was filled with a regret that was personal in its poignancy. He knew exactly what such a loss meant to Billy Duncan, who earned his living with his hands and gloried in his strength—independent young Billy Duncan an object of pity in his mutilated manhood! Dan Treu could not entirely realize it yet.

Lamb met him at the hospital door as though he had awaited his coming.

"Blood-poisonin' set in," he began with a haste which seemed due to excitement. "Developed sudden. Had to amputate to save his life. He was willin' enough; he knew it was for the best, his only chance in fact."

Dan Treu was seized with a sudden aversion for Lamb's shifty, dark-circled eyes, his unconvincing nasal voice.

"Blood-poisonin' set in, you say?" He eyed Lamb steadily.

"His habits, you know, battin' around and all that. Bad blood."

"Bad blood—hell!" said Dan Treu sharply. "His blood was as good as yours or mine, and his habits too."

He made to step inside, but Lamb stopped him.

"He hasn't come out of the ether yet—I'll let you know when you can see him."

There was nothing more to say, so Dan Treu turned on his heel and walked away, angry, sceptical—without exactly knowing why.

The aversion which Lamb had inspired was still strong within him when he stopped on a street corner to ruminate and incidentally roll a cigarette.

"When he gets close I feel like I do when a wet dog comes out of the crick and is goin' to shake." The deputy felt uncommonly pleased with the simile which so well described his feelings.

Dan Treu did not receive the promised notification that Billy Duncan was in a condition to be seen, which was not strange, since Billy Duncan was dying—dying because a man and woman whose diplomas licensed them to juggle with human life and limb were unable in their ignorance and inexperience to stop the flow of blood. Vital, life-loving, happy-go-lucky Billy Duncan lay limp on his narrow bed in the bare, white room, filled with a great heart-sickness at the uselessness of it, the helpless ignominy of dying like a stuck pig! With a last effort he turned his head upon his pillow and through the window by his bedside watched the colors of the distant foothills change from gold to purple—purple like the shadows of the Big Dark for which he was bound. And when at last the night shut out the world he loved so well, Billy Duncan coughed—a choking, strangling cough and died alone.

Nell Beecroft learned it first when she brought the soup and prunes which she was pleased to call his supper. She set the tray upon the bed and stood with arms akimbo looking down upon him. The boyish look of him as he lay so still brought the thought home to her for the first time that somewhere in the world there was some one—a mother—a woman like herself who loved young Billy Duncan. She stooped and with rough gentleness brushed a lock of fair hair from his forehead.

"Poor devil!" she murmured.

"He's dead." She conveyed the news shortly when Lamb came to make his nightly round.

"Who?"

"The kid—Billy Duncan."

Lamb looked startled. It had come sooner than he thought. Recovering himself, he wagged his head and sighed in his pious whine:

"Ah, truly, 'the wages of sin is death.' Altogether a most unfortunate affair, but no human skill could save him." His voice faltered a little, at the end, for pretence seemed ridiculous beneath Nell Beecroft's hard eyes, and her unpleasant laugh nettled him as she strode back to the kitchen.

Yes, Billy Duncan was dead—there was no doubt about that—perfectly and safely dead. There was no question of it in Dr. Lamb's mind when he slipped his hand beneath the pillow and withdrew the $90 which Billy Duncan had so obstinately refused to turn over toward his hospital expenses. Ninety dollars; yes, it was all there; Lamb counted it carefully. Little enough for the trouble and anxiety he had been. The eminent surgeon's waistcoat bulged with the gift of Billy Duncan's friends when he closed the door behind him.

A curious stillness came over Dan Treu when Lamb himself brought the news that Billy Duncan was dead. His jaw dropped slightly and he forgot to smoke.

"The shock—his weakened condition—it was to be expected, though we hoped for the best." Lamb found it something of an effort to speak naturally beneath the Deputy-sheriff's fixed gaze. "But he wanted for nothing. Me and the nurse was with him at the last."

A mist blurred Dan Treu's eyes and he turned abruptly on his heel.

"Wait a minute! Ahem! there's one thing more."

The deputy halted.

"You will arrange with the County about his funeral expenses?"

"With the County? Billy Duncan's no pauper."

"Why ain't he? I've been around and found out he's got nothin' in the bank."

"You have?" He eyed Lamb for a moment. "Billy Duncan will not be buried by the County," he finished curtly.

"I'm glad to hear that," said Lamb conciliatingly, and added: "Of course you're not counting on that $90?"

"There must be some left."

"Oh, no—nothing. Arm amputations are a $100. We are really out $10—more than that with his board and all, but"—his tone was magnanimity itself—"let it go."

When the Deputy-sheriff went out on the works and raised $125 more among Billy Duncan's friends, he handed it to Lutz, the hospital undertaker, and said—

"The best you can do for the money, Lutz. I've got to go to the County seat on a case and I can't be here myself. Billy was a personal friend of mine, so treat him right."

"Sure; we can turn him out first-class for that

money; a new suit of clothes and a tony coffin. Any friend of yours I'll handle like he was my own."

There was something slightly jocular in his tone, a flippancy which Dan Treu felt and silently resented. He looked at Lutz in his shiny, black diagonals, undersized, sallow, his meaningless brown eyes as dull as the eyes of a dead fish, and he thought to himself as he walked away—

"That feller's in the right business, and, by gosh, he's thrown in with the right bunch."

The grave-digger's mouth puckered in a whistle when Lutz went to his home to notify him that his services were needed.

"What! Another?"

The undertaker grinned.

"I'm about used up from gittin' robbed of my rest," complained the grave-digger. "This night-work ain't to my taste."

"It's no use kickin'; you know what Lamb says—that these daylight buryin's makes talk amongst the neighbors."

"Should think it would," retorted the grave-digger," with them typhoids dyin' like flies."

"I thought of a joke, Lem."

"Undertakin' is a comical business; what is it?"

"When an undertaker's sick ought he to go to the doctor what gives him the most work or the least?"

"You got me; I'll think it over and let you know."

In spite of his garrulous complaints the grave-digger was at work in a new grave on the sagebrush flat a mile or more from town when the undertaker and the liveryman drove up at midnight with all that remained of Billy Duncan jolting in the box of a lumber wagon.

The coffin of unplaned lumber was unloaded at the grave and the liveryman hastened away, for he himself had no liking for these nocturnal drives, but neither was he the man to quarrel with his own interests. If the Health Officer and His Honor, the mayor, asked no questions when the hospital deaths went unreported, he felt that these frequent midnight pilgrimages were no concern of his.

The undertaker peered into the shallow grave.

"This hole looks like a chicken had been dustin' itself."

"You'd think it was deep enough if you was diggin' in these rocks and drawin' only $5.00 for it," was the tart reply. "I told you I wouldn't dig but three feet for that money. 'Tain't like diggin' in nice, easy Nebrasky soil. Gimme $10 a grave an' I'll dig 'em regalation depth."

"Quit jawin' and take holt of this here box."

"Is he heavy?"

"Never heard of any of 'em comin' out of there fat. Slide the strap under your end."

"He's heavier than most," grunted the grave-digger. "He couldn't a been in there long."

Lutz laughed.

"They made a quick job of this one. Steady now—let her slide."

The grave-digger was sleepy and cross and careless. The strap slipped through his fingers and the box fell with a heavy thud. It fell upon its side and the lid came off.

"My God!" The grave-digger was staring into the hole with all his bulging eyes.

"You fool! You clumsy, blunderin' fool!"

The epithet passed unheard, for the grave-digger

was looking at the stark body rolled in a soiled blanket now lying face downward in the dirt of the grave.

"Jump in there and put him back!" cried Lutz excitedly.

The grave-digger backed off and shook his head emphatically.

"Not *me!*"

"What are you here for—you?"

"Not for jobs like this; this sure don't look right to me."

"What do I care how it looks to you! Get busy and help me roll him back and be quick about it!"

"I ain't paid for no such crooked work as this."

"Crooked?"

"I've heard it straight that every pauper had a suit o' clothes, a coffin, a six-foot grave, and a head-board comin' to him from the County. That's the law."

"Look here, Lem, use a little sense. Now what's the use spendin' County money on these paupers from God knows where? That's a good blanket."

"Oh, yes, that's a peach of a blanket. Kind of a shame to waste such a good blanket, ain't it? Why don't you take it off him? He'll never tell. But say, are you sure the County don't pay for that suit of clothes and coffin and six feet of diggin' he didn't git?"

"Are you goin' to lend a hand here or not?"

"Not." The grave-digger picked up his shovel and started off looking like a gnome in the moonlight under his high-crowned Stetson.

"Come back here! Don't be a fool."

"I'm not the man you're lookin' for," he replied stubbornly.

The undertaker started after him and laid a hand roughly upon his arm.

"See here, Lem, you goin' to blab this all over town?"

Remembering the graves he had dug for $5.00, the grave-digger began to enjoy Lutz's anxiety.

"Can't tell what I'll do when I get a few drinks in me."

"You start somethin' and you'll be sorry." Lutz's tone was threatening.

"I'm naturally truthful; I aims to stick strictly to facts if I does talk."

"Facts don't cut any ice in a libel suit," replied the undertaker significantly.

Libel suit! That sounded like the law and the grave-digger had a poor man's fear of the law. There was less assurance in his voice when he asserted—

"No man don't own me."

"I don't want to see you get in trouble, Lem, and I'm tellin' you for your own good that you better keep your trap shut on this. Who'd believe you if you'd tell any such story? You couldn't prove anything with the mayor and town officer against you if it was anything likely to get out and hurt the town. Who of Lamb and Harpe's friends that see them pikin' off to church every Sunday, singin' their sa'ms and the first at the altar of a Communion Sunday, who, I say, would believe us if we'd tell what we knew about that hospital and the whole lot more that we suspect? They could bluff you out because you haven't got the money it would take to prove you're right. Come back here and behave yourself and I'll try and get you that $10."

"If I wasn't a family man——" mumbled the grave-digger.

"But you are, and it's no use bein' squeamish over somethin' that's none of your business. This is your bread and butter."

It was the argument which has tied men's tongues since the world began and it never grows less effective. The shovel dropped from the grave-digger's shoulder.

"Hop in here and help me roll him back."

The grave-digger reluctantly obeyed.

"This looks fierce to me." He wiped the cold perspiration from his forehead.

"Take a rock and hammer in them shingle-nails and forget it!"

When Dan Treu returned from his business trip to the County seat the undertaker met him smilingly.

"I made a fine show for the money, Dan; you'd have been pleased. Everything was plain but good and went off without a slip. I handled him as I promised—like he was my own."

The few in Crowheart who heard the story laughed openly at the statement which Giovanni Pelezzo made when he returned to camp one day and declared that while seated in the doorway of the operating room of the hospital he had turned in time to see Dr. Harpe take five dollars and some small change from the pocket of his cousin Antonio Pelezzo, whom she had etherized for a minor operation.

Although Antonio turned his empty pockets inside out to verify Giovanni's stoutly reiterated assertion, the camp ridiculed their story and none laughed more heartily at the absurdity of the tale than Dr. Harpe herself. When she declared that it was only one illustration of the lengths to which ignorant and suspicious foreigners would go, her listeners agreed that she must indeed have much with which to contend in practising her profession among such a class of people as were employed upon the project.

The only person who did not laugh, beside the countrymen of the two Italians, was Dan Treu. He made no comment when he heard the tale, but he sat for a long time on the corner of the White Elephant's billiard table, holding a cigarette which he forgot to smoke.

XXI

Turning a Corner

Andy P. Symes was much occupied with his own thoughts, he was not sleeping well and all food tasted much alike, while the adulation of his fellow-townsmen did not afford him the usual pleasure. These symptoms are most frequently associated with lack of funds, and in this respect Mr. Symes's case was not a peculiar one, the fact being that the total of the month's payroll exceeded the amount in the treasury—with no relief in sight—interest in the great Symes Irrigation Project having seemed suddenly to lag in financial circles.

"Maybe I imagine it," Mudge, the promoter, had written, "but it looks to me as though Capital was giving us the frosty mitt. They won't even listen. I can't raise a dollar among the stockholders or sell a bond. Could anybody have been knocking the proposition?"

Symes had written back—

"Ridiculous! Who would knock? I have no enemies of sufficient importance to hurt me, and particularly back there. Do your utmost, for the situation is growing critical here—desperate, in fact."

And desperate was the word when Symes contemplated going into his own pocket for money to make up the deficit—money which he had told himself he would salt away against that rainy day with which he had become all too familiar.

Symes's private bank account had grown to quite a respectable sum since that memorable morning when he had received word that his balance was in the red.

If he was given a confidential discount upon machinery for which he charged the company full price, was he not entitled to the difference? If he received a modest revenue from his manipulation of the commissary, and the hospital contract contributed its mite, was it not all in the game? Wasn't it done every day by men in similar positions and as honest as himself? It was legitimate enough, certainly, and, if he did not mention it, it was because it was his own affair.

The longer and harder Symes walked the floor the more he realized that payday must be met. Labor was not an account which could wait. Nothing would so arouse suspicion and hurt his credit as a dilatory payday. Local merchants would come down upon him like a thousand of brick for the settlement of the large accounts which at the present moment they were rather proud of his owing.

The impression was general that the affairs of the Symes Irrigation Company were entirely satisfactory, and Symes's credit had only been limited by the local merchants' own credit.

Heretofore the treasury had been replenished through the activities of Mudge, but it was now disturbingly low and payday was close, while instead of the expected check from the promoter came his disquieting letter.

"Mudge is losin' his grip; he's gettin' timid," Symes thought irritably. "I may have to go back myself and raise the wind." His success with J. Collins Prescott had given him added confidence in his abilities along this line.

The estate which Prescott represented were now the largest bondholders and at the time of the purchase Symes had chortled—

"If we can just get this crowd in deep enough they won't dare lay down if we get in a hole. They've got to see the proposition through to save themselves."

"Yes," Mudge had agreed doubtfully," but you gotta be careful." And added in the tone of a specialist in the delicate art of handling capital: "You can't force or crowd 'em, for once they get their necks bowed they'd sooner drop their pile than give an inch."

The question which Symes was now trying to decide was whether it was better to meet payday with his own money and trust Mudge to raise sufficient to reimburse him and meet the next payday or to bare the situation to the stock and bondholders and make an imperative demand for funds.

In the end Symes's own money met the payroll, and the sensation of checking it out was much like parting with his heart's blood. Though it was a relief to feel that his credit was still good and that he could continue to shine in the community for another month as its one large, luminous star, it also brought the cold perspiration out on him when he woke up in the night and remembered where this noble act had placed him. He was worse than penniless if Mudge could not raise more money, but this he refused to believe a possibility.

In the days which followed, the circles deepened beneath his eyes, his high color faded and Mudge's laconic messages "Nothing doing" were not calculated to restore it. As the time shortened toward another payday there were moments when Symes felt that his overtaxed nerves nearly had reached their limit. There was no rest or solace for him in his home, for when Augusta was not away with Dr. Harpe the latter was there to remind him of the skeleton jangling in his closet. He came and went beneath the cold eyes of the one and the half-contemptuous glances of the other, like, as he told himself, a necessary but objectionable boarder.

He no longer found diversion in his nightly game of "slough" in the card room of the Terriberry House, for they became only occasions to remind him that he owed his fellow-players more than he could ever hope to pay if Mudge did not dispose of more bonds quickly or the stockholders did not "come through," as he phrased it. He knew fairly well the financial resources of those whom he had favored with his liberal patronage and realized that they were doomed to go down with him to that limbo provided for the over-sanguine and the over-trusting.

At last the black day came when the treasury could not meet the smallest bills. Delay was no longer possible. He must play his last card. An imperative call must be made upon the stockholders and Symes telegraphed Mudge to this effect.

Symes dreaded the reply, yet he tried to bolster his courage with the argument which had seemed so potent at the time he used it, namely, that they were all in too deep to refuse aid at this crisis. Symes imagined that he could almost see himself growing old in the hours of suspense which followed the sending of the telegram.

Symes's hand shook noticeably when he took the yellow sheet from the operator who delivered it in person. The message read:

> Turned down cold. Something wrong. Letter follows.
>
> MUDGE

Symes's towering figure seemed to crumple in the office chair.

Abe Tutts to whom he owed $2500 for hay and grain waved a genial hand as he passed the door.

"How goes it?" he called.

"Great!" and the boastful reply sickened him.

Great—when he was ruined!

It was the sentence "Something wrong" which gave Symes that weak feeling in his knees. To what did Mudge refer, to the stock and bondholders or to the project and himself? Must he go about for the four days which must intervene before a letter could reach him with that sinking sensation in the pit of his stomach, that curious limpness of his spine?

He lived through it somehow without betraying himself and when Mudge's letter came it read in part:

"Your theory regarding the extraction of funds from stockholders is all right only it don't work. When I called a meeting and suggested that they raise more money among themselves to relieve the present situation and protect their interests, they cut me off at the pockets.

"That Fly-trap King of yours said, 'If that's all you got us together for, Mudge, we might as well get to hell out of here because I, for one, don't propose to put another cent into the proposition—"My Wife Won't Let Me."'

"The air was so chilly I could see my own breath and my last winter's chilblains began to hurt.

"'Gentlemen,' I said, 'I don't understand your attitude in this matter. We've got to raise this money to save ourselves. The proposition is as good as it ever was.'

"'We don't doubt that,' says Prescott in that infernally quiet way of his that makes your ears tingle, and a grin like a slice of watermelon went round.

"I tell you, Symes, something or somebody has queered us here and if you can find out who or what it is you can do more than I've been able to do. Haven't you got some powerful enemy? Is there any weak spot in the proposition? Rack your brains and let me know the result.

"These fellows don't seem worried and that's the strange part of it, for I know that some of them have got in a whole lot more than they can afford to lose.

"Whatever's at the bottom of it, it's mighty effective, for I'm up against a blank wall. I've exhausted every resource and I can't raise a dollar. If only we dared advertise the land and get some purchasers to make part payments down it would keep things moving for a while, but I suppose this is out of the question."

Was it? Symes laid the letter down. It was against the law to sell land before the water was actually upon it, but was it out of the question?

In his desperation Symes decided that it was not.

Casually imparting the information to the Crowheart *Courier* that he was going out to meet a party of millionaires who were anxious to invest, Symes packed his suitcase and arrived in the State Capital as soon as an express train could get him there.

When he appeared before the State Land Board the arguments he used to that body never were made public, but they were sufficiently convincing to enable him to send a guarded telegram to Mudge that night telling him to prepare additional literature and commence a campaign of advertisement. Also to arrange with the railroad for a Homeseekers' Excursion at as early a date as possible.

The telegram restored Mudge's faith in Symes,

revived his waning enthusiasm and courage. He composed a pamphlet for distribution among Eastern and Middle West farmers, from which he quoted extracts to his wife in the middle of the night, awakening her for that purpose.

"Extend a hand to Nature and she meets you with outstretched arms! Tickle the soil and it laughs gold!"

"Wouldn't that start a man-milliner to raising alfalfa?" demanded Mudge upon such occasions.

"Where the clouds never lower and the sun shines always. Where the perfumed zephyrs fan the cheeks of men and brothers. The Perfect Climate found at last! Crowheart the Gem of the Rockies! within easy reach. Buy a ticket for $29.50 and breath the Elixir of Life while you look over our unequalled proposition."

"That ought to catch all the lungers in the world," averred Mudge.

That the promoter's confidence in the merits of his pamphlet was justified was soon evidenced by the flood of inquiries and requests for additional information which came by mail while his office became a mecca for the restless and the "land hungry" who read his vivid description of the great Symes irrigation project which was making the desert bloom like the rose.

They came in droves to ask questions and to stare at the twenty-pound beet which sat conspicuously upon Mudge's desk and their jaws dropped when he explained carelessly—

"A runt from under the Mormon ditch; we raise bigger on *our* land."

They studied the map of the neatly plotted townsite of Symes with its substantial bank building, its park, its boulevards, its public school building and band-stand.

"That's goin' to be some town," Mudge told each with a confidential air, "and you've got a chance to make something if you gobble up a corner lot or two before prices soar. Quick turns while the boom is on is the way to do it in the West."

Mudge believed all that he said, because he believed in Symes; that is, he was convinced that all would be as he represented as soon as Symes could be provided with money to complete the project, and if he permitted his imagination to take liberties with the truth, it was solely because he felt that the end justified the means. He assured himself that all would be forgotten and forgiven in the ultimate success of the enterprise and so great was his faith in it and its efficient management that his own money paid for the pamphlets and the half-page newspaper advertisements which told the world of the Homeseekers' Excursion to the great Symes Irrigation Project where the desert was blooming like the rose. If at times there came to him, as there did to Symes, chilling thoughts of the exact meaning of failure should their plans miscarry, he did not allow them to long dampen his ardor.

"We'll put it through *somehow!*" he declared vehemently. "There'll be a trainload of these Homeseekers, and, out of a bunch like that, surely *some* of 'em will stick even if it isn't—well—not quite exactly in the shape they expect to find it. They'll see the merits of the proposition and make allowances for my enthusiasm; and if we can work this once we can work it again." Mudge insisted to himself resolutely, "I'm not the man to be stumped by a few obstacles, I can't afford to be identified with failures and we'll put this thing through if S. B. Mudge goes broke trying."

The stock and bondholders had something of the attitude of blasé spectators at a circus, regarding Mudge's sensational efforts calmly, without applause or protest. A curious attitude, Mudge thought, for persons so vitally concerned, and there were times, after a chance meeting with Prescott, for instance, when Mudge wondered if they really were as indifferent as they seemed. That Prescott had an amazing knowledge of the situation for one in a position to know so little was evidenced by an occasional pertinent comment. But Mudge was too busy getting his Homeseekers in line to attempt the solution of any mysteries on the side.

In Crowheart the coming excursion of Homeseekers was the chief theme. Its citizens were elated at the wide publicity which the Company's advertising campaign was giving to the town, and increased deference to Symes was the result, for the merchants of Crowheart made no secret of the fact among themselves that without the payroll of the Symes Irrigation Project real money would be uncommonly scarce, and should the project fail—the remote possibility made them shudder. Gradually it had dawned upon these venturesome pioneers from "way back East in Nebraska" that the surrounding country had few if any resources and without the opening of fresh territory Crowheart's future was one they preferred not to contemplate.

If they wondered somewhat at the elasticity of the law, Symes's ability to stretch it only demonstrated still further his power, his ability to bend men and things to his iron will, and their awe of him increased proportionately. To the isolated community of obscure persons Symes seemed very nearly omnipotent. They had no criticism to make of the law's adaptability to Symes's needs; it was enough for them that Crowheart was in the limelight and the influx of settlers meant their individual prosperity.

It soon became obvious from the sale of excursion tickets that the Terriberry House would not be able to accommodate the Homeseekers.

"Not a carload but a trainload!" said Symes jubilantly to the editor of the Crowheart *Courier,* and Sylvester dashed off a double leaded plea to the first families of Crowheart to "throw open their homes" and do their utmost to make the strangers feel that they would be received upon terms of equality and find a welcome in their midst.

Crowheart's citizens responded magnificently to the appeal. The Percy Parrotts threw open their three-roomed residence and made arrangements to sleep in the hay, while their self-sacrificing example was quickly followed by others. Neither the Cowboy Band nor the neighbors knew either rest or sleep until they had mastered a Sousa March, while Mrs. Tutts showed her public spirit by rehearsing Crowheart's talented amateurs in an emergency performance of the "Lady of Lyons" for the strangers' evening entertainment.

Every available vehicle was engaged by Symes to convey the excursionists to the project and a committee chosen to meet them on the cinders at the station, himself to greet them in a few neat words.

With so much upon his mind, so many responsibilities upon his shoulders, it is small wonder that the little formality of payday should slip by without being properly observed. When it was called to his attention his explanation sounded reasonable enough.

"I'm just so busy now, boys, that I haven't the time to attend to your checks. But your money's as safe as though it was in the Bank of England, and if you'll oblige me by waiting until this excursion is over I'll greatly appreciate it."

"Sure!" they replied heartily, and indeed it was a pleasure to do Andy P. Symes a favor when he asked it in his big, genial voice. "Take your time, Mr. Symes, we are in no rush." In his magnetic presence they had quite forgotten that they were in a rush; besides, it was plain that he had more than one man should be expected to attend to, and no one dreamed that a dollar dropped in the treasury would have echoed like a rock falling in a well.

Like Mudge, Symes was convinced that out of a trainload of Homeseekers some of them would "stick." The inducement to do so was the privilege of the first choice of the 160-acre tracts—for a substantial deposit.

But those who did not stick?—those who were strongly under the impression that the water was already flowing through the ditch or that it was so near completion that it would do so shortly—would they be—irritated? As the day of the excursion approached the disquieting thought came with increasing frequency to Symes that they *would* be—irritated.

XXII

Crowheart's First Murder Mystery

The postmaster's curt "nothing" was like a judge's sentence to Essie Tisdale, for it meant to her the end of things. And now the marriage ceremony was over. She looked at the gold band upon her finger with a heavy, sinking heart. She must wear it always, she was thinking, to remind her that she had sold herself for a place to lay her head and thirty thousand sheep.

The jocose congratulations of the burly Justice of the Peace went unanswered and her eyes swept the smirking, curious faces of the bystanders without recognition. She heard Dubois's guttural voice saying—

"Go there to ze hotel, my dear, and get your clothes. Ze wagon is at ze shop for repairs and there you meet me. I've got to get back to ze sheep for awhile. You will haf good rest in ze hills."

The lonely hills with Dubois for company! A shiver like a chill passed over her. Returning to the hotel she found that the news had preceded her, for Mrs. Terriberry rushed down upon her with outstretched arms.

"Why didn't you tell me last night, Essie?"

The girl withdrew herself from the plump embrace.

"I didn't know it last night."

"I declare, if this isn't romantic!" Mrs. Terriberry fanned herself vigorously with her apron. "You'll be the richest woman around here when Dubois dies." She added irrelevantly, "And I've been like a mother to you, Ess."

"Why don't you and Dubois stay in town a few days and make us a visit?" Mr. Terriberry's voice rang with cordial hospitality.

The girl looked at him with embarrassing steadiness. The thirty thousand sheep were doing their work well.

"We are going to the camp to-day," she answered and turned upstairs.

When her few belongings were folded in a canvas "telescope" she looked about her with the panic-stricken feeling of one about to take a desperate, final plunge. The tiny, cheaply furnished room had been her home, her refuge, and she was leaving it, for she knew not what.

Every scratch upon the rickety washstand was familiar to her and she knew exactly how to dodge the waves in the mirror which distorted her reflection ludicrously. She was leaving behind her the shabby kid slippers in which she had danced so happily—was it centuries ago? And the pink frock hung limp and abandoned on its nail.

She walked to the window where she had sat so often planning new pleasures, happy because she was young and merry, and her heart brimmed with warmth and affection for all whom she knew, and she looked at the purple hills which shut out that wonderful East of which she had dreamed of seeing some time with somebody that she loved. She turned from the window with a lump in her aching throat and looked at the flat pillow which had been so often damp of late with her tears.

"It's over," she whispered brokenly as she picked up the awkward telescope, "everything is ended that I planned and hoped for. There's no happiness or love or laughter in the long, hot alkali road ahead of me. Just endurance—only duty."

She closed the door behind her, the door that always had to be slammed to make it fasten, and, drooping beneath the weight of the heavy bag trudged down the street toward the blacksmith shop.

It was less than an hour after the sheep-wagon had rumbled out of town with Dubois slapping the reins loosely upon the backs of the shambling grays that the telegraph operator, hatless, in his shirt-sleeves, bumped into Dr. Harpe as she was leaving the hotel.

"Have they gone?"

"Who?"—but her eyes looked frightened.

"Essie and old Dubois."

"Ages ago."

"I'm sorry, I hoped I'd catch her; perhaps I've something she ought to have."

Dr. Harpe looked at the telegram. Perhaps it was something she ought to have also.

"Look here, I've got a call to make over in the direction of Dubois's sheep camp and I'll take the message."

"Will you, Doc?" he said in relief. "That's good of you." He looked at the telegram and hesitated. "I didn't stop for an envelope."

"Oh, I won't read it."

"I know that, Doc," he assured her. "But——"

She was already hastening away for the purpose.

"Whew!" Dr. Harpe threw open her coat in sudden warmth. "I'm glad she didn't get *that!*"

She re-read the message—

Have heard nothing from you. Am anxious. Is all well with you? Telegraph answer to address given in letter.

Dr. Harpe tore the telegram in bits and watched the pieces flutter into the waste-basket.

"The Old Boy certainly looks after his own, Harpe," she murmured, but her fingertips were cold with nervousness.

Dr. Harpe had paid her professional visit and her horses were dragging the buggy through the deep sand in the direction of Dubois's sheep-ranch, where she contemplated staying for supper and driving home in the cooler evening. The small matter of being unwelcome never deterred Dr. Harpe when she was hungry and could save expense.

There was no one in sight nor human habitation within her range of vision; the slow drag was monotonous; the flies were bad and the heat was great; she was both drowsy and irritable.

"Lord! how I hate the smell of sheep!" she said fretfully as the odor rose strong from a bedding-ground, "and their everlastin' bleat would set me crazy. Gosh! it's hot! Wonder how she'll enjoy spending her honeymoon about forty feet from Dubois's shearing-pens," she sniggered. "Well, no matter what comes up in the future, I've settled *her;* she's out of the way for good and all, and I've kept my word—she'll never marry Ogden Van Lennop!"

Yet she was aware that there was hollowness in her triumph—that it was marred by a nameless fear which she refused to admit. Van Lennop was still to be reckoned with. His telegram had reminded her forcibly of that.

The muffled sound of galloping hoofs in the sand caused her to raise her chin from her chest and her mind became instantly alert. It would be a relief to exchange a word with some one, she thought, and wondered vaguely at the swiftness of the gait upon so hot a day. She could hear the labored breathing of the horses now and suddenly two riders flashed into sight around the curve of the hill. Instantly they pulled their horses on their haunches and swung them with rein and spur into the deep washout in the gulch where the giant sagebrush hid them.

It was so quickly done that Dr. Harpe had only a glimpse of flashing eyes, swarthy skins, and close-cropped, coal-black hair, but the glimpse was sufficient to cause her to say to herself—

"Breeds—and a long way from the home range," she added musingly. "Looks like a get-away—what honest men would be smokin' up their horses in heat like this?"

A barking sheep-dog ran up the road to greet her when, after another hour of plodding, she finally reached the ridge where she could look down upon the alkali flat where Dubois had built his shearing-pens, his log store house and his cabin of one room.

"No smoke. Darned inhospitable, I say, when it's near supper time and company comin'."

There was no sign of life anywhere save the sheep-dog leaping at her buggy wheels.

"Can it be the turtle-doves don't know it's time to eat?" she sneered. "Get ep!"

The grating of the wheels against the brake as she drove down the steep pitch brought no one around the corner of the house, which faced the trickling stream that made the ranch a valuable one.

They were somewhere about, she was sure of that, for she had recognized gray horses feeding some distance away and the sheep-wagon in which they had left town was drawn up close to the house. She tied her fagged team to the shearing-pens and sauntered toward the house, but with something of uncertainty in her face. There was a chance that she had been seen and the new Mrs. Dubois did not mean to receive her.

A faint, quavering moan stopped her at the corner of the house. She listened. It was repeated. She stepped swiftly to the doorway and looked inside. The girl was lying in a limp heap on the bunk, her face, her hands and wrists, her white shirtwaist smeared horribly with blood, while an unforgettable look of terror and repulsion seemed frozen in her eyes. The sight startled even Dr. Harpe.

"What's the matter? What's happened?" She shook her roughly by the shoulder, for the half-unconscious girl seemed about to faint. "Where's Dubois?"

She bent her head to catch the answer.

"Outside."

Dr. Harpe was not gone long, but returned to stand beside the bunk, looking down upon Essie with eyes that in the dimness of the illy-lighted cabin shone with the baleful gleam of some rapacious feline.

"You did a good job, Ess; he's dead as a mackerel."

The answer was the faint, broken moan which came and went with her breath.

"I'll go to town for help——"

The girl opened her eyes and looked at her beseechingly.

"Don't leave me alone!"

Dr. Harpe ignored the whispered prayer.

"Don't touch anything—leave everything just as it is," she said curtly; "it'll be better for *you.*"

Before she untied her team at the shearing-pens she

walked around the house and looked once more at the repulsive object lying upon a dingy quilt. Death had refused Dubois even the usual gift of dignity. His mouth was open, and his eyes; he looked even more than in life the brute and the miser.

"Two shots; and each made a bull's eye. One in the temple and another for luck. Either would have killed him."

She covered his face with a corner of the "soogan" and glanced around. The short, highly polished barrel of a Colt's automatic protruded from a clump of dwarf cactus some few feet away. She swooped swiftly down upon it and broke it open. The first cartridge had jammed and every other chamber was filled. Dr. Harpe held it in the palm of her hand, regarding it reflectively. Then she took her thumb nail and extracted the jammed cartridge and shook a second from the chamber. These she kept. The gun she threw from her with all her strength.

She lost no time in urging her fagged horses up the steep hill opposite the ranch house on the road back to Crowheart. At the top she let them pant a moment before they started up another almost as steep.

Dr. Harpe removed her hat and lifted her moist hair with her fingers. The sun was lowering, the annoying gnats and flies were beginning to subside, it soon would be cool and pleasant. Dr. Harpe looked back at the peaceful scene in the flat below—the sheep-wagon with its canvas top, the square, log cabin, the still heap beside it—really there was no reason why she should not enjoy exceedingly the drive back to town.

Out of the hills behind her came a golden voice that had the carrying qualities of a flute.

"Farewell, my own dear Napoli, farewell to thee, farewell to thee."

The smile faded from her face.

"The devil!" She chirped to her horses. "Where'd *he* come from?"

Those of Crowheart's citizens who yawned at 8 and retired at 8.30 were aroused from their peaceful slumbers by the astounding news that Essie Tisdale had shot and killed old Edouard Dubois, and the very same day that she had married him for his money. As a result, Crowheart was astir at dawn, bearing every evidence of a sleepless night and a hasty toilette.

This was the town's first real murder mystery. To be sure, there was the sheep-herder, who was found with his throat cut and his ear taken for a souvenir; but there was not much mystery about that, because he was off his range and had been duly warned. Also there had been plain killings over cards and ladies of the dance hall—surprising sometimes, but only briefly interesting—certainly never anything mysterious and thrilling like this.

Sylvanus Starr in that semi-conscious state midway between waking and sleeping, composed a headline which appeared on the "Extra" issued shortly after breakfast.

"A Man, a Maid, a Marriage and a Murder" read the headline, and while the editor made no definite charges, he declared in double-leaded type that the County should spare no expense to bring the assassin to justice *regardless of sex,* and the phrase "the dastardly murder of a good citizen and an honorable man" passed from lip to lip unmindful of the fact that in life Dubois had not been regarded as either.

That portion of Crowheart which was pleased to

speak of itself as the "sane and conservative element" endeavored to suspend sentence until the deputy-sheriff should return with further details, but even they were forced to admit that, from the meagre account furnished by Dr. Harpe, "it certainly looked bad for Essie Tisdale."

Dan Treu and the coroner, who was also the local baker, started immediately for the sheep-ranch, and Dr. Harpe accompanied them. "Ess looked about 'all in,'" she said in explanation.

They found the girl and the Dago Duke waiting by the fire which he had built outside the cabin. Huddled in a blanket which he had thrown about her shoulders she sat staring into the fire with the shocked look which never left her eyes. Utter, utter weariness was in her flower-like face and over and over again her subconsciousness was asking her tired brain, "What next? What horrible thing can happen to me next? What is there left to happen?" She felt crushed in spirit, unresentful even of Dr. Harpe's presence, for she felt herself at the mercy of whosoever chose to be merciless. But the Dago Duke was unhampered by any such feelings. He commented loudly as Dr. Harpe swaggered toward them with her hands thrust deep in the pockets of the man's overcoat which she wore on chilly drives—

"The ghouls are arriving early."

"There's another word as ugly," Dr. Harpe retorted significantly.

"I can't imagine—unless it's quack."

"Or accomplice," she suggested with a sneer.

Dan Treu frowned.

With the surprising tact and gentleness which

blunt men of his type sometimes show, the deputy-sheriff drew from the girl her story of the murder.

"I went to the creek—down the trail there—to get some water. I was only gone a moment; I was bending down—dipping with the pail—I heard two shots—close together. I thought he was shooting at prairie dogs—I did not hurry. When I came back—he was lying near the wagon. It was horrible! I called and called. He was dead. The blood was running everywhere. I got a quilt and dragged and dragged until I got him on it somehow. I saw no one. I heard no one."

Her slender hands were clenched tightly and she spoke with an effort. There was silence when she finished, for her story seemed complete; there seemed nothing more that she could tell. It was Dr. Harpe who asked—

"But his gun—where's his gun? He's always kept a gun—I've seen it—a Colt's automatic?"

The girl shook her head.

"I don't know."

"And, Doctor,"—it was the Dago Duke's suave voice that asked the question—"you saw no one—passed no one while driving through the hills?"

She looked at him steadily.

"I saw no one."

His eyelids slowly veiled his eyes.

"Why do you ask that?" His faint smile irritated her. "Don't you suppose I would have said so long before this?"

"Let's look for that gun," the deputy interrupted. "He had a gun—I'm sure of that; every sheepman packs a gun."

With the aid of a lantern and the glare of a huge

sagebrush fire they searched in the immediate vicinity for the gun and in the hope of finding some accidental clue.

"We can't expect to do much till morning," the deputy opined as with his light close to the ground he looked for some strange footprint in the dust of the dooryard.

It was behind the cabin that Dan Treu stooped quickly and brought the lantern close to a blurred outline in a bit of soft earth close to a growth of cactus. He looked at it long and intently and when he straightened himself his heavy, rather expressionless face wore a puzzled look.

"Come here," he called finally to the coroner. He pointed to the indistinct outline. "What does that look like to you?"

The coroner was not long from Ohio.

"It looks to me like somebody had made a track in his stockin' feet."

The deputy was born near the Rosebud Agency.

"Does it?" he added. "I guess we won't walk around any more until morning."

The track was a moccasin print to him.

It was the coroner who said to Dan Treu in an undertone as they sat by the fire waiting for the daylight—

"Did you ever see a woman act like Doc? By Gosh! did you ever see anybody act like Doc? She's enjoyin' this—upon my soul she is! She makes me think of a half-starved hunting dog that's pulled somethin' down and has got a taste of blood."

The deputy nodded with an odd smile.

The Dago Duke said nothing. But he seemed vastly interested in watching Dr. Harpe. He observed her every movement, her every expression, with a purposeful look upon his face which was new to it.

They found the gun in the morning, caught in a giant sagebrush where it hung concealed until accidentally jarred loose by no less a person than Mr. Percy Parrott, who had arrived early to give his unsolicited aid to the deputy-sheriff.

The Colt's automatic was easily identified as Dubois's gun, and two shells were missing.

"A pretty rough piece of work," commented Dr. Harpe as she looked at the empty chambers.

"As raw as they make it," agreed the Dago Duke for once.

"Don't run away, Dago," said the sheriff, "I may want you."

"Run?—when I go I'll fly."

All the town turned out to look when Dan Treu drove into town with the girl sitting bolt upright and very white upon the seat beside him.

They stopped at the Terriberry House and her old room was assigned to her, but all the gaping crowd considered her a prisoner.

XXIII

Symes Meets the Homeseekers

Andy P. Symes awoke from a night of troubled dreams with the impression still strong upon him that he was the exact centre of a typhoon in the China Seas. He realized gradually that the house was alternately shivering and rocking, that the shade of the slightly lowered window was flapping furiously, that his nose and throat were raw from the tiny particles of dust which covered the counterpane and furniture, that pebbles were striking the window-panes like the bombardment of a gattling gun. There was a wailing and shrieking from the wires which anchored his kitchen flue, a rattling and banging outside which conveyed the knowledge that the sheet-iron roof on his coal-house was loose, while a clatter from the street told his experienced ears that some one's tin garbage-can was passing.

He groaned. This was the day the Homeseekers' Excursion was due—coming to view the land "where the perfumed zephyrs fanned the cheeks of men and brothers!" Coming to breathe "the Elixir of Life," while they inspected that portion of the desert which was "blooming like the rose!"

Even the elements were against him it seemed.

Symes shoved up the shade to see the lovely Pearline Starr, with her head tied in a nubia, fighting her way through his front gate. She was bearing ahead of her some garment on the end of a stick. Mr. Symes dressed hastily that he might respond to her knock.

When Mr. Symes opened the door Miss Starr was

clinging, breathless, to a pillar of the veranda in order to keep her footing. She cast down her eyes as she extended her offering.

"Are these yours, Mr. Symes? We found them around a sagebrush in the backyard."

"If they were," said Mr. Symes shortly, "I'd be in bed. They look like Tuttses."

The air was filled with flying papers, shingles, pans, and there were times when he could not see across the street. Alva Jackson was in his corral distributing hay among his horses from a sack instead of a pitchfork. The Perfect Climate! Symes watched Miss Starr dig in her heels and depart lying back horizontally on the breeze. Then he slammed the door, but not before he saw Parrott's coal-house making its way toward his lot. He already had a cellar-door and a chicken coop which did not belong to him, while a "wash" he did not recognize was lodged in his woodpile of jack-pine and ground-cedar in the backyard.

The Homeseekers' Excursion arrived at last—hours late—delayed by the worst dust-storm in months. The committee of prominent citizens met it where the cinder platform had been before it blew off.

The excursionists looked through the car-windows to see members of the Cowboy Band with one arm locked around the frame-work of the water-tank and with the other endeavoring to keep divers horns, trombones and flutes in their mouth. No sound reached the ears of the excursionists owing to the fact that they were on the windward side of the band and the stirring notes of "Hot Time in the Old Town" were going the other way.

Mr. Symes's neat speech of welcome was literally blown out of his mouth, so he contented himself with shouting a warning to "look out for his hat" in the ear of the first Homeseeker to venture from the car, and led the way to the Terriberry House.

Crowheart found itself in the position of the boy at the double-ringed circus who suffers from the knowledge that there is something he must miss. It could not give its undivided attention to the strangers and at the same time attend the funeral of old Edouard Dubois, which was to be held under the auspices of the beneficiary society of which he had been a member.

To extend the warm, western hand of fellowship to the Homeseekers and find out where they came from, what their business was, and how much money they had was a pleasure to which the citizens of Crowheart had long looked forward, but also it was a pleasure and a duty to walk down the Main street in white cotton gloves and strange habiliments, following the new hearse. The lateness of the train had made it impossible to do both.

They were a different type, these Homeseekers, from the first crop of penniless adventurers who had settled Crowheart, being chiefly shrewd, anxious-eyed farmers from the Middle West who prided themselves upon "not owing a dollar in the world" and whose modest bank accounts represented broiling days in the hay field and a day's work before dawn, by lantern light, when there was ice to chop in the watering trough and racks to be filled for the bawling cattle being wintered on shares.

A trip like this had not been undertaken lightly by these men, but Mudge's alluring literature had stirred even their unimaginative minds, and the more impulsive had gone so far as to dispose of farming implements and stock that they might send for their families without delay when the purchase of the land was consummated.

In the long journey across the plains, one man had been tacitly assigned the position of spokesman for the excursionists. He was big, this prosperous looking stranger who seemed so unconscious of his leadership, as big as Andy P. Symes himself, and as muscular. He was a western type, yet he differed noticeably from his companions in that his clothes fitted him and his cosmopolitan speech and manner were never acquired in Oak Grove, Iowa. His eyes were both humorous and shrewd. He compelled attention and deference without demanding it. They explained him with pride, the Homeseekers, to inquiring citizens of Crowheart.

"That fellow? Why he controls all kinds of money beside what he's got himself; cattleman, banker, land, money to burn. He's representin' some farmers from his section that want to invest if the proposition's good."

This was enough for Crowheart, and Andy P. Symes, who was attracted to Capital by an instinct as sure as a law of Nature, flew to him and clung like a bit of steel to a magnet.

"Murder case," explained Symes for conversational purposes as he and the banker stood at the front window in the office of the Terriberry House and watched a mad race between Lutz, the undertaker, and a plume which had blown off the hearse.

"Yes?"

"Pretty raw piece of work," continued Symes, while the banker searched in his case for a cigar. "Old sheepman shot dead in his tracks the same day he was married to a girl young enough to be his granddaughter. Married him for his money and there's no doubt in anybody's mind but that she killed him for the same purpose. She may get away with it, though, for she'll be able to put up a fight with old Dubois's coin."

"Whose?" The banker's hand stopped on its way to scratch a match on the window-sill.

"French Canadian; signed himself 'Edouard Dubois.' Name familiar?"

The banker's face was a curious study as his mind went galloping back through the years.

"You say he was murdered—shot?"

"Dead as a door nail." Symes was pleased to have found a topic interesting to the stranger. "Each shot made a bull's-eye, one through the forehead and the other in his heart. She's a good shot, this girl, her one accomplishment."

"Does she admit it?"

Symes laughed.

"Oh, no; she tells some tale about having gone for water and hearing two shots—just about the sort of a yarn she *would* tell, but there was blood on her clothing and Dubois's own gun with two empty chambers was found where she had thrown it. They had a row probably and she beat him to his gun or else she waited and got the drop on him."

"But have they looked for strange footprints or any clues to corroborate her story?" persisted the banker.

Symes returned indifferently—

"I suppose so, but it's an open and shut case and the girl is practically a prisoner here in the hotel. The sheriff is hanging back about her arrest—western chivalry, you know, but it can't stand in the way of justice, and the people are pretty sore. Hurts a town, a thing like this," continued Symes feelingly, "gets in all the eastern papers, and when we appear in print we wish it to be in connection with something creditable.''

The banker agreed absent-mindedly, and asked—

''Do you know her—this Mrs. Dubois?''

''In a way—as one person knows another in a small town''—he hesitated delicately—''not socially at all. She was never in society.''

The banker looked at Symes sidewise through a cloud of smoke and his lips twitched suspiciously at the corners. He said merely:

''No?'' and continued to stare at the pall-bearers clinging to the wheels of the hearse while they waited outside the undertaking establishment for Lutz to beat his way back with the plume.

''I'd like to have a look at this man Dubois, if it's possible,'' he said suddenly.

''Why, yes,'' said Symes not too willingly. ''They're going to the Hall now to hold the services.'' He hated to be separated from Capital even for so short a time, besides he had a hope that his ''magnetic personality'' and personal explanations might go a long way toward softening any criticisms he might make when he noted the discrepancies between Mudge's statements and the actual conditions.

Symes had been quick to recognize this man's leadership and importance; simultaneously his sanguine temperament had commenced to build upon the banker's support—perhaps even to the extent of financing the rest of the project.

The banker followed the morbid crowd up the steep stairs to the Hall and seated himself on one of the squeaking folding chairs beside Mrs. Abe Tutts and Mrs. Alva Jackson, who were holding hands and stifling sobs which gave the impression that their hearts were breaking.

The ugly lodge room whose walls were decorated with the gaudy insignias of the Order was filled to overflowing with the citizens of Crowheart, whose attendance was prompted by every other reason than respect. But this a stranger could not know, since the emotion which racked Mrs. Percy Parrott's slender frame and reddened Mrs. Hank Terriberry's nose seemed to spring from overwhelming grief at the loss of a good friend and neighbor.

Mrs. Jackson's rose-geranium had blossomed just in the nick of time, and Mrs. Parrott, who did beautiful work in paper flowers, had fashioned a purple pillow which read "At Rest" and reposed conspicuously upon the highly polished cover of a sample coffin. Nor could the stranger, who found himself dividing attention with the casket, know that the faltering tributes to the deceased taxed the young rector's ingenuity and conscience to the utmost. Indeed, as he saw the evidences of esteem and noted the tears of the grief-stricken ladies, he regretted the impulse which had prompted him to go, for he could not conceive the removal of the Dubois of his acquaintance being the occasion of either private or public sorrow.

But even the sermons of young rectors must end, and at last Lutz, in the tremulous, minor, crepe-trimmed voice and drooping attitude which made the listeners feel that undertakers like poets are born, not made, urged those who cared to do so to step forward and pass around to the right.

Yes, it was he; there was no doubt about that; the brutal, obstinate face had altered very little in twenty years. Twenty years? It was all of that since he had seen old "Ed" Dubois betting his gold-dust on an Indian horse race—twenty years since young Dick Kincaid had floundered through the drifts in a mountain pass to see how the Canuck saved flour gold. Once more he was on the trail, scuffling rocks which rolled a mile without a stop. Before him were the purple blotches which the violets made and he could smell the blossoms of the thorn and service berry bushes that looked like fragrant banks of snow. He felt again the depression of the silence in the valley below—the silence in which he heard, instead of barking dogs and laughing children, the beating of his own heart. He never had forgotten the sight that met his eyes, and he recalled it now with a vividness which made him shudder, and he heard with startling clearness the childish voice of a half-naked, emaciated boy saying without braggadocio or hysteria—

"I'm goin' to find him, m'sieu, and when I do I'll get him, *sure!*"

Twenty years is a long time to remember an injury, but not too long for Indian blood. It was a good shot—the purple hole was exactly in the centre of the low, corrugated forehead—it had been no boyish, idle threat. His son had "got him, *sure!*" Neither had Dick Kincaid forgotten his own answer—

"If you do, boy, and I find it out, I don't know as I'll give you away."

He had learned to save flour gold and he was known as Richard H. Kincaid in the important middle west city where he had returned with his fortune. Time and experience had cooled his blood, yet, deep down, his heart always responded to the call of the old, primitive justice of the mining camps—"An eye for an eye; a tooth for a tooth."

Kincaid became conscious that he was being eyed in curiosity and impatience by the eager folk behind. He heard Mrs. Tutts's rasping whisper as he moved along—

"She ain't shed a tear—not even gone into black. I'll bet she don't aim to view the corp' at all!"

Kincaid followed Mrs. Tutts's disapproving gaze.

That was the suspect! That slim, young girl with her delicately cut features hardened to meet the concentrated gaze of a procession of staring, unfriendly eyes? Why, as he glanced about him, she looked the only lady in the room!

Essie sat with the feeling that ice had formed about her heart, trying to bear unflinchingly the curious or sneering looks of those she had known well enough to call by their first names. It was torture for the sensitive girl who saw in each cold eye the thought that she had killed a man—killed a human being—for money!

A feeling of overwhelming pity surged over Kincaid as he looked at her, a feeling so strong that when she raised her eyes and gazed squarely into his he wondered if he had spoken aloud. They were blue and beautiful, her eyes, as two mountain forget-me-nots, like two bruised flowers, he thought, that had been hurt to death. He could remember having seen only one other pair like them.

An impulse so strong, a resolve so sudden and violent that it sent the blood in a crimson wave above his collar and over his face seized him, and he whispered to himself as he moved toward the door—

"I'll see her through, by George! I'll stand by her till there's skating in the place that don't commonly freeze!"

XXIV

The Dago Duke and Dan Treu Exchange Confidences

"They were shod horses and they were goin' some. See how deep the corks sunk. Look at the length of the jumps." The sheriff followed the hoof tracks with his eye until they turned at an angle and dropped into the gulch.

"Pft!—like that—and they were gone," said the Dago Duke, with an expressive gesture. "Over there, where I was reposing under the scant shade of a sagebrush, I opened my eyes just in time to see the top of their black hats disappear. Her buggy was turning the hill."

The sheriff stepped off the distance.

"Less than a hundred yards. She must have seen them plainly."

"Certainly; that's when they swung into the gulch."

"Well, sir, it gets me." With the admission the sheriff thrust his hands deep in his trousers pockets and looked frankly nonplussed.

"She denied as plain as she could say it in English that she had seen or met anybody and she'll probably do the same under oath."

"No doubt about it," replied the Dago Duke.

"But why should she?" demanded the sheriff in frowning perplexity. "I can think of no reason, yet she must have one. Do you suppose she knew the men—that she's protecting them at the girl's expense?"

The Dago Duke shrugged his shoulders.

"It's possible, but not probable if they were Indians."

"If them wasn't moccasin tracks around the camp, I'll eat 'em," Dan Treu declared with conviction. "I've run with Injuns and fit 'em, too, enough to know their tracks in the dark, but, man, there ain't an Injun within two hundred miles of here, and besides they never got away with anything, there was nothin' gone, and Reservation Injuns ain't killin' for fun these days. That's right, too, about her not knowin' them if they were Injuns. I'll tell you, Dago, I never run up agin' a proposition just like this."

The Dago Duke looked reflectively at the end of his cigarette.

"It seems as though that little girl's fate depends upon this woman."

"You say they are urging you to arrest her?"

The sheriff's face darkened.

"Oh, yes, they've got it all cut and dried just how it happened. They make me think of a pack of wolves that's got a weak one down; he's outnumbered and can't fight back, so jump him! tear him! They're roarin' at me to 'do somethin''—Tinhorn Frank, Symes, Parrott, the whole outfit of 'em. Say, Dago, I wasn't raised to fight women."

"Does your chivalry extend to the lady doc?"

"No, by gum! it don't," replied the sheriff, with a promptness which made the other laugh. "If I knew any way short of choking her to get the truth I'd do it."

"You mean to try?"

"To choke her?"

"To get the truth."

"I'm goin' to appeal to her first."

The Dago Duke laughed sardonically.

"You think it won't work?"

"Not for a minute."

"I'll see what bull-dozing will do, then."

"Better save your breath."

"Why?"

"It's a question of veracity. She'll see that. Her word against mine. Even you must admit, Dan, that I haven't her spotless reputation. A communicant of the church versus the town drunkard. She'd merely say that instead of Gila monsters I was 'having' assassins. This chronic cloud under which I live has its drawbacks. The fact that I haven't had a drink in six weeks wouldn't have the slightest weight if she chooses to persist in her denial that she met these men."

"I suppose you're right," the sheriff admitted reluctantly, "and if this wind keeps up we won't even have tracks to back up your story."

"Besides," added the Dago Duke, "if there is not great friendship between them there is, at least, no open quarrel to furnish a plausible reason for her silence. We would only make ourselves absurd, Dan, by any public charge. But there is some way to get the truth. Try your methods and then—well, I'll try mine."

This was in the forenoon. That evening the Dago Duke leaned against the door-jamb of the White Elephant Saloon and watched Dan Treu coming from Dr. Harpe's office with failure written upon his face. His white teeth gleamed in a smile of amusement as he waited for the sheriff.

"Don't swear, Dan. Never speak disrespectfully of a lady if you can help it."

"Dago," said the sheriff, with his slow, emphatic

drawl, "I wish she was a man just for a minute—half a minute—one second would do."

"She laughed at you, yes?"

"She laughed at me, yes? Well, I guess she did. She gave me the merry ha! ha! I told her you had seen two men on horseback pass her out there in the hills, that I had seen the mark of her buggy wheels and the tracks of the two horses on the run and that the print of moccasins led from the sheep-wagon into the brush. She looked at me with that kind of stare where you can see the lie lying back of it and said—

"I didn't see anybody. I've told you that and I'll swear to it if necessary."

"'Look here, Doc,' I says, 'if you don't tell that you saw these men we'll tell it for you.'"

"That's when she laughed, cackled would be a better word, it sure wasn't a laugh you'd call ketchin', and says—

"'You fly at it. Try startin' something like that and see what happens to you. I got some pull in this town and you'll find it out if you don't know it. You'll wake up some mornin' and find yourself out of a job. Who do you think would take that drunken loafer's word against mine? And beside, why should I keep anything back that would clear Essie Tisdale? You're crazy, man! Why, she's a friend of mine.'

"You called the turn on her all right, Dago; she said just about what you said she would say."

"You haven't got the right kind of a mind, Dan, to sabe women of her sort. It takes a Latin to do that. There's natural craft and intrigue enough of the feminine in the southern races to follow their illogical reasoning and to understand their moods and caprices as an Anglo-Saxon never can. You are like a big, blundering, honest watch-dog, Dan, trying to do field work that requires a trained hunting dog with a fine nose and hereditary instincts. If this was a horse-stealing case, or cattle rustling, or a sheep raid, and you were dealing with men all around——"

The deputy-sheriff's jaw set grimly.

"I'd have the truth or he'd be in the hospital. I'm handicapped here because there's no money in the treasury to work with. This county's as big as a State and only two or three thousand in it, so we are about as flush as grasshopper year in Kansas. The people are howling about bringin' the murderer to justice at any cost, but if I'd ask 'em to dig up a hundred apiece in cold cash for expense money they'd subside quick."

"This is one of the few occasions when my past extravagances and habits fill me with regret," replied the Dago Duke, with half-humorous seriousness. "My remittance which has shrunk until it is barely sufficient to sustain life, is already spoken for some months ahead by certain low persons who consider themselves my creditors. Tinhorn Frank, who drew to a straight and filled, is one of them, and Slivers, inside, has a mortgage on my body and soul until an alleged indebtedness is wiped out.

"Financially and socially I am nil; mentally and physically my faculties are at your disposal. Do you happen to know anything in the lady's past or present that she would not care to have exploited? Blackmail, yes? I have no scruples. What do you know?"

The deputy gave the Dago Duke a curious look, but did not answer.

"There's something," guessed the other quickly.

"Yes, Dago, there is," said Dan Treu finally with awkward hesitation. "It's something so fierce that I hate to tell it even to you for fear there might be some mistake. It's hard to believe it myself. It sounds so preposterous that I'd be laughed at if I told it to anyone else in Crowheart."

"I'll not laugh," said the Dago Duke. "It's the preposterous—the most unlikely thing you can think of that is frequently true. I've studied that woman, with my comparatively limited opportunities, until I know her better than you think and far, far better than she thinks."

"Dago," the big deputy squirmed as he asked the question:

"Could you believe her a petty thief?"

"Without the least difficulty," replied the Dago Duke composedly.

"That she would rifle a man's pockets—roll him like any common woman of the street?"

"If it was safe—quite, quite safe."

Slowly, even reluctantly, Dan Treu told the Dago Duke the story of the Italians as he had heard it in their broken English from their own lips. Through it all the Dago Duke whistled softly, listening without emotion or surprise. He still whistled when the deputy had finished.

"Do you believe it?" the sheriff asked anxiously, at last.

"Emphatically I do. Let me tell you something, Dan: a woman that will stoop to the petty leg-pulling, sponging, grafting that she does to save two bits or less has got a thief's make-up. Her mania for money, for getting, for saving it, is a matter of common knowledge.

"You know and I know that she will do any indelicate thing which occurs to her to get what she wants without paying for it. When she wants a drink, which the good God knows is often, she asks any man she happens to know and is near to buy it for her. Her camaraderie flatters him. She habitually 'bums' cigarettes and I've known her to go through a fellow's war-bag, in his absence, for tobacco. When she's hungry, which I should judge was all the time, she drops in casually upon a patient and humorously raids the pantry—all with that air of nonchalant good fellowship which shields her from much criticism, since what in reality is miserliness and gluttony passes very well for amusing eccentricity."

Dan Treu laughed.

"You've got her sized up right in that way, Dago. I know a fellow that was sick and had to cache the chocolate and things his folks sent him from the East under the mattress when he saw her coming and he always locked the fruit in his trunk after she had cleaned him out a dozen times as though a flock of seventeen-year locusts had swarmed down upon him. One night about two or three in the morning when she couldn't sleep, she called on a typhoid patient under the pretext of making a professional visit, and got the nurse to fry her some eggs. She's as regular as a boarder at Andy P. Symes's when meal-time rolls around. I wonder sometimes that he stands for it."

The Dago Duke looked at him oddly, but observed merely:

"Do you?"

"And you don't think the dagos made a mistake or misunderstood something through not talkin' English much? It sounded straight to me the way they told it, but a thing like this is something you don't want to repeat unless you just about saw it for yourself."

"If they told you they had $5.50 taken from them you can bet it's so. Italians of that class know to a penny what they have sent home, what they have in the bank, what there is in their pockets to spend. Generations of poverty have taught them carefulness and thrift. Americans call them ignorant and stupid because their unfamiliarity with the language and customs make them appear so, but they are neither too ignorant nor stupid to misunderstand an incident like this. Are the men still on the works?"

The deputy nodded.

"If you'll loan me your horse I'll ride out and see them myself. My understudy can perhaps stand another day with the sheep without going crazy. When I come back I may be in a better position to call upon the lady doc and talk it over. She's fond of me, you know."

"So I've noticed." Dan Treu grinned as he recalled the invariable exchange of personalities when they met.

XXV

Crowheart Demands Justice

The utterly insignificant telegraph operator at an equally insignificant railway station in Mexico loomed a person of colossal importance to Ogden Van Lennop, who had calculated that the reply to his telegram was considerably more than a week overdue. As he went once more to the telegraph office, the only reason of which he could think for being glad that he was the principal owner in the only paying mine in the vicinity was that the operator did not dare laugh in his face.

"Anything for me?"

"Nothing; not yet, sir."

The operator's voice and manner were respectful, but Van Lennop saw his teeth gleam beneath his dark mustache. He had found it quite useless to assure Van Lennop that he need not trouble himself to call as any telegram would be delivered immediately upon its receipt, also he had been long enough in the service to know that young Americans of Van Lennop's type did not ordinarily become so intense over a matter of business.

"Could it have gone astray—this infernal name—it looks like a piece of barbed wire when it's spelled out—is there another place of the same name in Mexico?

"Not in the world, sir."

"I didn't think so," returned Van Lennop grimly. He continued: "I want you to telegraph the operator in Crowheart and find out positively if the message was delivered to the person to whom it was sent."

"I'll get it off at once, sir."

So this was being "in love?"—this frenzy of impatience, this unceasing anxiety which would not let him sleep! It seemed to Van Lennop that he had nearly run the emotional gamut since leaving Crowheart and all that remained to be experienced was further depths of doubt and dark despair. Had he been too sure of her, he asked himself; had something in his letter or the sending of his telegram displeased her? Was she ill?

He reproached himself bitterly for not telling her before he left, and thought with angry impatience of the caution which had kept him silent because he wanted to be sure of himself.

"Sure of myself!" he repeated it contemptuously. "I should have been making sure of her! The veriest yokel would have known that he was completely—desperately in love with her, but I, like the spineless mollusk that I am, must needs wait a little longer—'to be sure of myself'!"

To shorten the long hours which must intervene before he could expect a reply from Crowheart, Van Lennop ordered his saddle horse and rode to the mine, where a rascally superintendent had stripped the ore chute and departed with everything but the machinery. Van Lennop had the tangled affairs of the mine fairly well straightened out and the new superintendent was due that day, so the end of his enforced stay was in sight in a day or two more—three at the most.

As his horse picked its way over the mountain trail the fresh air seemed to clear his brain of the jumble of doubts and misgivings and replace them with a growing conviction that something had gone wrong—

that all was not well with Essie Tisdale. His unanswered letter and telegram was entirely at variance with her sweet good-nature. What if she were needing him, calling upon him now, this very minute? He urged his horse unconsciously at the thought. Some accident—he could think of nothing else—unless a serious illness.

The employees at the mine observed that the young American owner was singularly inattentive that day to the complaints and grievances to which heretofore he had lent a patient ear.

His horse was sweating when upon his return he threw the reins to an idle Mexican in front of his hotel and hurried into the office.

Yes; there was a telegram for Señor Van Lennop—two, in fact.

He tore open the envelope of one with fingers which were awkward in their haste. The telegram read:

> Message addressed to Miss Essie Tisdale received and delivered.
>
> OPERATOR

Van Lennop stood quite still and read it again, even to the unintelligible date-line. He felt suddenly lifeless, listless, as though he wanted to sit down. It was all over, then. She had received his letter and his telegram, and her reply to his offer of his love and himself was—silence? It was not like her, but there seemed nothing more for him to do. He could not force himself and his love upon her. She knew her own mind. His conceit had led him into error. It was done.

He opened the other telegram mechanically. It was from Prescott and partially in code. It was a long one for Prescott to send, but Van Lennop looked at it without interest. He would translate it at his leisure—there was no hurry now—the game had lost its zest.

Van Lennop turned to the dingy register. A train had arrived in his absence and perhaps Britt, the new superintendent, had come. His name was there—that was something for which to be grateful, as he could the sooner get back into the world where he could find in business something better than his own wretched thoughts to occupy his mind.

He walked languidly over the stone flagging to his room and dropped listlessly int. a chair. It was not long before he heard Britt's alert step in the corridor quickly followed by his brisk rap upon the door. He always had liked the ambitious young engineer and they shook hands cordially.

"I'm more than glad to see you."

Britt laughed.

"I dare say. A week in a place like this is much like a jail sentence unless you're hard at work. Are things in pretty much of a mess?"

Van Lennop went over the situation briefly, and concluded—

"I'll stay over a day or so, if you desire."

"There's no necessity, I think," said Britt, rising. "I'll keep in touch with you by wire. Crowheart again?"

Van Lennop shook his head.

"I'm going east from here."

"Here's a late paper; perhaps you'd like to look it over. When I'm in a place like this I can read a patent medicine pamphlet, and enjoy it."

Van Lennop smiled.

"Much obliged. There's the supper gong. Don't wait for me; I'll be a little late."

Van Lennop had no desire for food, much less for conversation, so he picked up the travel-worn newspaper which Britt had tossed upon the table and glanced at the headlines.

The stock market was stronger. Nevada Con was up three points. The girl with the beautiful eyebrows had married that French jackanapes after all. Another famine in India. A Crowheart date-line caught his eye.

WEALTHY SHEEPMAN MURDERED
EDOUARD DUBOIS SHOT AND KILLED AT HIS CAMP
BRIDE OF A DAY TO BE ARRESTED

The story of Essie Tisdale's marriage with Dubois followed, and even the news editor's pencil could not eliminate Sylvanus Starr's distinctive style. He had made the most of a chance of a lifetime. "An old man's darling"—"Serpent he had warmed in his bosom"—"Weltering in his blood"—all the trite phrases and vulgarisms of country journalism were used to tell the sensational story which sickened Van Lennop as he read:

"The arrest of the murdered patriarch's beautiful bride is expected hourly, as the leading citizens of Crowheart are clamoring for justice and are bringing strong pressure to bear upon Sheriff Treu, who seems strangely reluctant to act."

The paper dropped from Van Lennop's nerveless hand and he sat staring at it where it lay. He picked it up and read the last paragraph, for his dazed brain had not yet grasped its meaning. But when its entire significance was made clear to him it came with a rush:

it was like the instantaneous effect of some powerful drug or stimulant that turned the blood to fire and crazed the brain. The blind rage which made the room swing round was like the frenzy of insanity. Van Lennop's face went crimson and oaths that never had passed his lips came forth, choking-hot and inarticulate.

"The leading citizens of Crowheart, the outcasts and riff-raff of civilization, the tinhorn gamblers, the embezzlers, ex-bankrupts and libertines, the sheep-herders and reformed cattle-thieves, the blackmailers and dance-hall touts swollen by prosperity, disguised by a veneer of respectability, want justice, do they? By God!" Van Lennop shook his clenched fist at the empty air, "the leading citizens of Crowheart shall HAVE justice!"

He smoothed Prescott's crumpled telegram and reached for his code-book.

When he had its meaning he pulled a telegraph-blank toward him, and wrote:

Carry out my instructions to the letter. Do not neglect the smallest detail. Leave no stone unturned to accomplish the end in view.

VAN LENNOP

XXVI

Latin Methods

"Oh, Doc!" It was the telegraph operator, hatless, in his shirt-sleeves, hurrying toward her from the station as she passed.

Doctor Harpe stood quite still and waited, not purposely but because a sudden weakness in her knees made it impossible for her to meet him half-way. She was conscious that the color was leaving her face even as her upper lip stretched in the straight, mirthless smile with which she faced a crisis. She knew well enough why he called her, the dread of this moment had been with her ever since her foolish boast of Van Lennop's letter and the destruction of his telegram.

"You gave that message to Essie? She got it all right, didn't she, Doc?"

She had prepared herself a hundred times to answer this question, but now that it was put she found it no easier to decide on a reply; to know what answer would best save her from the consequences of the stupid error into which her hatred had led her.

If she said that she had lost it and subsequent events had driven it from her mind, he would duplicate the message. If she said she had delivered it and her falsehood was discovered, her position was rendered more dangerous, ten-fold. She decided on the answer which placed discovery a little farther off.

"Sure, she got it; I gave it to her that afternoon."

Her assurance closed the incident so far as the telegraph operator was concerned; it was the real beginning of it to Doctor Harpe, whose intelligence enabled her to realize to the utmost the position in which she now had irrevocably placed herself. She turned abruptly and walked to her office with a nervous rapidity totally unlike her usual swagger.

When the door was closed behind her she paced the floor with excited strides. It was useless to attempt to hide from herself the fact that she was horribly, cravenly afraid of Ogden Van Lennop; for she recognized beneath his calm exterior a quality which inspired fear. She was afraid of him as an individual, afraid of his money and the power of his influence if he chose to use them, for Dr. Harpe had brains enough, worldly wisdom enough, to know that he was beyond her reach.

In Crowheart, she believed that through her strong personality and the support of Andy P. Symes she could accomplish nearly anything she undertook; but she knew that in the great world outside where she had discovered Van Lennop was a factor, she would be only an eccentric female doctor, amusing perhaps, mildly interesting, even, but entirely inconsequential.

Her thoughts became a chaotic jam of incoherent explanations as she thought of an accounting to Van Lennop should he return, and again she raged at herself for the insane impulse which had led her to boast of a farewell letter to her. The sleepless hours in which she had gone over and over the situation with every solution growing more preposterous than the last, had been telling upon the nerves which never had quite recovered from the shock and the incidents which followed Alice Freoff's death. The slightest excitement seemed to set them jangling of late.

They were twitching now; her eyelids, her shoulders, her mouth seemed never in repose when she was alone. Her hand shook uncontrollably as she refilled a whiskey glass and rolled and smoked another cigarette. It was no new thing, this nervous paroxysm, being nearly always the climax to a night of exaggerated fear. The necessity for self-possession and outward calmness in public made it a relief to let her nerves go when alone.

"If he comes back, I'm ruined! He'll cut loose on me in public and he'll sting; I know him well enough for that." Her hands grew clammy at the thought. "It'll put a crimp in my practice. If it wasn't for the backin' of Symes I'd as well pull my freight—but he hasn't come yet. It's not likely he ever will with no word from her and this scandal comin' close on the heels of her silence. I'm a fool to worry—to let myself get in such a state as this."

She no longer entertained the hallucination that she might attract Van Lennop to herself; to save herself from public exposure, should he by any chance return, was her one thought, her only aim. And always her hopes simmered down to the one which centred in Symes's influence in Crowheart and his compulsory protection of herself. He dared not desert her.

"Let him try it!" She voiced her defiant thoughts. "Let him go back on me if he dare! If I get in a place where I've absolutely nothing to lose—if he throws me down—Andy P. Symes and Crowheart will have food for thought for many a day. But, pshaw! I'm rattled now; I've pulled out before and I'll——"

A hand upon the door-knob startled her. Hastily she shoved the glass and bottle from sight and pulled herself together.

"Oh, it's you?" Her tone was not cordial, as the Dago Duke stood before her.

"Did you think it was your pastor," inquired that

person suavely as he sniffed the air, "come to remonstrate with you upon your intemperate habits?"

She laughed her short, harsh laugh as she took the bottle from its hiding-place and shoved it toward him.

"Help yourself."

She had long since learned that it was useless to pretend before the Dago Duke. His mocking, comprehending eyes made pretence ridiculous even to herself. She dreaded meeting him in public because of the flippant disrespect of his manner toward her; privately she found a certain pleasure in throwing off the cloak which hid her dark, inner-self from Crowheart. He assumed her hypocrisy as though it were a fact too obvious to question and she had been obliged to accept his estimate of her.

"How like you, my dear Doctor!" He picked up the bottle and read the label. "Your womanly solicitude for my thirst touches me deeply, but,"—he replaced the bottle upon her desk—"since I've stood off the demon Rum for six weeks now I'll hold him at bay until I finish my little talk with you."

"If you're here on business, cut it short," she said curtly.

"I can't imagine myself here on any other errand" he returned placidly. "Say, Doc,"—there was a note in his wonderful speaking voice which made her look up quickly—"why don't you give back that $5.00 and four bits you pinched from Giovanni Pellezzo?"

The moment showed her remarkable self-control. She could feel her overtaxed nerves jump, but not a muscle of her face moved.

"What are you driving at?" she demanded.

"The name is not familiar to you?"

"Not at all."

"I'm not surprised at that, since your interest in your contract patients extends no further than their pockets."

"If you're here to insult me——"

"I couldn't do that," returned the Dago Duke composedly; "I've tried."

"You've got to explain."

"That's what I came for." He smiled pleasantly.

"Well?" She tapped her foot.

"Don't rush me, Doc. I have so few pleasures, you know that, and the enjoyment I'm extracting from your suspense makes me desire to prolong it. You *are* anxious, you must admit that, although you really conceal it very well. But you're gray around the mouth and those lines from your nose down look like—yes, like irrigation laterals—furrows—upon my soul, Doc, you've grown ten years older since I came in. You should avoid worry by all means, but I can understand exactly how you feel when you're not quite sure to which case I may refer."

Her tense nerves seemed suddenly to snap. She struck the desk with her open palm, and cried—

"I'm *sick* of this!"

He looked at her critically.

"I can believe it. Temper adds nothing to your appearance. But, Doc, with your intelligence and experience, how did you come to rifle a man's pocket with a witness in the room?"

She jumped to her feet.

"I won't stand this! I don't have to stand it!"

The Dago Duke crossed his legs leisurely.

"No—you don't have to, but I believe I would if I were you. The fact is, Doc, I dropped in merely to make a little deal with you."

"Blackmail!" she cried furiously.

"In a way—yes. Strictly, I suppose, you might call it blackmail."

"You're broke again—you want money!"

The Dago Duke shuddered.

"Oh, Doc! how can you be so indelicate as to taunt me with my poverty; to suggest, to hint even so subtly, that I would fill my empty pockets from your purse?" He looked at her reproachfully.

"What *do* you want, then?"

The Dago Duke's voice took on a purring, feline softness which was more emphatic and final than any loud-mouthed vehemence—

"What do I want? I want you to tell the officers that you passed two men riding on a run from Dubois's sheep-camp—two Indians or 'breeds' in moccasins—and I want you to do it quick!"

"You want me to perjure myself and you 'want me to do it quick,'" she mimicked.

He paid no attention.

"I want you to help clear that girl; if you refuse, Giovanni Pellezzo will swear out a warrant for your arrest, charging you with the theft of $5.50 while he was etherized for a minor operation."

They regarded each other in a long silence.

She said finally—

"You know, of course, that this Italian will have to go after this?"

"You'll have him discharged?"

"Certainly."

"He needs a rest."

"He'll get it."

Another pause came before she asked—

"Do you imagine for a moment that an ignorant foreigner can get a warrant for me on such a charge?"

"I foresee the difficulty."

"You mean to persist?"

He nodded.

She flung at him—

"Try it!"

"If we fail in this," continued the Dago Duke evenly, "there's the case of Antonio Amato, whose hand the nurse, acting under your instructions, held after thrusting a pencil in his limp fingers and signed a check when he was dying and unconscious. Which check you cashed after his death, in violation of the State banking laws from which perhaps even you are not exempt if this man's relatives choose to bring you to account for the irregularity."

"It is a lie!"

"It is not impossible," he continued, "to get the nurse who left you before Nell Beecroft came, saying that she knew enough about you both to 'send you over the road.' It is not too difficult to bring to light the examples of your incredible incompetency which prove you unfit to sign a death certificate, nor is your record in Nebraska hard to get."

She moistened her colorless lips before she spoke.

"And where is the money coming from to do all this?"

She had touched the weak spot in his attack, but he replied with assurance.

"It will be ready when needed."

"This is persecution—a plot to ruin me on the trumped-up charges of irresponsible people."

The Dago Duke's keen ear detected the faint note of uncertainty and agitation beneath the defiance of her tone.

"These things are true—and more," he returned unemotionally. "But consider, even if you beat us at every turn through personal influence, you will pay dearly for your victories in money, in peace, in reputation. These things will leave a stigma which will outlast you. It will arouse suspicion of your ability and skill among your private patients who now trust you. You'll have to fight every inch of the road to retain your ground, or any part of it, against the new and abler physicians who must come with the growth of the country. You'll not be wanted by your best friends when it comes to a case of life and death. You'll become only a kind of licensed midwife rushing about from one accouchement to another, and, even for this, you must finesse and intrigue in the manner which has made the incompetents of your sex in medicine the bête noir of the profession."

The sneering smile she had forced faded as he talked. It was like the deliberate voice of Prophecy, drawing pictures which she had seen in waking nightmares that she called the "blues" and was wont to drive away with a drink or a social call outside.

She raised her chin from her chest where it had sunk, and summoned her courage.

"You have taken a great deal of trouble to inform yourself upon the subject of the medical profession and my unfitness for it."

The Dago Duke hesitated and an expression which was new to it crossed his face, a look of mingled pride and pain.

"I have gone to less trouble than you think," he answered finally. "I was reared in the atmosphere of medicine. My father was a beloved and trusted physician to the royal family of my country. I was to have followed in his footsteps and partially prepared myself to do so. The reason that I have not is not too difficult to guess since it is the same which sends me sheep-herding at $40 a month."

"But my identity is neither here nor there." The Dago Duke threw up his hand with a characteristic, foreign gesture as though dismissing himself from the conversation and half regretting even so much of his personal history. "It serves but one purpose and that is that you may know that the degrees which I have earned, not bought, qualify me to speak of your ability, or lack of it, with rather more authority than the average layman's." He arose languidly and sauntered across the room where he stood looking up at her framed diploma, and added, "To judge, too, of the value of a sheepskin like that. How much did you pay for it, Doc?" Seeming to expect no reply, he continued serenely, "Well I'll have to be going. Stake me to a cigarette paper? I haven't talked so much or been so strongly moved since my remittance was reduced to $100 a month. I can't get drunk like a gentlemen on that—you couldn't yourself—and it's an inhuman outrage. It may drive me to reform—I've thought of it. You're such a sympathetic listener, Doc. It makes me babble." His hand was on the door-knob. "Since you've nothing to say I suppose you mean to stick to your story, but you must admit, Doc, I've at least been as much of a gentleman as a rattlesnake. I'm rattling before I strike."

The door had closed upon his back when she tore it open.

"Wait a minute!" She was panting as though she had been running a distance. He saw, too, the desperation in her eyes. "Give me—a little—time!"

The Dago Duke's tone was one of easy friendliness.

"All you need, but don't forget the suspense is hard on Essie Tisdale."

XXVII

Essie Tisdale's Moment.

Mrs. Sylvanus Starr, who was indisposed, sat up in her *robe de nuit* of pink, striped outing-flannel and looked down into the street.

"Pearline," she said hastily, "turn the dish-pan over the roast beef and cache the oranges. Planchette, hide the cake and just lay this sweet chocolate under the mattress—the doctor's coming."

"She cleaned us out last time all right," commented Lucille.

"Her legs are hollow," observed Camille, "she can eat half a sheep."

"What's half a sheep to a growing girl?" inquired Mrs. Starr as she plucked at her pompadour and straightened the counterpane.

The Starrs were still tittering when Dr. Harpe walked in. Their hilarity quickly passed at the sight of her face. Another intelligence, a new personality from which they unconsciously shrank looked at them through Dr. Harpe's familiar features. The Starrs were not analytical nor given to psychology, therefore it was no subtle change which could make them stare. It was as though a ruthless hand had torn away a mask disclosing a woman who only resembled some one they had known. She was a trifle more than thirty and she looked to-day a haggard forty-five.

A grayish pallor had settled upon her face, and her neck, by the simple turning of her head, had the lines of withered old age. Her lips were colorless, and dry, and drooped in a kind of sneering cruelty, while her restless, glittering eyes contained the malice and desperation of a vicious animal when it's cornered. The uneasiness and erratic movements of a user of cocaine was in her manner.

"What ails you now?" Her voice was harsh and Mrs. Starr flushed at the blunt question.

She saw that Dr. Harpe was not listening to her reply.

"Get this filled." The prescription she wrote and handed her was scarcely legible. "I'll be in again."

She stalked downstairs without more words.

The Starrs looked at each other blankly when she had gone.

"What's the matter with Dr. Harpe?"

Elsewhere throughout the town the same question was being asked. The clairvoyant milliner cautiously asked the baker's wife as they watched her turn the corner—

"Have you noticed anything queer about Dr. Harpe?"

There was that about her which repelled, and those who were wont to pass her on the street with a friendly flourish of the hand and a "Hello, Doc," somehow omitted it and substituted a nod and a stare of curiosity. Her swaggering stride of assurance was a shamble, and, as she came down the street now with her head down, her Stetson pulled low over her eyes, her hand thrust deep in one pocket of her square cut coat, her skirt flapping petticoatless about her, she looked even to the wife of the baker, who liked her, and to the clairvoyant milliner, who imitated her, a caricature upon womankind.

There was a look of evil upon her face at the moment not easy to describe. She and Augusta had quarrelled—for the first time—and when she could least afford to quarrel.

She had spoken often of Andy P. Symes as "the laziest man in Crowheart" and Augusta always had giggled; to-day she had resented it. Was it, Dr. Harpe asked herself, that she was losing control of Augusta because she was losing her own? Nothing more disastrous could happen to her at this time than to lose her footing in the Symes household. Her power over Symes went with her prestige, for her word would have little weight if the Dago Duke even partially carried out his threats. Her disclosure would appear but the last resort of malice and receive little credence.

As she walked down the street with bent head she was asking herself if the props were to be pulled from beneath her one by one, if the invisible lines emanating from her own acts were tightening about her to her undoing?

With a fierce gesture she pushed these thoughts from her as though they were tangible things. No, no! she would not be beaten! Insomnia, narcotics and stimulants had unnerved her for the time, but she was strong enough to pull herself together and stay the circumstances which threatened to swamp her midway in her career. Bolstered for the moment by this resolve, she threw back her head and raised her eyes.

The Dago Duke, Dan Treu, and an important looking stranger were crossing the street and she felt intuitively that it was for the purpose of meeting her face to face. The Dago Duke bowed with his exaggerated salutation of respect as they passed, the deputy-sheriff with an odd constraint of manner, while the stranger who raised his hat in formal politeness gave her a look which seemed to search her soul. It frightened her. Who was he? She had seen him at old Dubois's funeral. Was he some new factor to be reckoned with, or was it merely her crazy nerves that made her see fresh danger at every turn, a new enemy in every stranger?

She climbed the stairs to her office in a kind of nervous frenzy. She felt like screaming, like beating upon the walls with her bare fists. Inaction was no longer possible. She must do something, else this agony of uncertainty and suspense would drive her mad. She strode up and down at a pace which left her breathless, clenching and unclenching her hands, while thickly, between set teeth, she raved at Essie Tisdale, upon whom her vonom concentrated.

"I could throttle her!" She looked at her curved, outspread fingers, tense and strong as steel hooks. "I could choke her with my own hands till she is black! Curse her—curse her! She's been a stumbling block in my way ever since I came. The sight of her is a needle in my flesh. I'd only want a minute if I could get my fingers on her throat! I'd shut that baby mouth of hers for good and all. God! How I hate her!" She hissed the words in venomous intensity, racked with the strength of her emotions, weak from it, her ghastly face moist with perspiration.

"I've humiliated her!" she gasped. "I've made her suffer. I've downed her, but there's something left yet that I haven't crushed! I'm not satisfied; I haven't done enough. I want to break her spirit, to break her heart, to finish her for all time!"

She groped for the door-knob as one who sees dimly, and all but ran down the corridor. Even as she went the thought flashed through her mind that she was making a fool of herself, that she was being led by an impulse for which she would be sorry.

But she was at a pitch where the voice of caution had no weight; she wanted what she wanted and in her heart she knew that she was going to Essie Tisdale with the intention of inflicting physical pain. Nothing less would satisfy her. Yet, when the door opened in response to her knock, her upper lip stretched in its straight, mirthless smile.

"Hello, Ess!" She stepped back a bit into the dimly lighted corridor and the girl all but shrank from the malice glowing in her eyes.

Essie did not immediately respond, so she asked in mock humility—

"Can't I come in, Mrs. Dubois?"

She saw the girl wince at the name by which no one as yet had called her.

"Why this timidity, this unexpected politeness, when it's not usual for you even to knock?"

She stepped inside and closed the door behind her.

"True enough, Mrs. Dubois, but naturally a poor country doctor like me would hesitate before bolting in upon the privacy of a rich widow."

"If you use 'poor' in the sense of incompetent I am afraid I must agree with you," was the unexpected answer.

"Ah, beginning to feel your oats, my dear." She slouched into the nearest chair and flung her hat carelessly upon the floor.

"You notice it, my dear?" mimicked Essie Tisdale.

"When a range cayuse has a few square meals he gets onery."

"While they merely give a well-bred horse spirit."

Dr. Harpe looked at her searchingly. There was

a change in Essie Tisdale. She had a new confidence of manner, a cool poise that was older than her years, while that intangible something which she could never crush looked at her more defiantly than ever from the girl's sparkling eyes. She had a feeling that Essie Tisdale welcomed her coming. Certainly her assurrance and animation was strangely at variance with her precarious positon. What had happened? Dr. Harpe intended to learn before she left the room.

"At any rate you've paid high for your oats, Ess," she said finally.

The girl agreed coolly—

"Very."

"And you're not done paying," she added significantly.

"That remains to be seen."

Dr. Harpe's eyes narrowed in thought.

"Ess," in a patronizing drawl, "why don't you pull your freight? I'll advance you the money myself."

"Run away? Why?"

"You're going to be arrested—that's a straight tip. You may get off, but think what you'll have to go through first. Skip till things simmer down. They'll not go after you."

The girl flashed a smile of real merriment at her, which almost cost Dr. Harpe her self-control. The young and now glowing beauty of the girl before her, the unconscious air of superiority and confidence which had its wellspring in some mysterious source was maddening to her. The interview was taxing her self-control to the limit and she felt that in some inexplicable way the tables were turning.

"You—won't go, then?" Her voice held a menace.

"Why should I, since I am innocent? Take a vacation yourself, Dr. Harpe, with the money you so generously offer me. You need it."

She followed the girl's dancing eyes to the mirror opposite which was tilted so that it reflected the whole of her uncouth pose. Slid far down in the chair with her heels resting on the floor and wrinkling hose exposed above her boottops, a knot of dull, red hair slipped to one side with shorter ends hanging in dishevelment about her face, she looked—the thought was her own—like a drab of the streets in the magistrate's court in the morning. She was startled, shocked by her own appearance. Was she, Emma Harpe, as old, as haggard, as evil-looking as that!

She had clung with peculiar tenacity to the hallucination that she still had youthful charm of face and figure. As she stared, it seemed as though the sand was sliding a little faster from beneath her feet. She shoved the loose knot of hair to its place and straightened herself, growing hot at the realization that she had betrayed to Essie Tisdale something of her consternation.

She turned upon her fiercely—

"Look here, Ess, if you want to be friends with me, and have my influence to get you out of this mess, you'd better change your tactics."

"Haven't I yet made it clear to you that I care no more for your friendship than for your enmity? Do you imagine that you can frighten liking, or force respect after the occasion which we both remember?"

"There's one thing I can do—I can make Crowheart too hot to hold you!" Her grip on herself was going fast.

Essie Tisdale stood up and, folding her arms, drew

herself to her slim height while she looked at her in contemptuous silence.

"I know there is no low thing to which you would not stoop to make good your boast. You make me think of a viper that has exhausted its venom. You have the disposition to strike, but you no longer have the power."

"You think not? And why? Do you imagine that your position in Crowheart will be changed one iota by the fact that you've got a few dollars that are red with blood?" She flung the taunt at her with savage insolence.

"My position in Crowheart is of no importance to me. But"—her voice cut like finely tempered steel—"don't goad me too far. Don't forget that I know you for what you are—a moral plague—creeping like a pestilence among people who are not familiar with your face. I know, and you *know* that I know you are in no position, Dr. Harpe, to point a finger at the commonest women in the dance hall below."

The woman sprang from her chair and walked to her with the crouching swiftness of a preying animal. She grasped Essie Tisdale's wrist in a grip which left its imprint for hours after.

"How dare you!"

Essie Tisdale raised her chin higher.

"How dare I?" She smiled in the infuriated woman's face. "It takes no courage for me to oppose you now. When I was a biscuit-shooter here, as you lost no opportunity to remind me, you loomed large! That time has gone by. Crowheart will know you some day as I know you. Your name will be a byword in every saloon and bunk-house in the country!"

"I'll *kill* you!"

The tense fingers were curved like steel hooks as she sprang for Essie Tisdale's slender throat, but even as the girl shoved her chair between them a masculine voice called "Esther" and a rap came upon the door.

Doctor Harpe's arms dropped to her side and she clutched handfuls of her skirt as she struggled for self-control.

Essie Tisdale walked swiftly to the door and threw it wide. The towering stranger stood in the corridor looking in amazement from one woman to the other.

The girl turned and said with careful distinctness:

"You have been so occupied of late that perhaps you have not heard the news. My uncle—Mr. Richard Kincaid—Dr. Harpe."

XXVIII

The Sweetest Thing in the World

Dr. Harpe standing at her office window saw the lovely Pearline Starr, curled and dressed at ten in the morning, trip down the street bearing a glass of buffalo berry jelly in her white-gloved hands, while Mrs. Percy Parrott sitting erect in the Parrotts' new, second-hand surrey, drove toward the hotel, carefully protecting from accident some prized package which she held in her lap. Mrs. Parrott was wearing her new ding-a-ling hat, grass-green in color, which, topping off the moss-colored serge which, closely fitting her attenuated figure, gave Mrs. Parrott a surprising resemblance to a katydid about to jump.

Dr. Harpe could not see Mrs. Abe Tutts walking gingerly across lots carrying a pot of baked beans and brown bread in her two hands, nor Mrs. Alva Jackson panting up another street with a Lady Baltimore cake in the hope of reaching the hotel before her dearest friend and enemy Mrs. Tutts, but Dr. Harpe knew from what she already had seen and from the curious glances cast at the windows of the Terriberry House, that the town was agog with Essie Tisdale's romantic story and her newly established relationship to the important looking stranger. Mrs. Terriberry could be trusted to attend to that and in her capable hands it was certain to lose nothing in the telling.

The story was simple enough in itself and had its counterpart in many towns throughout the West. Young Dick Kincaid had run away from his home on the bank of the Mississippi River to make his fortune in the mining camps of the far West. He did not write, because the fortune was always just a little farther on. The months slipped into years, and when he returned with the "stake" which was to be his peace offering, the name of Kincaid was but a memory in the community, and the restless Mississippi with its ever-changing channel flowed over the valuable tract of black-walnut timber which had constituted the financial resources of the Kincaids. The little sister had married a westerner as poor as he was picturesque, and against her parents' wishes. They had gone, never to be heard from again, disappeared mysteriously and completely, and Samuel Kincaid had died, he and his wife, as much of loneliness and longing as of age.

The triumphant return of his boyish dreams was, instead, an acute and haunting remorse. The success that had been his, the success that was to be his in the near-by city, never erased the bitter disappointment of that home-coming. He had searched in vain for some trace of the little sister whom he had loved. He had never given up hoping and that hope had had its weight in influencing him to make the tedious trip to Crowheart.

And then, as though the Fates had punished him enough for his filial neglect, his sister's eyes had looked out at him from the flower-like face at the funeral of old Edouard Dubois. He had followed up his impulse, and the rest is quickly told, for all Crowheart knew the story of Essie Tisdale's miraculous rescue and of the picture primer which had furnished the single clue to her identity.

With the news of Essie Tisdale's altered position—and Mrs. Terriberry missed no opportunity to convey the impression that Kincaid's resources were unlimited—the tide turned and the buffalo berry jelly, the Lady Baltimore cake, baked beans and Mrs. Parrott's tinned lobster salad, were the straws which in Crowheart always showed which way the wind was blowing. That the ladies bearing these toothsome offerings had not been speaking to Essie for some months past was a small matter which they deemed best to forget.

Not so Mrs. Terriberry.

Mrs. Terriberry not only had Essie Tisdale's score to pay off but her own as well, and who knows but that the latter was the sharper incentive? To have been obliged to watch through a crack in the curtain the fashionable world rustle by on its way to Mrs. Alva Jackson's euchre had occasioned a pang not easily forgotten. To have knowledge of the monthly meetings of Mrs. Parrott's Shadow Embroidery Class only through the Society Column of the Crowheart *Courier* and to be deprived of the privilege of hearing Mrs. Abe Tutts's paper upon Wagnerian music at the Culture Club were slights that rankled.

She was suspiciously close at hand when the ladies appeared in the office of the Terriberry House with their culinary successes; also she was wearing the red foulard which never went out of the closet except to funerals and important functions.

Although the most conspicuous thing about these early callers was the parcels they carried, Mrs. Terriberry chose to ignore them.

"Why, how do you do, Mrs. Parrott, and Miss Starr, too. It's a lovely day to be out, isn't it?" Her voice was distinctly patronizing and she extended a languid hand to Mrs. Jackson. "And usin' your brain like you do, Mrs. Tutts, writin' them pieces for the Culture Club, I suppose you have to git exercise."

"I've brought Essie some lobster salad from a receipt that mamma sent me," said Mrs. Parrott when she could get an opening, "and while it's canned lobster, it's really delicious!"

"The whites of sixteen aigs I put in this Lady Baltimore cake, and it's light as a feather."

Mrs. Terriberry made no offer to take the package which Mrs. Jackson extended.

"Just a little taste of buffalo berry jelly for Essie," said Miss Starr, with her most radiant smile. "Her uncle might enjoy it."

"I ain't forgot," said Mrs. Tutts, "how fond Ess is of brown bread, so I says to myself I'll just take some of my baked beans along, too. Tutts says I beat the world on baked beans. Where's Ess? I'd like to see her."

"Yes; tell her we're here," chorused the others.

Mrs. Terriberry's moment had come. She drew herself up in a pose of hauteur which a stout person can only achieve with practice.

"Miss Tisdale," she replied with glib gusto, "is engaged at present and begs to be excused. But," she added in words which were obviously her own, "you can put your junk in the closet over there with the rest that's come."

Dr. Harpe understood perfectly now the meaning of the Dago Duke's confident smile and the stranger's cold, searching look of enmity. He was no weakling, this new-found relative of Essie Tisdale's, and the Dago Duke's threats were no longer empty boastings.

If only she could sleep! Sleep? Was it days or weeks since she had slept? Forebodings, suspicions of those whom she had been forced to trust, Nell Beecroft, Lamb, and others, were spectres that frightened sleep from her strained eyes. A tight band seemed stretched across her forehead. She rubbed it hard, as though to lessen the tension. There was a dull ache at the base of her brain and she shook her head to free herself from it, but the jar hurt her.

Some one whistled in the corridor. She listened.

"Farewell, my own dear Napoli, Farewell to Thee, Farewell to Thee——" How she hated that song! The Dago Duke was coming for his answer.

He stood before her with his hat in his hand, the other hand resting on his hip smiling, confident, the one long, black lock of hair hanging nearly in his eyes. He made no comment, but she saw that he was noting the ravages which the intervening hours had left in her face. Beneath his smile there was something hard and pitiless—a look that the executioner of a de Medici might have worn—and for a moment it put her at a loss for words. Then with an attempt at her old-time camaraderie, she shoved a glass toward him—

His white teeth flashed in a fleeting smile—

"If you will join me—in my last drink?"

For answer she filled his glass and hers.

He raised it and looked at her.

"I give you—the sweetest thing in the world."

Her lip curled.

"Love?"

His black eyes glittered between their narrowed lids.

"The power to avenge the wrongs of the helpless."

He set down his empty glass and fumbled in his pocket for a paper which he handed her to read.

"It's always well to know what you're signing," he said, and he watched her face as her eyes followed the lines, with the intent yet impersonal scrutiny of a specialist studying his case.

She looked, as she read, like a corpse that has been propped to a sitting position, with nostrils sunken and lips of Parian marble. Her hand shook with a violence which recalled her to herself, and when she raised her eyes they looked as though the iris itself had faded. The Dago Duke seemed absorbed in the curious effect.

He could hear the dryness of her mouth when she asked at last—

"You expect me—to put my name—to this?"

He inclined his head.

"It is—*impossible!*"

He replied evenly:

"It is necessary."

"You are asking me to sign my own death warrant."

He lifted his shoulders.

"It is your reputation or Essie Tisdale's."

The name seemed to prick her like a goad. Her hands and body twitched nervously and then he saw swift decision arrive in her face.

"I'll not do it!"

As moved by a common impulse they arose.

"It's the lesser of two evils."

"I don't care!" She reiterated in a kind of hopeless desperation, "I don't care—I'll fight!"

He eyed her again with a recurrence of his impersonal professional scrutiny.

"You can't go through it, Doc; you haven't the stamina, any more. You don't know what you're up against, for I haven't half showed my hand. I have no personal grievance, as you know, but the wrongs of my countrymen are my wrongs, and for your brutality to them you shall answer to me. Fight if you will, but when you're done you'll not disgrace your profession again in this or any other State."

While this scene was occurring in Doctor Harpe's office, Andy P. Symes in his office was toying impatiently with an unopened letter from Mudge as Mr. Percy Parrott, hat in hand, stood before him.

"It's not that I'm worried at all, Mr. Symes"—every line of Parrott's face was deep-lined with anxiety as he spoke—"but, of course, I've made you these loans largely upon my own responsibility, I've exceeded my authority, in fact, and any failure on your part——" Mr. Parrott finding himself floundering under Symes's cold gaze blurted out desperately, "Well, 'twould break us!"

"Certainly, certainly, I know all that, but, really, these frequent duns—this Homeseekers' Excursion has put me behind with my work, but as soon as things are straightened out again——"

"Oh, of course. That's all right. I understand, but as soon as you conveniently can——"

Mr. Parrott's lengthened jaw rested between the "white wings" of his collar as he turned away. It might have reached his shirt-stud had he known the number of creditors that had preceded him.

Even Symes's confident assurances that the complete failure of the Homeseekers' Excursion was relatively a small matter, could not entirely eradicate from the minds of Crowheart's merchants the picture presented by the procession of excursionists returning with their satchels to the station, glowering at Crowheart's citizens as they passed and making loud charges of misrepresentation and fraud.

When the door closed behind him Symes dropped the catch that he might read Mudge's bulky letter undisturbed. Mudge's diction was ever open to criticism, but he had a faculty for conveying his meaning which genius well might envy.

The letter read:

MY DEAR SYMES:

Are you the damnedest fool or the biggest scoundrel out of jail? Write and let me know.

I told you there was something wrong; that some outside influence was queering us all along the line and I let myself be talked out of my conviction by you instead of getting busy and finding out the truth.

The stock and bond-holders have had a meeting and are going to ask the court to appoint a Receiver, and when he gets through with us we'll cut as much ice in the affairs of the Company as two office-boys, with no cause for complaint if we keep out of jail.

There's been a high-priced engineer doing detective work on the project for days and his report would n't be apt to swell your head. The bond-holders know more about the Symes Irrigation Company and conditions under the project than I ever did.

They know that your none too perfect water-right won't furnish water for a third of the land under the ditch. They know that if you had every water-right on the river that there's some ten thousand acres of high land that could n't be reached with a fire-hose. They know that there's another thousand or so where the soil is n't deep enough to grow radishes, let alone sugar-beets. They know, too, that instead of the $250,000 of your estimate to complete the ditch it will require nearly half a million, and they're on to the fact that in order to get this estimate you cut your own engineer's figures in two, and then some, upon the cost of making cuts and handling loose rock.

Rough work, Symes, raw even for a green hand. You've left a trail of blood a yard wide behind you.

Furthermore, the report contained the information that

the wide business experience which you lost no occasion to mention consisted chiefly of standing off your creditors in various sections of the country.

I trust that I have made it quite plain to you that we 're down and out. I have about as much weight in financial circles as a second-story man, and am regarded in much the same light, while you are as important as a cipher without the rim.

And the man behind all this, the largest bond-holder, the fellow that has pulled the strings, is not the Fly-Trap King, or even J. Collins Prescott, but the man he works for, Ogden Van Lennop, whose present address happens to be Crowheart.

What 's the answer? Why has a man like Van Lennop who is there on the ground and has long been familiar with conditions, why has he become the largest investor? Why should he tie up money in a project which the engineer reports will never pay more than a minimum rate of interest upon the investment even when the Company is re-organized and the ditch pushed to completion under economical and capable management? Why has he come in the Company for the one purpose of wrecking it? Why has he stuck the knife between your short ribs and mine—and turned it? What 's the answer, Symes, you must know?

We might as well buck the Bank of England as the Van Lennops, or match our wits against the Secret Service. They 've got us roped and tied and I'd advise you not to squeal.

Truly yours,

S. B. MUDGE

Symes laid down the letter and smoothed it carefully, setting a small brass crocodile exactly in the centre. Wiping his clammy palms upon one of the handkerchiefs purchased on his wedding tour, the texture of which always gave him a pleasurable sense of refinement and well-being, he read again the line which showed below the paper-weight:

There 's one thing sure—we 're down and out.

Symes's head sunk weakly forward. Down and out! Not even Mudge knew how far down and out!

Stripped of the hope of success, robbed of the position which he had made for himself, his self-esteem punctured, his home-life a mockery, no longer young—it was the combination which makes a man whose vanity is his strength, lose his grip. To be little where he had been big; to be the object of his ruined neighbors' scorn—men have blown their brains out in his mood, and for less.

What Mudge and the Company regarded as wilful misrepresentations had in the beginning been due to inexperience and ignorance of an undertaking which it required scientific knowledge to successfully carry out. When the truth had been gradually borne in upon him as the work progressed, he felt that it was too late to explain or retract if he would raise more money and keep his position. The real cost he believed would frighten possible investors and with the peculiar sanguineness of the short-sighted, he thought that it would work out somehow.

And all had gone well until Mudge's unheeded warning had come that some subtle but formidable influence was at work to their undoing.

The dull red of mortification crept slowly over Symes's face as he realized that Ogden Van Lennop, before whom he had boasted of his lineage, and patronized, was a conspicuous member of a family whose name was all but a household word throughout the land!

But why, Symes asked the question that Mudge had asked, why should Van Lennop thrust the knife between his short ribs—and turn it? It could not be because Van Lennop had resented his patronage and his vaporings to any such extent as this; he was not that kind. No; he had been touched deeper than his pride or any petty vanity.

Another question like an answer to his first flashed through his mind. Could it be—was it possible that his attentions to Essie Tisdale, the biscuit-shooter of the Terriberry House, had been sincere?

Symes rose in sudden excitement and paced the floor.

He believed it was! The belief grew to conviction and he dropped again into his chair. If this was it he need expect no quarter. As his thoughts flashed back over the past the fact began to stand out clearly that nearly every unfriendly act he had shown the girl had been instigated by Doctor Harpe and accomplished through Augusta.

"That woman!" The veins swelled in his temples. "Always that woman!" and as though in answer to her name he saw her pass the window and shake the latched door.

"Let me in!" It was a peremptory demand.

Symes threw the catch back hard.

"Yes, Dr. Harpe, I'll let you in. I've business with you. For the first time in my life I want to see you." His tone was brutal. "Sit down!" He laid his huge hand upon her shoulder and thrust her into a chair.

Towering above her in the red-faced, loud-voiced fury of a man who has lost his self-control, he shouted:

"I want you to get out! To quit! To leave this town! Twenty-four hours I'll give you to get your traps together. Do you hear? If you don't, so help me God, I'll put you where you belong! Don't speak," he raised his hand as though to forestall her,

HE LAID HIS HUGE HAND UPON HER SHOULDER AND THRUST HER INTO A CHAIR.

"lest I forget your sex." He went on, inarticulate with passion: "I've protected you as long as I can—as long as I'm going to. Do you understand? I'm done. I've got some little self-respect left; not much, but enough to see me through this. And you can tell Augusta Symes that if she wants to go, every door is open wide! Tell her—tell her that for me!"

He stopped, choked with the violence of his feelings, and in the pause which followed she sat looking up at him unmoved. The shock seemed to quiet her. Then, too, it was so like another scene indelibly engraved upon her memory that she wanted to laugh—actually to laugh. Yet Symes's violence cut her less than had the cool, impersonal voice of the coroner back there in that little Nebraska town. She found his blazing eyes far easier to meet than the cold unfriendliness in the gaze of the man who had delivered that other ultimatum. Perhaps it was because she believed she had less to fear. Symes dared not—*dared* not, she told herself—enforce his threats.

Symes read something of this thought in her face and it maddened him. Was it not possible to make her comprehend? Was she really so callous, so thick-skinned that she was immune from insult? His hand dropped once more upon her shoulder.

"I'm ruined—do you understand?" He shook her. "I'm down and out. I'm broke; and so is Crowheart!" She winced under his tightening grip. "The smash was due when Van Lennop said the word. He's said it." He felt her start at the name and there was something like fear in her face at last. "Van Lennop," he reiterated, "Van Lennop that you've made my enemy to gratify your personal spite and jealousy." He continued through clenched teeth:

"From the beginning you've used me to further your petty ends. It's plain enough to me now, for, with all your fancied cleverness, you're transparent as a window-pane when one understands you're character. You've silenced me, I admit it, and blackmailed me through my pride and ambition, but you've reached the limit. You can't do it any more. I've none left.

"You expect to cling to my coat-tails to keep yourself up. You look to my position for shelter, but let me make it clear to you that you can't hide behind my prestige and my position any longer. You human sponge! You parasite! Do you think I'm blind because I've been dumb? Go! you—DEGENERATE! By God! you go before I kill you!"

In his insane fury he pulled her to her feet by the shoulders of her loose-cut coat where she stood looking at him uncertainly, her faded eyes set in a gray mask.

"See here, Mr. Symes, see here——" she said in a kind of vague belligerence.

Symes pushed her toward the door as Adolph Kunkel passed.

"Will you go?" Symes shouted.

She turned on the sidewalk and faced him. The gray mask wore a sneer.

"Not alone."

"Hi, Doc!" Kunkel pointed to a straight, black pillar of smoke rising at the station, and yelled in local parlance: "Look there! Your beau's come That's the Van Lennop Special!"

XXIX

"The Bitter End"

"She ain't here." Nell Beecroft, with arms akimbo, blocked the hospital door.

"Upon your honor, Nell?"

She looked the sheriff squarely in the eyes.

"Upon my honor, Dan."

She saw the doubt lying behind his look, but she did not flinch.

"When she comes, send me word. No," on second thought, "you needn't; I'll be back." He tapped the inside pocket of his coat significantly. " I want to see Dr. Harpe most particular."

" I'll tell her," the woman answered shortly. She watched him down the street. "He knows I'm lyin'," she muttered, and though the heat was unusual, she closed the door behind her.

The muffled sound of beating fists drew her to the cellarway.

"Nell—let me out! Quick! Open the door!"

Nell Beecroft took a key from her apron pocket and demanded harshly as she turned it in the lock:

"What's the matter with you, anyhow?"

Dr. Harpe stumbled blinking into the light.

"Oh-h-h!" she gasped in relief.

"You'd better stay cached." Nell Beecroft eyed, with a look of contempt, the woman for whom she had lied. "Dan Treu was here; he's got a warrant."

"I don't care—I'll not go down there!" She pinned wildly at the loosened knot of dull red hair which lay upon her shoulders. " That was fierce!"

She looked in horror down the dusky cellarway.

"What ails you, Harpe?" There was no sympathy in the harsh voice.

Dr. Harpe laughed—a foolish, apologetic laugh.

"Spooks—Nell! I'm nervous—I'm all unstrung. Moses! I thought all the arms and legs we've amputated were chasin' me upstairs. Did you hear me scream?"

"No," the woman reiterated sharply. "Dan Treu was here. He wants to see you most particular."

"You didn't tell him——"

"Of course not."

"You won't go back on me, Nell?"

The woman regarded her in cold dislike.

"No, I'll not go back on you, Harpe. A man or a woman that ain't got some redeemin' trait, some one thing that you can bank on, is no good on earth, and stickin' to them I've throwed in with happens to be mine. What you goin' to do? stay and brazen it out—this mess you're in—or quit the flat?"

"Nell," she replied irrelevantly with a quick, uncertain glance around, "I'm *afraid.* Do you know what it is to be afraid?"

"I've been scart," the woman answered curtly.

"I've a queer, sinkin' feeling here," she laid her hand at the pit of her stomach, "and my back feels weak—all gone. My knees take spells of wobblin' when I walk. I'm afraid in the dark. I'm afraid in the light. Not so much of any one thing as of some big, intangible thing that hasn't happened. I can't shake off the feeling. It's horrible. My mind won't stop thinkin' of things I don't want to think of. My nerves are a wreck, Nell. I've lost my grip, my judgment. I'm not myself."

Nell Beecroft listened in hard curiosity, eyeing her critically.

"Oh, yes, you are, only you've never really seen yourself before. You've took your brass for courage. Lots of people do that till some real show-down comes."

"Look here, Nell,"—her voice held a whine of protest—" you haven't got me sized up right." Yet in her heart she knew that the woman's brutal analysis was true. Better even than Nell Beecroft she knew that what passed with her following for shrewdness and courage in reality was callousness and calculating cynicism.

The woman ignored the interruption and went on—

"So long as you could swagger around with Andy P. Symes to bolster you up and a crowd of old women to flatter you, you could put up a front, but you ain't the kind, Harpe, that can turn your back to the wall, fold your arms, and sling defiance at the town if they all turn on you."

"But they won't."

"You've got a kind of mulishness, and you've got gall, and when things are goin' your way you'll take long chances, but they ain't the traits that gives a person the sand to stand out in the open with their head up and let the storms whip thunder out of them without a whimper."

"It's my nerves, I tell you; they're shot to pieces —the strain I've been under—everything goin' wrong —pilin' on me like a thousand of brick."

"Is it goin' to be any better?"

"Some of my friends will stick," Dr. Harpe repeated stubbornly.

"Sure, they will. A woman like you will always

have a followin' among the igner'nt and weak-minded."

"What you roastin' me for like this?" The woman's brutal frankness touched her at last. "Who and what do you think you are yourself?"

"Nothin'," Nell Beecroft returned composedly. "Nobody at all. Just the wife of a horse-thief that's doin' time. But," and her hard, gray eyes flashed in momentary pride, "he learnt me the diffrunce between sand and a yellow-streak. They sent fifty men to take him out of the hills, and when he was handed his medicine he swallowed the whole dose to save his pardner, and never squeaked."

Nell Beecroft walked to the window swallowing hard at the lump which rose in her throat.

"If I could sleep—get one night's decent sleep——"

"When you collapse you'll go quick," opined the woman unemotionally.

"But I'm goin' to see it through —I'll stick to the bitter end—I'm no coward——"

"Ain't you?" Sudden excitement leaped into Nell Beecroft's voice and she stared hard down the street. "Unless I'm mistaken you're goin' to have as fine a chance to prove it as anybody I ever see. Come here." She pointed to a gesticulating mob which was turning the corner where the road led from the Symes Irrigation Project into town.

"The dagos!" Dr. Harpe's voice was a whisper of fear.

"They're on the prod," Nell Beecroft said briefly, and strode to the cellar-door. "Cache yourself!" She would have thrust Dr. Harpe down the stairway.

"No—no—not there! I can't! I'd scream!" She

shrank back in unfeigned horror. "I'm goin' to run for it, Nell! The Dago Duke has ribbed this up on me!" From force of habit she reached for her black medicine case as she swung her Stetson on her head. "If I can get to Symes's house—down the alley—they can't see me——"

Nell Beecroft, with curling lips, stood in the kitchen doorway and watched her go. Crouching, with her head bent, she ran through the alley, panting, wild-eyed in her exaggerated fear.

A big band of bleating sheep on the way to the loading pens at the station blocked her way where she would have crossed the street to Symes's house. She swore in a frenzy of impatience as she waited for them to pass in the cloud of choking dust raised by their tiny, pointed hoofs.

"Way 'round 'em, Shep!" The voice was familiar. "Hullo, Doc!" The Sheep King of Poison Creek waved a grimy, genial hand.

"Hurry your infernal woolers along, can't you?" she yelled in response.

That other cloud of dust rising above the road which led from the Symes Irrigation Project into town was coming closer. She plunged among the sheep, forcing a path for herself through the moving mass of woolly backs.

"You're in a desprit rush, looks like. They won't die till you get there!" The Sheep King was not too pleased as he ran to head the sheep she had turned.

"Like the devil was after her." He watched her bound up the steps of Symes's veranda and burst through the doorway.

The engineer had steam up and the last half dozen sheep were being prodded into the last car of the long train bound for the Eastern market when the Sheep King of Poison Creek drew his shirt sleeve across his moist forehead in relief and observed with feeling:

"Of all the contrary—onery—say, Bill, there's them as says sheep is fools!"

It took a moment for this surprising assertion to sink into his helper's brain.

"They as says sheep is fools——" Bill, the herder's voice rang with scorn, "them as says sheep is fools——" great mental effort was visible upon his blank countenace as he groped for some word or combination of words sufficiently strong to express his opinion of those who doubted the intelligence of sheep —"is fools themselves," he added lamely, finding none.

"Guess we're about ready to pull out. Get aboard, Bill." The Sheep King, squinting along the track where the banked cinders radiated heat waves, was watching, not the signalling brakeman, but a figure skulking in the shade of the red water-tank. "It looks like——"

The heavy train of bleating sheep began to crawl up the grade. The Sheep King stood at the door of the rear car looking fixedly at the slinking figure so obviously waiting for the caboose to pass.

Dr. Harpe threw her black medicine case upon the platform.

"Give us a hand." The words were a demand, but there was appeal in the eyes upturned to his as she thrust up her own hand.

"Sure." The cordiality in the Sheep King's voice was forced as he dragged her aboard; and in his curious looks, his constraint of manner, the sly glances and averted, grinning faces of his helpers inside, Dr. Harpe read her fate.

"Your name," Essie Tisdale had said, "will be a byword in every sheep-camp and bunk-house in the country."

Sick with a baffled feeling of defeat and the realization that the prophecy of the girl she hated already had come true, Dr. Harpe sat on the top step of the caboose, her chin buried in her hands, with moody, malignant eyes watching Crowheart fade as the bleating, ill-smelling sheep train crept up the grade.

XXX

"Thicker Than Water"

Essie Tisdale pulled aside the coarse lace curtains starched to asbesteroid stiffness which draped the front windows of the upstairs parlor in the Terriberry House, and looked with growing interest at an excited and rapidly growing group on the wide sidewalk in front of the post-office.

Such gatherings in Crowheart nearly always portended a fight, but since the hub of the fast widening circle appeared to be Mr. Percy Parrott gesticulating wildly with a newspaper, she concluded that it was merely a sensational bit of news which had come from the outside world. Yet the citizens of Crowheart were not given to exhibiting concern over any happening which did not directly concern themselves, and Dr. Lamb was running. From a hurried walk he broke into a short-stepped, high-kneed prance which was like the action of an English cob, while from across the street dashed Sohmes, the abnormally fat butcher, clasping both hands over his swaying abdomen to lessen the jar.

She turned from the window, and one of the waves of gladness which kept rising within her again swept over her as she realized that the affairs of Crowheart meant nothing to her now. A gulf, invisible as yet, but real as her own existence, lay between her and the life of which she had been a part such a little time before.

She looked about her at the cotton plush furniture of dingy red, at the marble-topped centre table upon whose chilly surface a large, gilt-edged family Bible reposed—placed there by Mrs. Terriberry in the serene confidence that its fair margins would never be defiled through use. Beside the Bible, lay the plush album with its Lombroso-like villainous gallery of countenances upon which transient vandals had pencilled mustaches regardless of sex. She looked at the fly-roost of pampas grass in the sky-blue vase on the shelf from which hung an old-gold lambriquin that represented the highest art of the Kensington cult—water lilies on plush—and at the crowning glory of the parlor, a pier glass in a walnut frame.

It was tawdry and cheap and offended her eye, but it was exclusively her own and she looked about her with a keen thrill of pleasure because of the condition which her occupancy of it represented. Somehow it seemed years ago that she had walked around the hole in the ingrain carpet in the bare room which looked out upon the heap of tin-cans and corrals of the Terriberry House.

Through the door which opened into her bed-chamber she saw the floor littered with boxes and papers, the new near-silk petticoat draping a chair, the new near-tailored suit which represented the "last cry" from the General Merchandise Store, the Parisian hat which the clairvoyant milliner had seen in a trance and trimmed from memory, but the lines of which suggested that the milliner's astral body had practised a deception and projected itself no further than 14th Street.

A fresh realization of what these things meant, namely the personal interest of some one who cared, brought a rush of tears to her eyes. They were still moist when Mr. Richard Kincaid appeared in the parlor, his eyes twinkling above a pillar of boxes and bundles which he carried in his arms.

"What's the matter, Esther? What has happened?" He dropped the packages and went to her side.

She threw her arms impulsively about his neck and laid her head upon his breast while she said between little sobs of tears and laughter—

"I'm so happy! happy! *happy!* Uncle Dick—that's all. And so grateful, too. I love you so much that I want to cry, and so happy that I want to laugh. So I do both. I didn't have to learn to love you. I did from the first. It came with a rush just as soon as I found out who you were—that we belonged to each other, you know. All at once I felt so different—so safe—so sure of you, and so secure—and so proud to think we were related. I can't explain exactly, but just being *me,* so long—not knowing who I was or where I came from—and belonging to no one at all—it seems a wonderful thing to have you!"

She turned her face to his shoulder and cried softly.

He patted her cheek and smiled—a smile that was of sadness and understanding.

"I know what you mean, Esther; I comprehend your feelings perfectly. It's the bond of kinship which you recognize, the tie of blood, and let me tell you, girl, there never was a truer saying than the old one that 'blood is thicker than water.' Disguise it as you will, and bitter family feuds would sometimes seem to give it the lie, but it's a fact just the same. It takes time to find it out—a lifetime often—but deep in the heart of every normal human being there's an instinctive, intimate, personal feeling for one's own flesh and blood that is like nothing else. Their successes and their failures touch us closer, for the pride of race is in us all.

"There's none who realize more strongly the limitations of strangers' friendships than those, who, like you and I, have been dependent upon them as a substitute for the affection of our own. But there, that's done with, loneliness is behind us, for we have each other now; and, bottled up within me, I've the longings of twenty years to spoil and pamper somebody. When I was the marrying age I was off in the hills; since then I've been too busy and too critical. So you see, Esther Kincaid Tisdale, you are filling a long-felt want."

He kissed her with a smack and she hugged his arm in ecstasy.

"I'm going to try and make up for what we both have lost. No harm can come to you so long as I have a dollar and the brains to make more."

"It's like stories I've dreamed!" she breathed happily.

"But tell me,"—some thought made him hold her at arms' length to read her face —" has there been no one, no one at all who has figured in these dreams of yours in a different way from which I do?"

He watched with something like consternation the tell-tale color rise in her face and her eyes drop from his own.

"There was—one," she faltered, "but he—I—misunderstood—I was vain enough to think he cared for me. It was a mistake—a stupid mistake of mine—he just liked me—he was lonely—I suppose—that's all." She swallowed hard to down the rising lump in her throat.

"Who was he?"

"I don't know exactly who he was; he just came here; rode in on horseback—for his health, he said. They used to say he was a hold-up getting the lay of the town to make a raid, or a gambler, but he wasn't, he *wasn't* anything like that. *You'd* have liked him, Uncle Dick, I know you would have liked him!" Her eyes were sparkling now. "He talked like you, and when he was interested enough to exert himself he had the same sure way of doing things. But he went away about three weeks ago and did not even say good-by."

"What's his name?"

She answered with an effort—

"Ogden Van Lennop."

"Van Lennop?" Kincaid's voice was sharp with astonishment. "Why, girl, he's here. He just got in and he's raising Cain in Crowheart! I meant to tell you, but this shopping business quite drove it from my head. The news has only come out that the Symes's Irrigation Company is going into a Receiver's hands and the bondholders will foreclose their mortgages. Look down in the street. There's a mob of workmen from the project and the creditors of your friend Symes considering how they best can extract blood from a turnip. For some reason of his own Van Lennop has gone after Symes's scalp and got it. Don't be too quick to judge him, Esther." But a glance at her face told him he need not plead Van Lennop's cause.

"He meant it, then!" she exclaimed breathlessly. "All that he said that day we rode together. I didn't understand his meaning, but this is it: 'I'll wear your colors in the arena where *men* fight—and win,' he said.

'I'll fight with the weapons I know best how to use.' "

"If he's the member of the family that I think he is," said Kincaid dryly, "it's almost unsportsmanlike for him to go after Symes; it's like a crack pigeon shot shooting a bird sitting."

"And he said," Essie went on, " 'Don't waste your energy in quarrelling with your enemies, concentrate—make money out of them.' "

"Did Van Lennop say that?"

She nodded.

"They'll pay tribute, then. Van Lennop will put this project through in his own good time; but let me prophesy they'll be pitching horse-shoes in the main street of Crowheart first."

The sound of a commotion on the stairs reached them.

"What's broken loose in this man's town now?"

As though in direct answer to Kincaid's question Mrs. Terriberry lunged down the corridor looking like a hippopotamus in red foulard.

"If anything more happens"—Mrs. Terriberry's voice rose shrill and positive—"I shall *die!*"

A lunge in his direction indicated that her demise might take place in Kincaid's arms, but a startled side-step saved him and she sank heavily upon the red plush sofa. Her teeth chattered with a touch of nervous chill and her skin looked mottled.

"She choked her! choked her almost to death! She'd a done it in a minute more only the hired girl broke her holt!"

"Who? What do you mean, Mrs. Terriberry?"

"Dr. Harpe! She choked Gussie Symes because Gussie wouldn't leave her home and go away with her! Did you ever hear such a thing!" She went on in disconnected gasps: "Crazy! Jealous! I don't know what—nobody does—and she's disappeared—they can't find her." Mrs. Terriberry's shudders made the sofa creak. "And her active in church work, which they say her langwudge was awful!"

But Essie Tisdale was listening to another step upon the stair and she trembled when she heard the steps hastening down the corridor.

Van Lennop saw only her as he came toward her with outstretched hands, speaking her name with the yearning tenderness with which he had spoken it to himself a hundred times—

"Essie—Essie Tisdale!"

He kissed her, and she yielded, as though there were no need for words between them.

"But my letter? My telegram? Why didn't you answer?"

Her eyes widened with astonishment.

"Your letter! Your telegram!"

"You didn't get them?"

"Not one."

"Who did then?"

She shook her head.

"No one knew you'd gone but Dr. Harpe."

"Dr. Harpe!"

"You wrote her!"

"I wrote Dr. Harpe?" He stared at her for one incredulous second. "I wrote Dr. Harpe! She said so?"

"She said you left a letter for her."

There leaped into his steel-gray eyes a look which reminded Kincaid of the play of a jagged flash of lightning. He spoke slowly and enunciated very carefully when he said—

"I knew Dr. Harpe had the instincts of a prying servant, but I scarcely thought she'd go as far as that."

"Essie," Kincaid tapped her on the shoulder, "don't forget that your old Uncle Dick is here and waiting to be noticed."

He laughed aloud at her confusion and said as he and Van Lennop shook each other's hand—

"Just as I think I'm fixed for life, by George! I'm shoved out in the cold again; for I am forced to believe"—his eyes twinkled as he looked at Van Lennop—"that I am not the only Homeseeker left in Crowheart."